TinkerBell
AND THE
GREAT FAIRY RESCUE

By Shiori Kanaki

TOKYOPOP®

HAMBURG // HONG KONG // LOS ANGELES // TOKYO

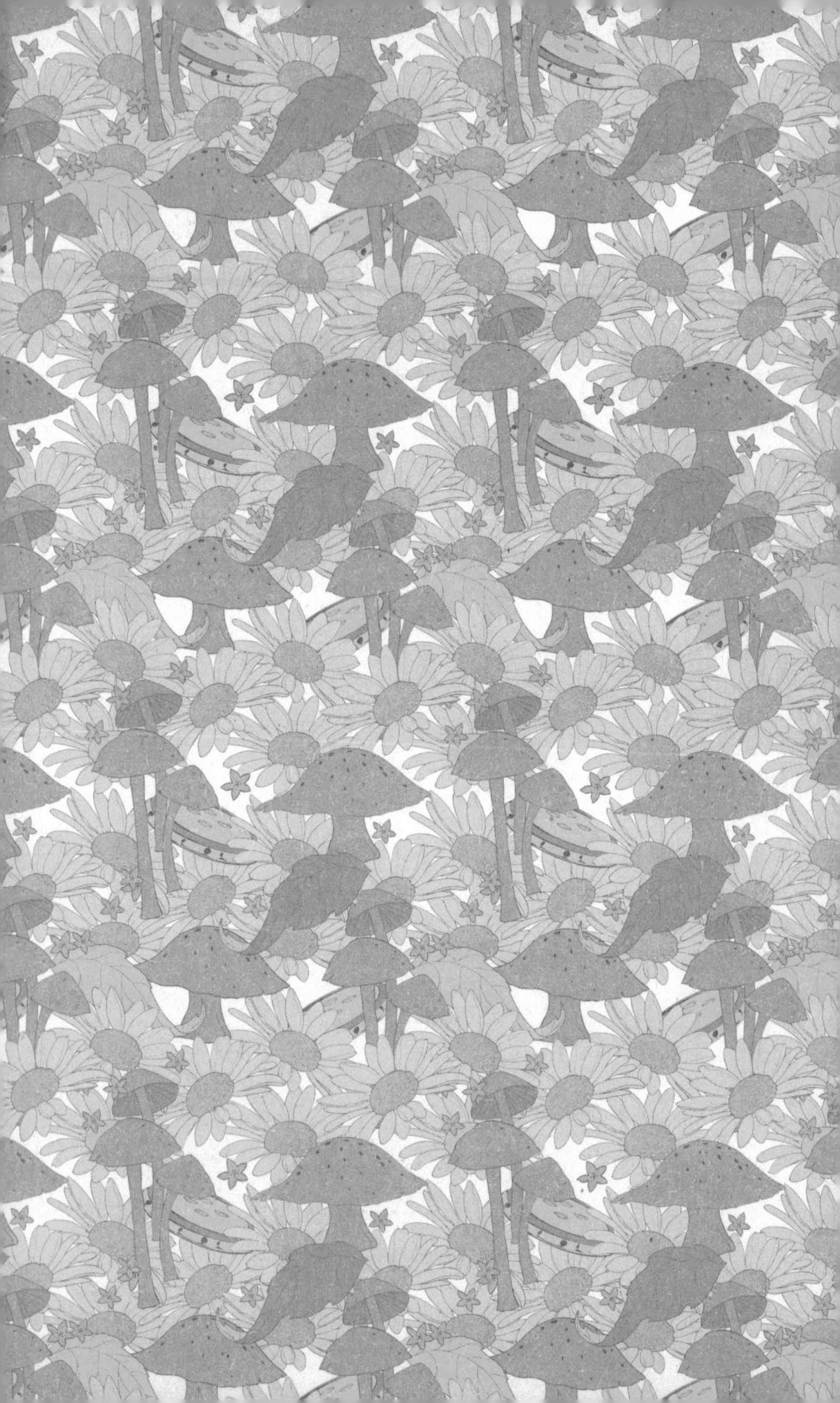

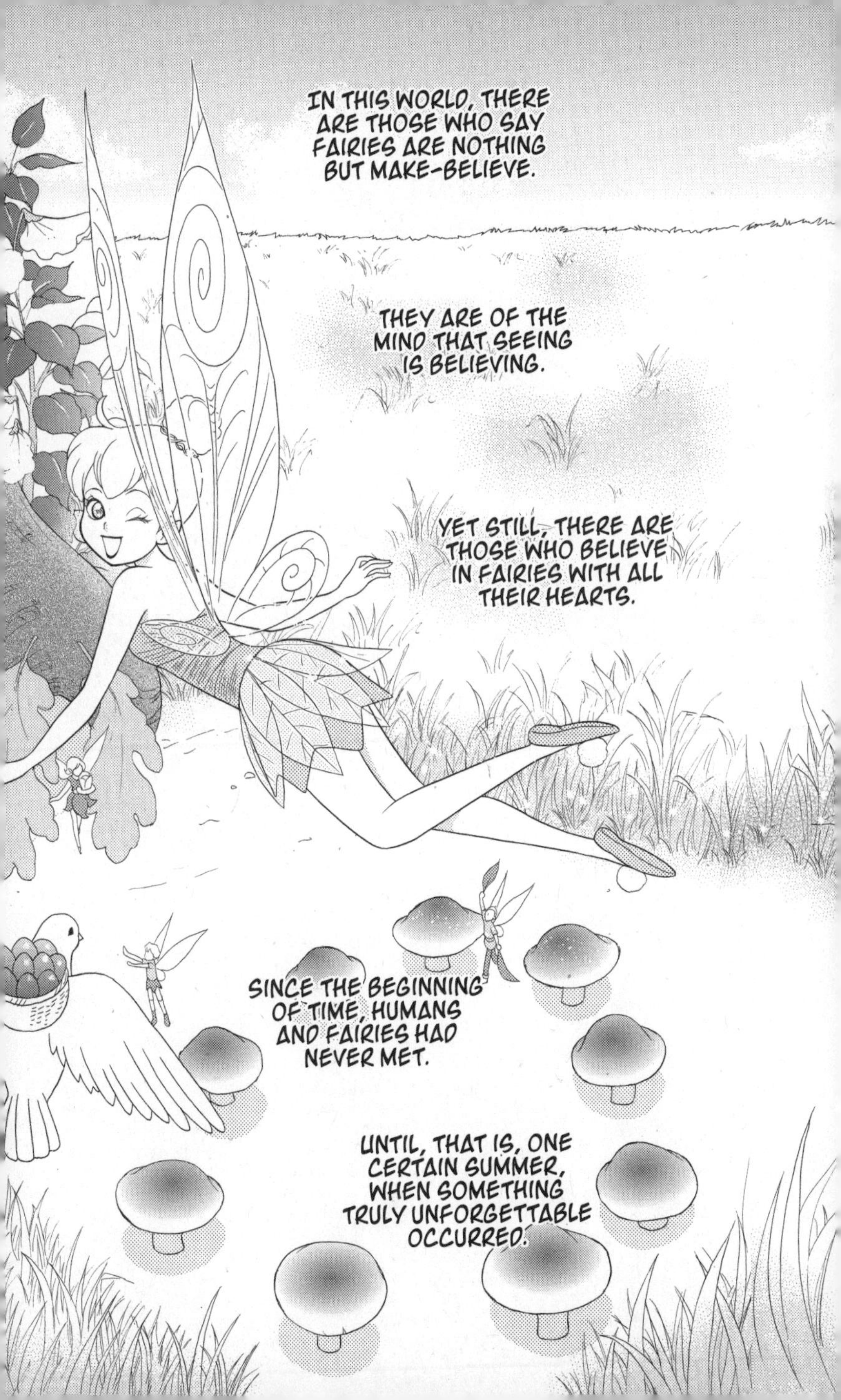
IN THIS WORLD, THERE ARE THOSE WHO SAY FAIRIES ARE NOTHING BUT MAKE-BELIEVE.
THEY ARE OF THE MIND THAT SEEING IS BELIEVING.
YET STILL, THERE ARE THOSE WHO BELIEVE IN FAIRIES WITH ALL THEIR HEARTS.
SINCE THE BEGINNING OF TIME, HUMANS AND FAIRIES HAD NEVER MET.
UNTIL, THAT IS, ONE CERTAIN SUMMER, WHEN SOMETHING TRULY UNFORGETTABLE OCCURRED.

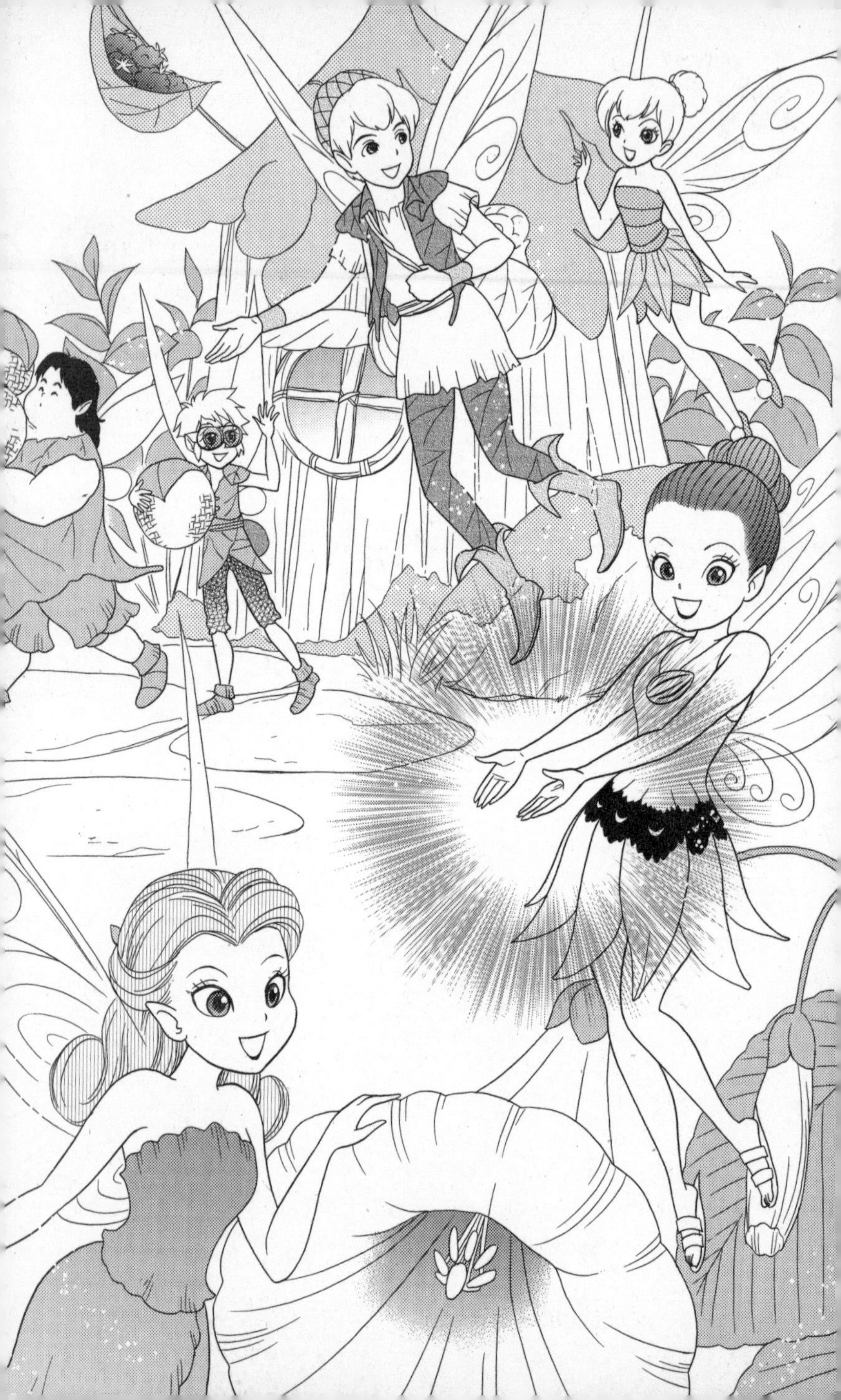

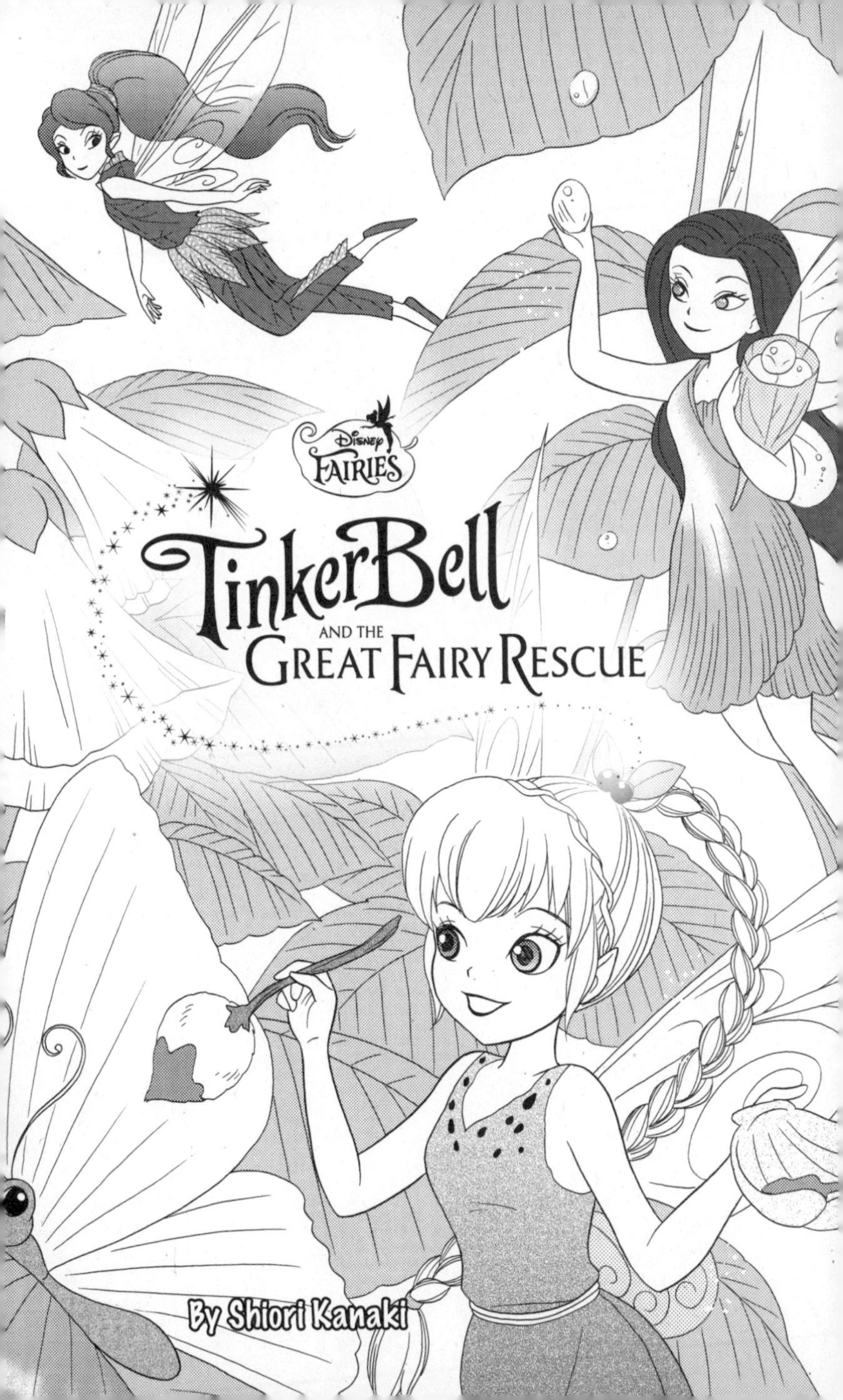
Disney Fairies
Tinker Bell
and the
Great Fairy Rescue
By Shiori Kanaki

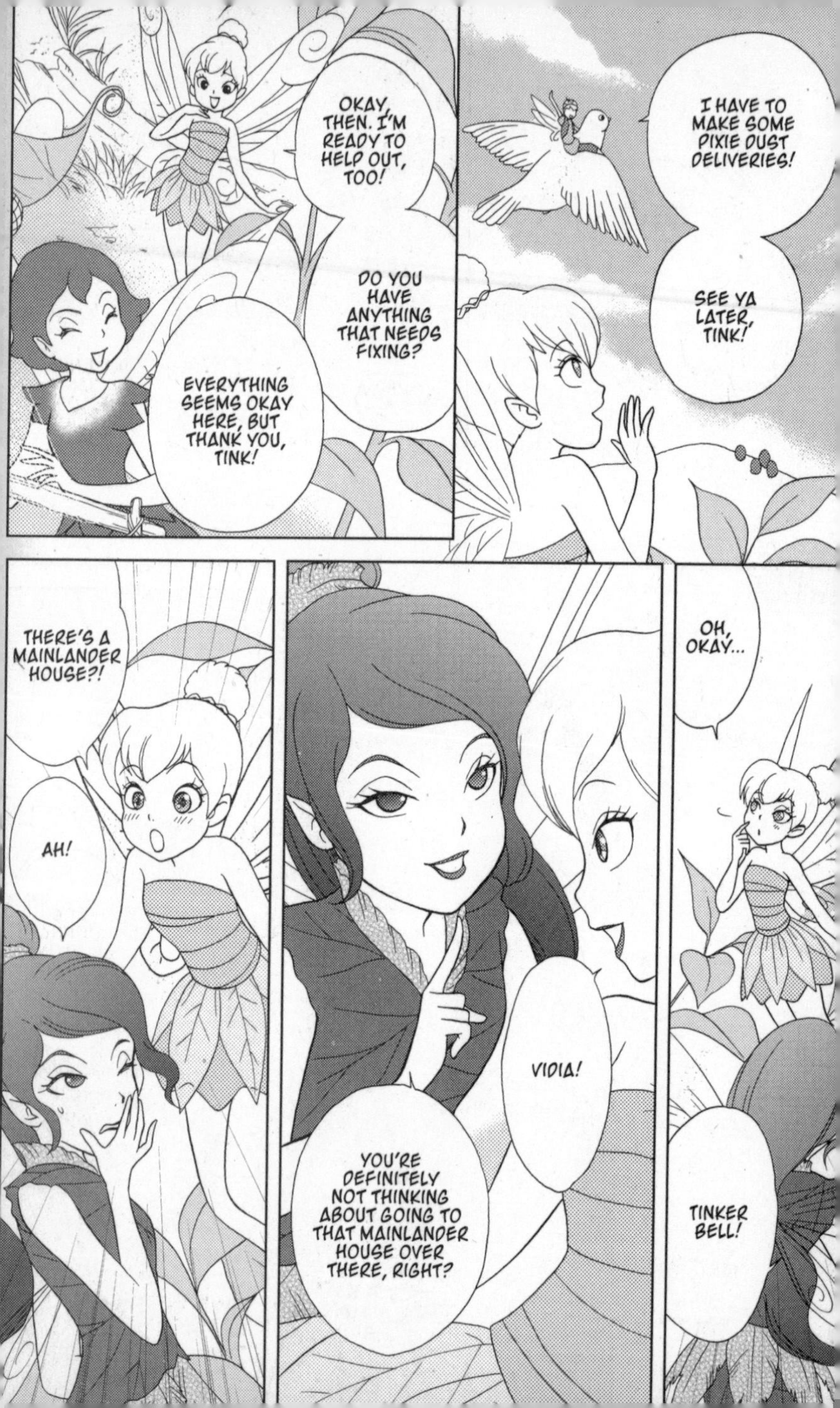
I HAVE TO MAKE SOME PIXIE DUST DELIVERIES!
SEE YA LATER, TINK!
OKAY, THEN. I'M READY TO HELP OUT, TOO!
DO YOU HAVE ANYTHING THAT NEEDS FIXING?
EVERYTHING SEEMS OKAY HERE, BUT THANK YOU, TINK!
OH, OKAY...
TINKER BELL!
VIDIA!
YOU'RE DEFINITELY NOT THINKING ABOUT GOING TO THAT MAINLANDER HOUSE OVER THERE, RIGHT?
THERE'S A MAINLANDER HOUSE?!
AH!

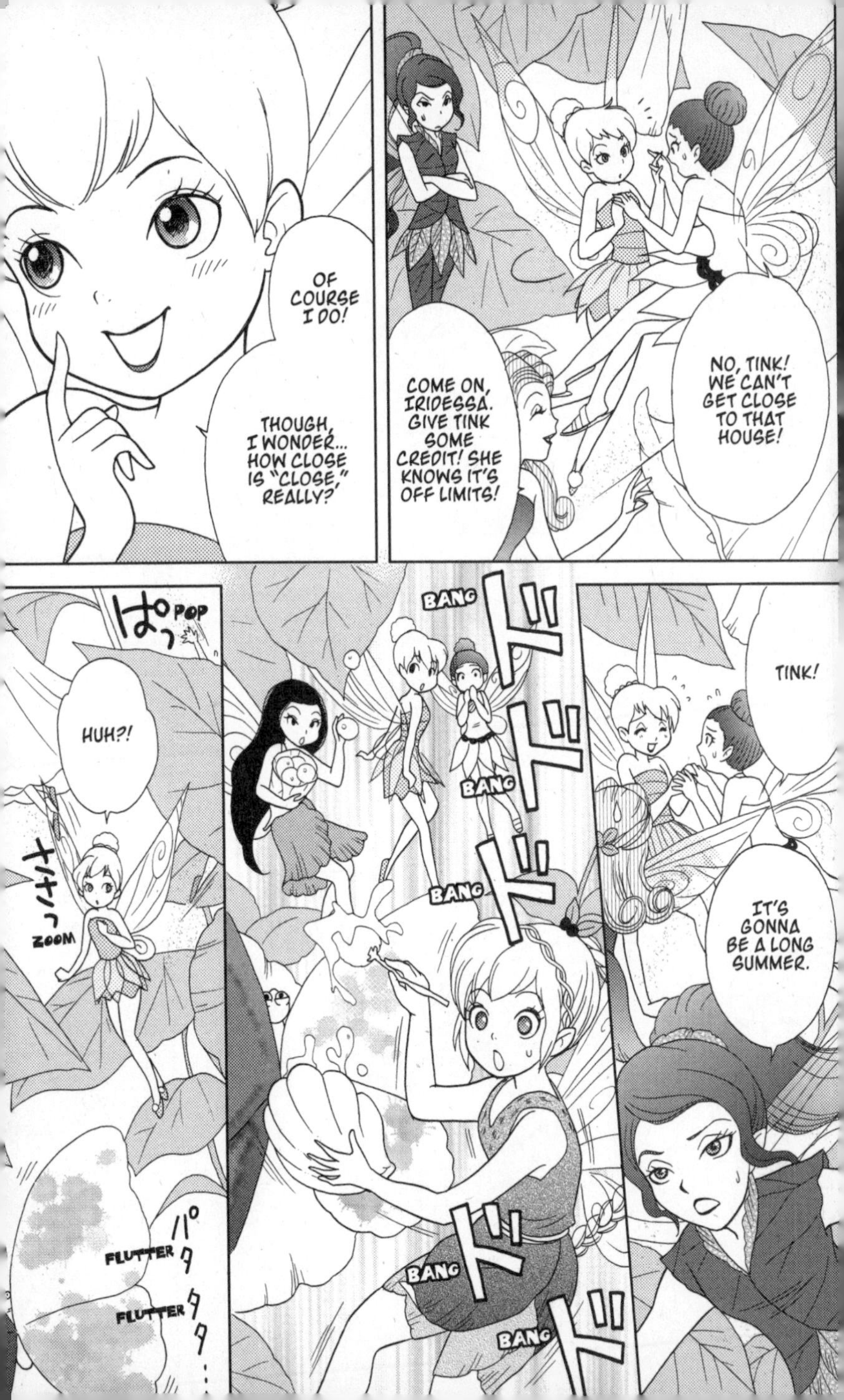
NO, TINK! WE CAN'T GET CLOSE TO THAT HOUSE!
COME ON, IRIDESSA. GIVE TINK SOME CREDIT! SHE KNOWS IT'S OFF LIMITS!
OF COURSE I DO!
THOUGH, I WONDER... HOW CLOSE IS "CLOSE," REALLY?
TINK!
IT'S GONNA BE A LONG SUMMER.
BANG
BANG
BANG
BANG
BANG
ぱっ POP
HUH?!
ZOOM
FLUTTER
FLUTTER

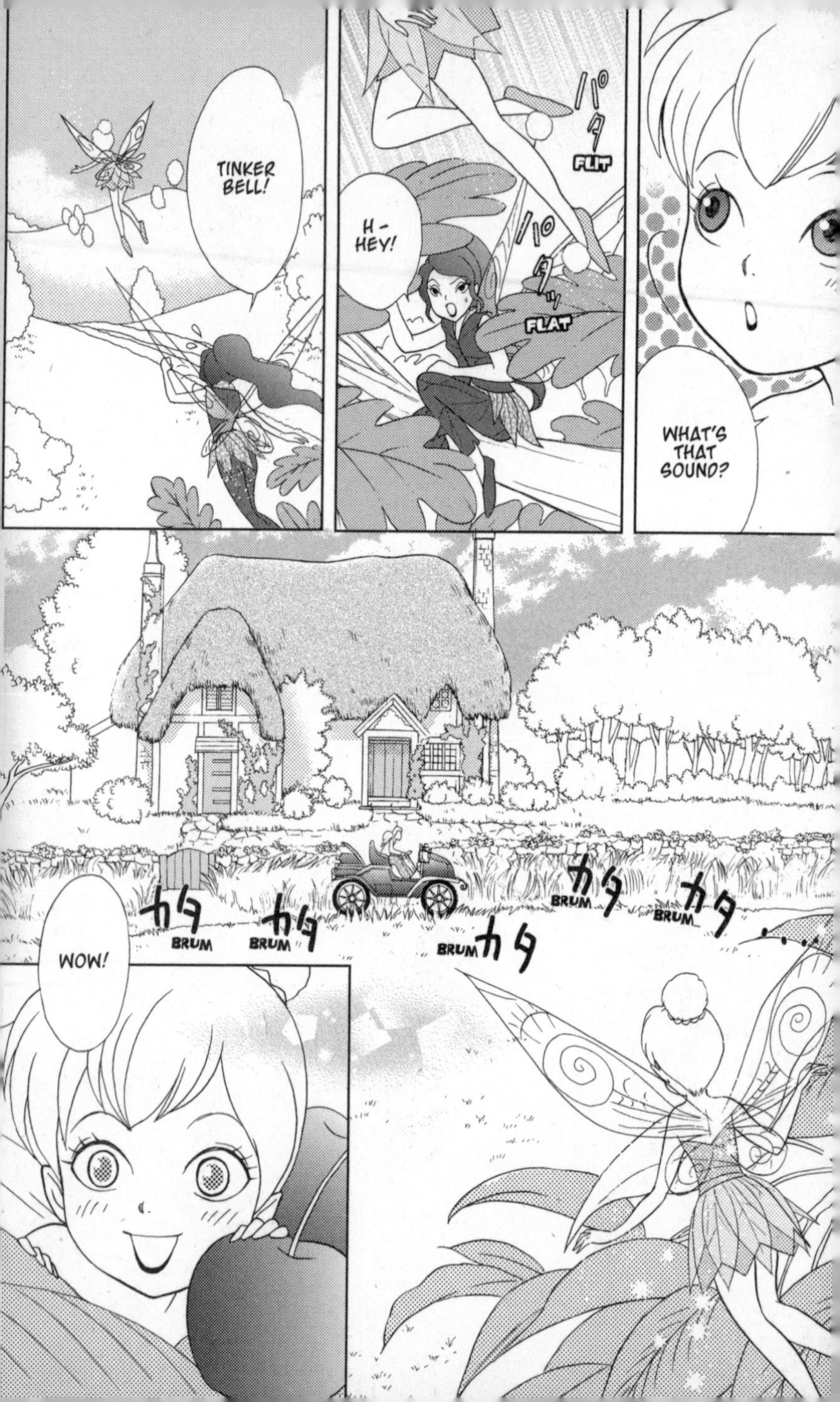
WHAT'S THAT SOUND?
パタ
FLIT
H-HEY!
パタッ
FLAT
TINKER BELL!
カタ
BRUM
カタ
BRUM
カタ
BRUM
カタ
BRUM
カタ
BRUM
...
WOW!

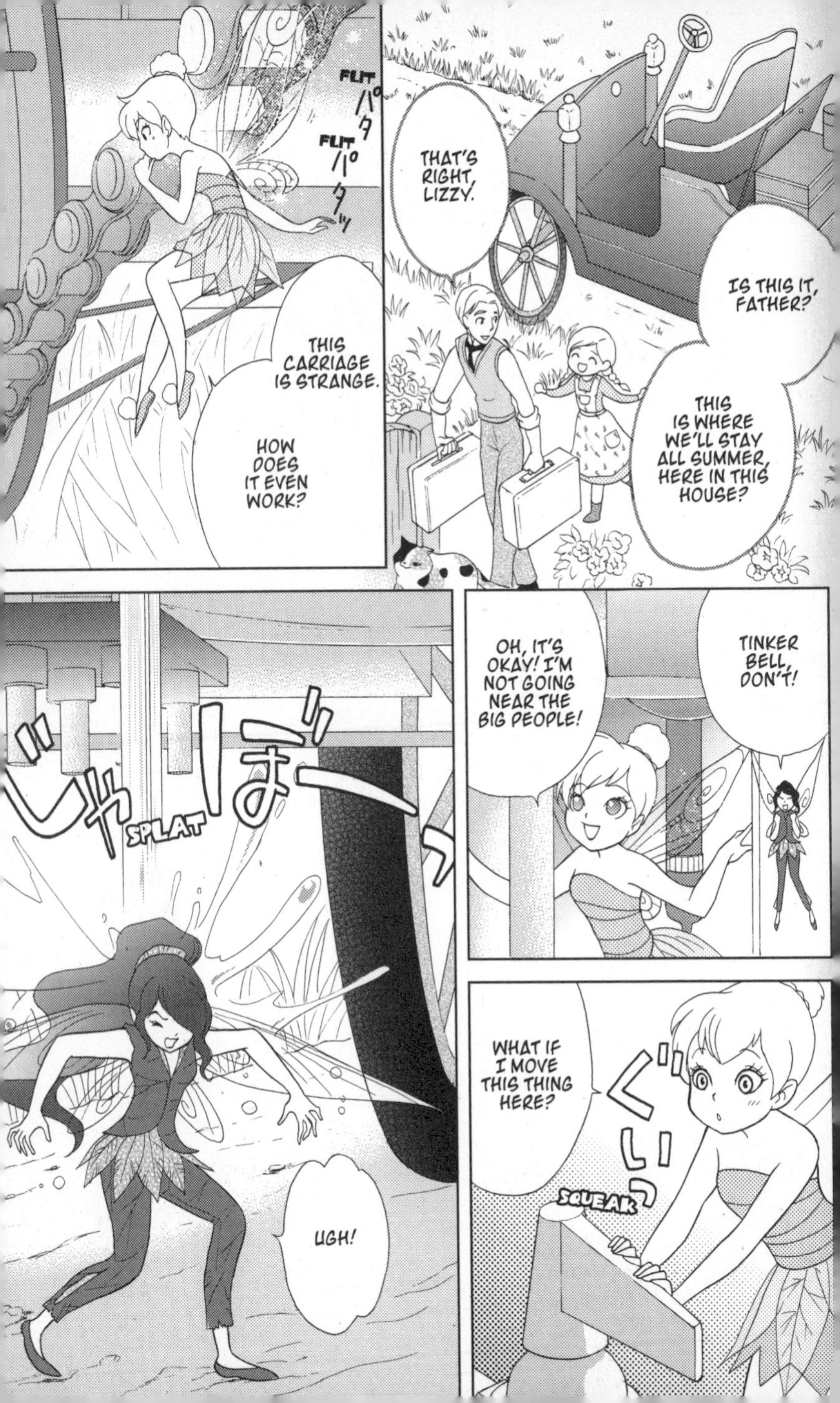
IS THIS IT, FATHER?
THIS IS WHERE WE'LL STAY ALL SUMMER, HERE IN THIS HOUSE?
THAT'S RIGHT, LIZZY.
FLIT パタ
FLIT パタッ
THIS CARRIAGE IS STRANGE.
HOW DOES IT EVEN WORK?
TINKER BELL, DON'T!
OH, IT'S OKAY! I'M NOT GOING NEAR THE BIG PEOPLE!
WHAT IF I MOVE THIS THING HERE?
ぐいっ
SQUEAK
じゃぼーっ
SPLAT
UGH!

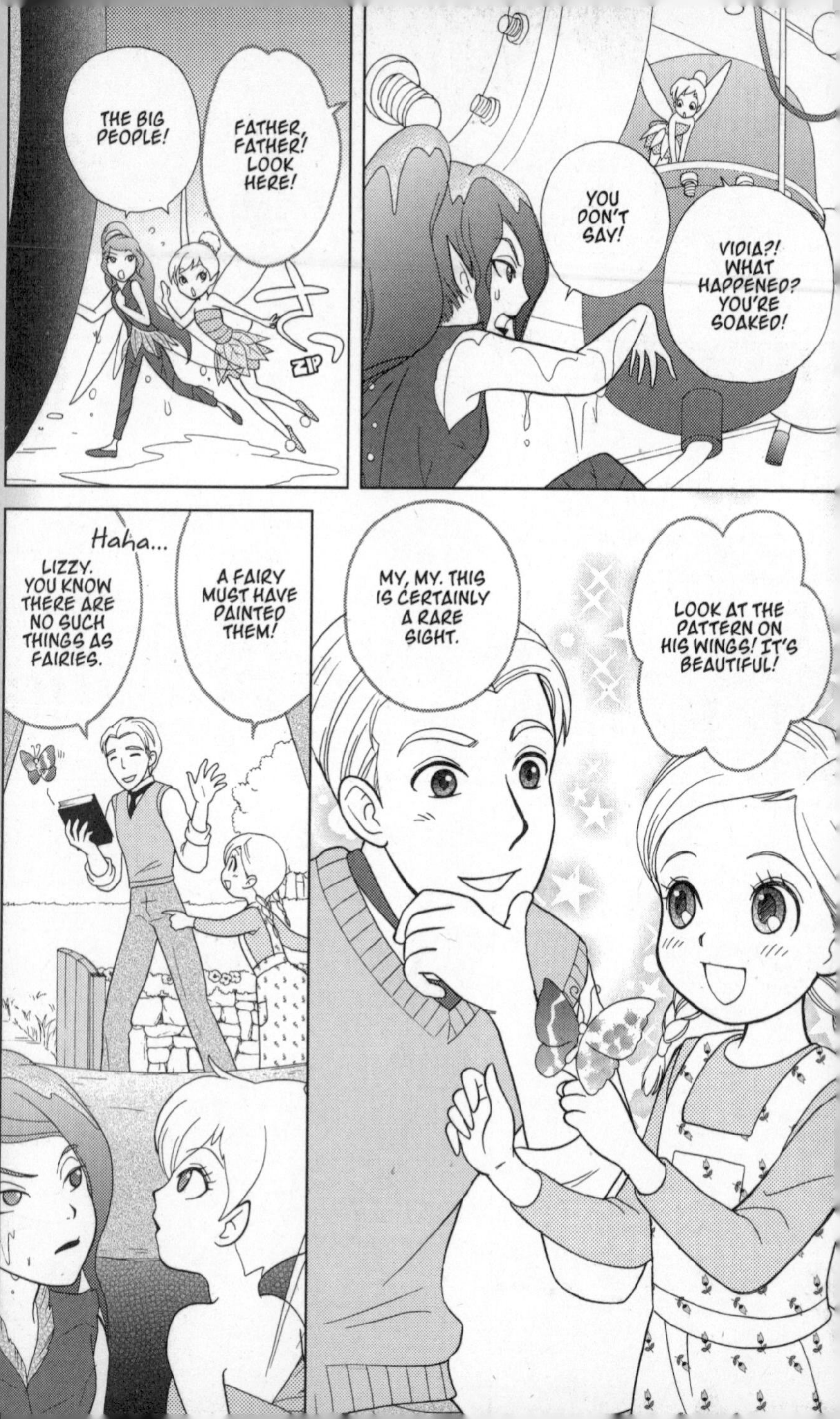
VIDIA?! WHAT HAPPENED? YOU'RE SOAKED!
YOU DON'T SAY!
FATHER, FATHER! LOOK HERE!
THE BIG PEOPLE!
ZIP
LOOK AT THE PATTERN ON HIS WINGS! IT'S BEAUTIFUL!
MY, MY. THIS IS CERTAINLY A RARE SIGHT.
A FAIRY MUST HAVE PAINTED THEM!
Haha...
LIZZY. YOU KNOW THERE ARE NO SUCH THINGS AS FAIRIES.

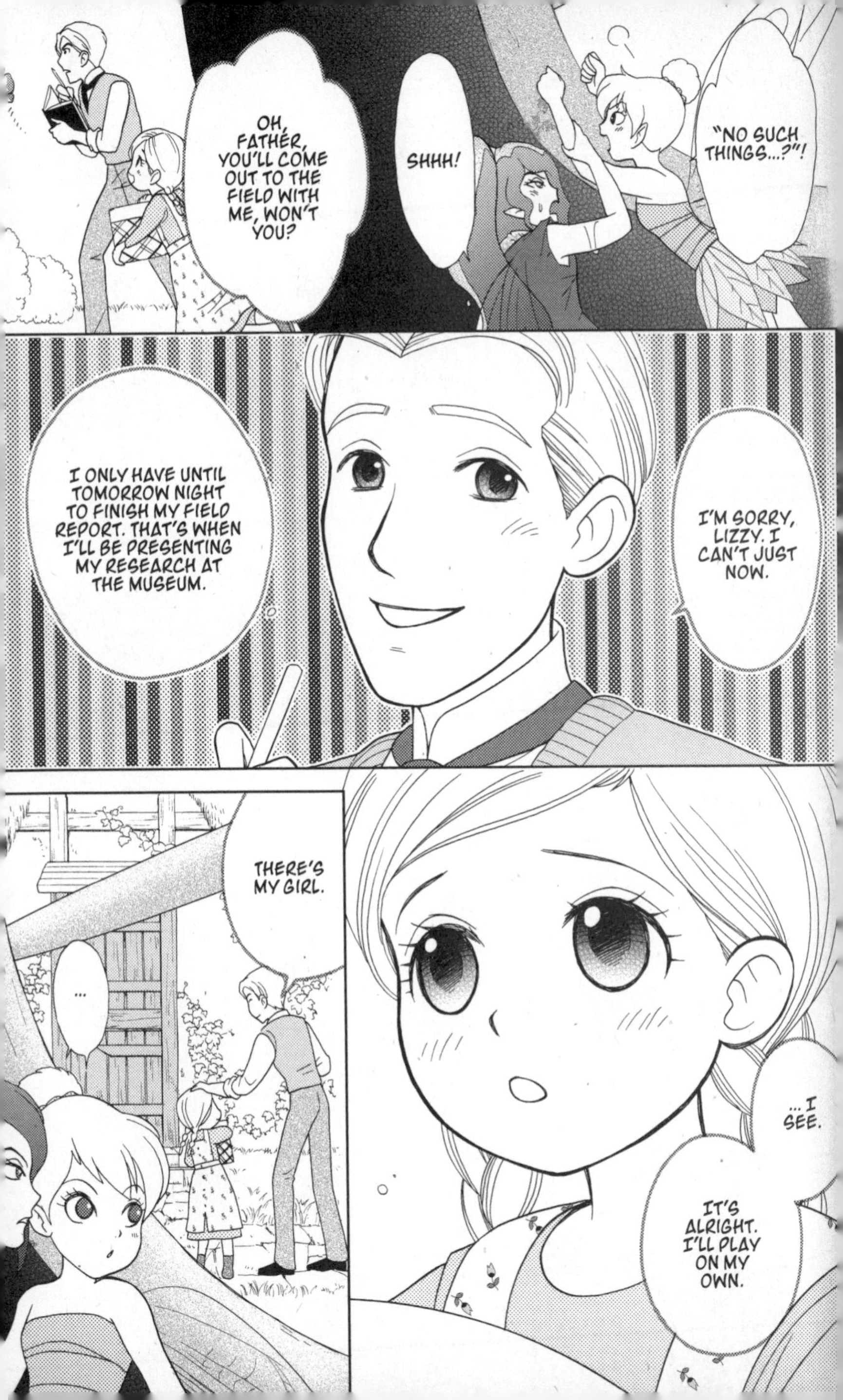
"NO SUCH THINGS...?"!
SHHH!
OH, FATHER, YOU'LL COME OUT TO THE FIELD WITH ME, WON'T YOU?
I'M SORRY, LIZZY. I CAN'T JUST NOW.
I ONLY HAVE UNTIL TOMORROW NIGHT TO FINISH MY FIELD REPORT. THAT'S WHEN I'LL BE PRESENTING MY RESEARCH AT THE MUSEUM.
... I SEE.
IT'S ALRIGHT. I'LL PLAY ON MY OWN.
THERE'S MY GIRL.
...

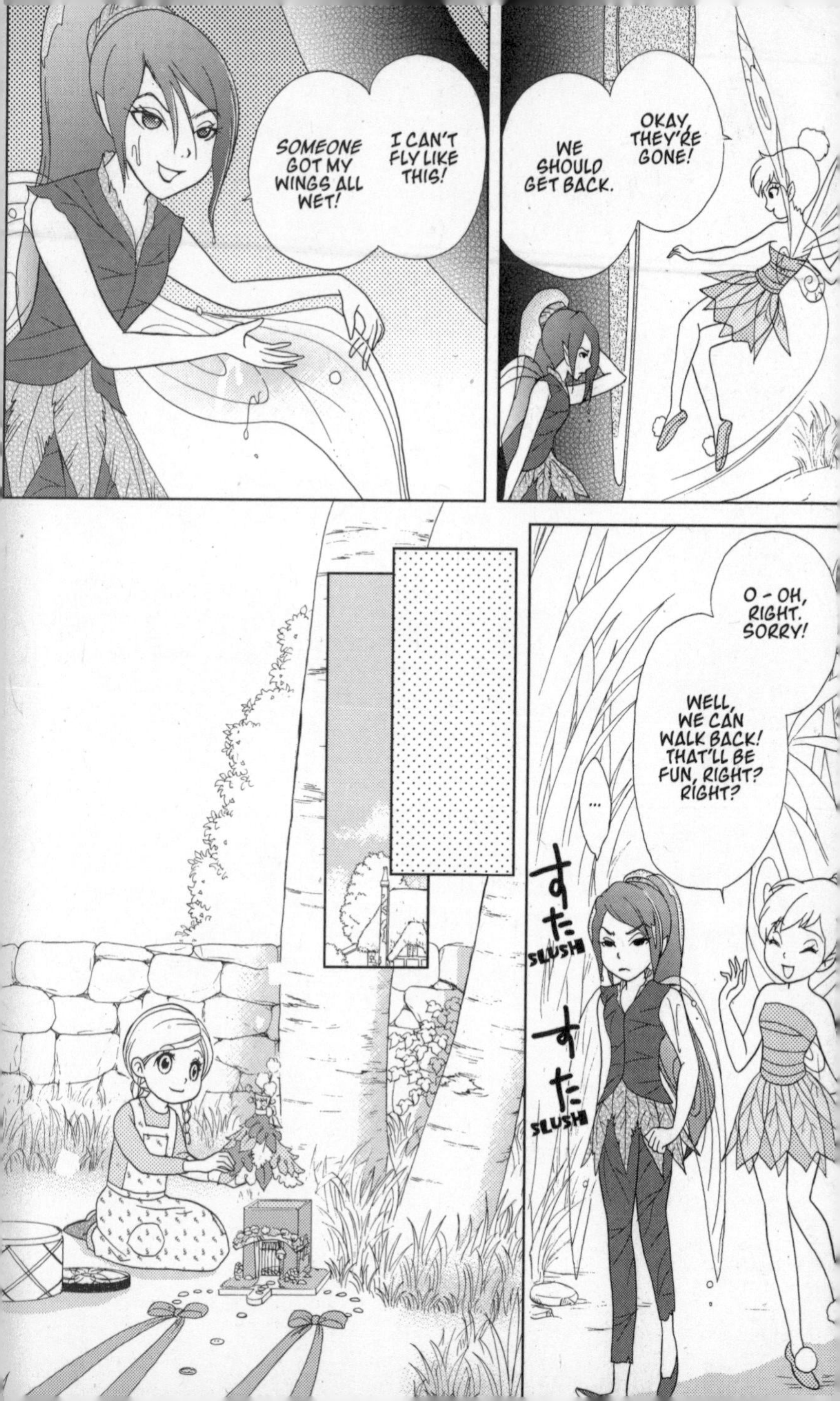
OKAY, THEY'RE GONE!
WE SHOULD GET BACK.
I CAN'T FLY LIKE THIS!
SOMEONE GOT MY WINGS ALL WET!
O - OH, RIGHT. SORRY!
WELL, WE CAN WALK BACK! THAT'LL BE FUN, RIGHT? RIGHT?
...
すた SLUSH
すた SLUSH

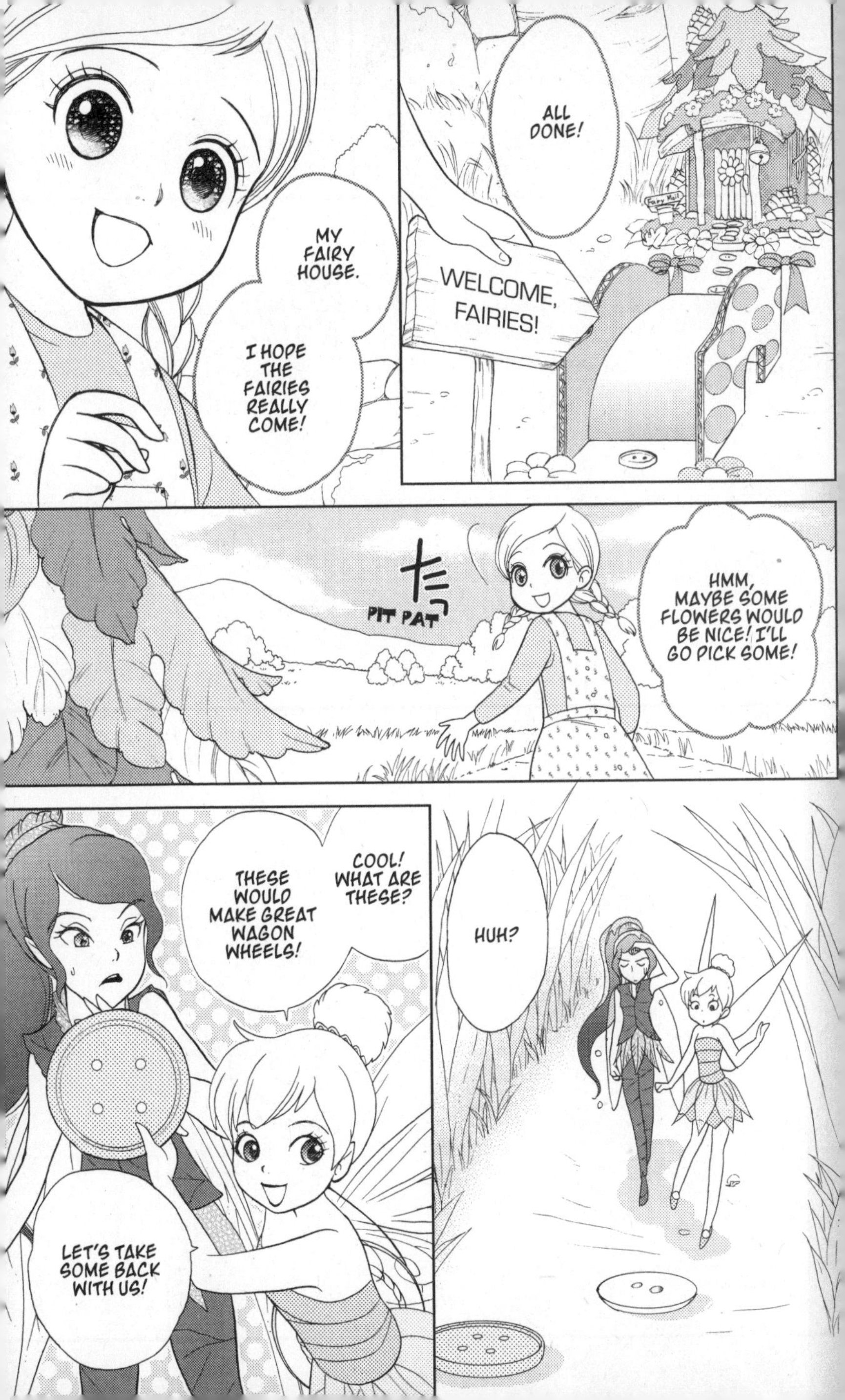
ALL DONE!
Fairy Mail
WELCOME, FAIRIES!
MY FAIRY HOUSE.
I HOPE THE FAIRIES REALLY COME!
HMM, MAYBE SOME FLOWERS WOULD BE NICE! I'LL GO PICK SOME!
PIT PAT
HUH?
COOL! WHAT ARE THESE?
THESE WOULD MAKE GREAT WAGON WHEELS!
LET'S TAKE SOME BACK WITH US!

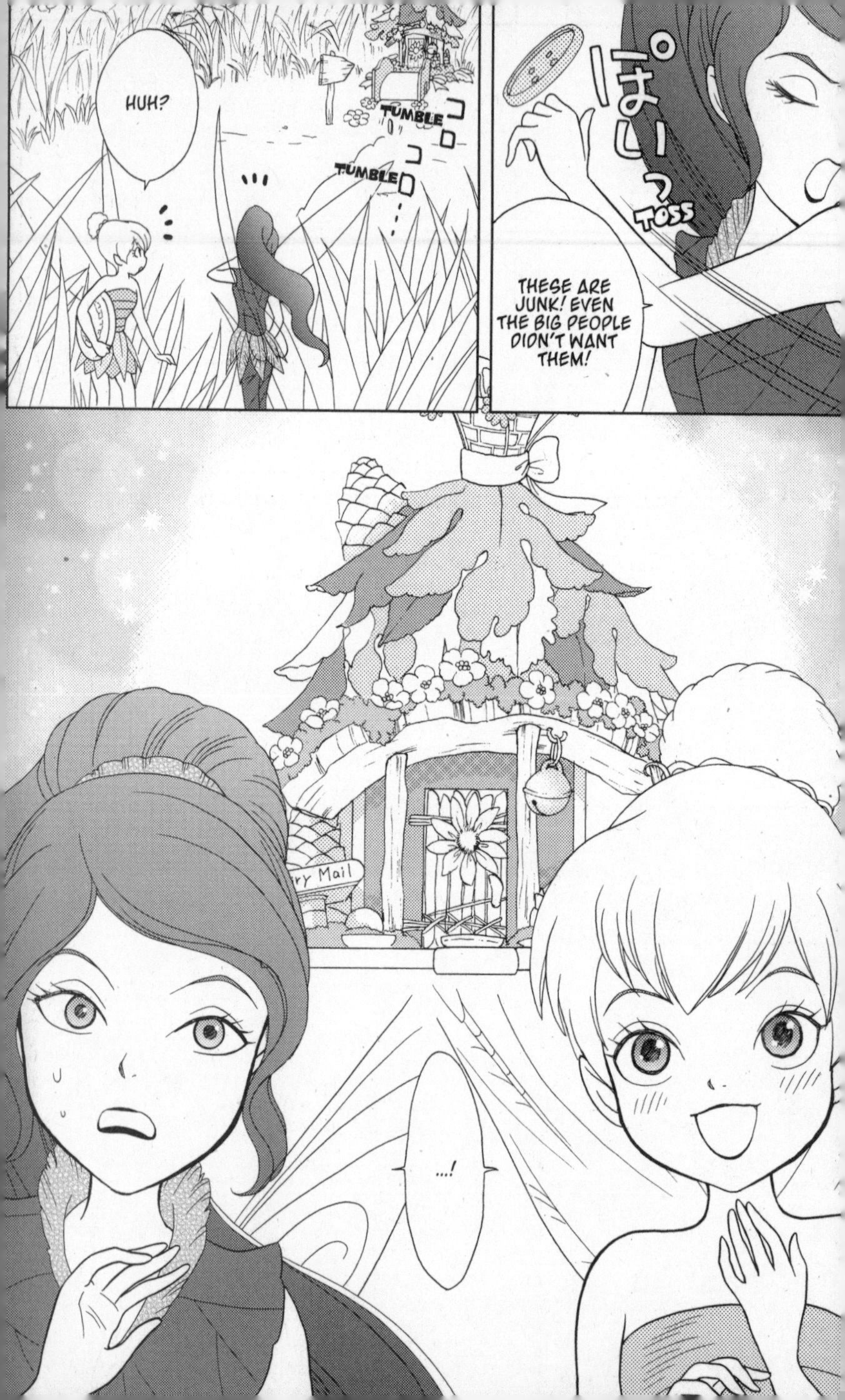
ぽいっ
TOSS
THESE ARE JUNK! EVEN THE BIG PEOPLE DIDN'T WANT THEM!
HUH?
TUMBLE コロ
TUMBLE コロ
...!

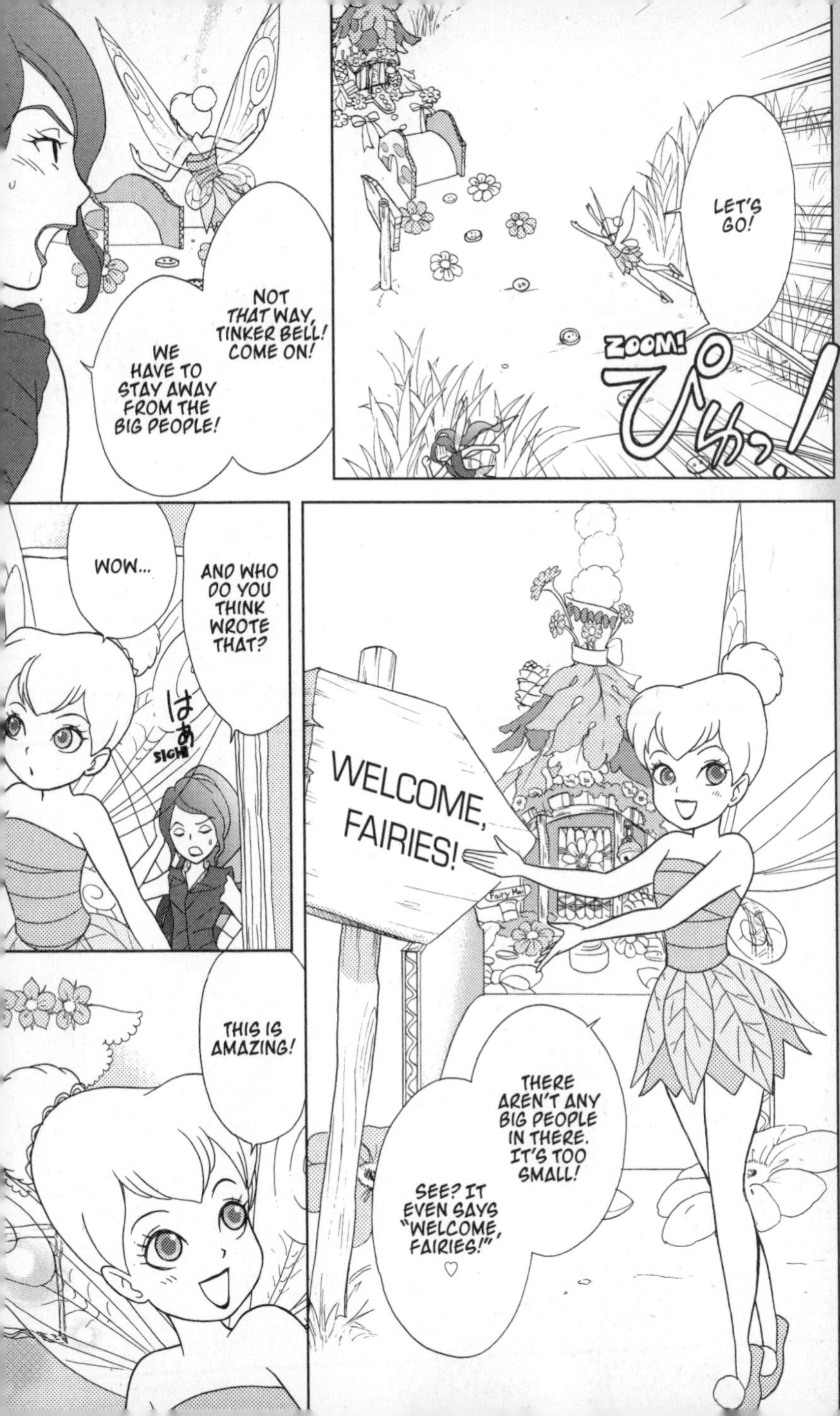
LET'S GO!
ZOOM!
ぴゅっ!
NOT THAT WAY, TINKER BELL! COME ON!
WE HAVE TO STAY AWAY FROM THE BIG PEOPLE!
WELCOME, FAIRIES!
Fairy Mail
THERE AREN'T ANY BIG PEOPLE IN THERE. IT'S TOO SMALL!
SEE? IT EVEN SAYS "WELCOME, FAIRIES!" ♡
AND WHO DO YOU THINK WROTE THAT?
WOW...
はあ
SIGH
THIS IS AMAZING!

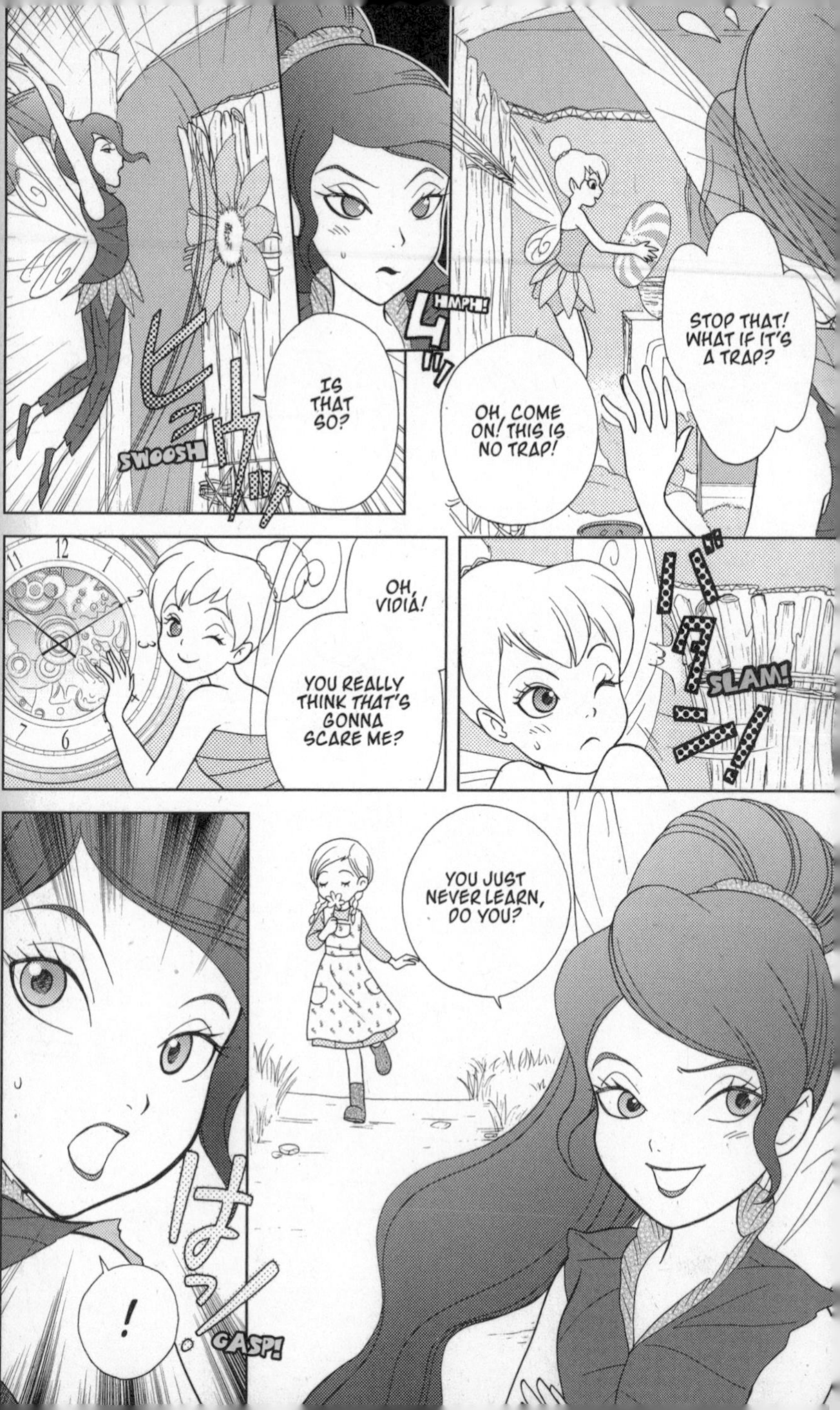
STOP THAT! WHAT IF IT'S A TRAP?
OH, COME ON! THIS IS NO TRAP!
HMPH!
IS THAT SO?
SWOOSH
SLAM!
OH, VIDIA!
YOU REALLY THINK THAT'S GONNA SCARE ME?
YOU JUST NEVER LEARN, DO YOU?
!
GASP!

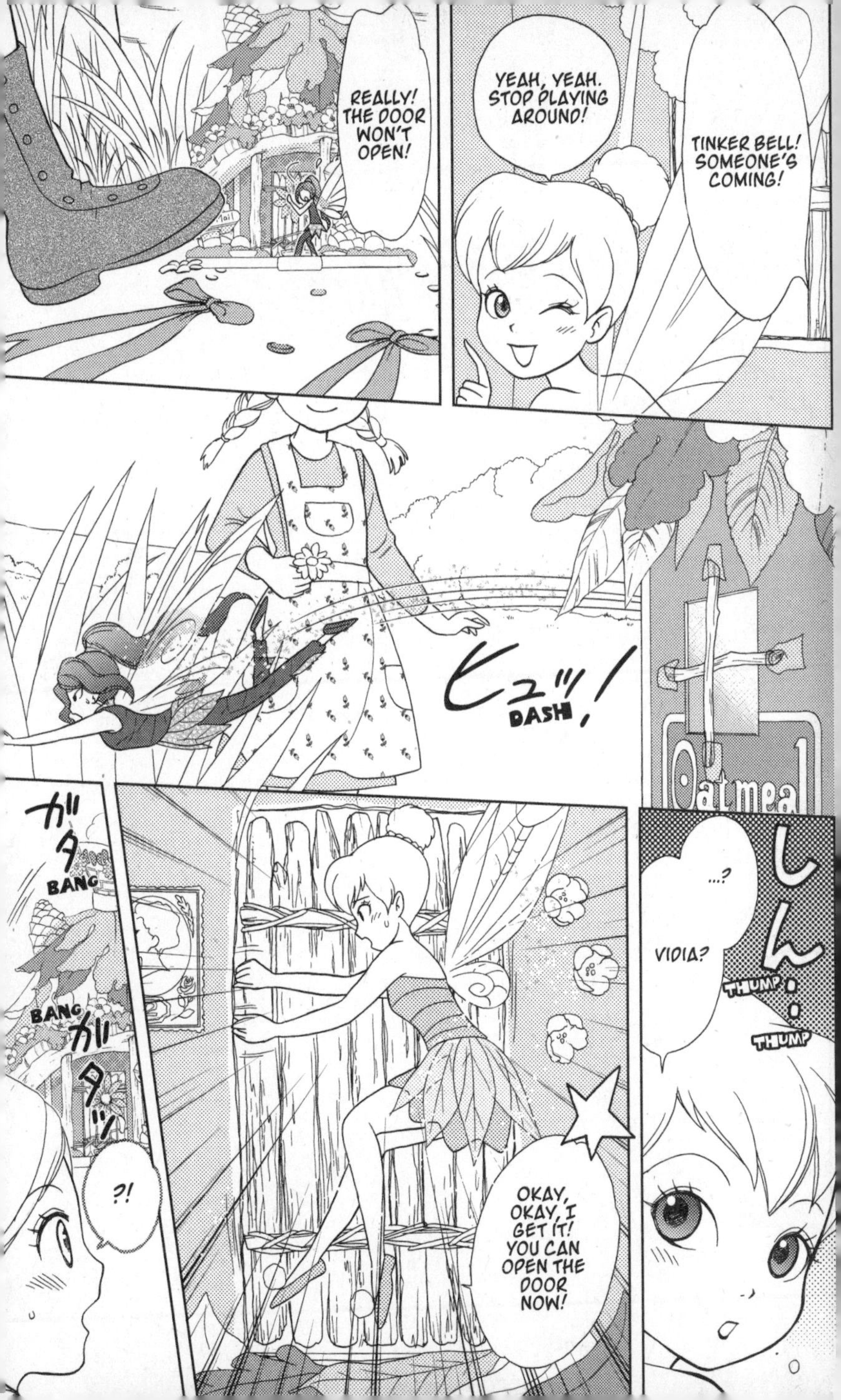
TINKER BELL! SOMEONE'S COMING!
YEAH, YEAH. STOP PLAYING AROUND!
REALLY! THE DOOR WON'T OPEN!
ヒュッ!
DASH!
しん…
THUMP THUMP
...?
VIDIA?
OKAY, OKAY, I GET IT! YOU CAN OPEN THE DOOR NOW!
ガタ
BANG
BANG
ガタタッ
?!

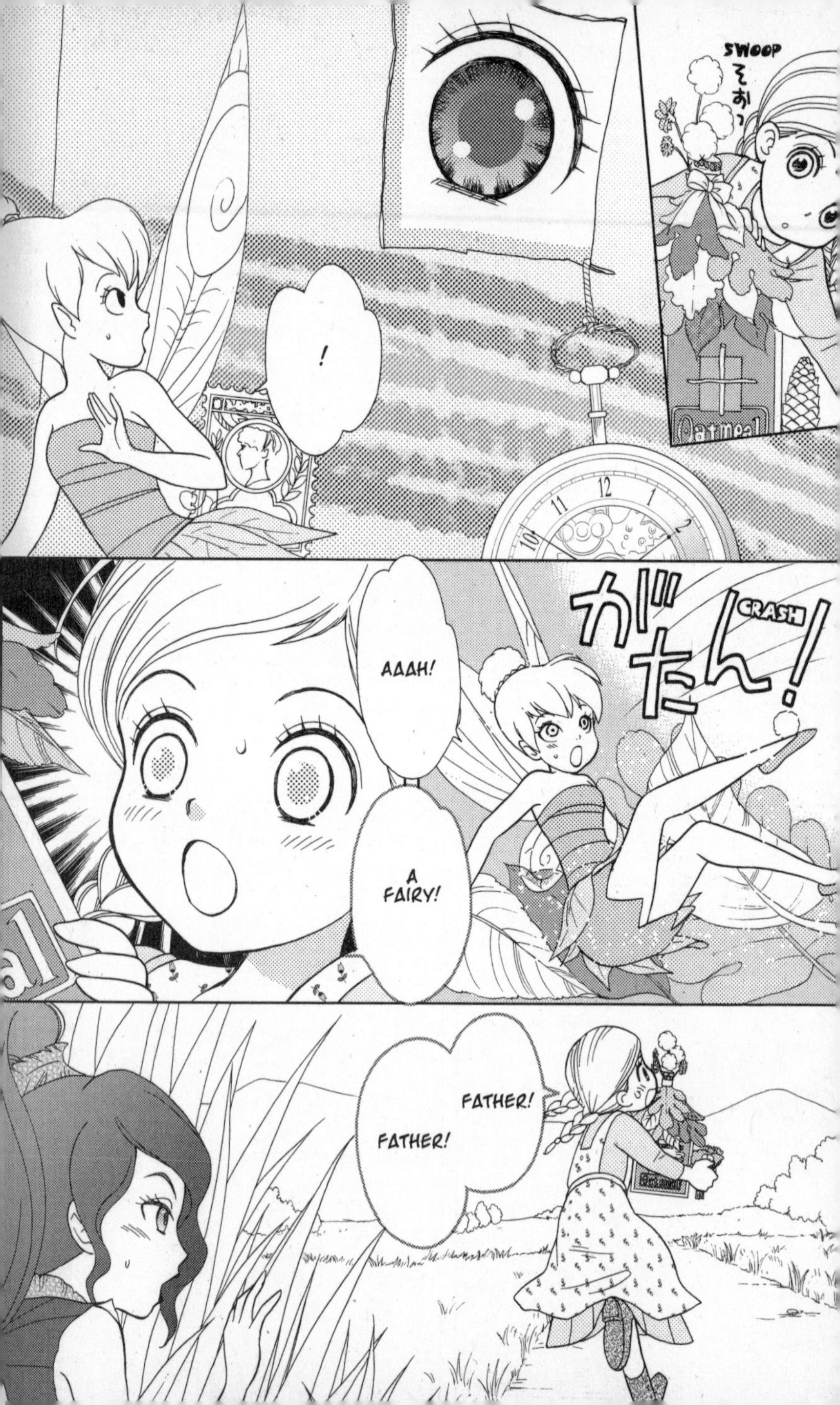
SWOOP
そおっ
Oatmeal
!
がたん!
CRASH
AAAH!
A FAIRY!
FATHER!
FATHER!

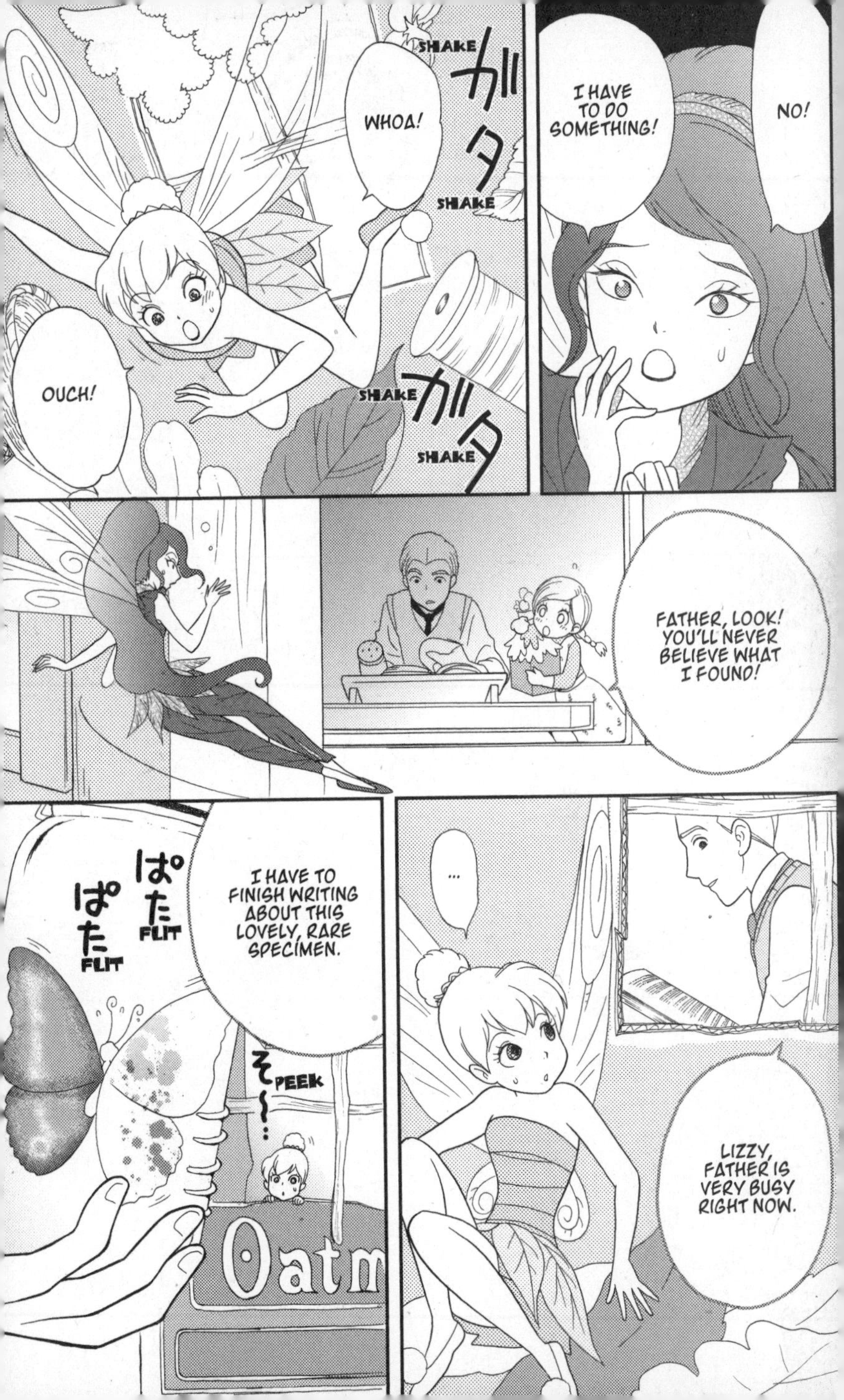
NO!
I HAVE TO DO SOMETHING!
SHAKE ガタ SHAKE
WHOA!
SHAKE ガタ SHAKE
OUCH!
FATHER, LOOK! YOU'LL NEVER BELIEVE WHAT I FOUND!
...
LIZZY, FATHER IS VERY BUSY RIGHT NOW.
I HAVE TO FINISH WRITING ABOUT THIS LOVELY, RARE SPECIMEN.
ぱた FLIT
ぱた FLIT
そ~… PEEK
Oatm

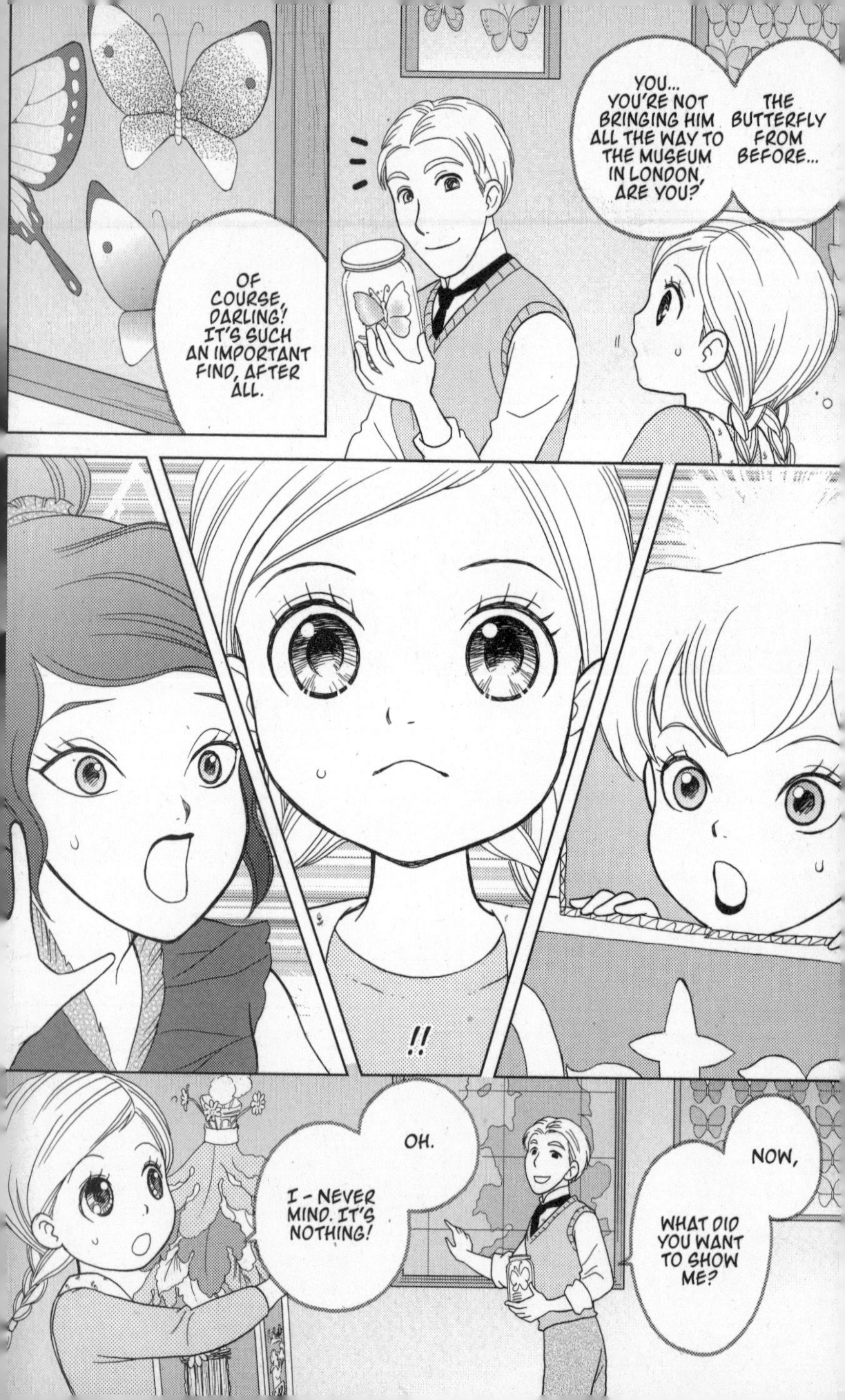
THE BUTTERFLY FROM BEFORE...
YOU... YOU'RE NOT BRINGING HIM ALL THE WAY TO THE MUSEUM IN LONDON, ARE YOU?
OF COURSE, DARLING! IT'S SUCH AN IMPORTANT FIND, AFTER ALL.
!!
NOW,
WHAT DID YOU WANT TO SHOW ME?
OH.
I- NEVER MIND. IT'S NOTHING!

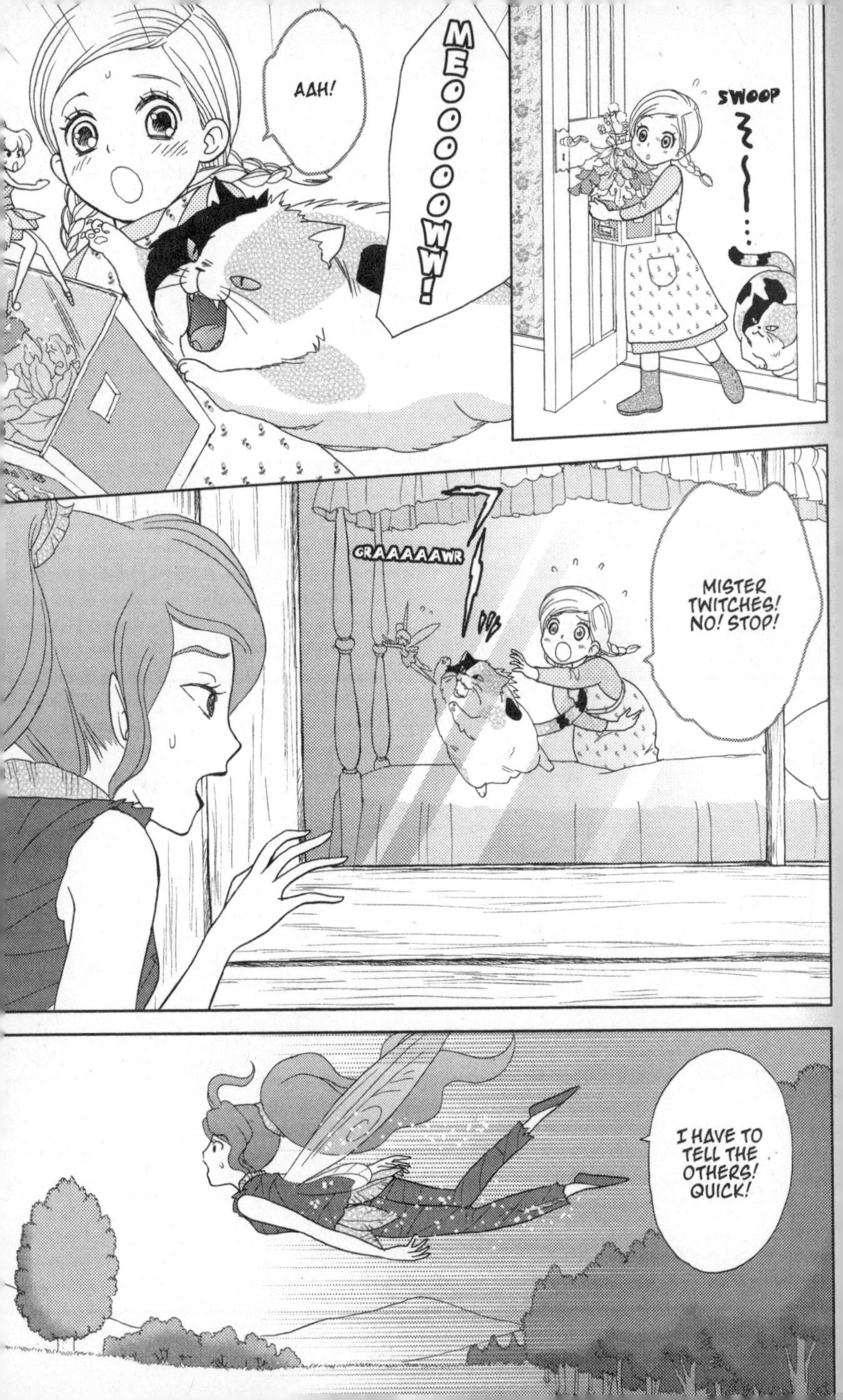
SWOOP
MEOOOOOOWW!
AAH!
MISTER TWITCHES! NO! STOP!
GRAAAAAWR
I HAVE TO TELL THE OTHERS! QUICK!

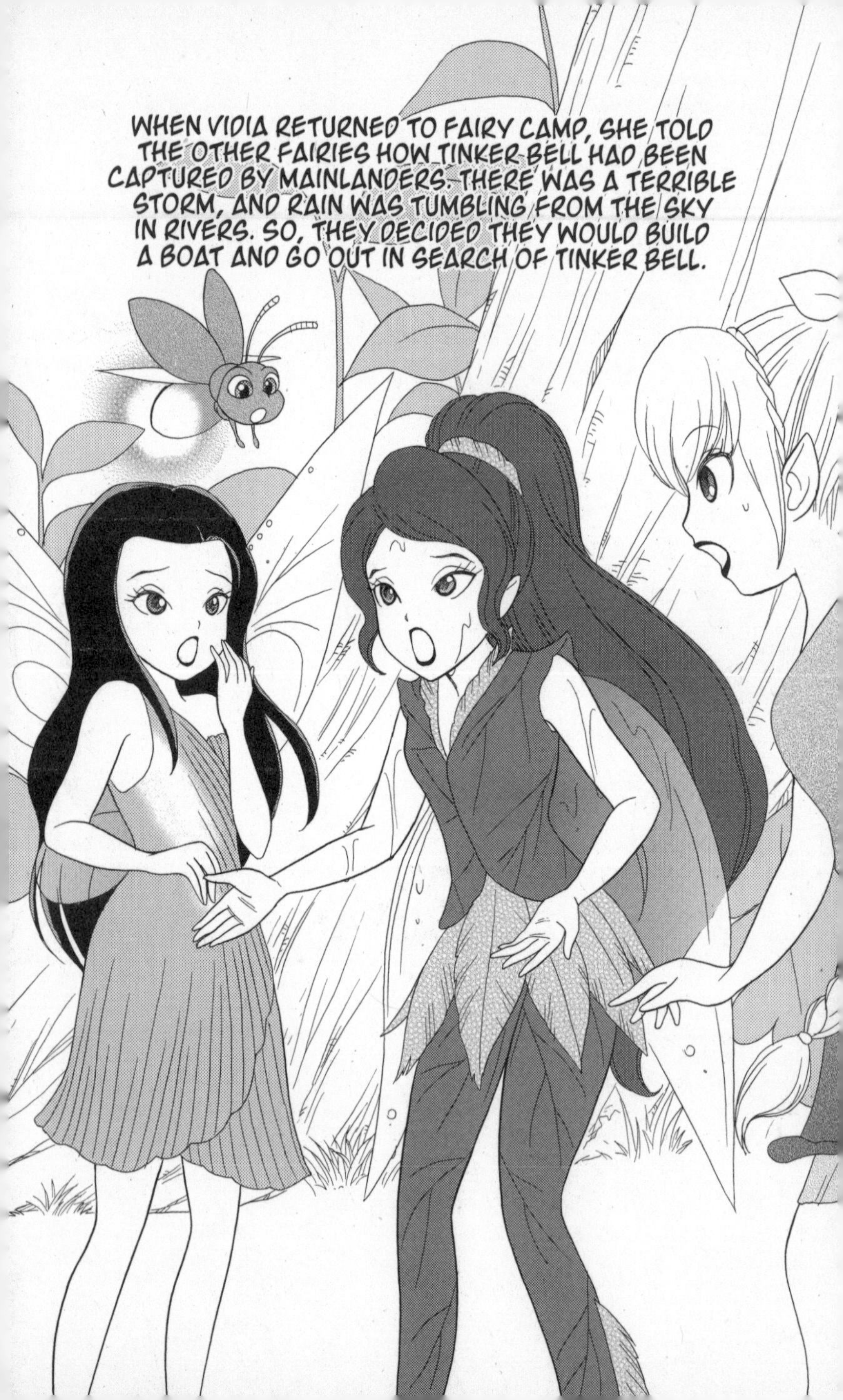
WHEN VIDIA RETURNED TO FAIRY CAMP, SHE TOLD THE OTHER FAIRIES HOW TINKER BELL HAD BEEN CAPTURED BY MAINLANDERS. THERE WAS A TERRIBLE STORM, AND RAIN WAS TUMBLING FROM THE SKY IN RIVERS. SO, THEY DECIDED THEY WOULD BUILD A BOAT AND GO OUT IN SEARCH OF TINKER BELL.

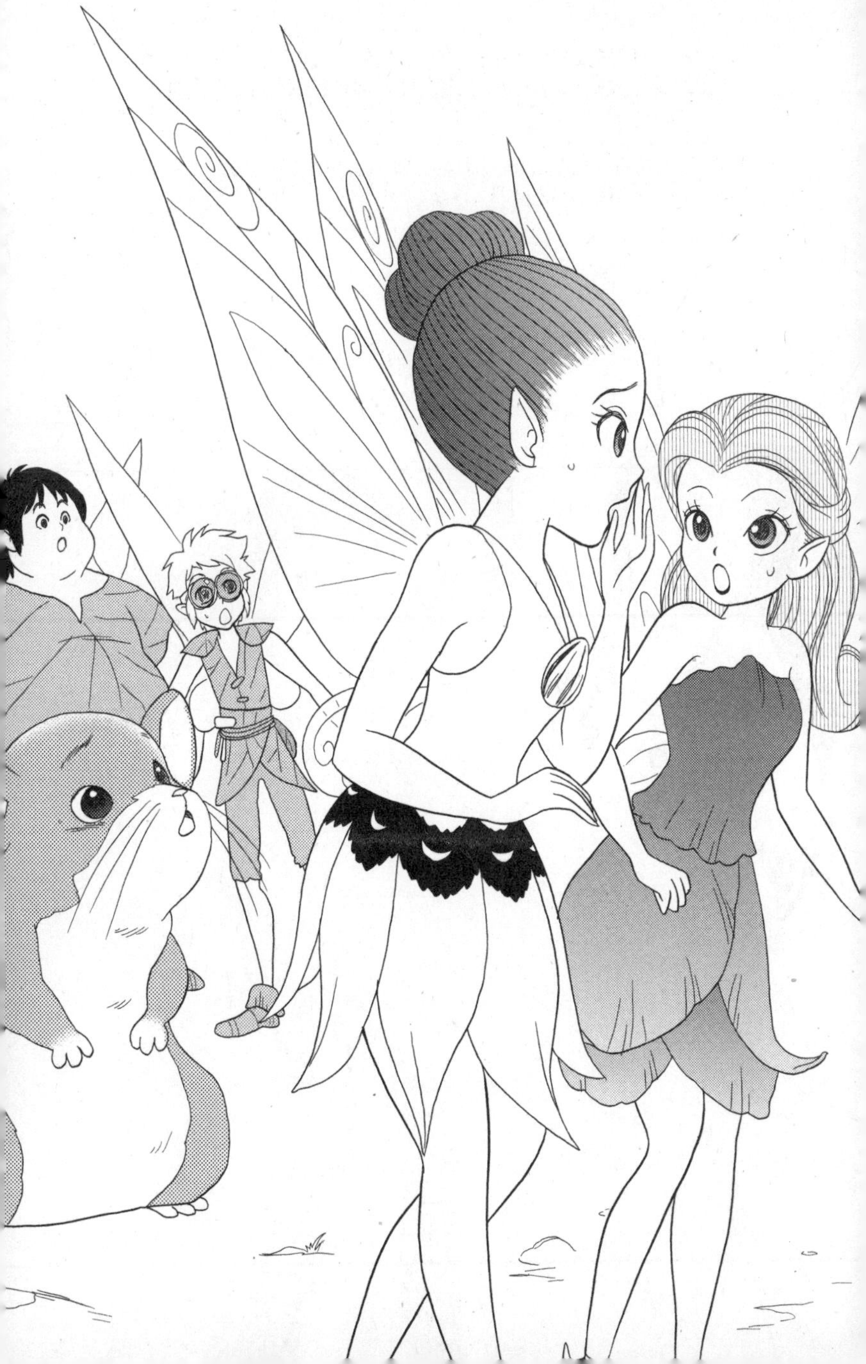

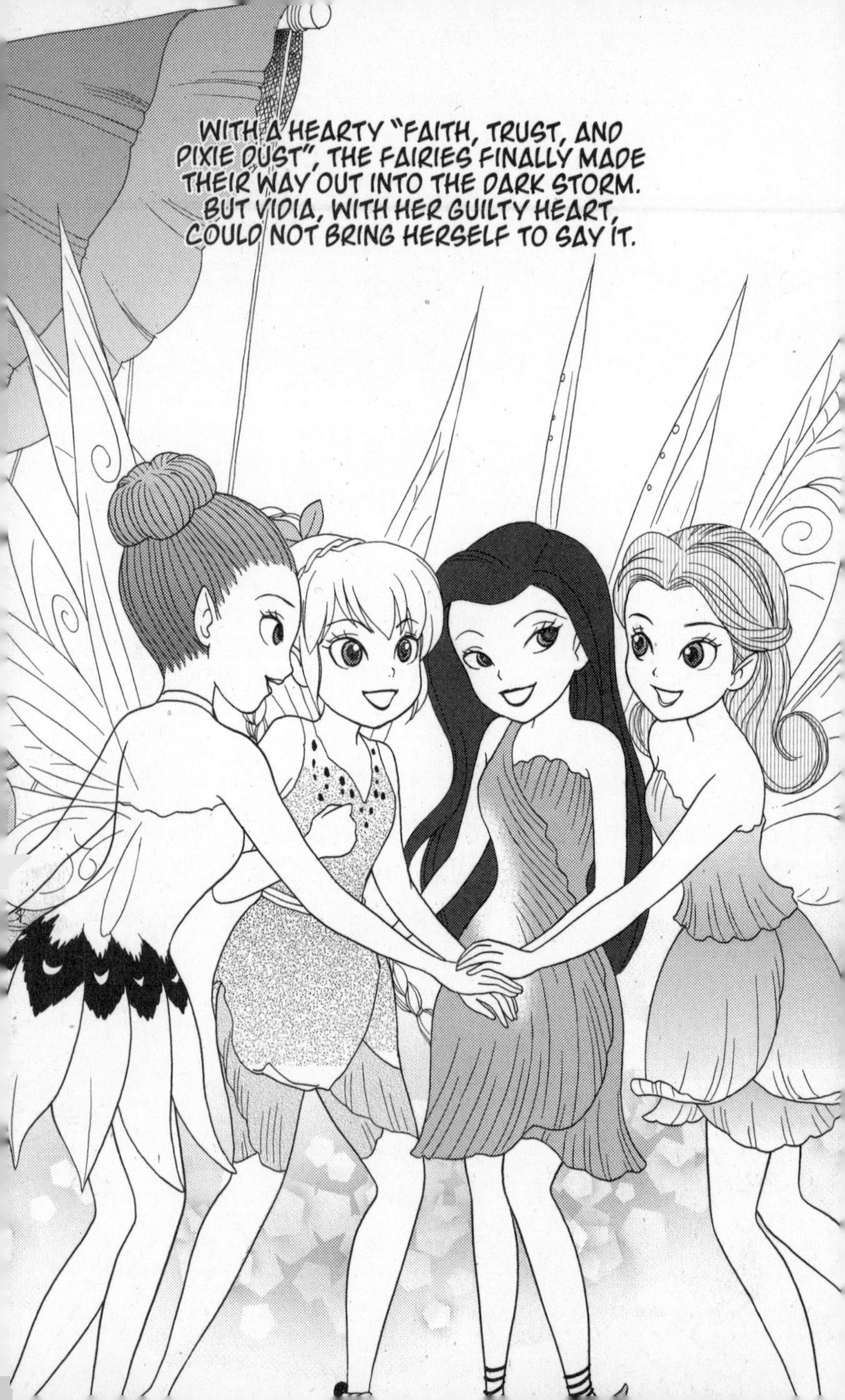
WITH A HEARTY "FAITH, TRUST, AND PIXIE DUST", THE FAIRIES FINALLY MADE THEIR WAY OUT INTO THE DARK STORM. BUT VIDIA, WITH HER GUILTY HEART, COULD NOT BRING HERSELF TO SAY IT.

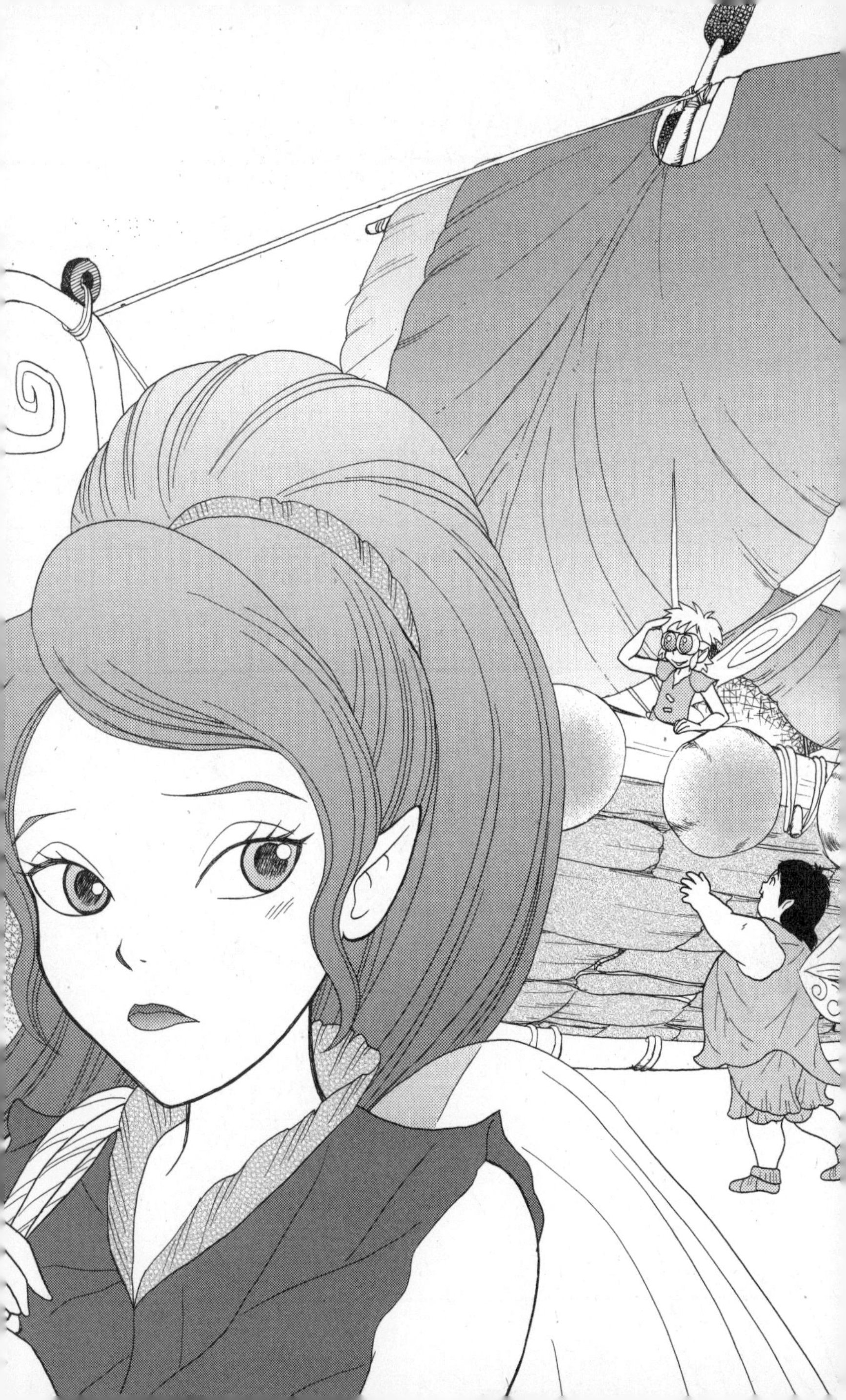

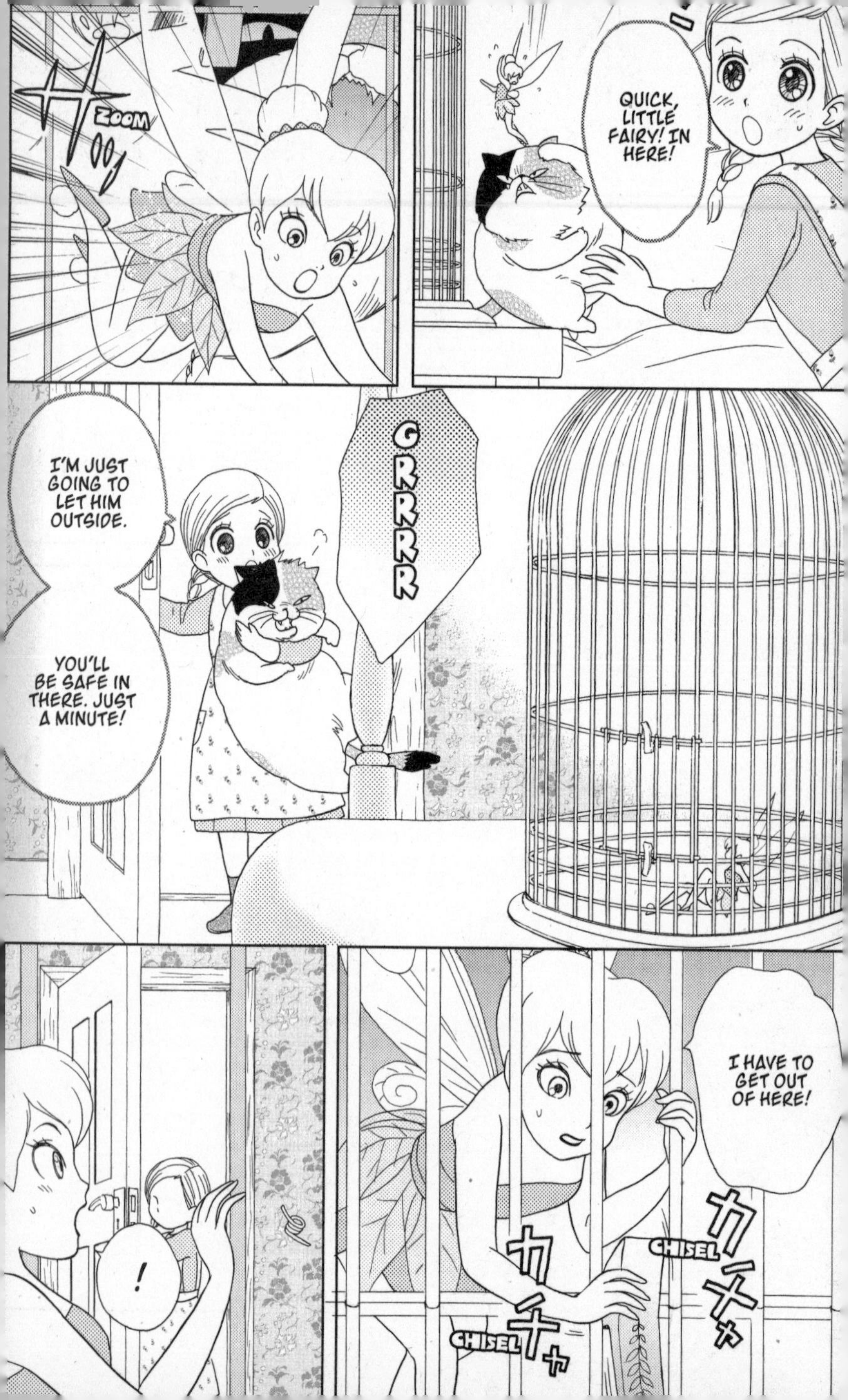
QUICK, LITTLE FAIRY! IN HERE!
ZOOM
GRRRR
I'M JUST GOING TO LET HIM OUTSIDE.
YOU'LL BE SAFE IN THERE. JUST A MINUTE!
I HAVE TO GET OUT OF HERE!
CHISEL
CHISEL
!

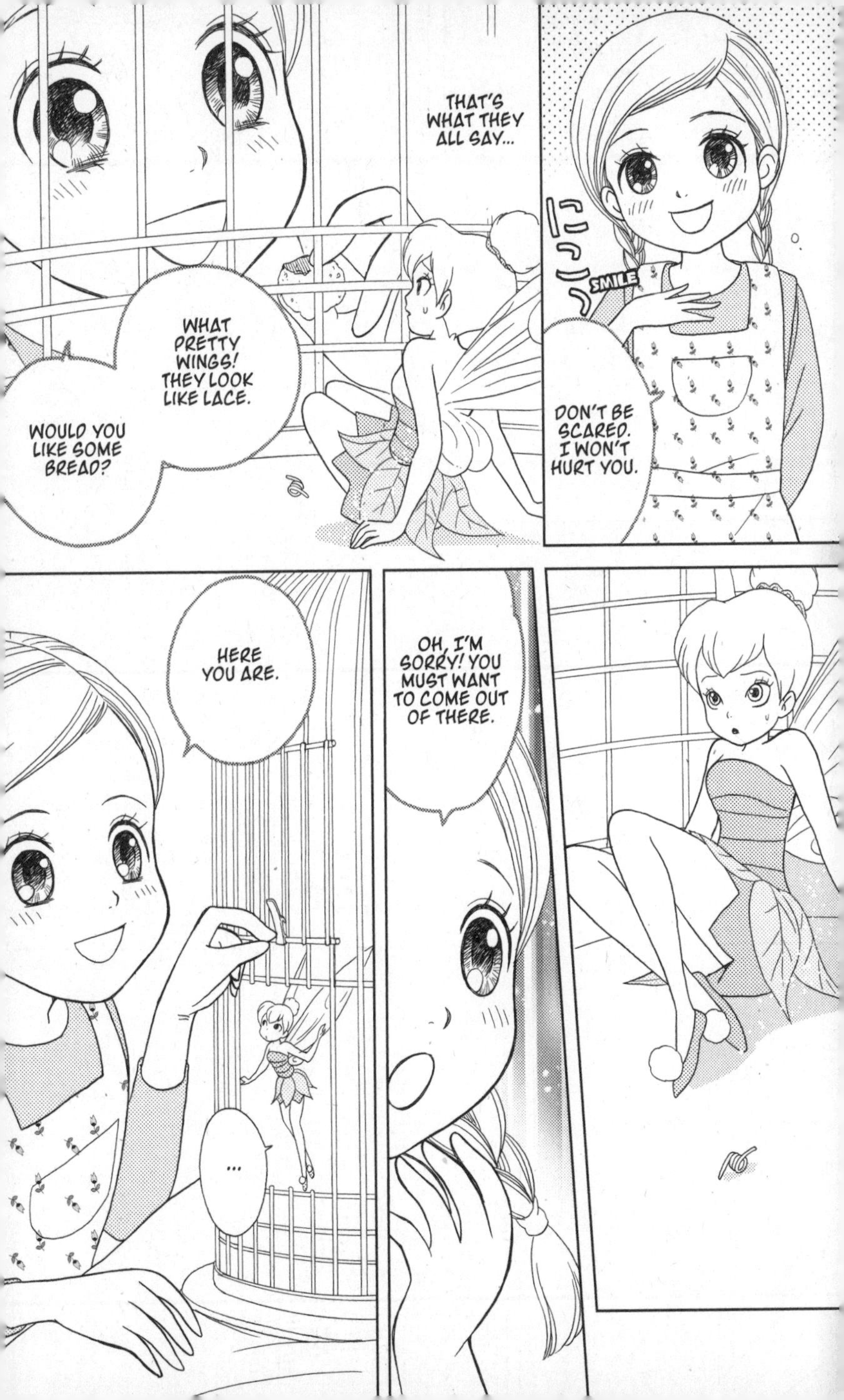
SMILE
DON'T BE SCARED. I WON'T HURT YOU.
THAT'S WHAT THEY ALL SAY...
WHAT PRETTY WINGS! THEY LOOK LIKE LACE.
WOULD YOU LIKE SOME BREAD?
OH, I'M SORRY! YOU MUST WANT TO COME OUT OF THERE.
HERE YOU ARE.
...

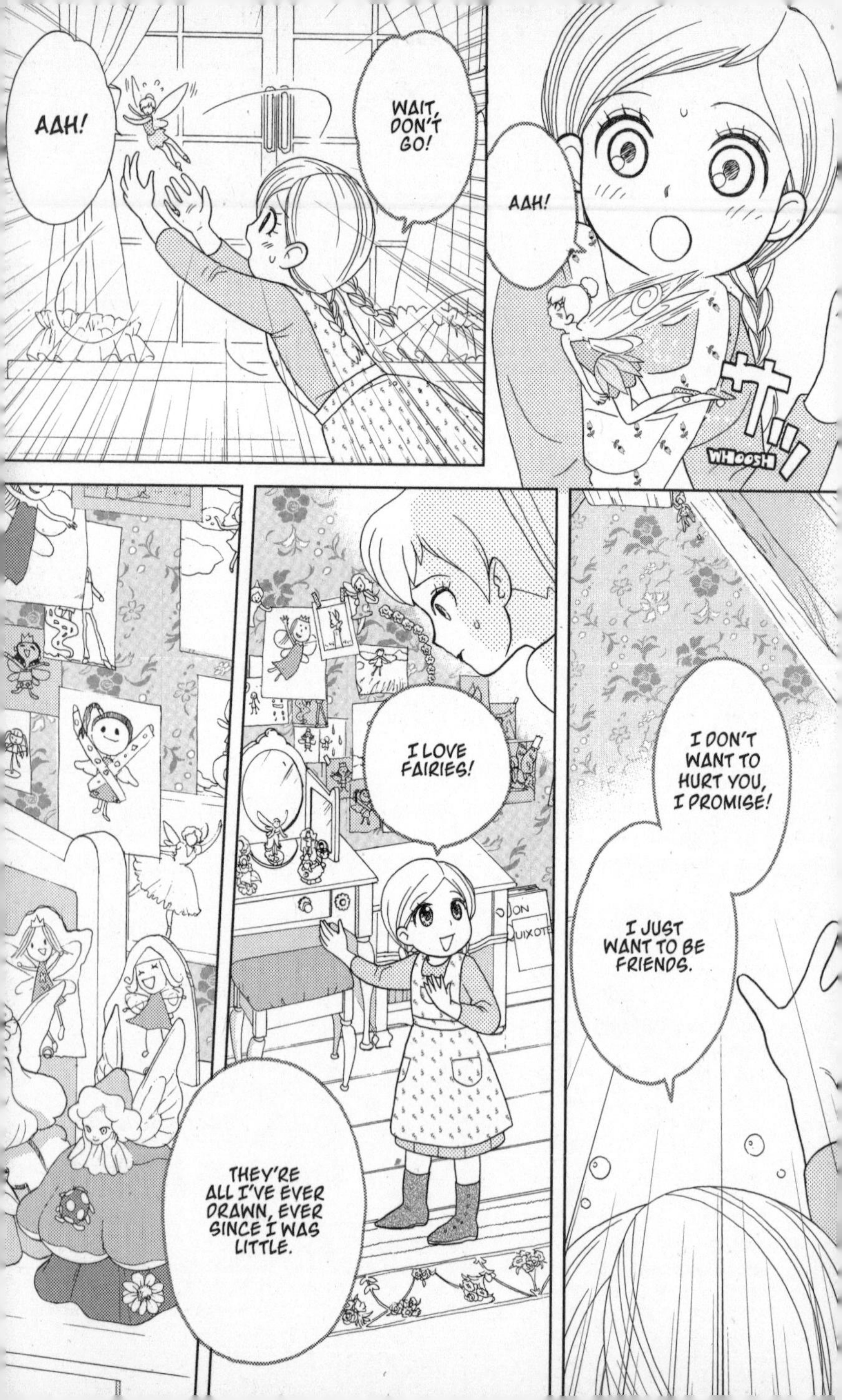
AAH!
WHOOSH
WAIT, DON'T GO!
AAH!
I DON'T WANT TO HURT YOU, I PROMISE!
I JUST WANT TO BE FRIENDS.
I LOVE FAIRIES!
THEY'RE ALL I'VE EVER DRAWN, EVER SINCE I WAS LITTLE.

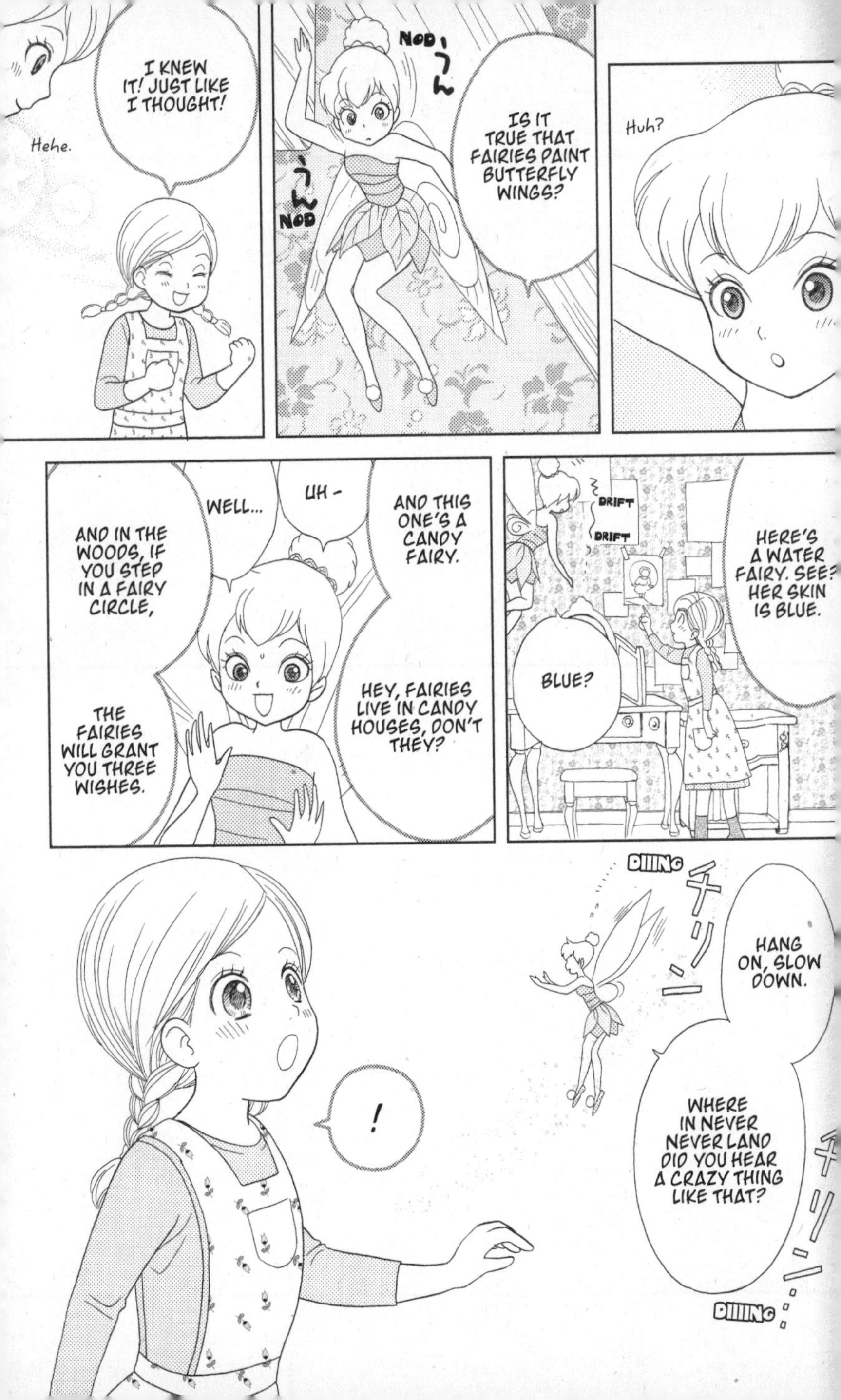

Huh?
NOD
うん
IS IT TRUE THAT FAIRIES PAINT BUTTERFLY WINGS?
うん
NOD
I KNEW IT! JUST LIKE I THOUGHT!
Hehe.
HERE'S A WATER FAIRY. SEE? HER SKIN IS BLUE.
DRIFT
DRIFT
BLUE?
AND THIS ONE'S A CANDY FAIRY.
UH -
HEY, FAIRIES LIVE IN CANDY HOUSES, DON'T THEY?
WELL...
AND IN THE WOODS, IF YOU STEP IN A FAIRY CIRCLE,
THE FAIRIES WILL GRANT YOU THREE WISHES.
DIIING
チリーン
HANG ON, SLOW DOWN.
WHERE IN NEVER NEVER LAND DID YOU HEAR A CRAZY THING LIKE THAT?
チリーン
DIIING
!

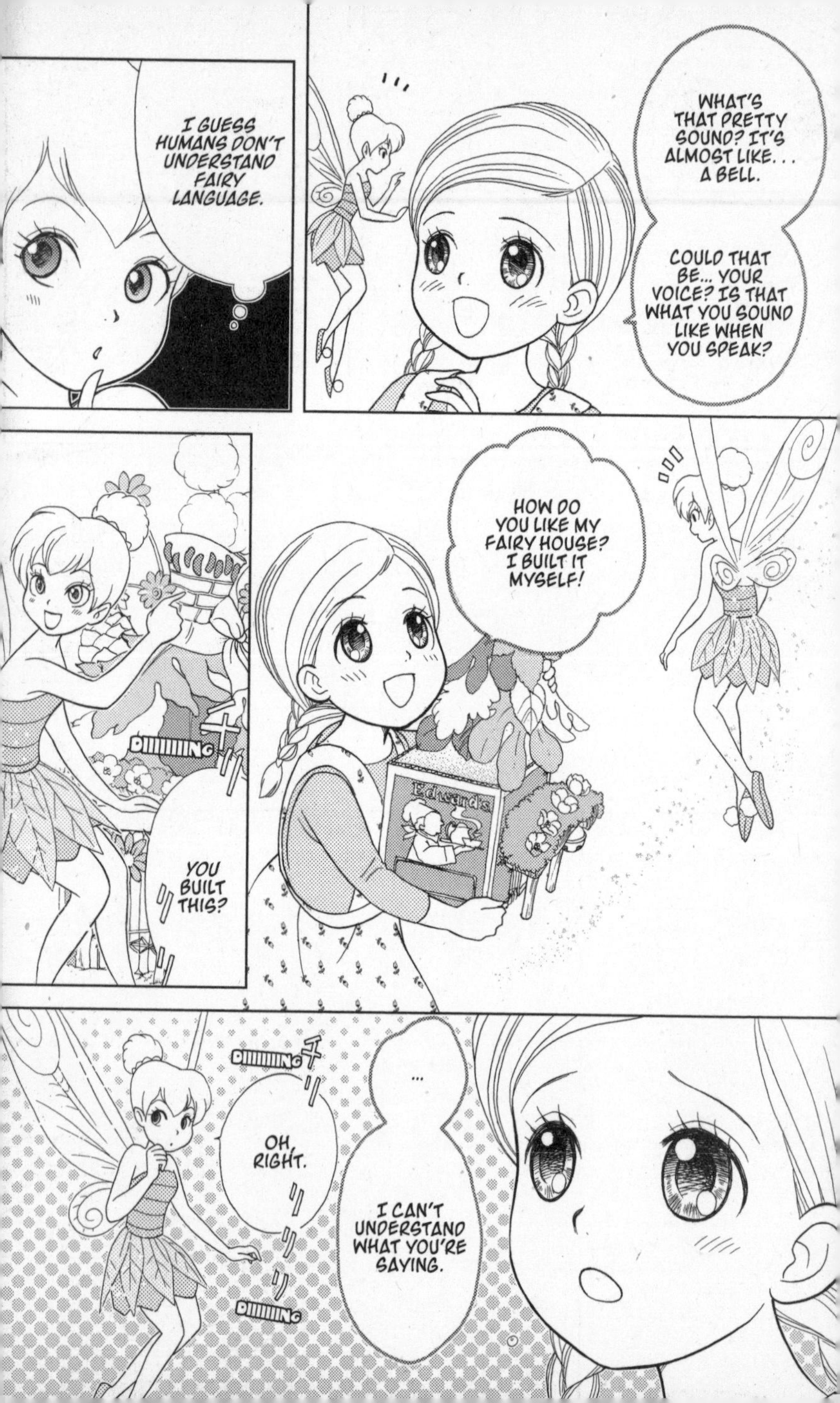
WHAT'S THAT PRETTY SOUND? IT'S ALMOST LIKE... A BELL.
COULD THAT BE... YOUR VOICE? IS THAT WHAT YOU SOUND LIKE WHEN YOU SPEAK?
I GUESS HUMANS DON'T UNDERSTAND FAIRY LANGUAGE.
HOW DO YOU LIKE MY FAIRY HOUSE? I BUILT IT MYSELF!
DIIIIIING
YOU BUILT THIS?
... I CAN'T UNDERSTAND WHAT YOU'RE SAYING.
DIIIIIING
OH, RIGHT.
DIIIIIING

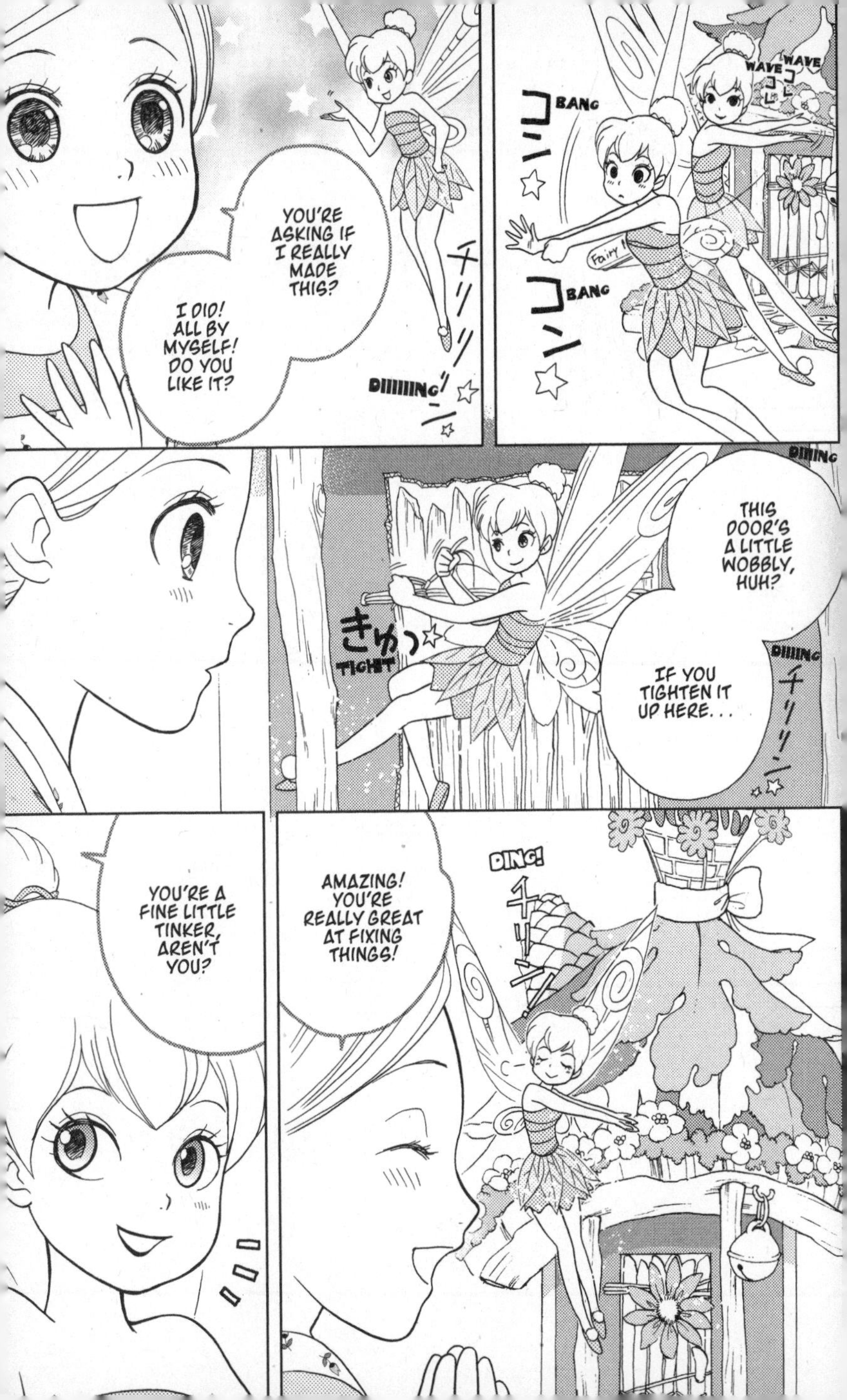

BANG
コン
BANG
コン
WAVE
WAVE
YOU'RE ASKING IF I REALLY MADE THIS?
I DID! ALL BY MYSELF! DO YOU LIKE IT?
チリリ
DIIIIING
DIIIING
THIS DOOR'S A LITTLE WOBBLY, HUH?
きゅっ
TIGHT
IF YOU TIGHTEN IT UP HERE. . .
DIIIING
チリリ
DING!
チリーン
AMAZING! YOU'RE REALLY GREAT AT FIXING THINGS!
YOU'RE A FINE LITTLE TINKER, AREN'T YOU?

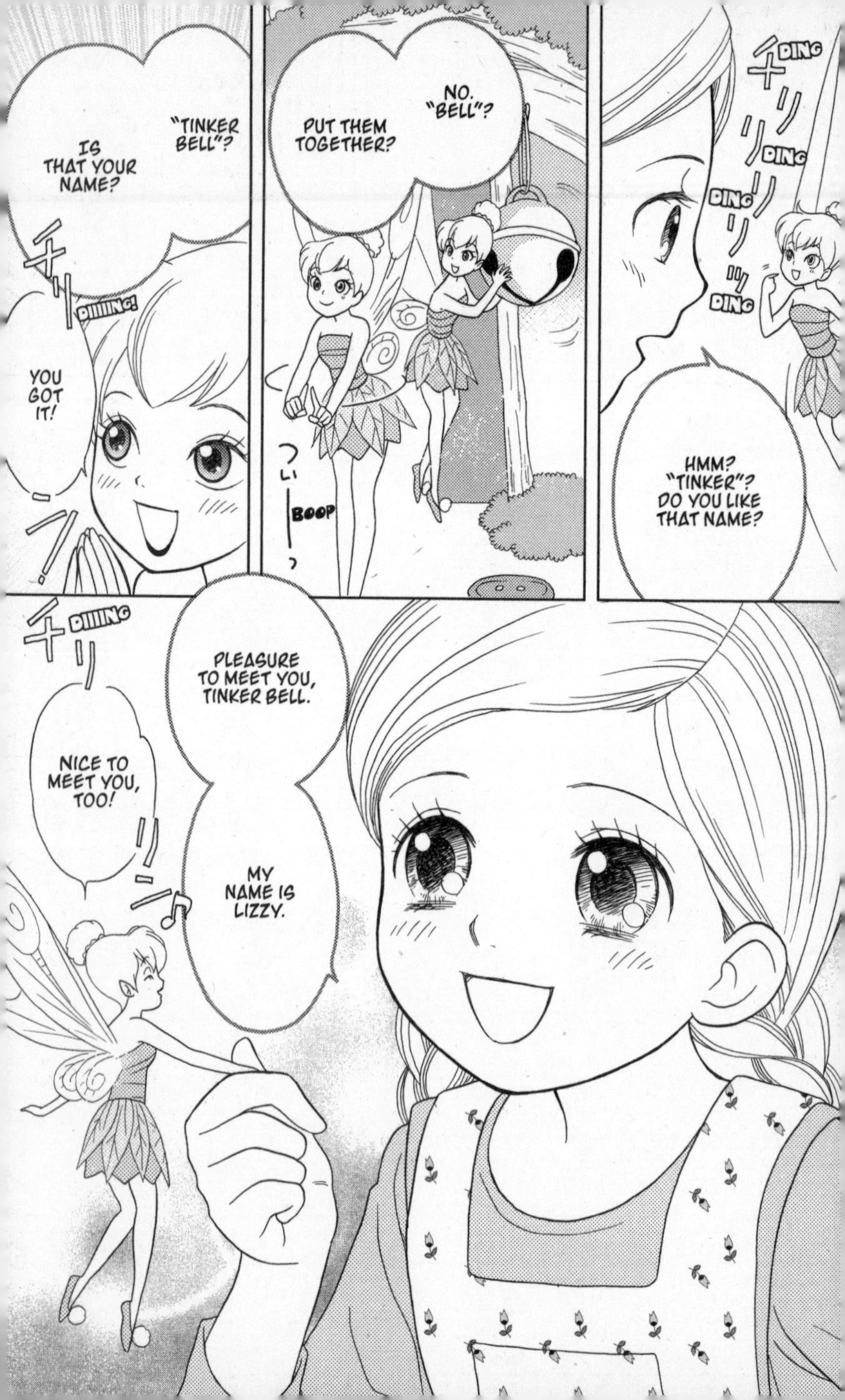
DING
DING
DING
DING
HMM? "TINKER"? DO YOU LIKE THAT NAME?
NO. "BELL"?
PUT THEM TOGETHER?
BOOP
"TINKER BELL"?
IS THAT YOUR NAME?
DIIIING!
YOU GOT IT!
PLEASURE TO MEET YOU, TINKER BELL.
MY NAME IS LIZZY.
DIIIING
NICE TO MEET YOU, TOO!

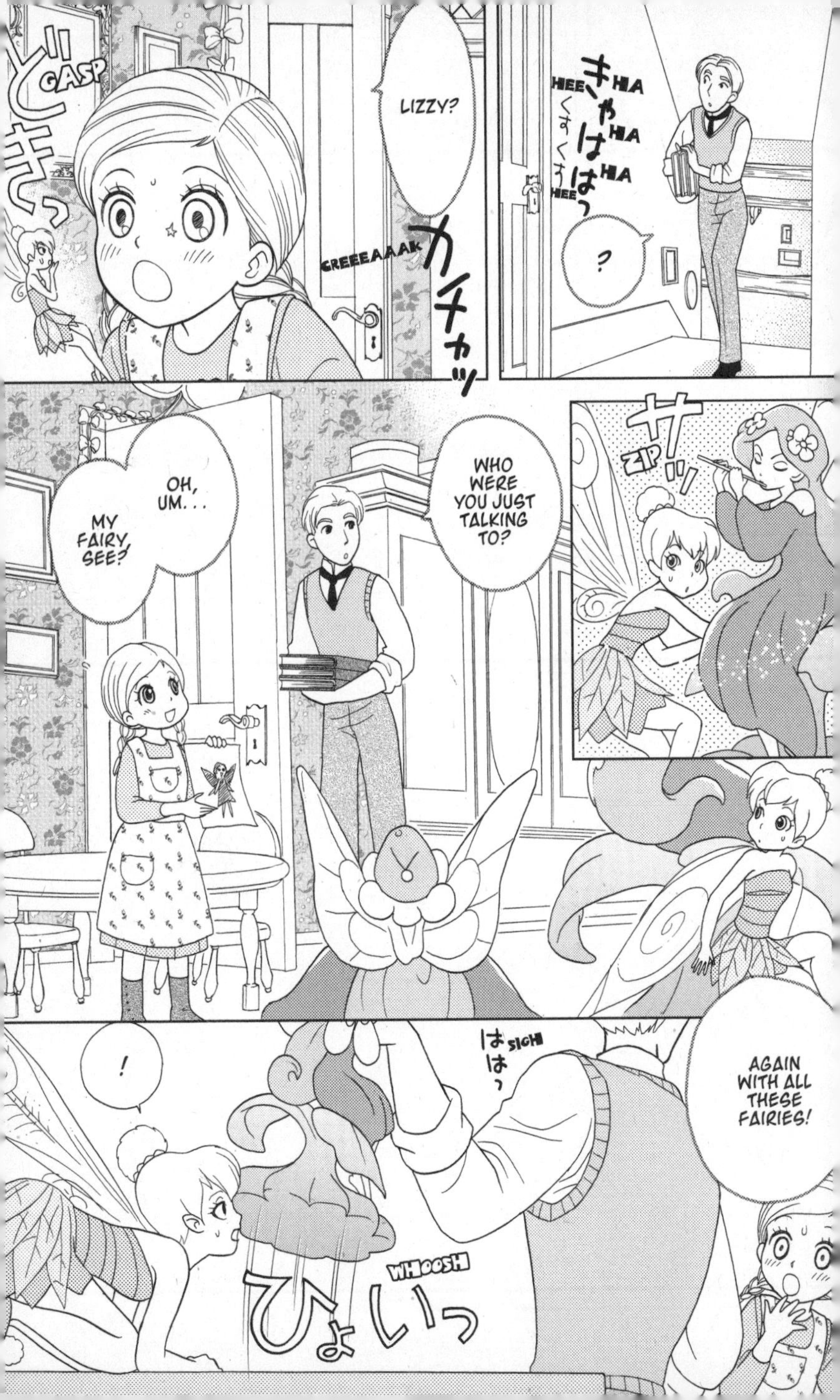

きゃははっ
HEE HA HA HA
くすくす
HEE
?
LIZZY?
カチャッ
GREEEAAAK
どきっ
GASP
ザッ
ZIP
WHO WERE YOU JUST TALKING TO?
OH, UM...
MY FAIRY, SEE?
AGAIN WITH ALL THESE FAIRIES!
ははっ
SIGH
!
ひょいっ
WHOOSH

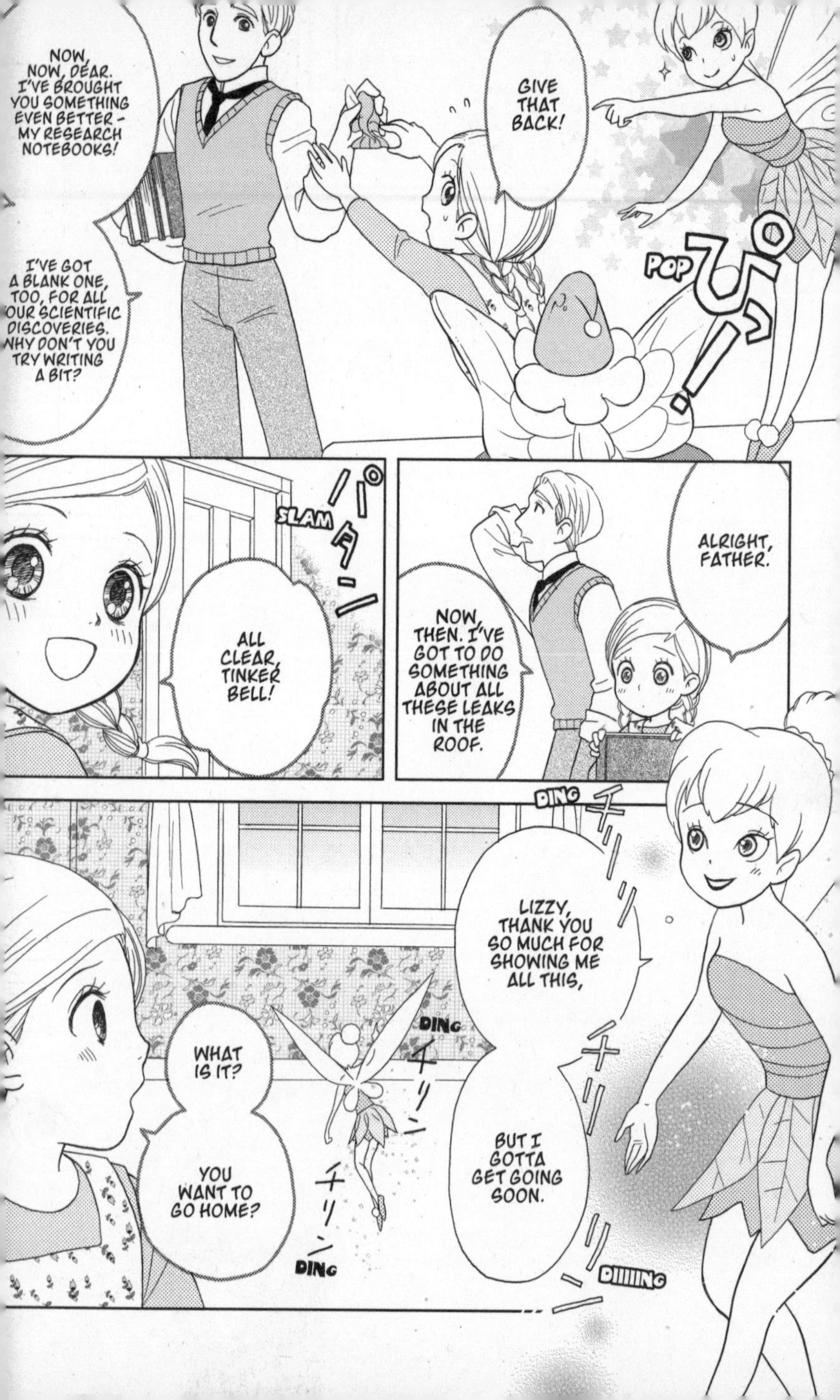
GIVE THAT BACK!
POP
NOW, NOW, DEAR. I'VE BROUGHT YOU SOMETHING EVEN BETTER - MY RESEARCH NOTEBOOKS!
I'VE GOT A BLANK ONE, TOO, FOR ALL OUR SCIENTIFIC DISCOVERIES. WHY DON'T YOU TRY WRITING A BIT?
ALRIGHT, FATHER.
NOW, THEN. I'VE GOT TO DO SOMETHING ABOUT ALL THESE LEAKS IN THE ROOF.
SLAM
ALL CLEAR, TINKER BELL!
DING
LIZZY, THANK YOU SO MUCH FOR SHOWING ME ALL THIS,
BUT I GOTTA GET GOING SOON.
DIIIING
DING
WHAT IS IT?
YOU WANT TO GO HOME?
DING

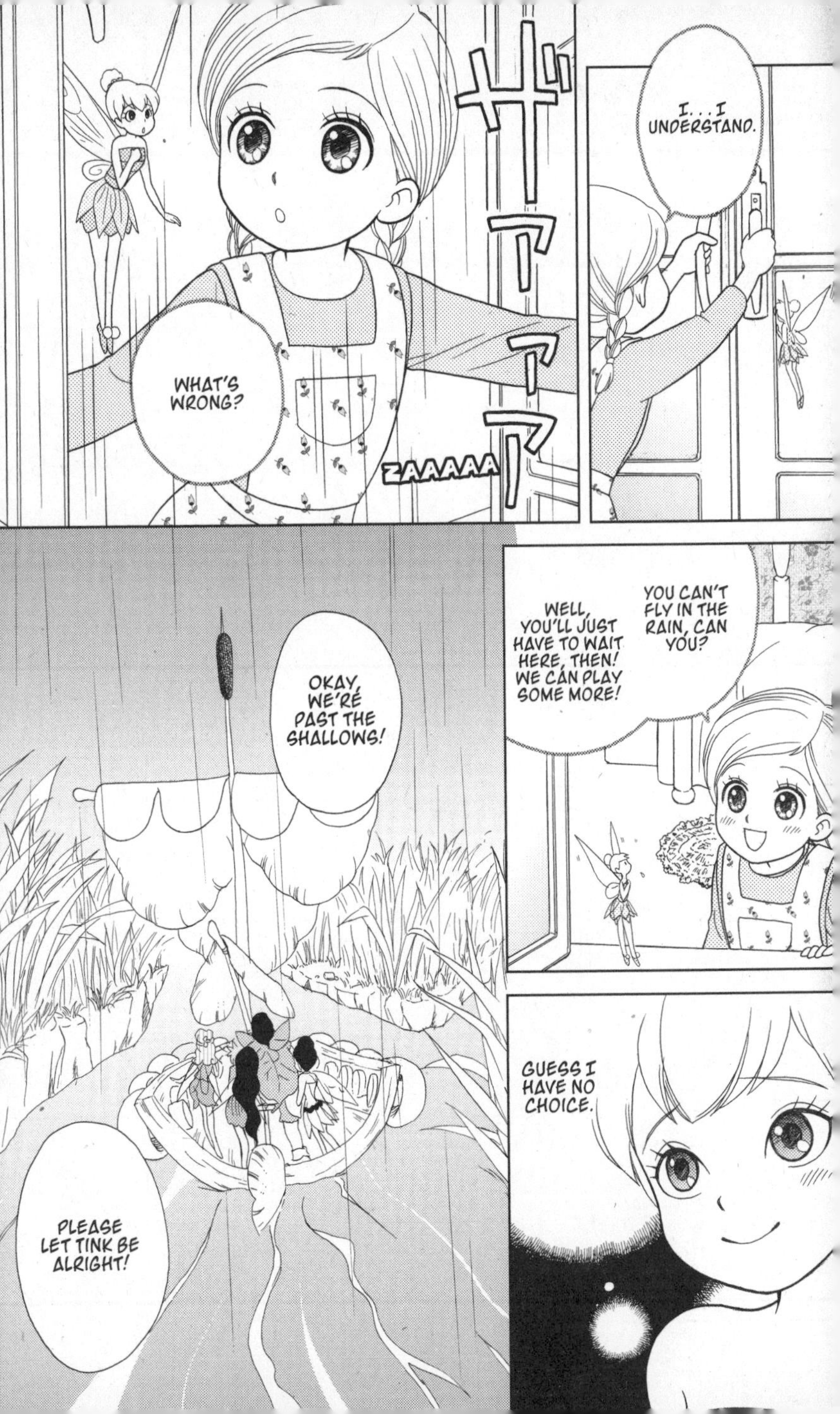
I... I UNDERSTAND.
WHAT'S WRONG?
ザァァァ
ZAAAAA
YOU CAN'T FLY IN THE RAIN, CAN YOU?
WELL, YOU'LL JUST HAVE TO WAIT HERE, THEN! WE CAN PLAY SOME MORE!
GUESS I HAVE NO CHOICE.
OKAY, WE'RE PAST THE SHALLOWS!
PLEASE LET TINK BE ALRIGHT!

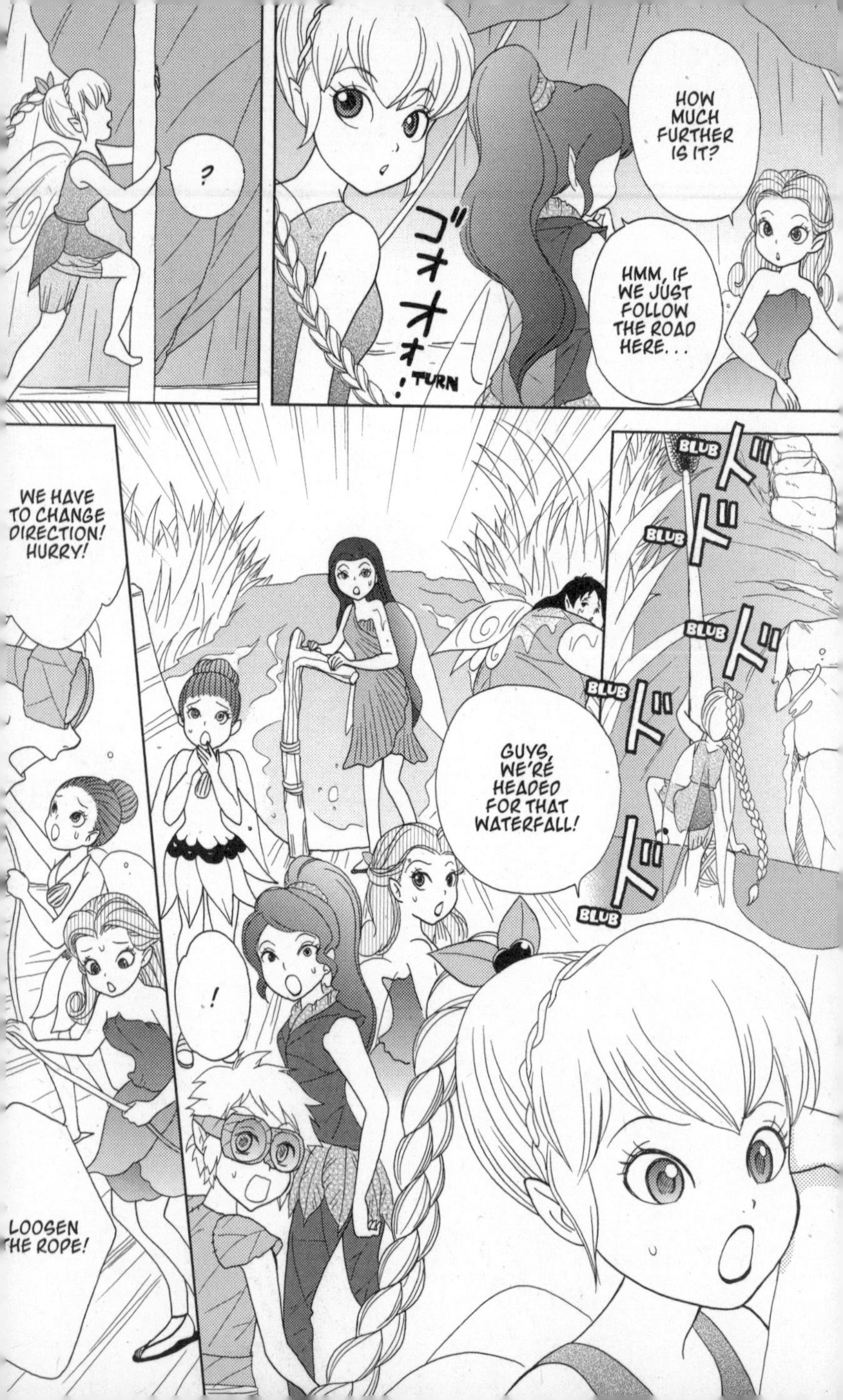

HOW MUCH FURTHER IS IT?
HMM, IF WE JUST FOLLOW THE ROAD HERE...
ゴオオォ!
TURN
?
BLUB
ドドドド
BLUB
BLUB
BLUB
BLUB
GUYS, WE'RE HEADED FOR THAT WATERFALL!
!
WE HAVE TO CHANGE DIRECTION! HURRY!
LOOSEN THE ROPE!

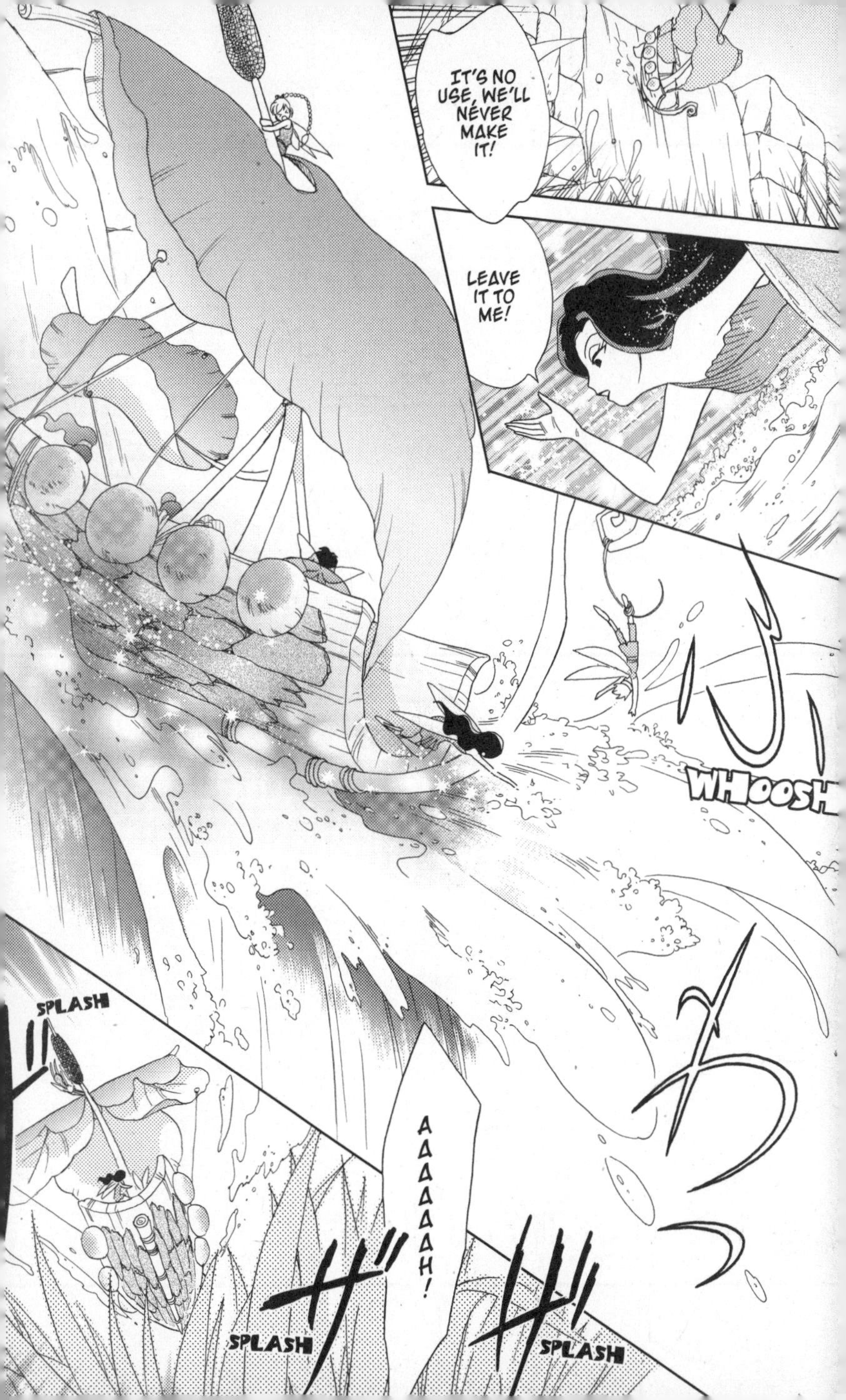
IT'S NO USE, WE'LL NEVER MAKE IT!
LEAVE IT TO ME!
WHOOSH
AAAAAAAAH!
SPLASH
SPLASH
SPLASH

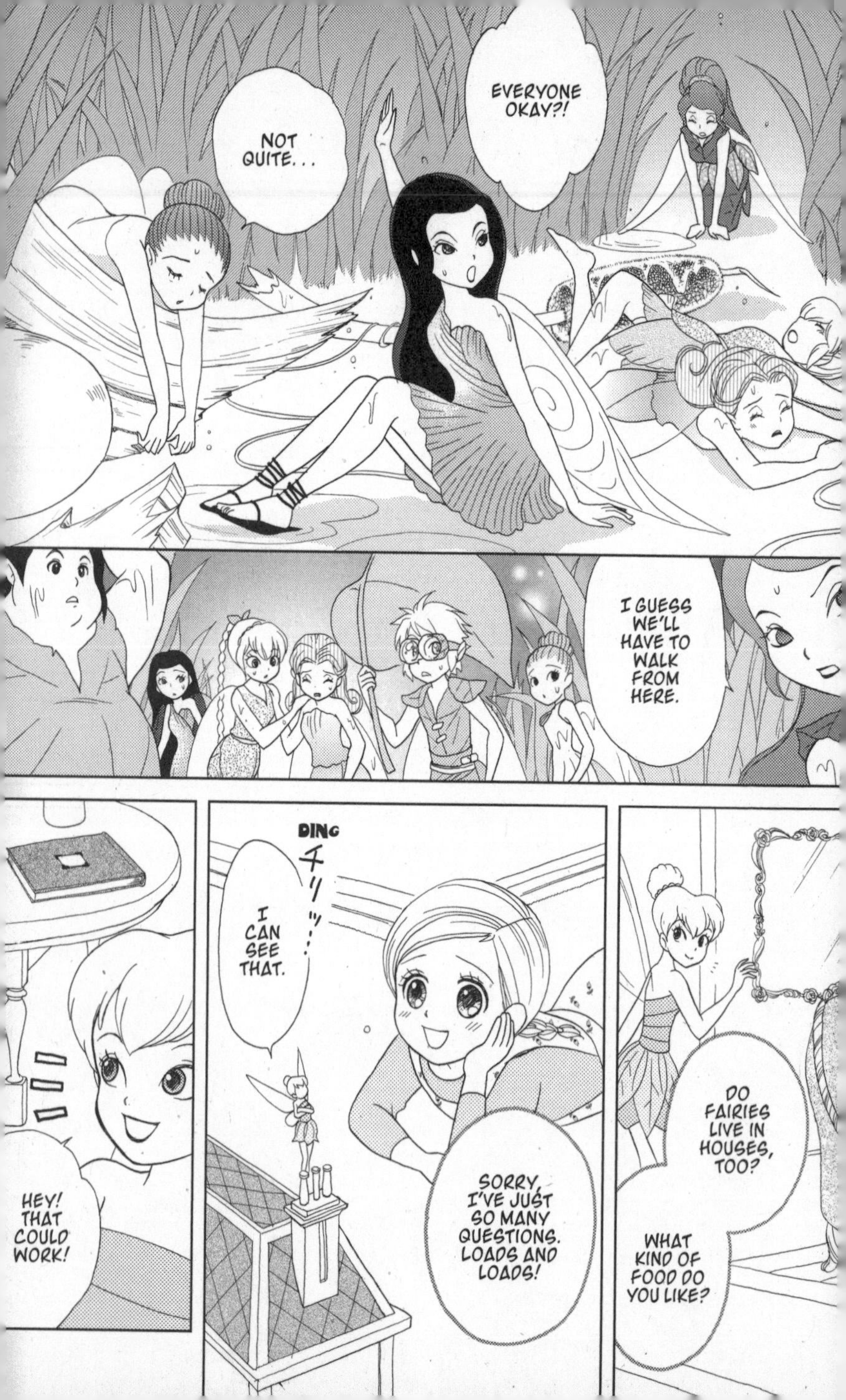
EVERYONE OKAY?!
NOT QUITE...
I GUESS WE'LL HAVE TO WALK FROM HERE.
DO FAIRIES LIVE IN HOUSES, TOO?
WHAT KIND OF FOOD DO YOU LIKE?
SORRY, I'VE JUST SO MANY QUESTIONS. LOADS AND LOADS!
DING
チリッ…
I CAN SEE THAT.
HEY! THAT COULD WORK!

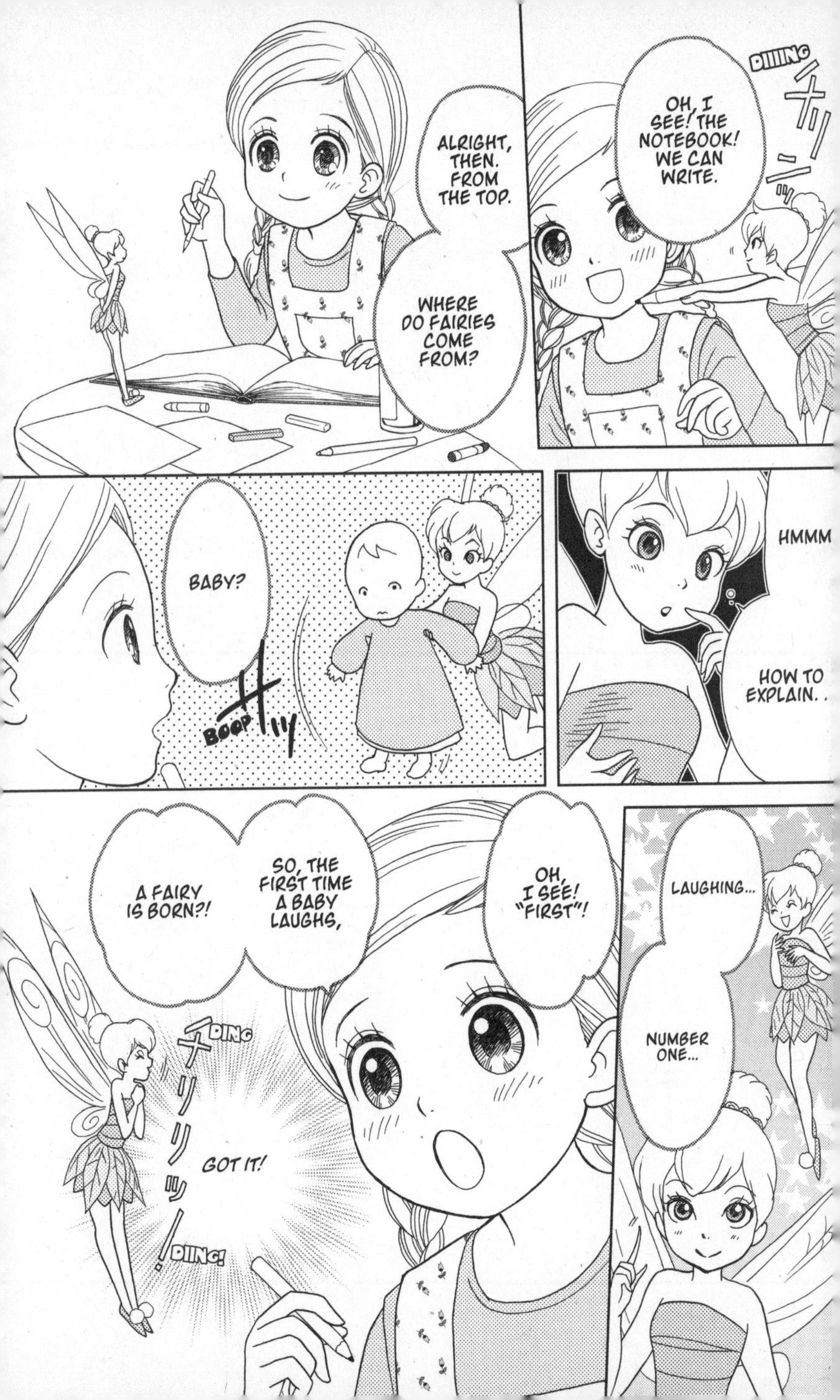
DIIING
OH, I SEE! THE NOTEBOOK! WE CAN WRITE.
ALRIGHT, THEN. FROM THE TOP.
WHERE DO FAIRIES COME FROM?
HMMM
HOW TO EXPLAIN. . .
BABY?
BOOP
LAUGHING...
NUMBER ONE...
OH, I SEE! "FIRST"!
SO, THE FIRST TIME A BABY LAUGHS,
A FAIRY IS BORN?!
DING
GOT IT!
DIING!

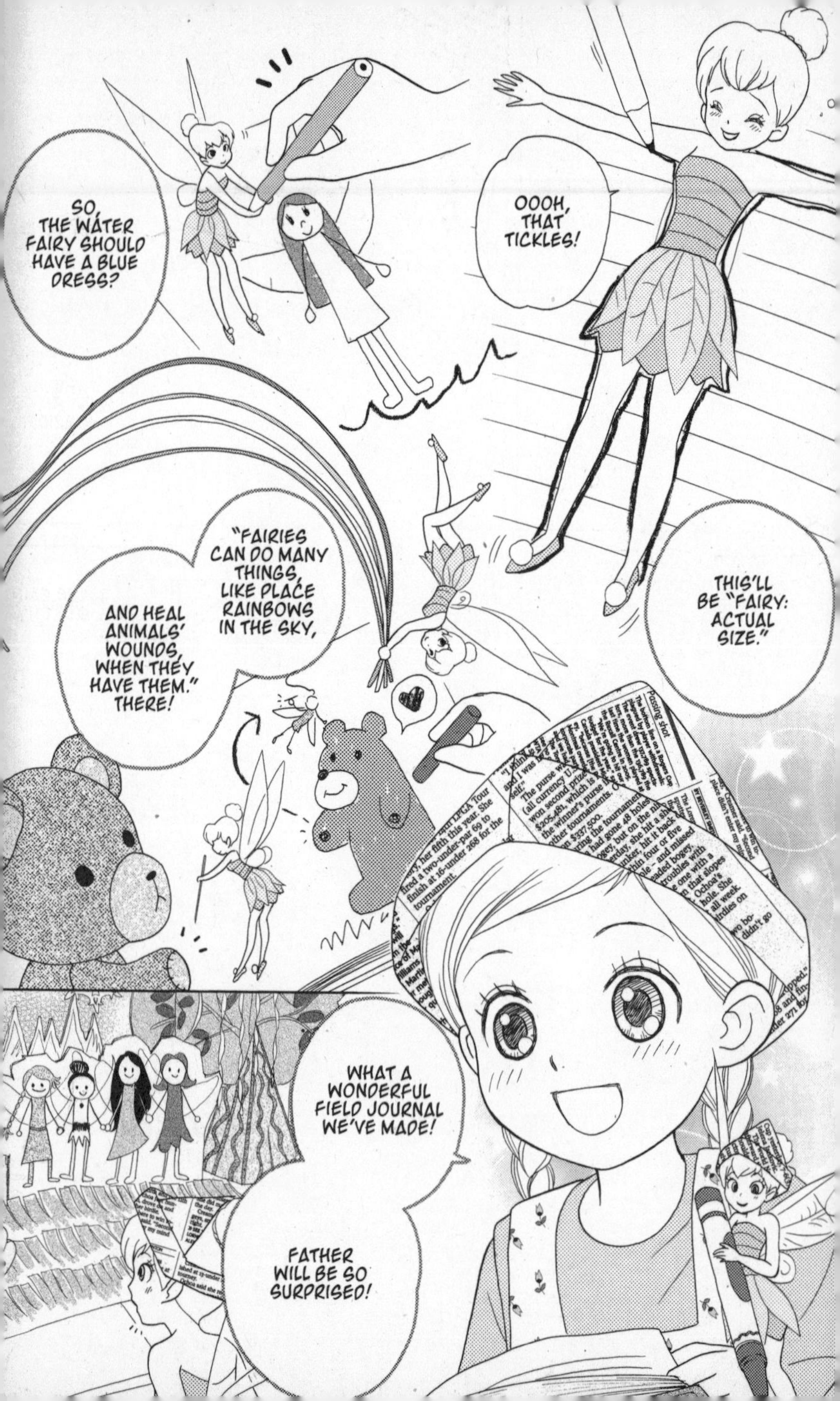
OOOH, THAT TICKLES!
THIS'LL BE "FAIRY: ACTUAL SIZE."
SO, THE WATER FAIRY SHOULD HAVE A BLUE DRESS?
"FAIRIES CAN DO MANY THINGS, LIKE PLACE RAINBOWS IN THE SKY,
AND HEAL ANIMALS' WOUNDS, WHEN THEY HAVE THEM." THERE!
WHAT A WONDERFUL FIELD JOURNAL WE'VE MADE!
FATHER WILL BE SO SURPRISED!

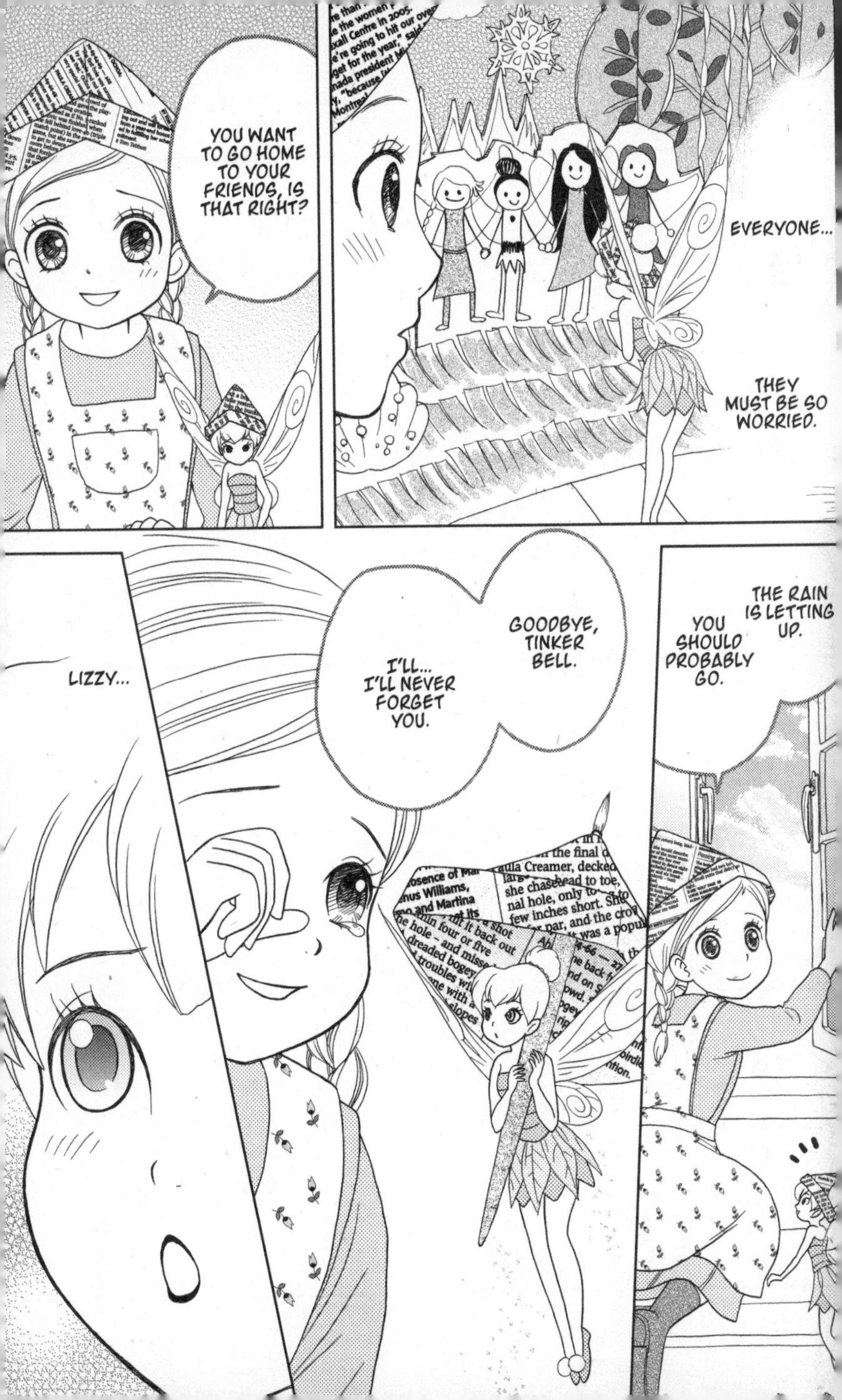

EVERYONE...
THEY MUST BE SO WORRIED.
YOU WANT TO GO HOME TO YOUR FRIENDS, IS THAT RIGHT?
THE RAIN IS LETTING UP.
YOU SHOULD PROBABLY GO.
GOODBYE, TINKER BELL.
I'LL... I'LL NEVER FORGET YOU.
LIZZY...

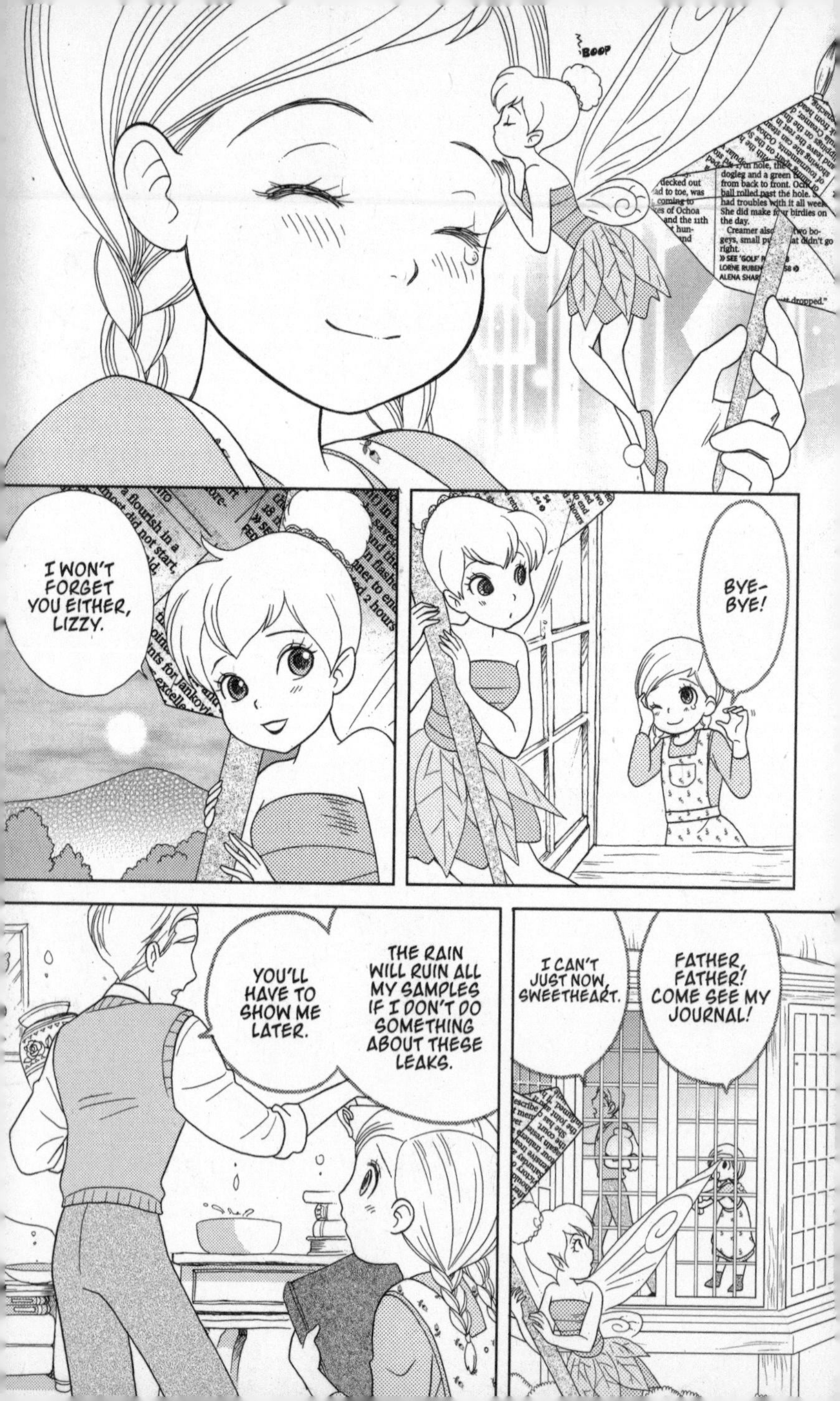
BOOP
BYE-BYE!
I WON'T FORGET YOU EITHER, LIZZY.
FATHER, FATHER! COME SEE MY JOURNAL!
I CAN'T JUST NOW, SWEETHEART.
THE RAIN WILL RUIN ALL MY SAMPLES IF I DON'T DO SOMETHING ABOUT THESE LEAKS.
YOU'LL HAVE TO SHOW ME LATER.

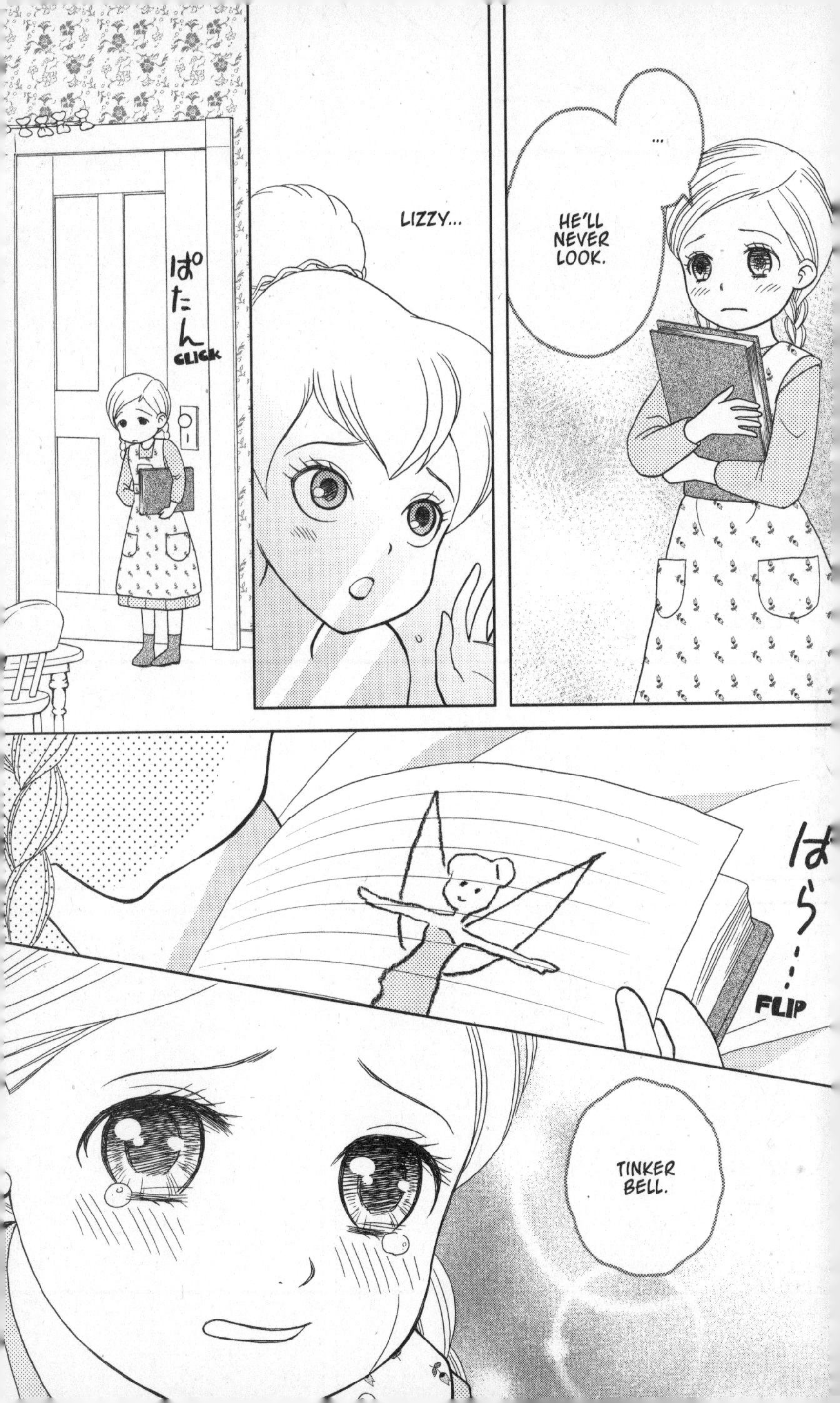

...
HE'LL NEVER LOOK.
LIZZY...
ぱたん
CLICK
はら…
FLIP
TINKER BELL.

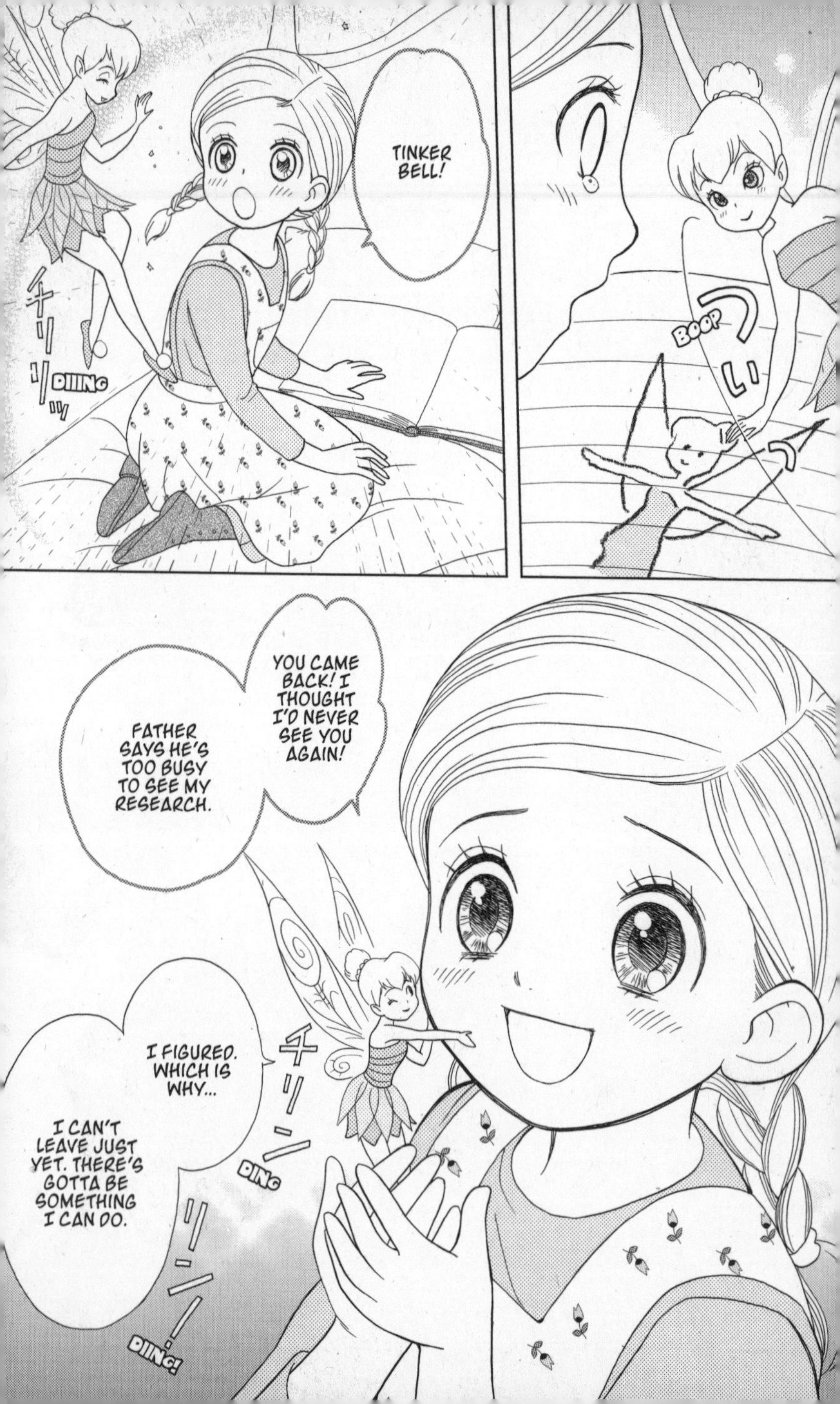
BOOP
TINKER BELL!
DIIING
YOU CAME BACK! I THOUGHT I'D NEVER SEE YOU AGAIN!
FATHER SAYS HE'S TOO BUSY TO SEE MY RESEARCH.
I FIGURED. WHICH IS WHY...
DING
I CAN'T LEAVE JUST YET. THERE'S GOTTA BE SOMETHING I CAN DO.
DIING!

WHERE'S TINK?

SILHOUETTE QUIZ

CUTE LITTLE TINK HAS A MATCHING SILHOUETTE DOWN BELOW. CAN YOU FIND HER?

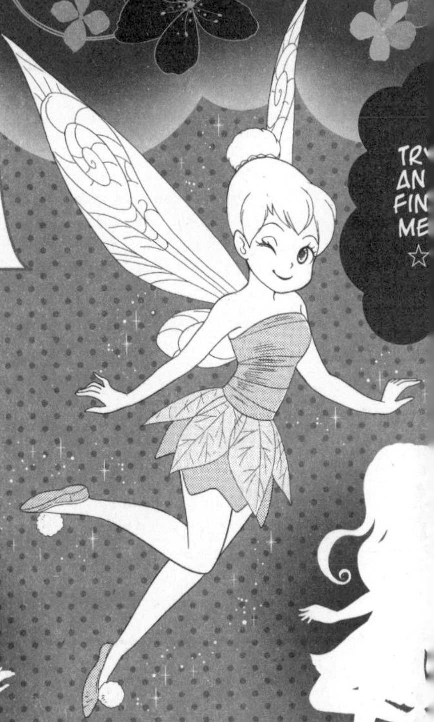

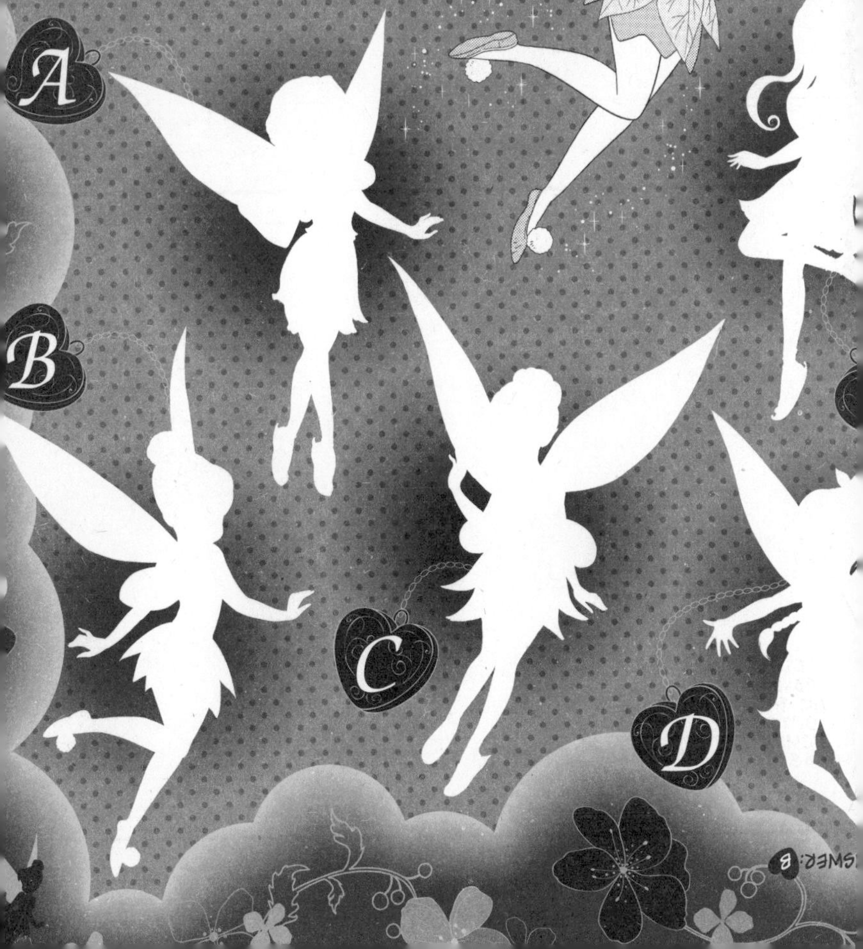
A
B
C
D

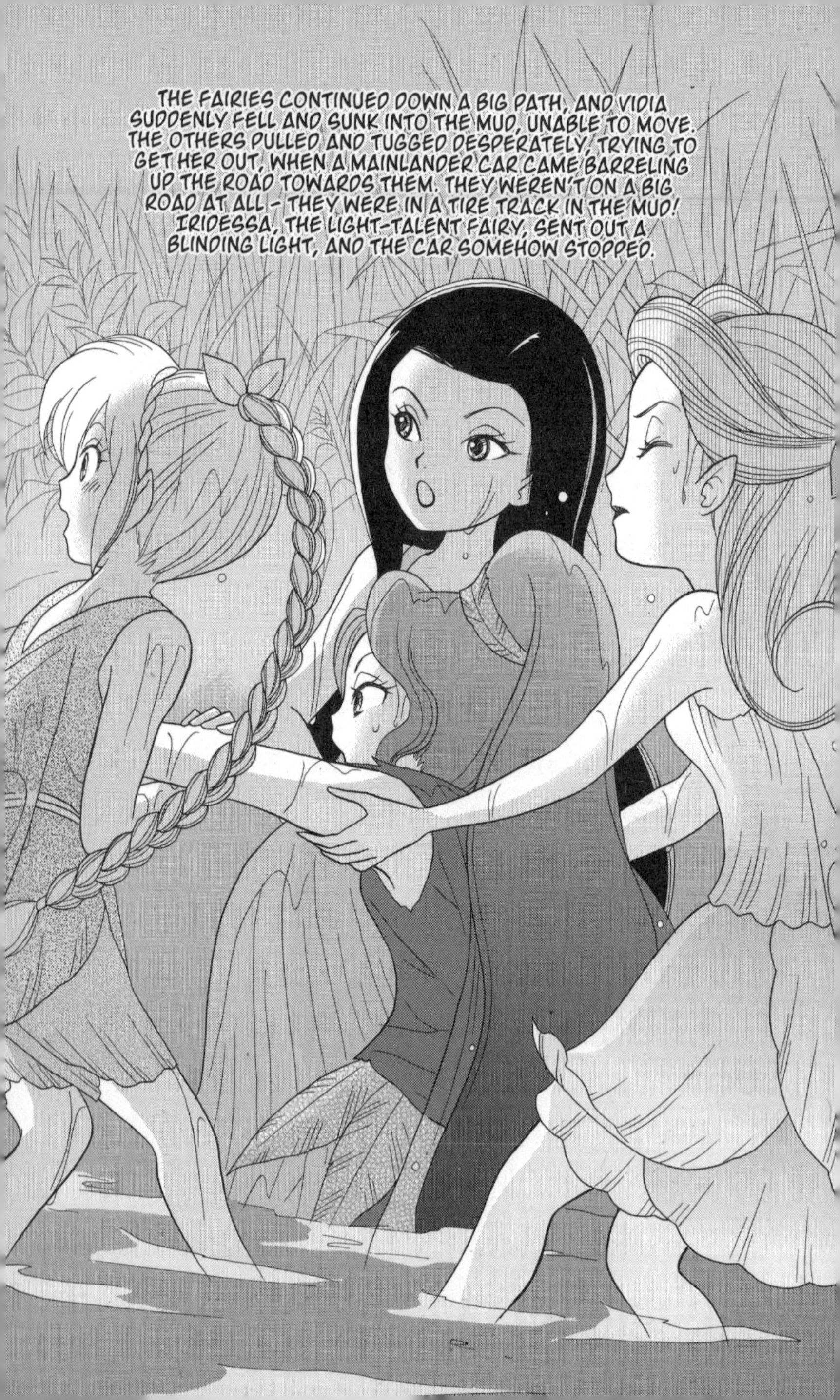
THE FAIRIES CONTINUED DOWN A BIG PATH, AND VIDIA SUDDENLY FELL AND SUNK INTO THE MUD, UNABLE TO MOVE. THE OTHERS PULLED AND TUGGED DESPERATELY, TRYING TO GET HER OUT, WHEN A MAINLANDER CAR CAME BARRELING UP THE ROAD TOWARDS THEM. THEY WEREN'T ON A BIG ROAD AT ALL - THEY WERE IN A TIRE TRACK IN THE MUD! IRIDESSA, THE LIGHT-TALENT FAIRY, SENT OUT A BLINDING LIGHT, AND THE CAR SOMEHOW STOPPED.

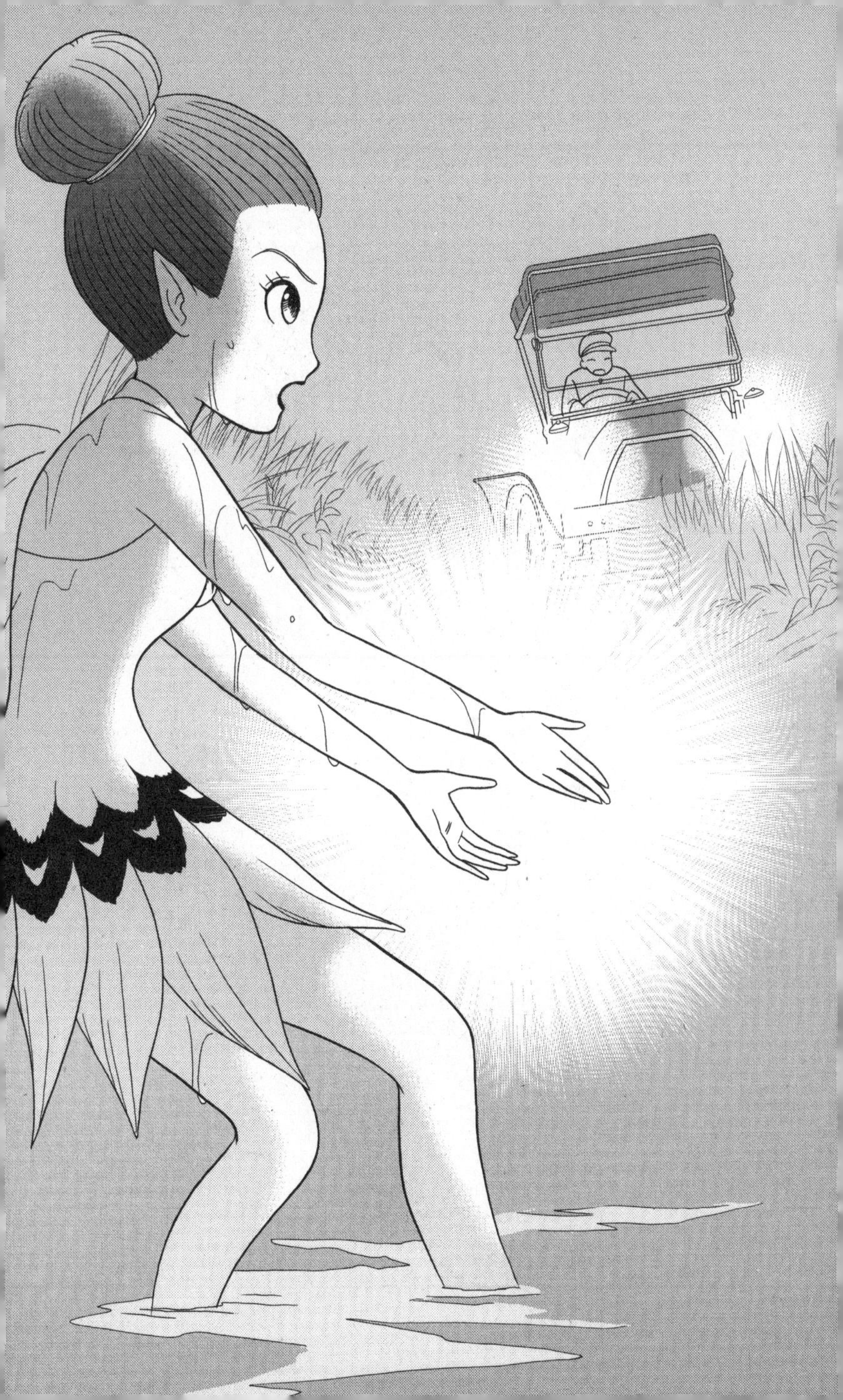

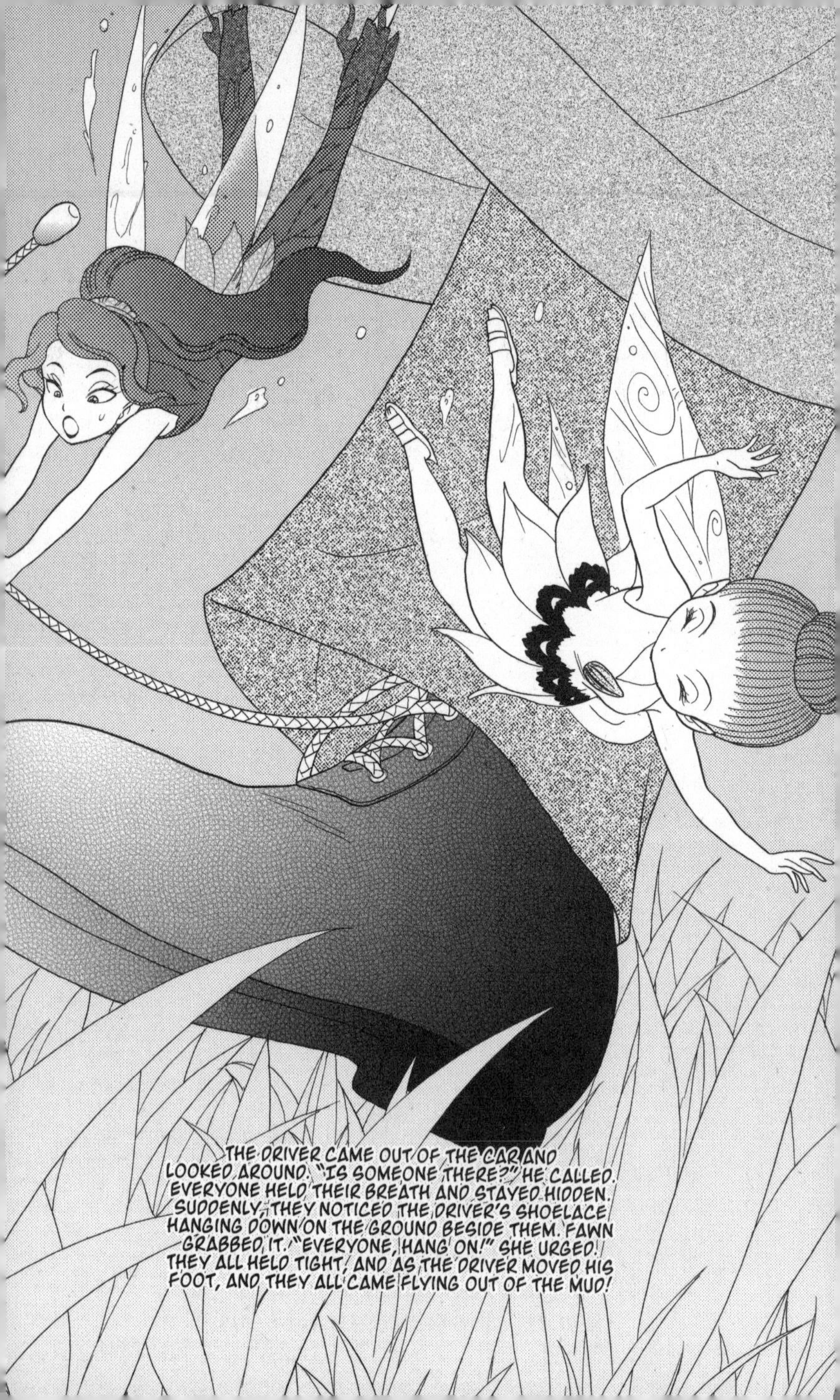
THE DRIVER CAME OUT OF THE CAR AND LOOKED AROUND. "IS SOMEONE THERE?" HE CALLED. EVERYONE HELD THEIR BREATH AND STAYED HIDDEN. SUDDENLY, THEY NOTICED THE DRIVER'S SHOELACE HANGING DOWN ON THE GROUND BESIDE THEM. FAWN GRABBED IT. "EVERYONE, HANG ON!" SHE URGED. THEY ALL HELD TIGHT, AND AS THE DRIVER MOVED HIS FOOT, AND THEY ALL CAME FLYING OUT OF THE MUD!

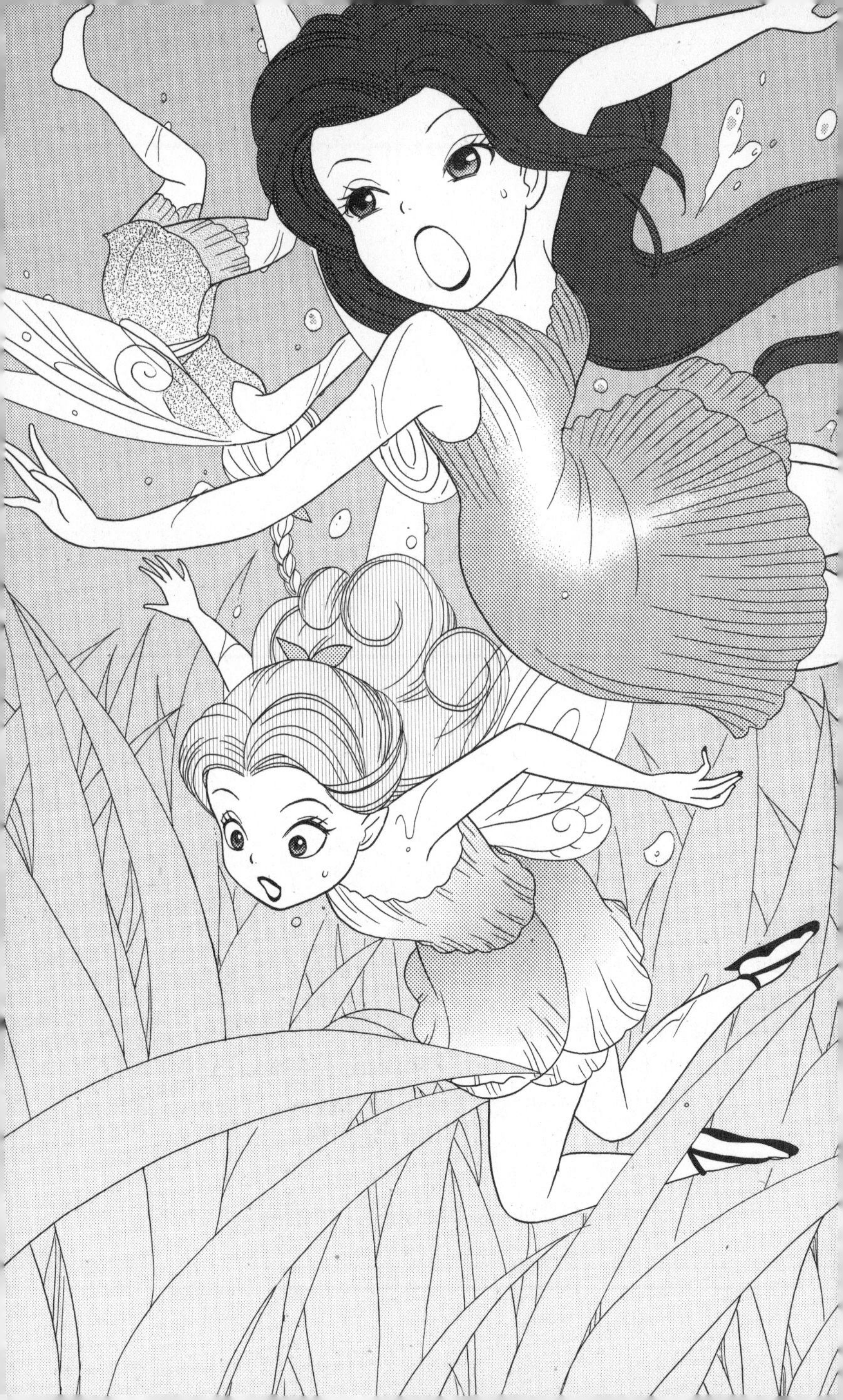

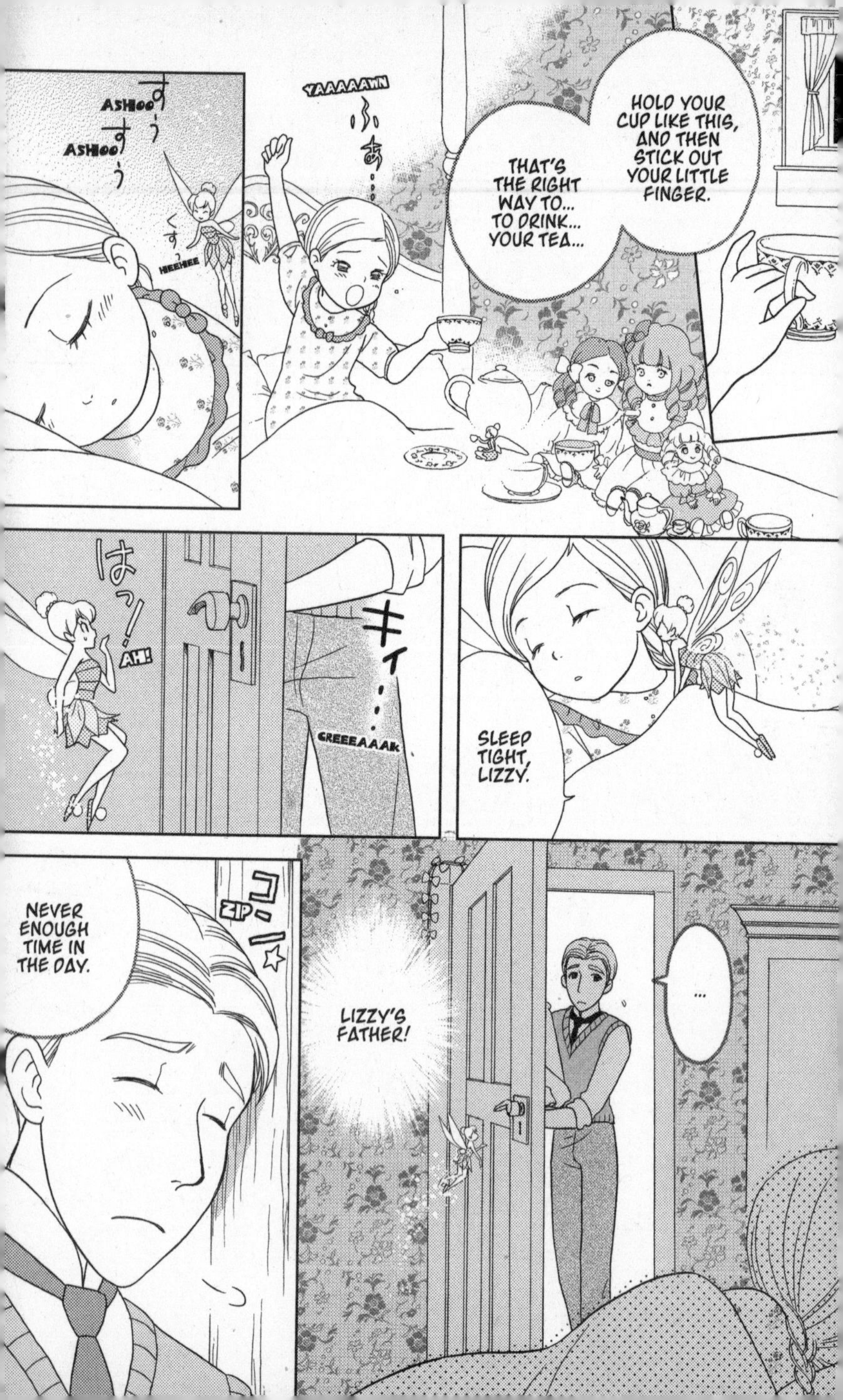
HOLD YOUR CUP LIKE THIS, AND THEN STICK OUT YOUR LITTLE FINGER.
THAT'S THE RIGHT WAY TO... TO DRINK... YOUR TEA...
YAAAAAWN
ASHOO
ASHOO
HEEHEE
SLEEP TIGHT, LIZZY.
CREEEAAAK
AH!
...
LIZZY'S FATHER!
ZIP
NEVER ENOUGH TIME IN THE DAY.

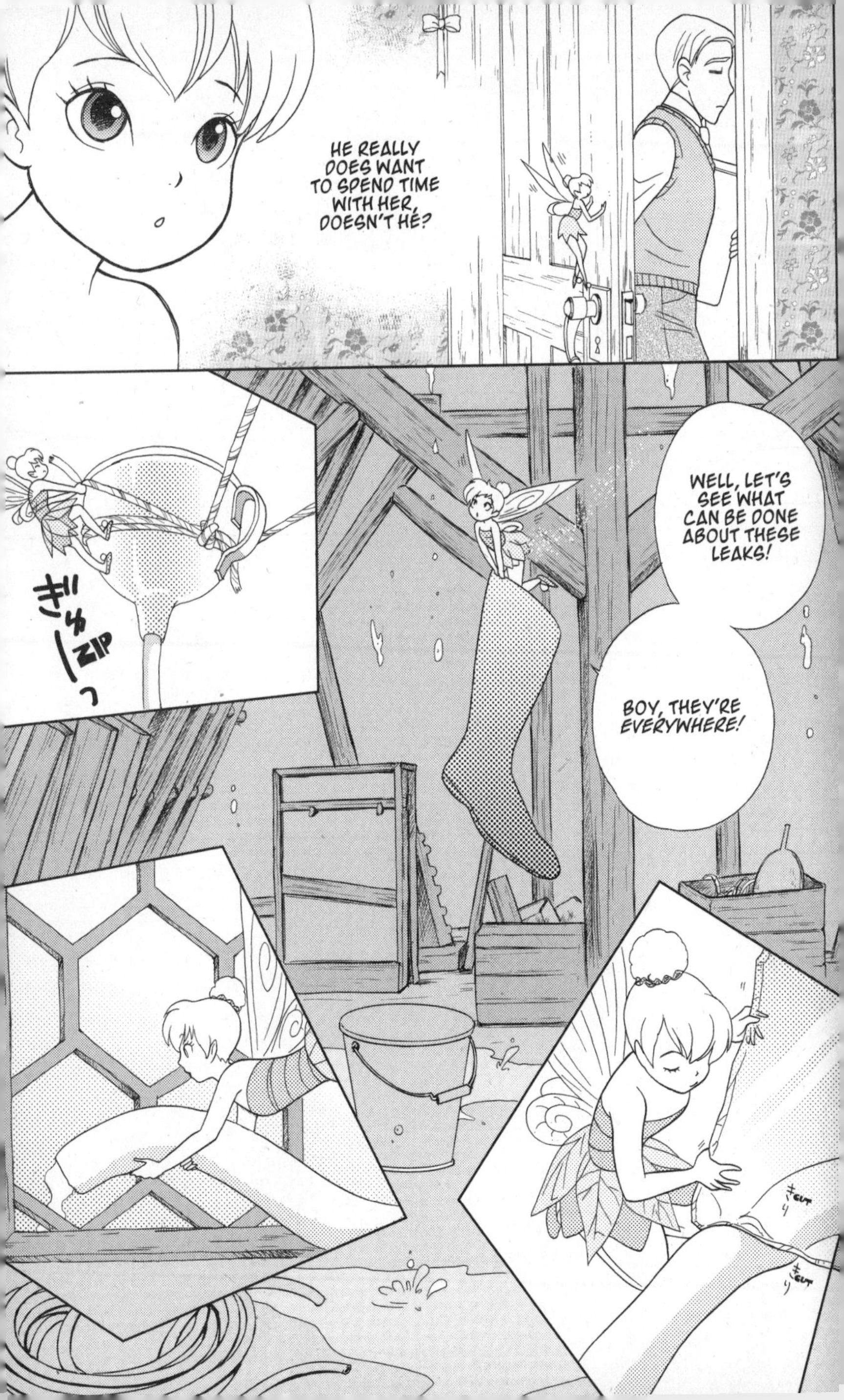
HE REALLY DOES WANT TO SPEND TIME WITH HER, DOESN'T HE?
WELL, LET'S SEE WHAT CAN BE DONE ABOUT THESE LEAKS!
BOY, THEY'RE EVERYWHERE!
ぎゅーっ ZIP
きり CUT
きり CUT

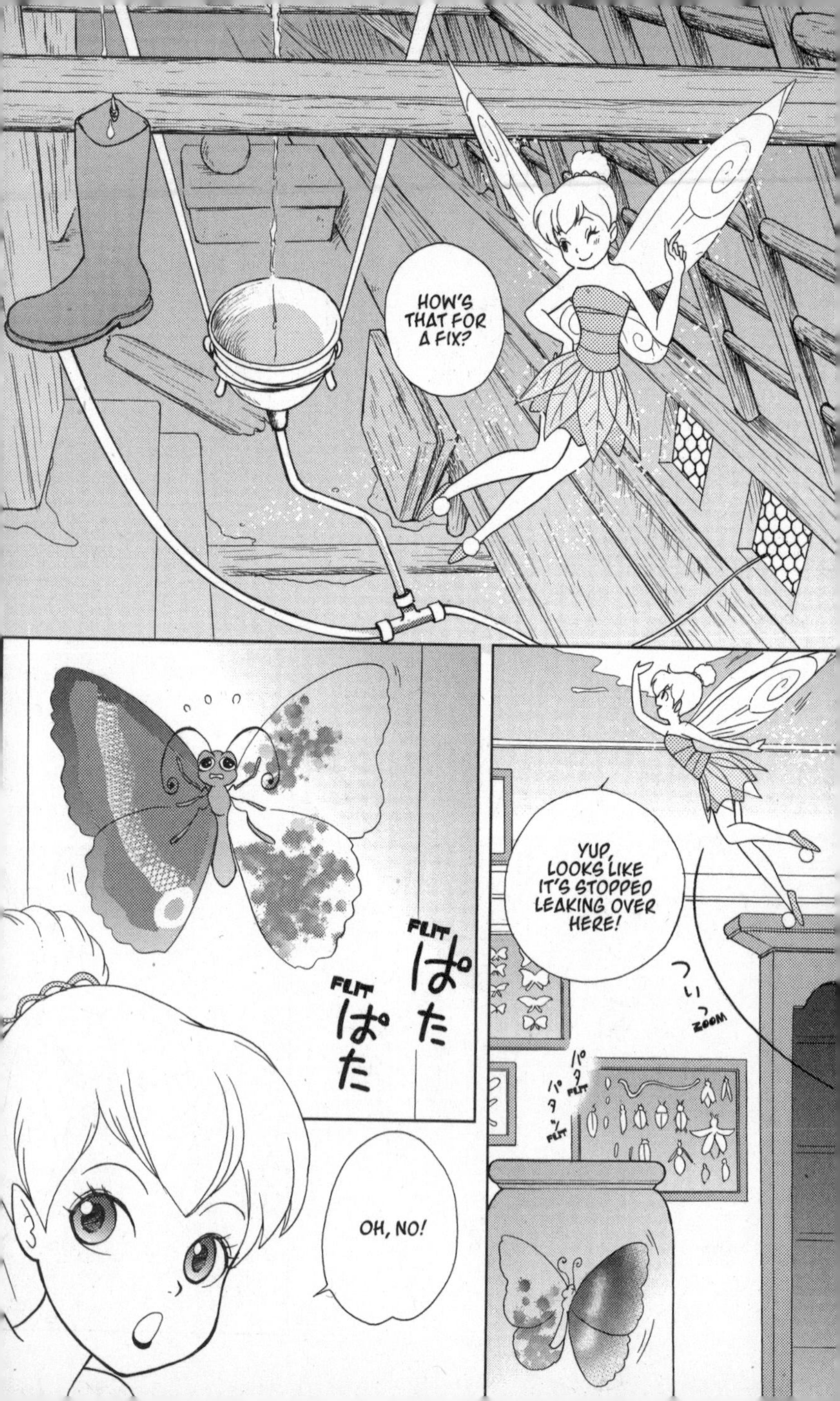
HOW'S THAT FOR A FIX?
YUP, LOOKS LIKE IT'S STOPPED LEAKING OVER HERE!
ついっ ZOOM
パタ FLIT
パタッ FLIT FLIT
ぱた FLIT
ぱた FLIT
OH, NO!

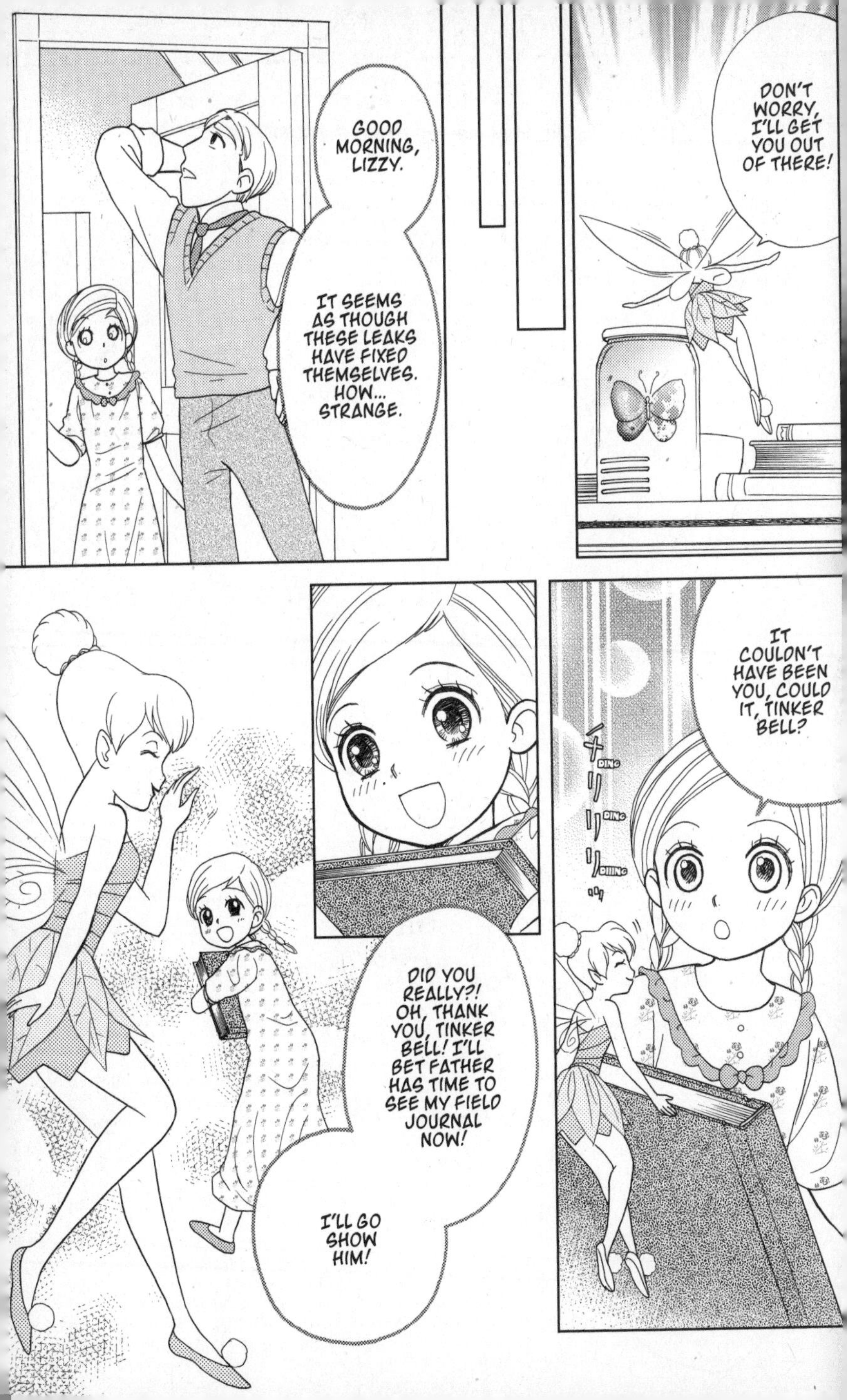
DON'T WORRY, I'LL GET YOU OUT OF THERE!
GOOD MORNING, LIZZY.
IT SEEMS AS THOUGH THESE LEAKS HAVE FIXED THEMSELVES. HOW... STRANGE.
IT COULDN'T HAVE BEEN YOU, COULD IT, TINKER BELL?
DING DING DIIING
DID YOU REALLY?! OH, THANK YOU, TINKER BELL! I'LL BET FATHER HAS TIME TO SEE MY FIELD JOURNAL NOW!
I'LL GO SHOW HIM!

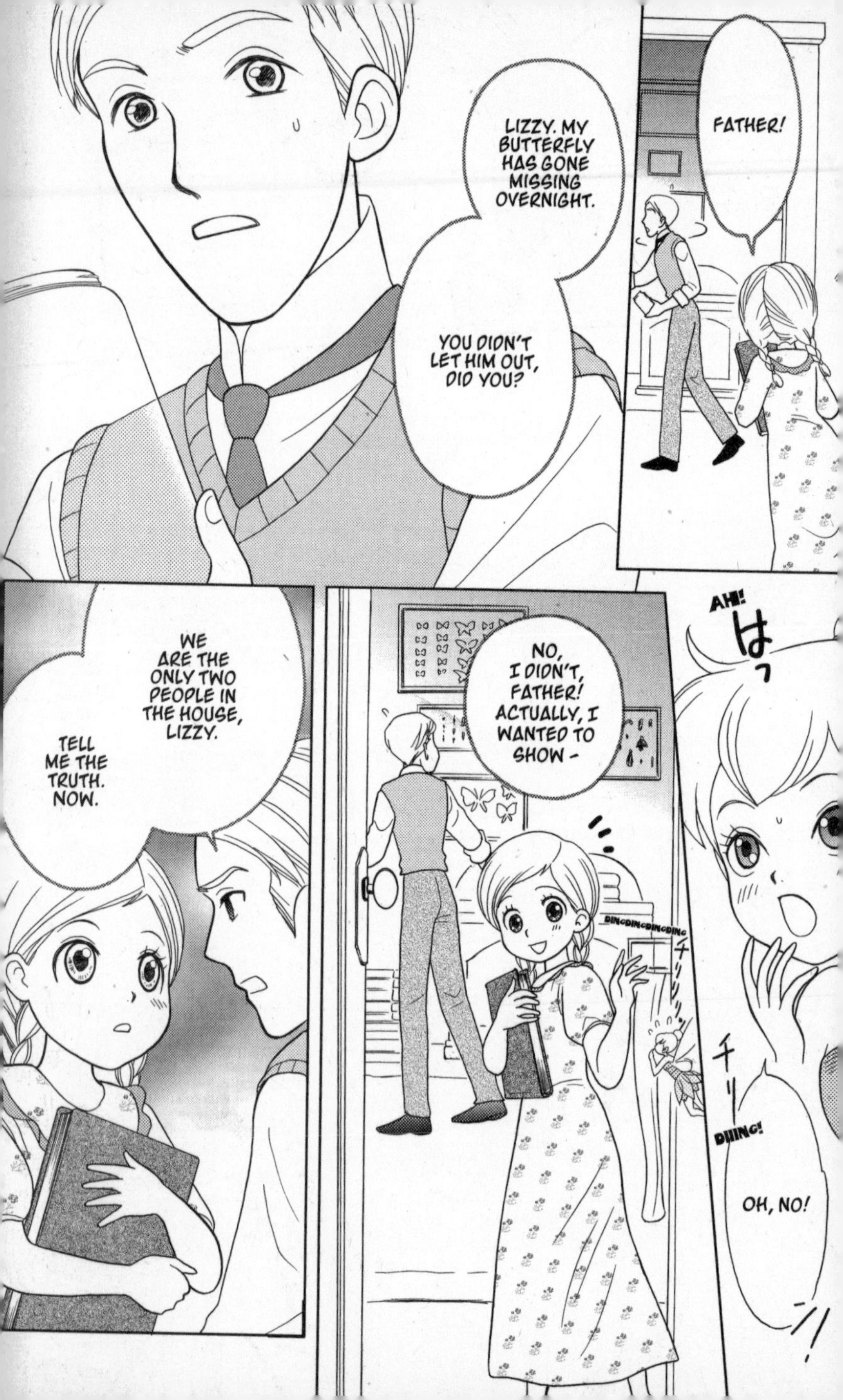
FATHER!
LIZZY. MY BUTTERFLY HAS GONE MISSING OVERNIGHT.
YOU DIDN'T LET HIM OUT, DID YOU?
AH! はっ
DIING! チリー
OH, NO!
NO, I DIDN'T, FATHER! ACTUALLY, I WANTED TO SHOW -
DINGDINGDINGDING チリリリ
WE ARE THE ONLY TWO PEOPLE IN THE HOUSE, LIZZY.
TELL ME THE TRUTH. NOW.

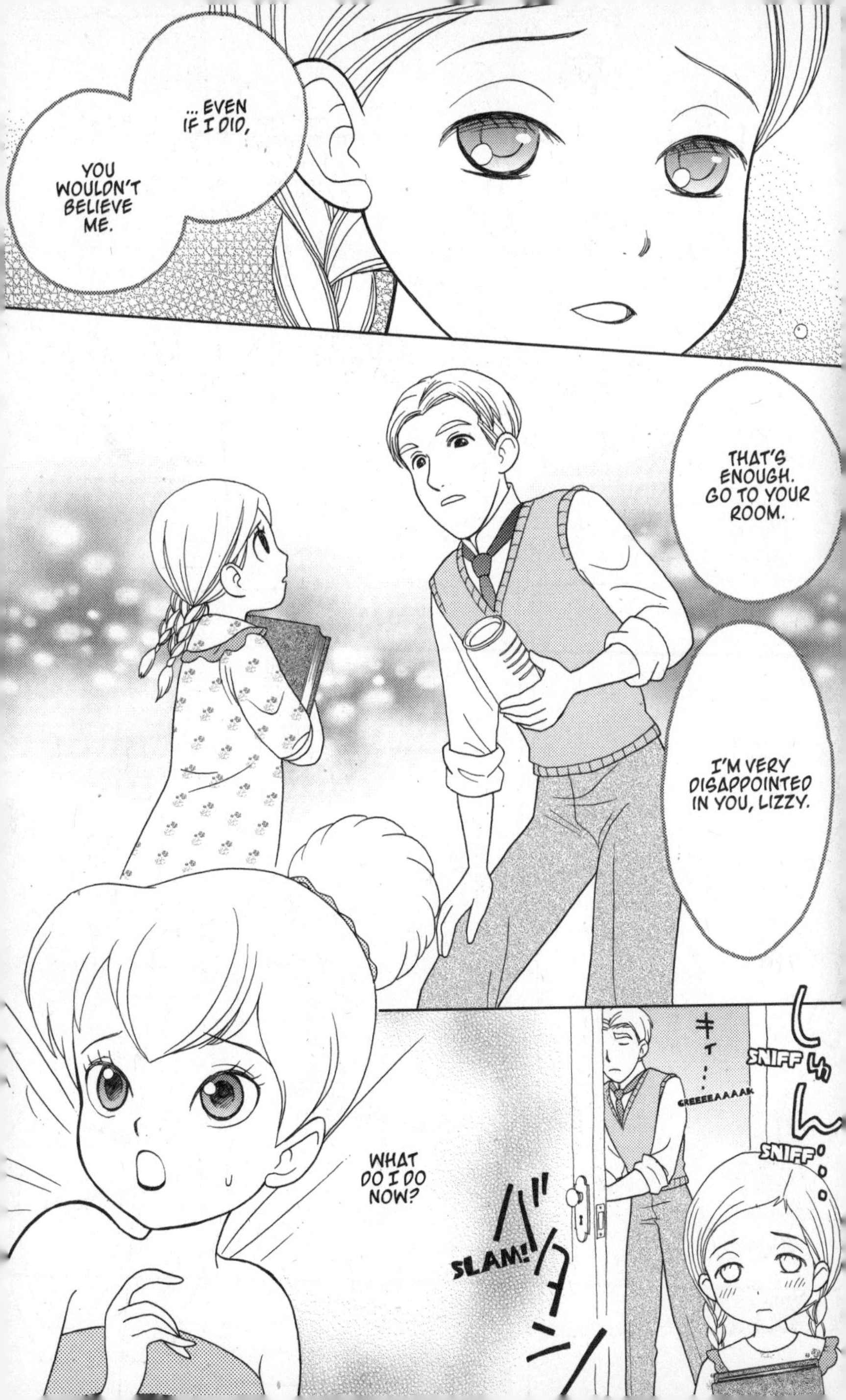

... EVEN IF I DID,
YOU WOULDN'T BELIEVE ME.
THAT'S ENOUGH. GO TO YOUR ROOM.
I'M VERY DISAPPOINTED IN YOU, LIZZY.
キィ…
GREEEEAAAAK
SNIFF
SNIFF
SLAM!
WHAT DO I DO NOW?

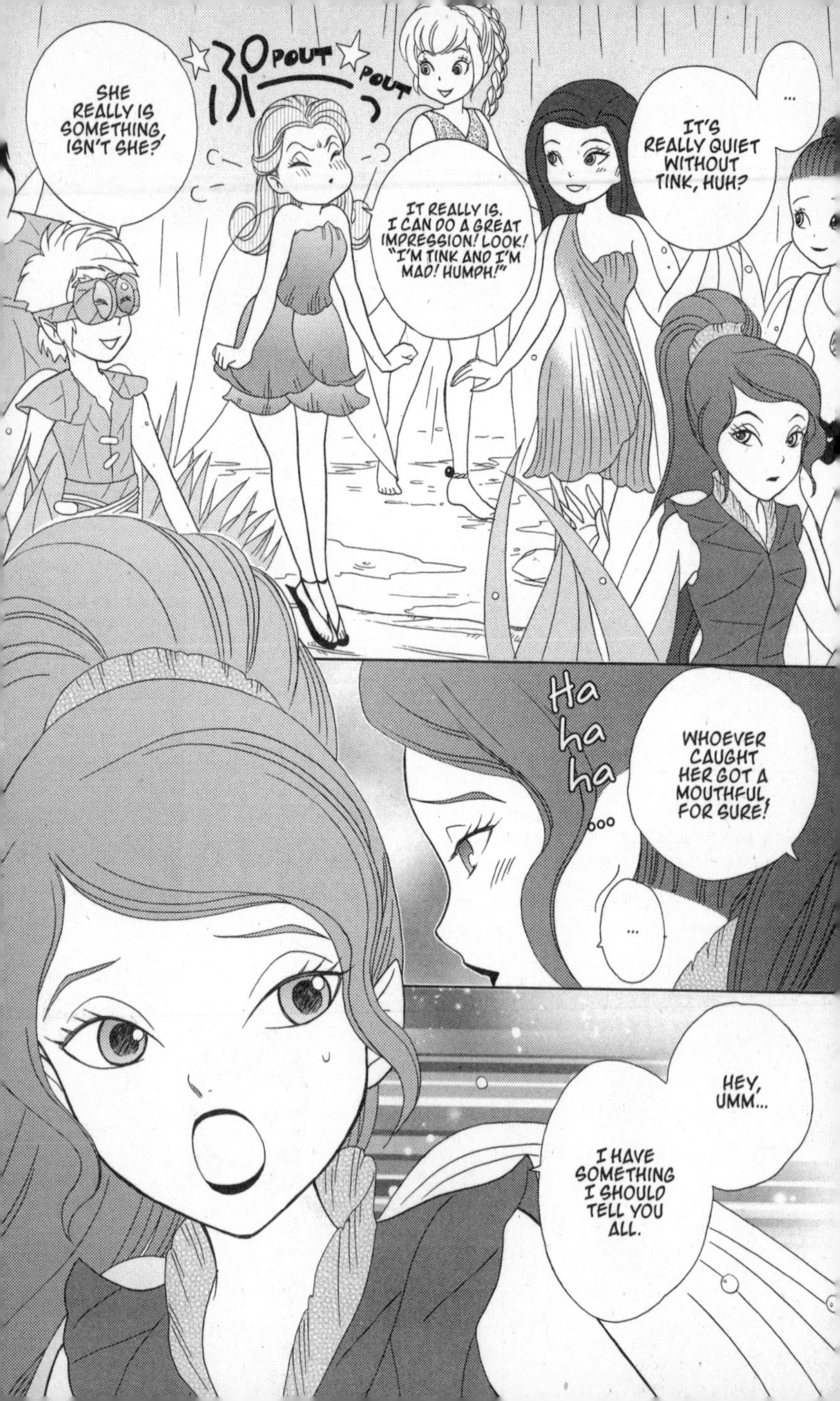
...
IT'S REALLY QUIET WITHOUT TINK, HUH?
IT REALLY IS. I CAN DO A GREAT IMPRESSION! LOOK! "I'M TINK AND I'M MAD! HUMPH!"
POUT POUT
SHE REALLY IS SOMETHING, ISN'T SHE?
WHOEVER CAUGHT HER GOT A MOUTHFUL, FOR SURE!
Ha ha ha
...
HEY, UMM...
I HAVE SOMETHING I SHOULD TELL YOU ALL.

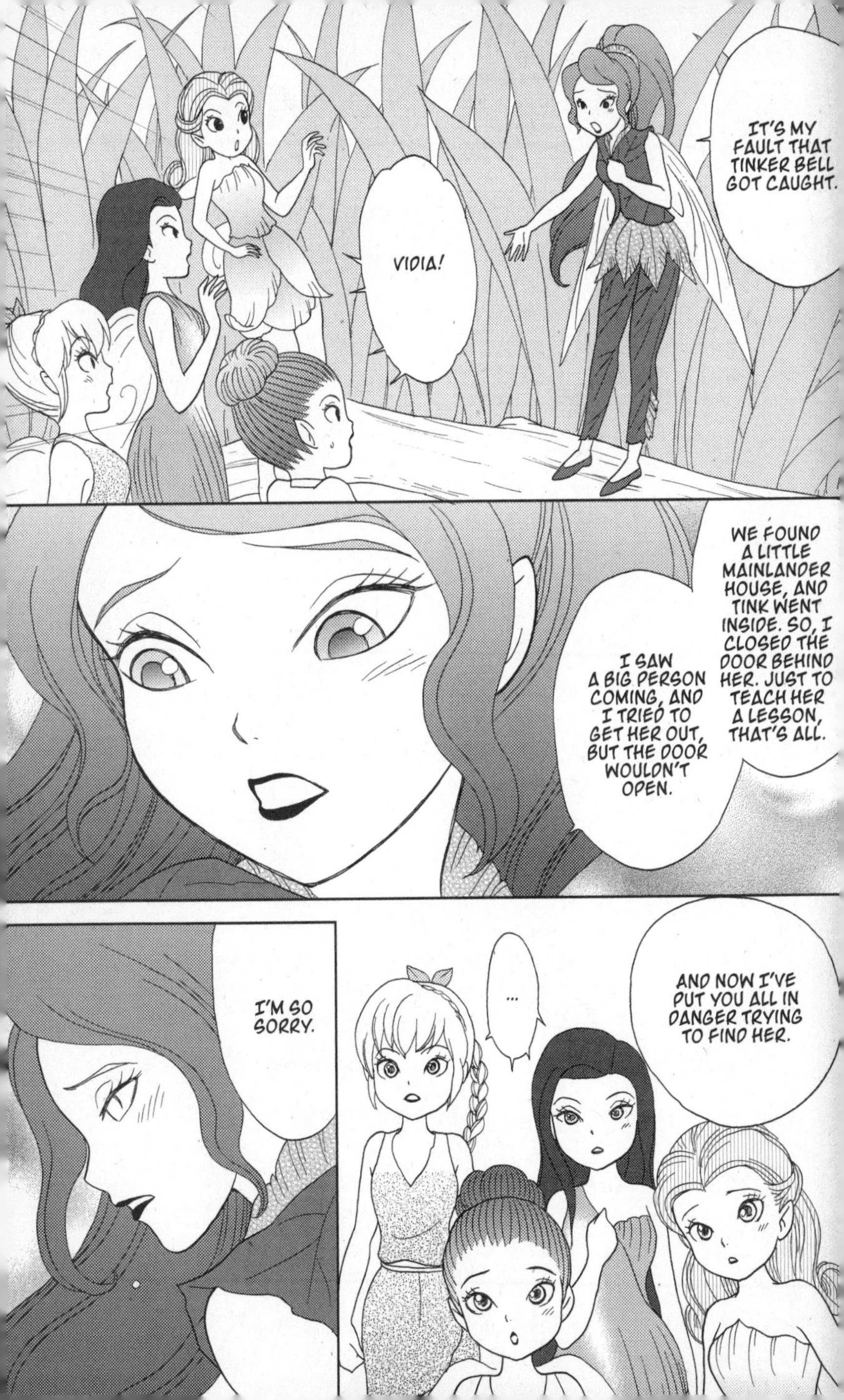
IT'S MY FAULT THAT TINKER BELL GOT CAUGHT.
VIDIA!
WE FOUND A LITTLE MAINLANDER HOUSE, AND TINK WENT INSIDE. SO, I CLOSED THE DOOR BEHIND HER. JUST TO TEACH HER A LESSON, THAT'S ALL.
I SAW A BIG PERSON COMING, AND I TRIED TO GET HER OUT, BUT THE DOOR WOULDN'T OPEN.
AND NOW I'VE PUT YOU ALL IN DANGER TRYING TO FIND HER.
...
I'M SO SORRY.

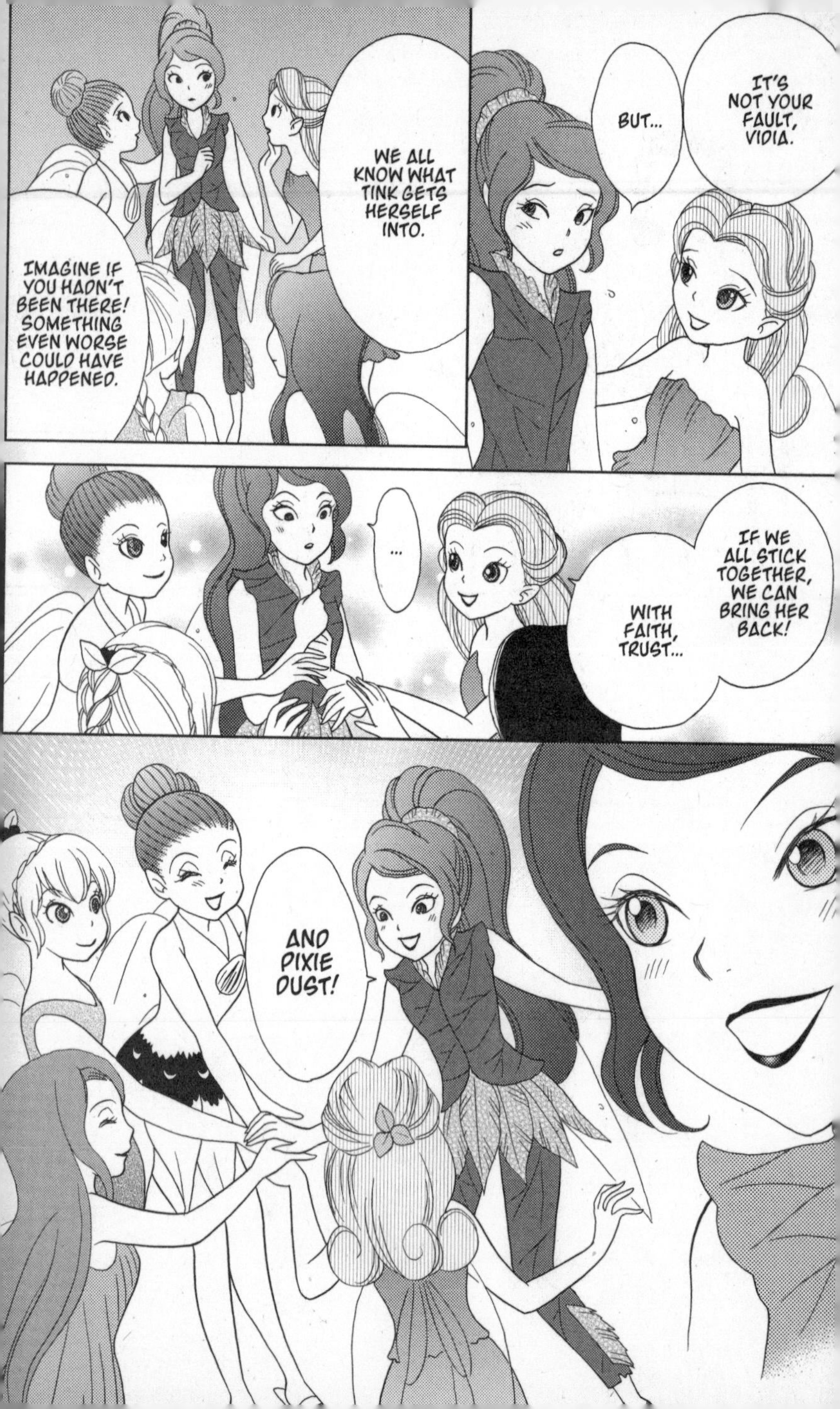
IT'S NOT YOUR FAULT, VIDIA.
BUT...
WE ALL KNOW WHAT TINK GETS HERSELF INTO.
IMAGINE IF YOU HADN'T BEEN THERE! SOMETHING EVEN WORSE COULD HAVE HAPPENED.
IF WE ALL STICK TOGETHER, WE CAN BRING HER BACK!
WITH FAITH, TRUST...
...
AND PIXIE DUST!

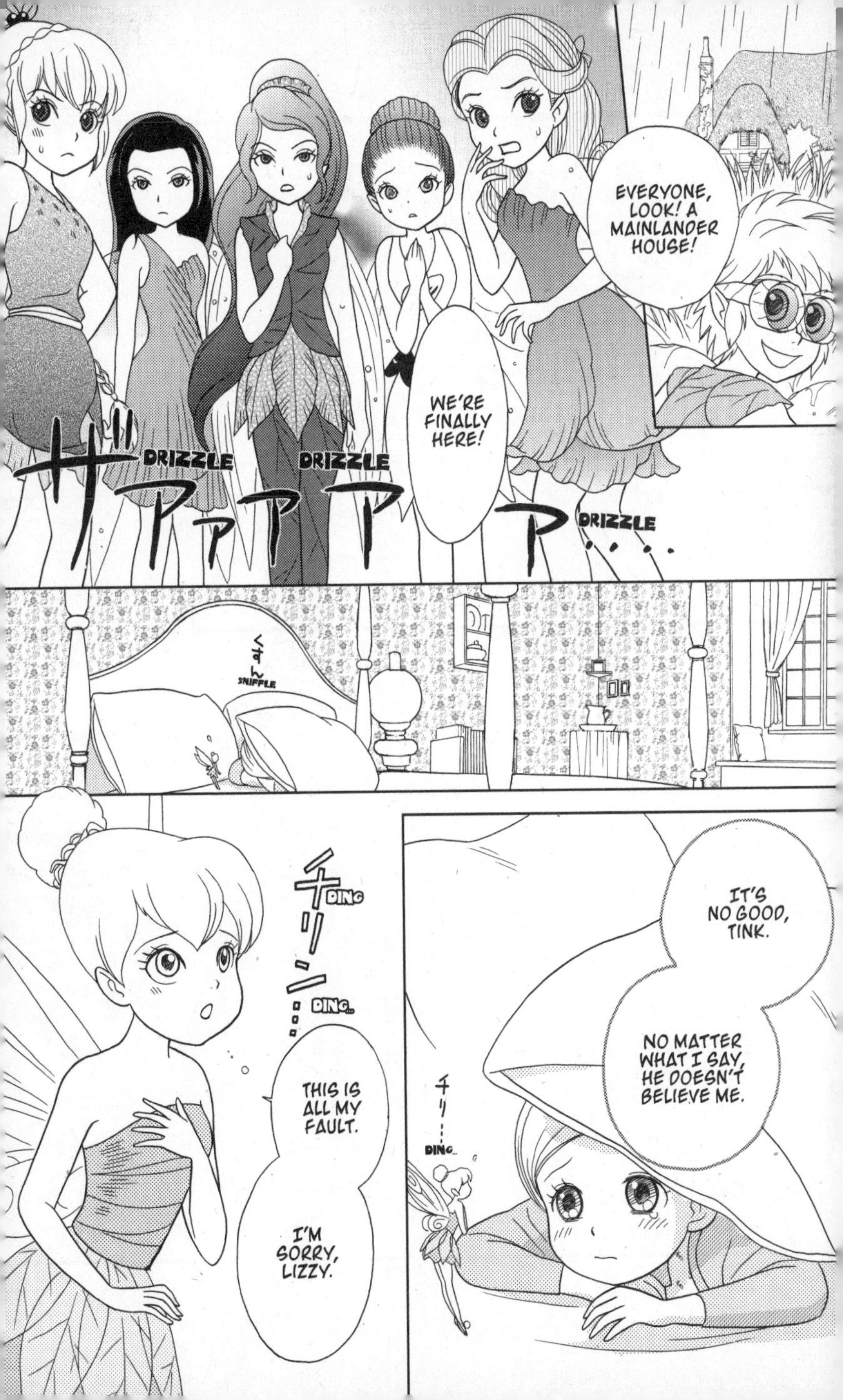
EVERYONE, LOOK! A MAINLANDER HOUSE!
WE'RE FINALLY HERE!
ザァァァ…
DRIZZLE DRIZZLE DRIZZLE
くすん
SNIFFLE
IT'S NO GOOD, TINK.
NO MATTER WHAT I SAY, HE DOESN'T BELIEVE ME.
チリ…
DING...
チリーン…
DING
DING...
THIS IS ALL MY FAULT.
I'M SORRY, LIZZY.

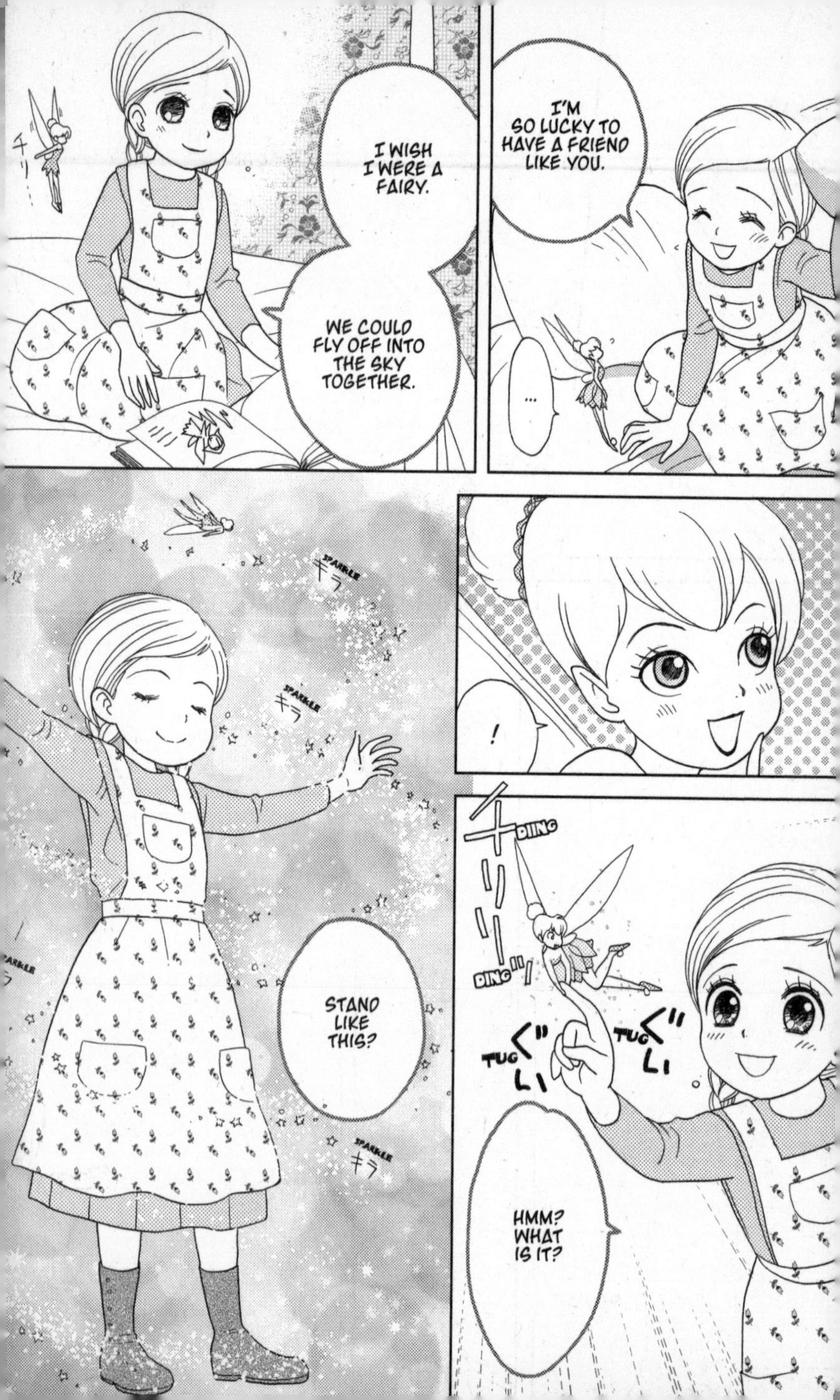
I'M SO LUCKY TO HAVE A FRIEND LIKE YOU.
...
I WISH I WERE A FAIRY.
WE COULD FLY OFF INTO THE SKY TOGETHER.
!
DIING
DING
TUG
TUG
HMM? WHAT IS IT?
SPARKLE
SPARKLE
SPARKLE
STAND LIKE THIS?
SPARKLE

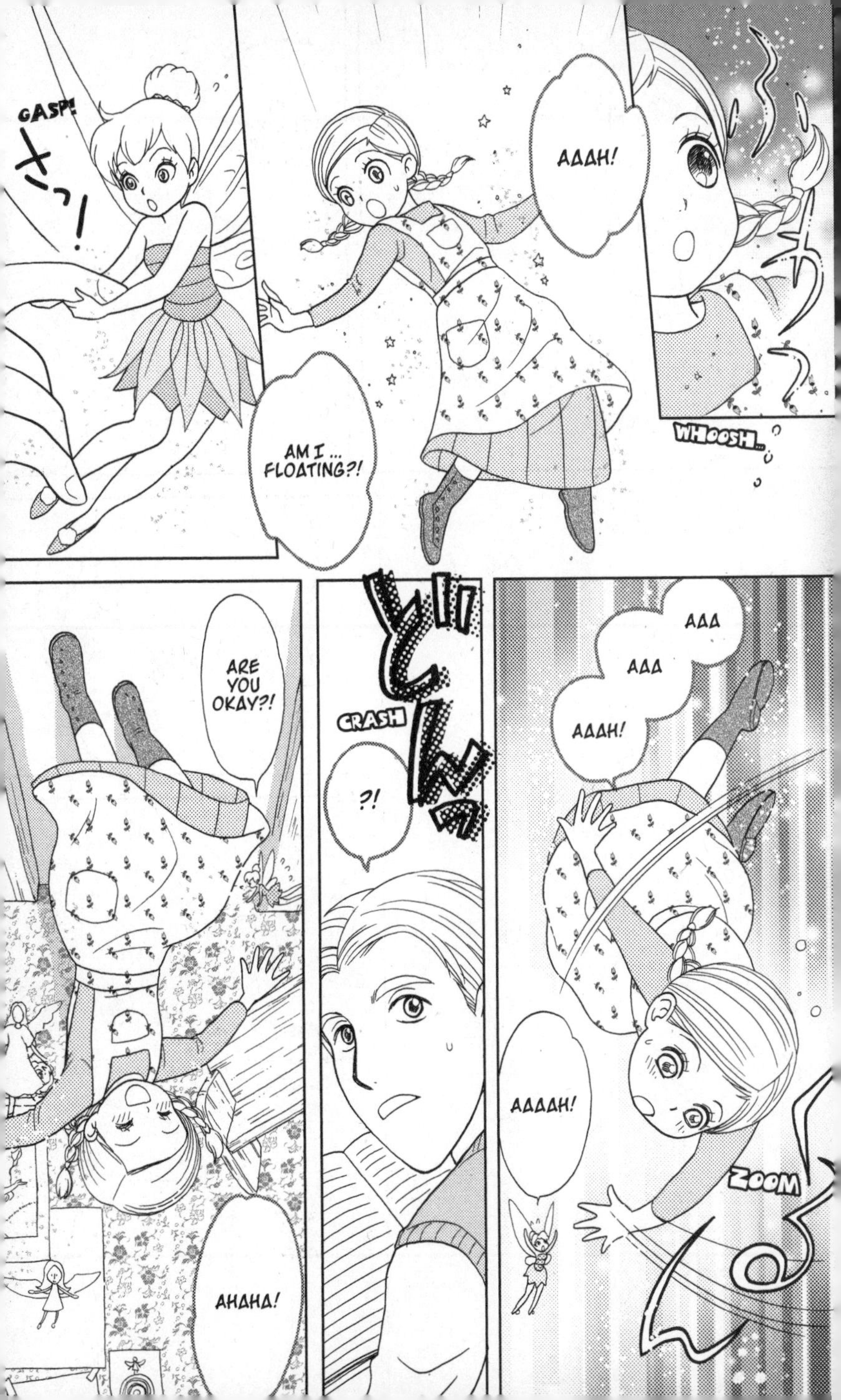
WHOOSH...
AAAH!
AM I ... FLOATING?!
GASP!
AAA
AAA
AAAH!
AAAAH!
ZOOM
CRASH
?!
ARE YOU OKAY?!
AHAHA!

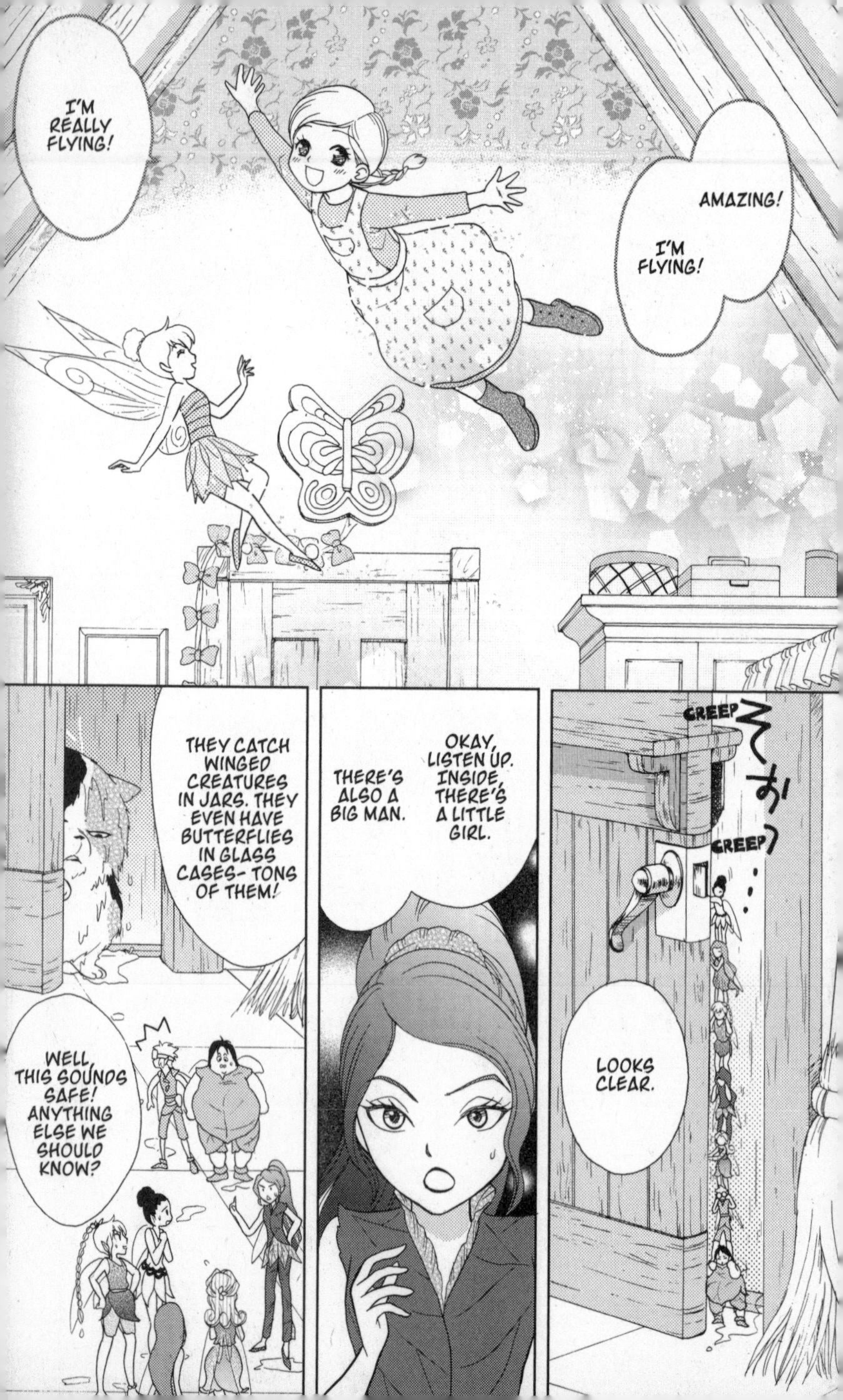
AMAZING! I'M FLYING!
I'M REALLY FLYING!
CREEP
そおっ
CREEP
LOOKS CLEAR.
OKAY, LISTEN UP. INSIDE, THERE'S A LITTLE GIRL.
THERE'S ALSO A BIG MAN.
THEY CATCH WINGED CREATURES IN JARS. THEY EVEN HAVE BUTTERFLIES IN GLASS CASES- TONS OF THEM!
WELL, THIS SOUNDS SAFE! ANYTHING ELSE WE SHOULD KNOW?

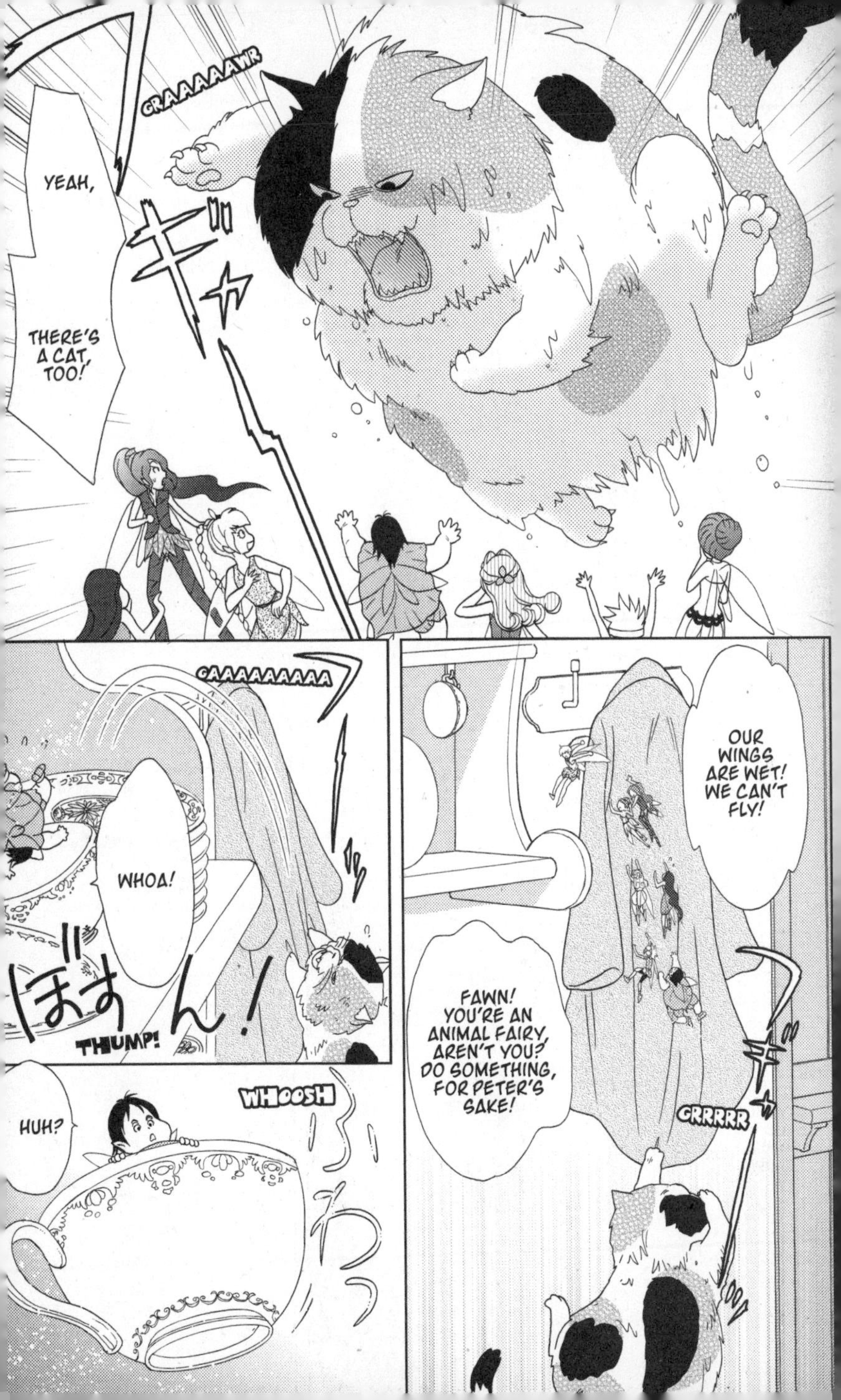
GRAAAAAWR
YEAH,
THERE'S A CAT, TOO!
OUR WINGS ARE WET! WE CAN'T FLY!
FAWN! YOU'RE AN ANIMAL FAIRY, AREN'T YOU? DO SOMETHING, FOR PETER'S SAKE!
GRRRRR
GAAAAAAAAA
WHOA!
ぼすん!
THUMP!
WHOOSH
HUH?

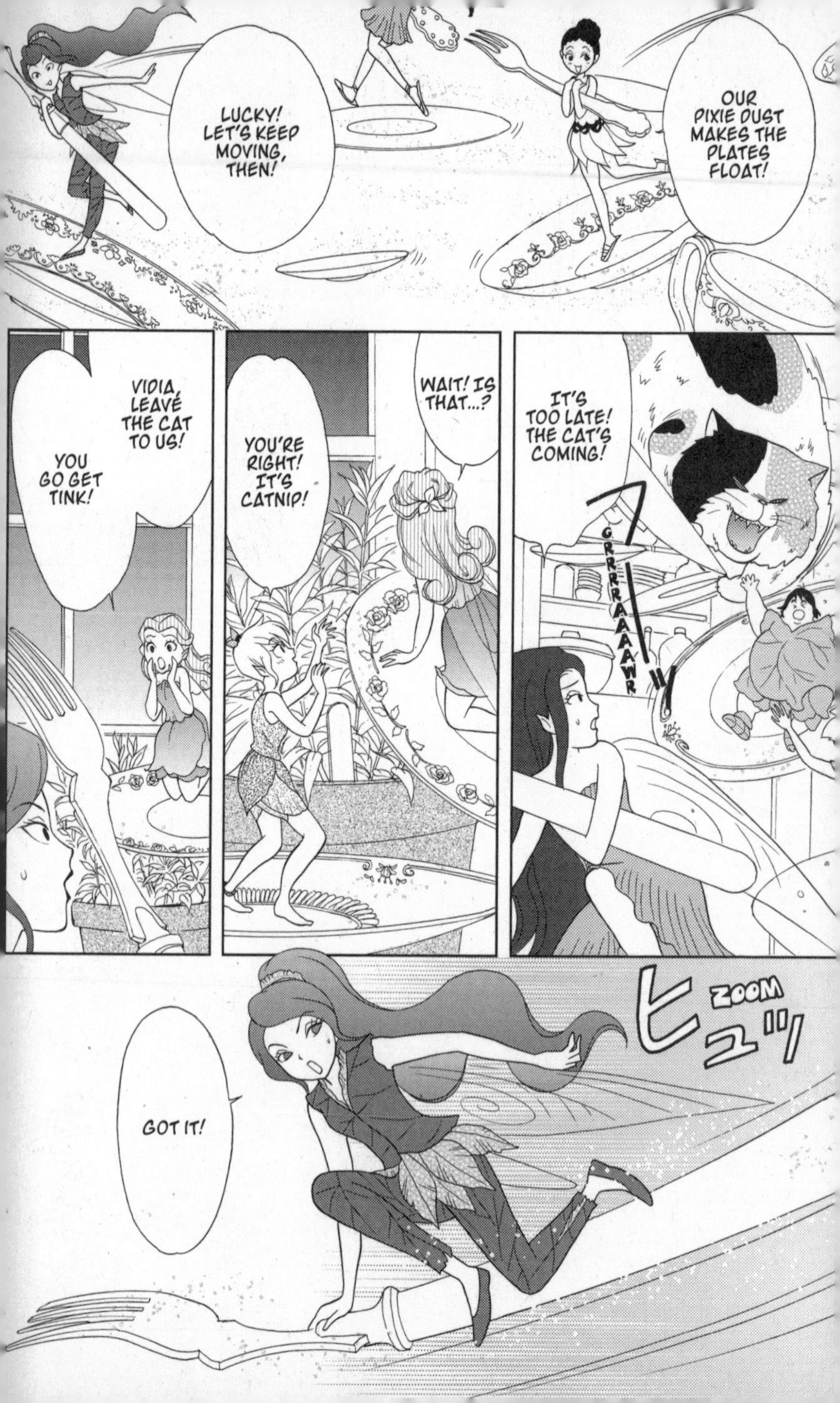
OUR PIXIE DUST MAKES THE PLATES FLOAT!
LUCKY! LET'S KEEP MOVING, THEN!
IT'S TOO LATE! THE CAT'S COMING!
GRRRRAAAAAWR
WAIT! IS THAT...?
YOU'RE RIGHT! IT'S CATNIP!
VIDIA, LEAVE THE CAT TO US!
YOU GO GET TINK!
ZOOM
ヒュッ
GOT IT!

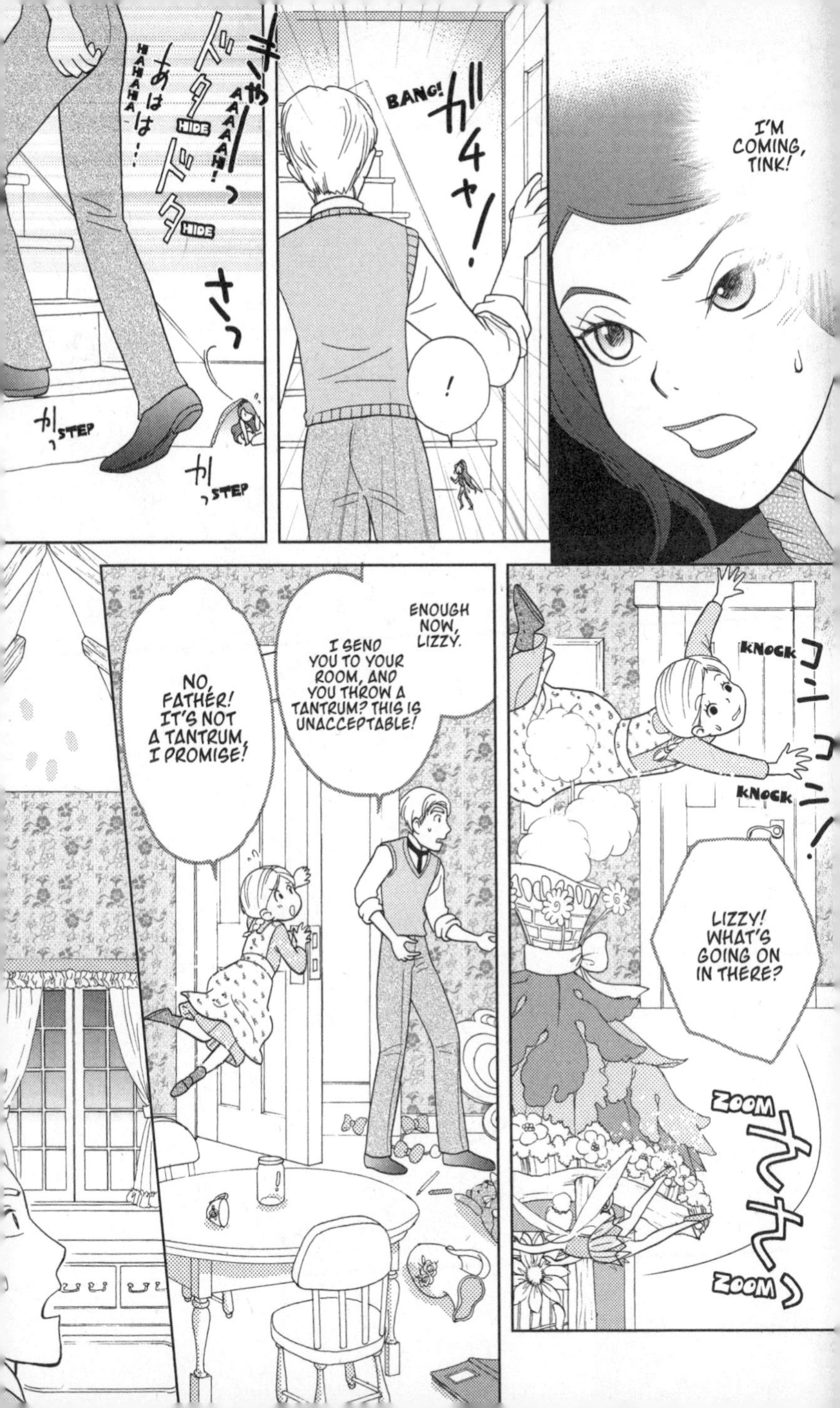
I'M COMING, TINK!
BANG!
!
AAAAAAH!
HIDE
HIDE
HAHAHA
STEP
STEP
KNOCK
KNOCK
LIZZY! WHAT'S GOING ON IN THERE?
ZOOM
ZOOM
ENOUGH NOW, LIZZY.
I SEND YOU TO YOUR ROOM, AND YOU THROW A TANTRUM? THIS IS UNACCEPTABLE!
NO, FATHER! IT'S NOT A TANTRUM, I PROMISE!
!

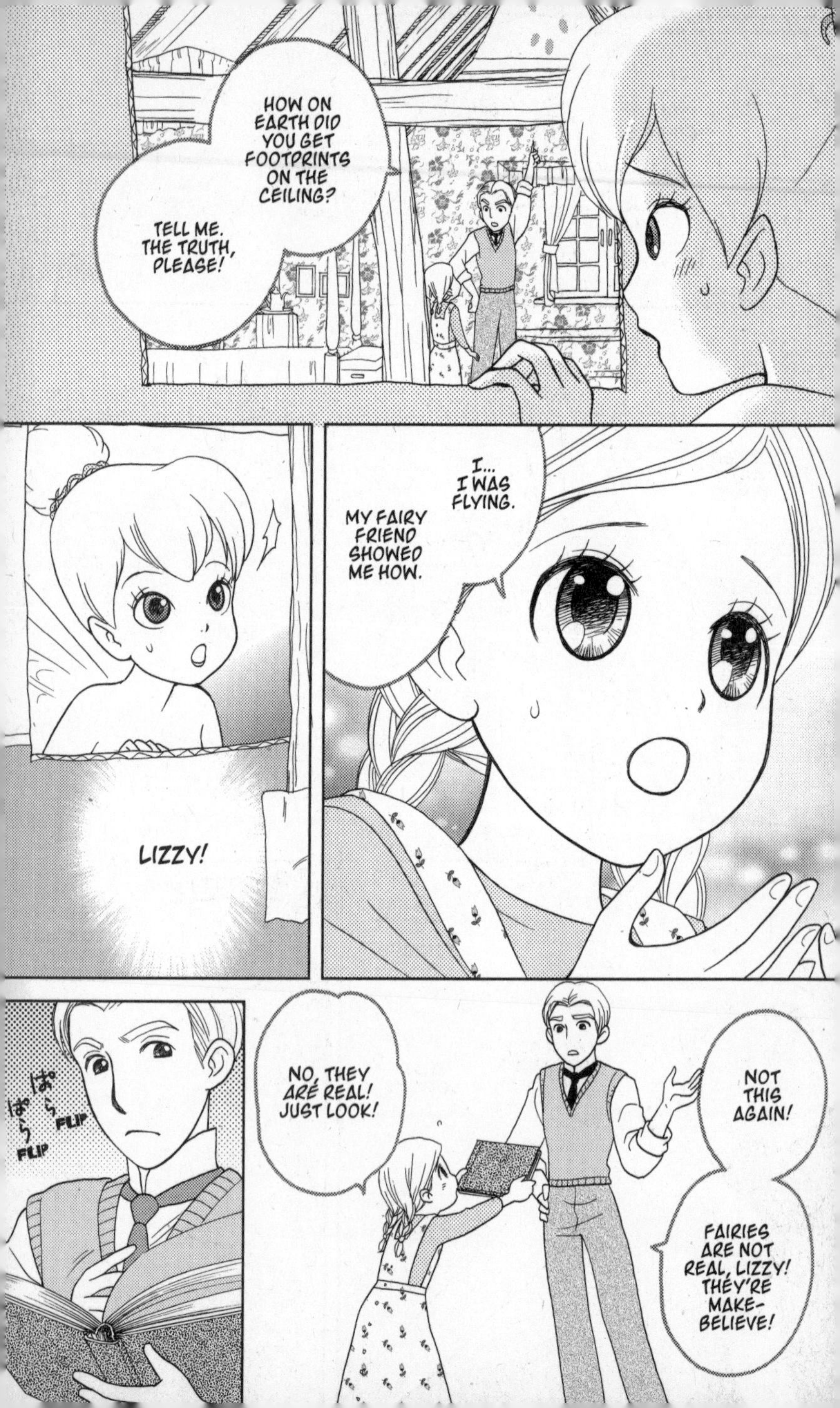
HOW ON EARTH DID YOU GET FOOTPRINTS ON THE CEILING?
TELL ME. THE TRUTH, PLEASE!
I... I WAS FLYING.
MY FAIRY FRIEND SHOWED ME HOW.
LIZZY!
NOT THIS AGAIN!
FAIRIES ARE NOT REAL, LIZZY! THEY'RE MAKE-BELIEVE!
NO, THEY ARE REAL! JUST LOOK!
ぱら
ぱら
FLIP
FLIP

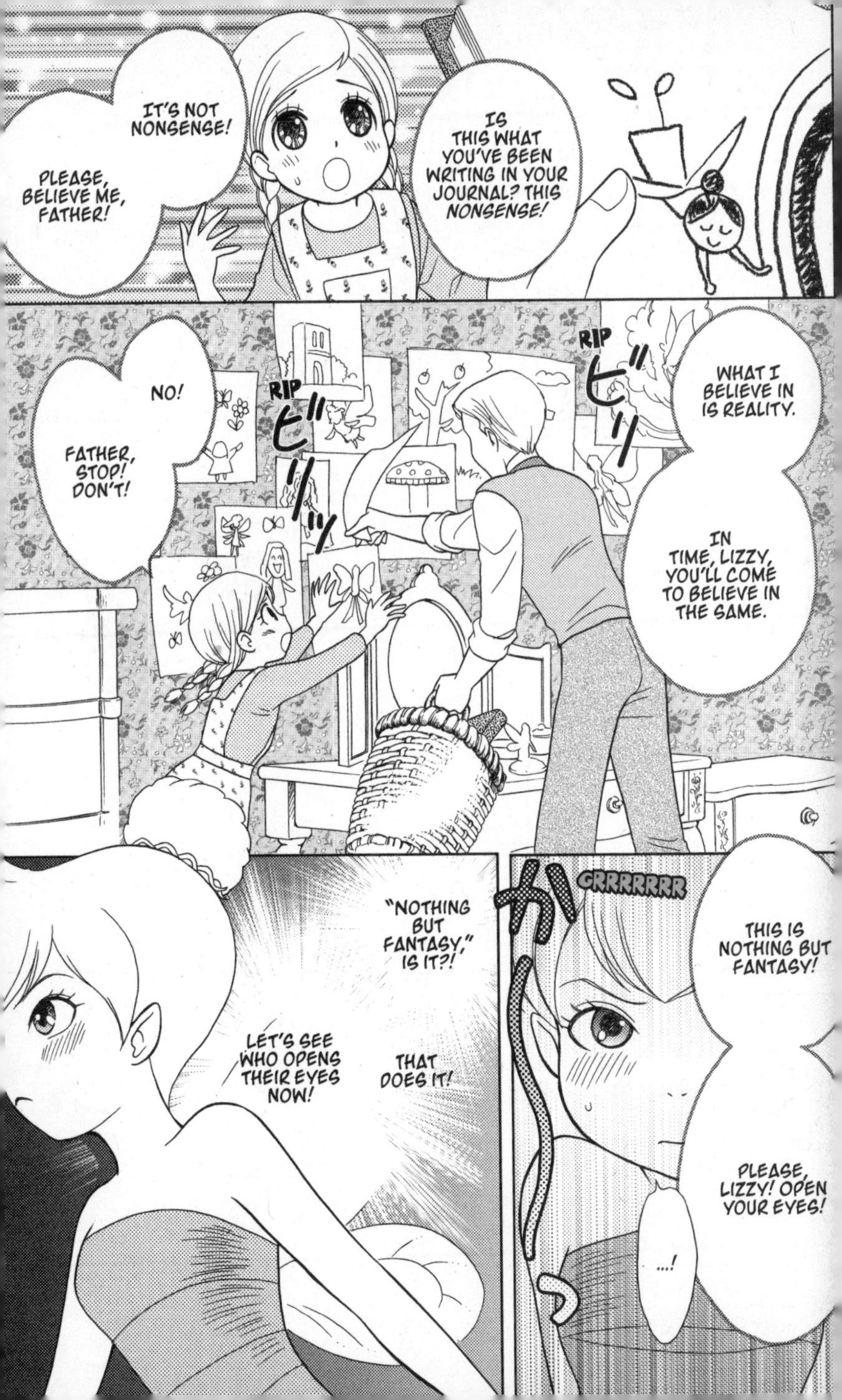
IS THIS WHAT YOU'VE BEEN WRITING IN YOUR JOURNAL? THIS NONSENSE!
IT'S NOT NONSENSE!
PLEASE, BELIEVE ME, FATHER!
WHAT I BELIEVE IN IS REALITY.
IN TIME, LIZZY, YOU'LL COME TO BELIEVE IN THE SAME.
RIP
RIP
NO!
FATHER, STOP! DON'T!
GRRRRRRR
THIS IS NOTHING BUT FANTASY!
PLEASE, LIZZY! OPEN YOUR EYES!
...!
"NOTHING BUT FANTASY," IS IT?!
THAT DOES IT!
LET'S SEE WHO OPENS THEIR EYES NOW!

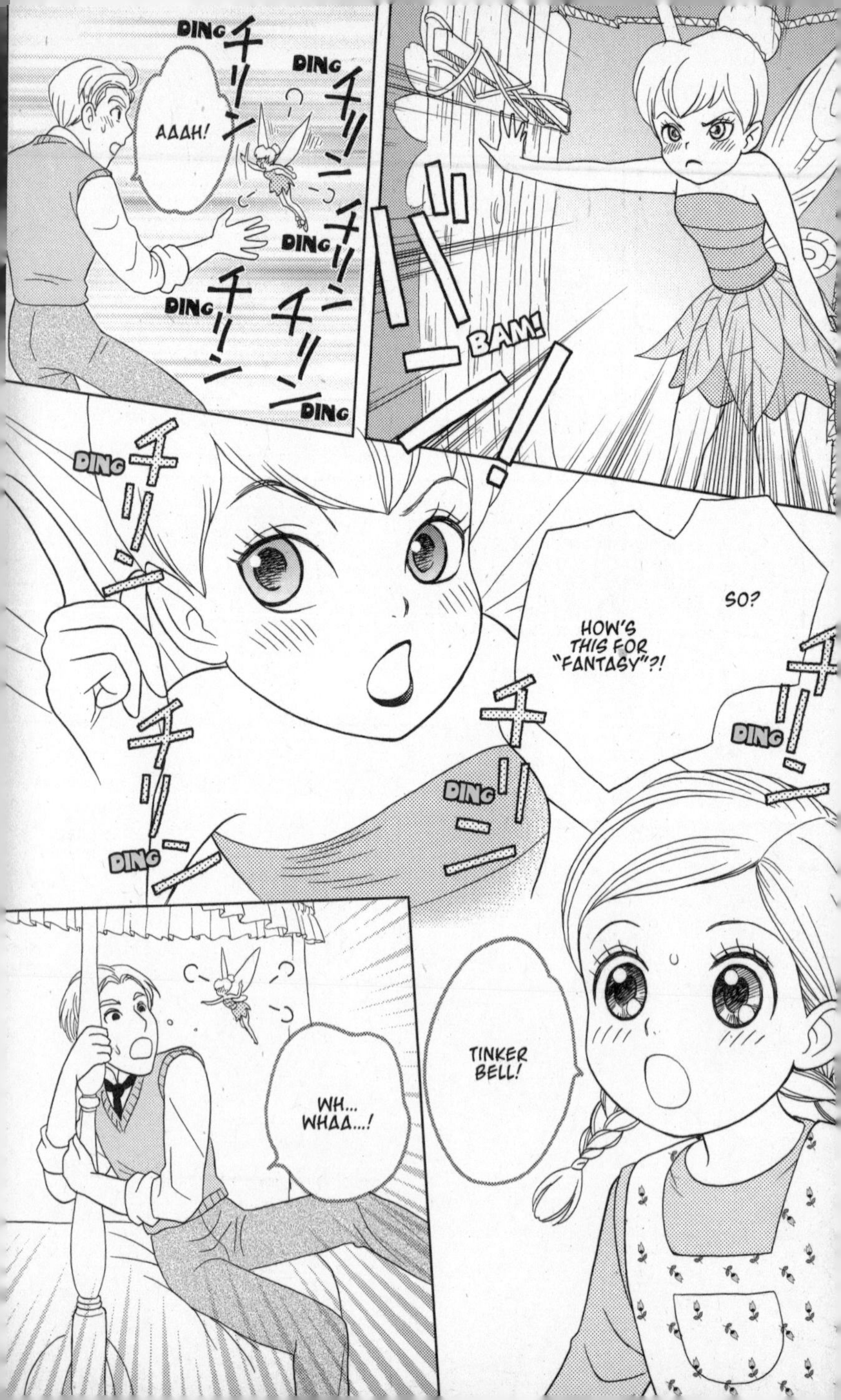
BAM!
DING
DING
AAAH!
DING
DING
DING
SO?
HOW'S THIS FOR "FANTASY"?!
DING
DING
DING
DING
TINKER BELL!
WH... WHAA...!

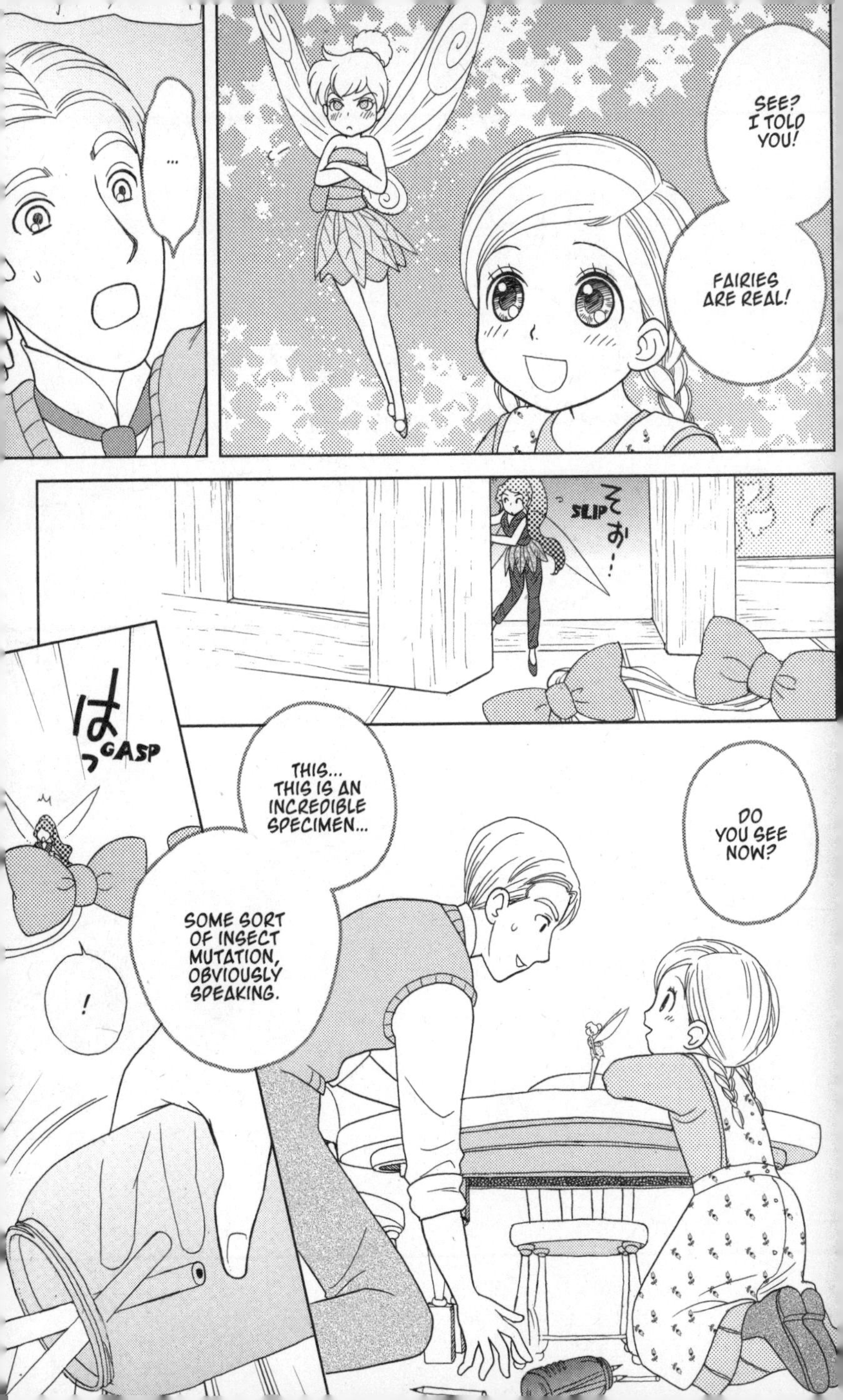
SEE? I TOLD YOU!
FAIRIES ARE REAL!
...
そお・・
SLIP
DO YOU SEE NOW?
THIS... THIS IS AN INCREDIBLE SPECIMEN...
SOME SORT OF INSECT MUTATION, OBVIOUSLY SPEAKING.
はっ
GASP
!

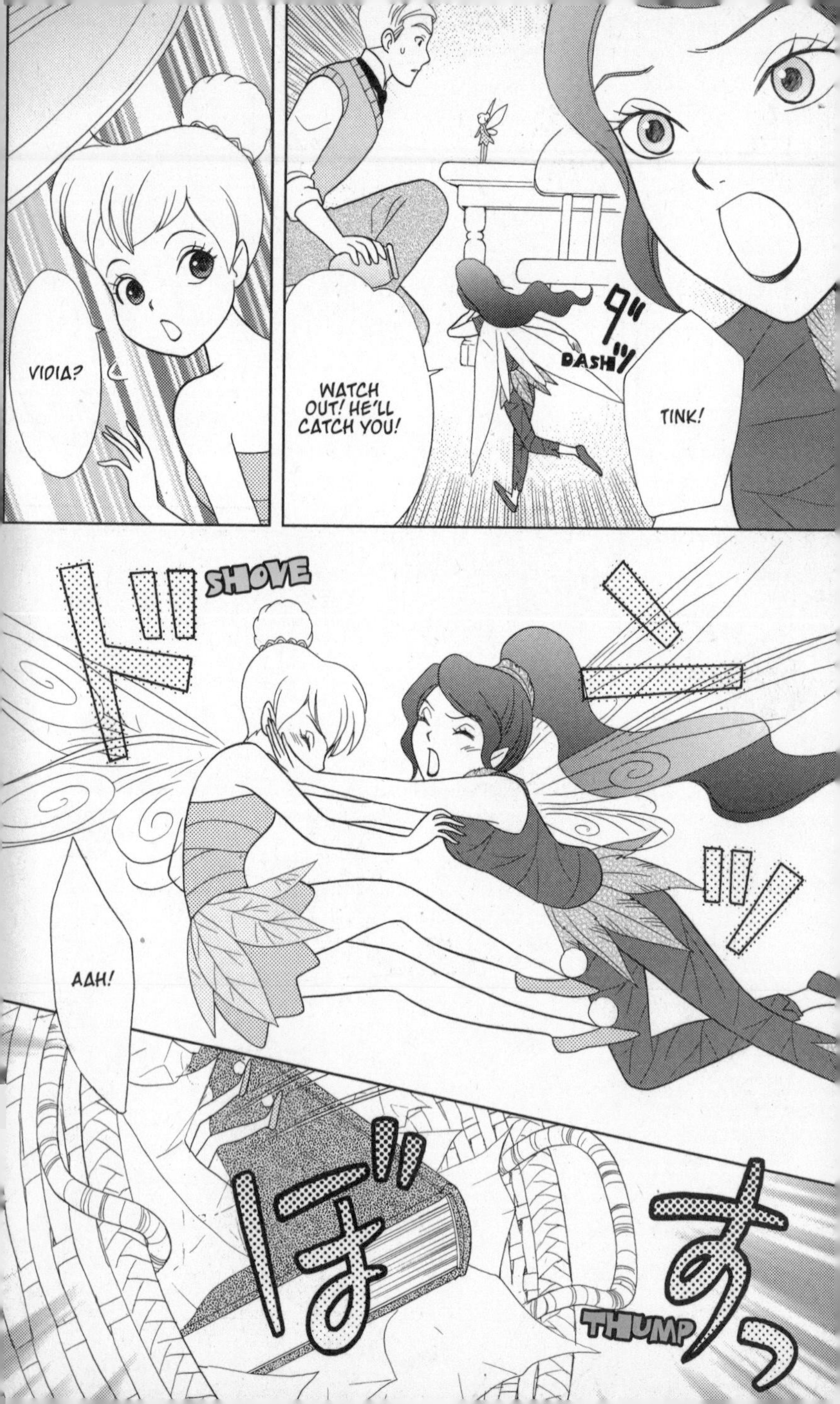
DASH
TINK!
WATCH OUT! HE'LL CATCH YOU!
VIDIA?
SHOVE
AAH!
THUMP

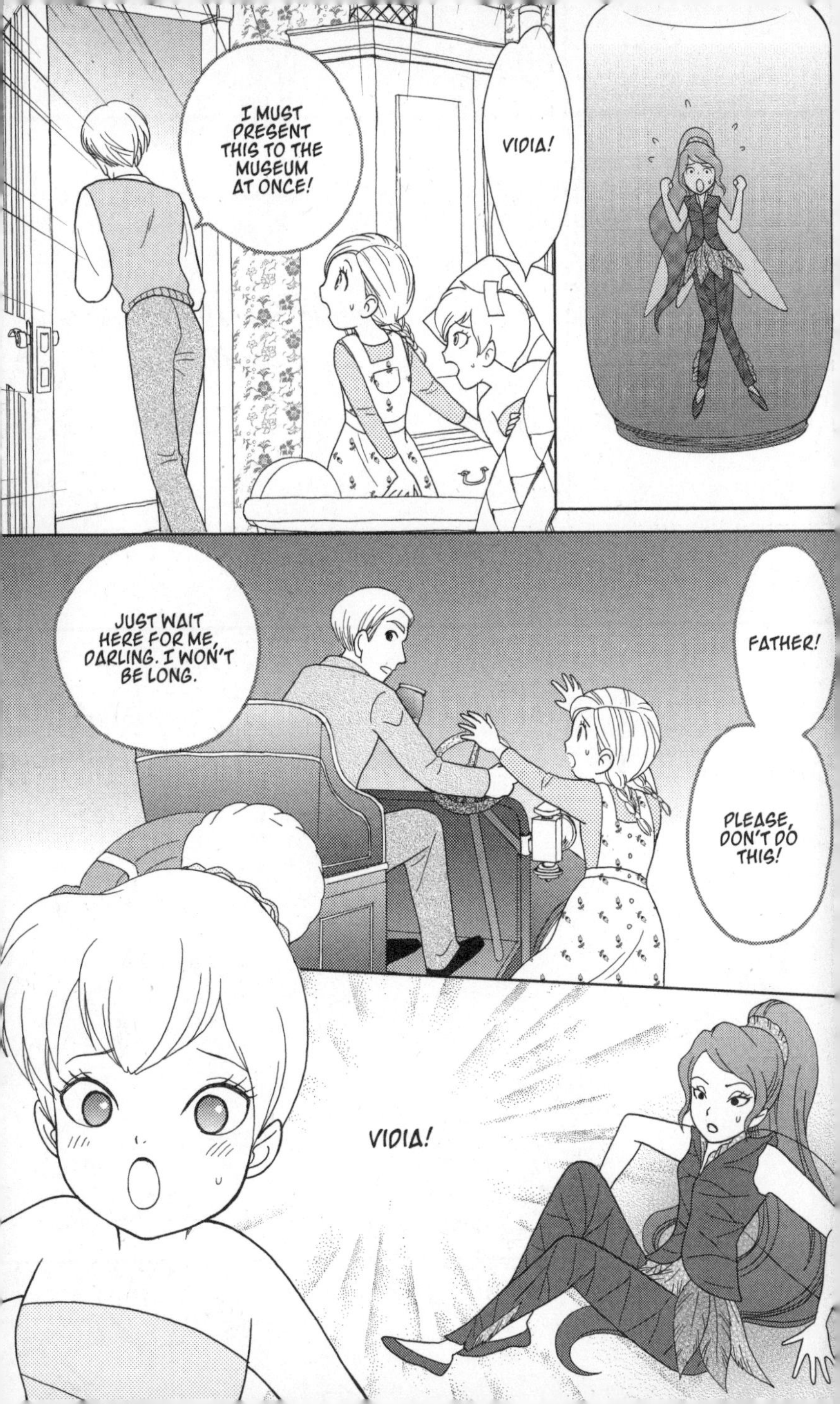
VIDIA!
I MUST PRESENT THIS TO THE MUSEUM AT ONCE!
FATHER!
PLEASE, DON'T DO THIS!
JUST WAIT HERE FOR ME, DARLING. I WON'T BE LONG.
VIDIA!

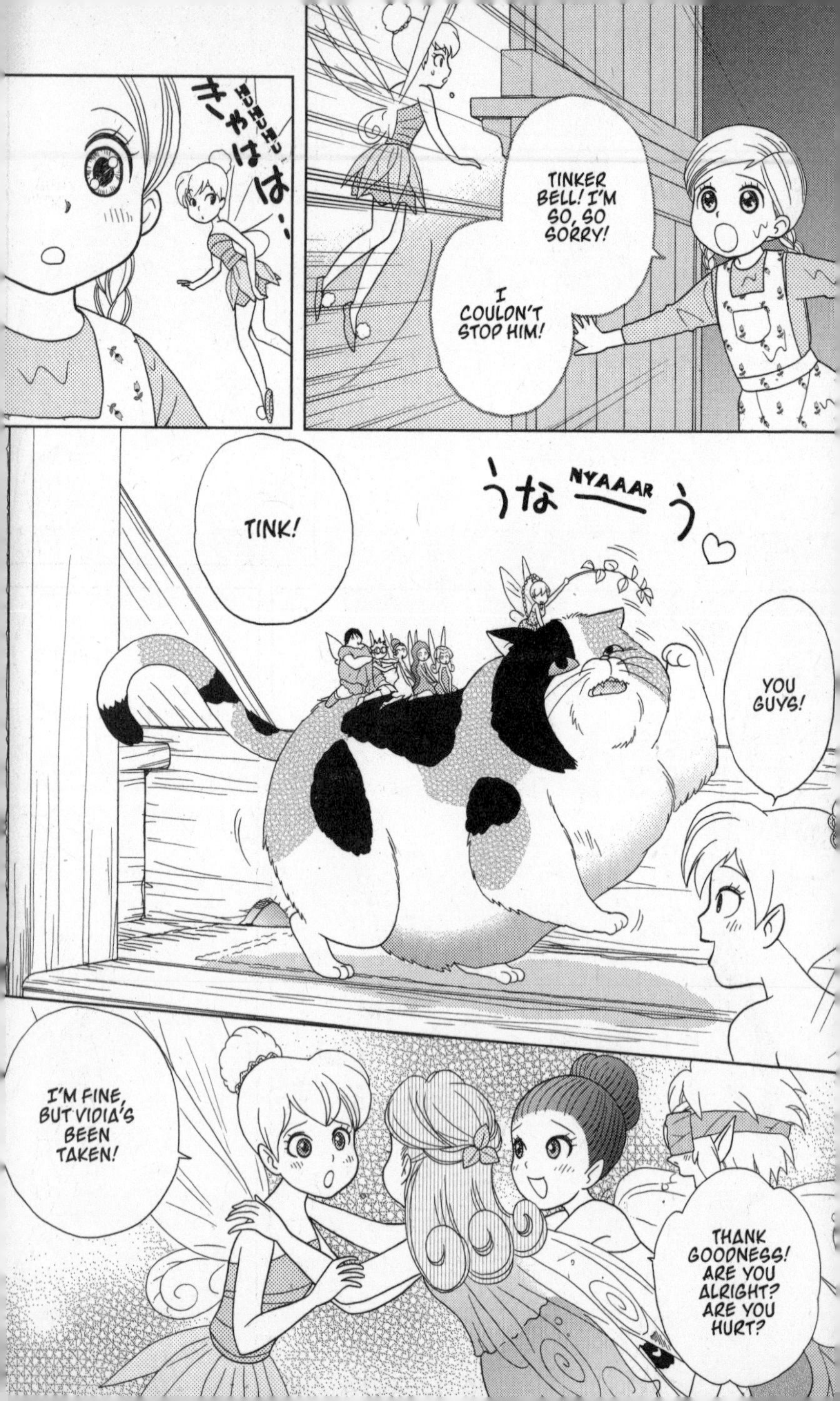
TINKER BELL! I'M SO, SO SORRY!
I COULDN'T STOP HIM!
きゃはは
HUHUHU
うなーう
NYAAAR
YOU GUYS!
TINK!
THANK GOODNESS! ARE YOU ALRIGHT? ARE YOU HURT?
I'M FINE, BUT VIDIA'S BEEN TAKEN!

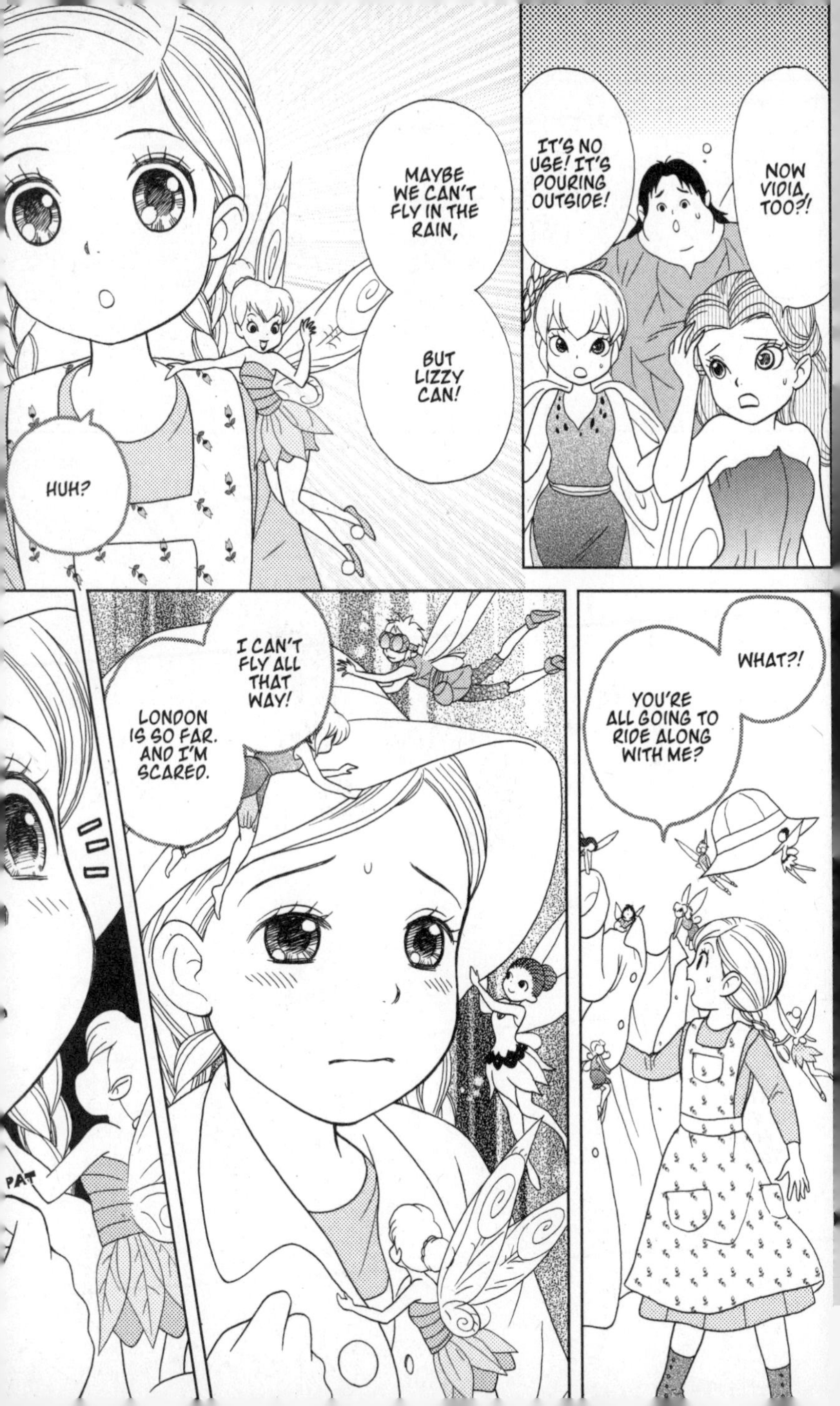
NOW VIDIA, TOO?!
IT'S NO USE! IT'S POURING OUTSIDE!
MAYBE WE CAN'T FLY IN THE RAIN,
BUT LIZZY CAN!
HUH?
WHAT?!
YOU'RE ALL GOING TO RIDE ALONG WITH ME?
I CAN'T FLY ALL THAT WAY!
LONDON IS SO FAR. AND I'M SCARED.
PAT

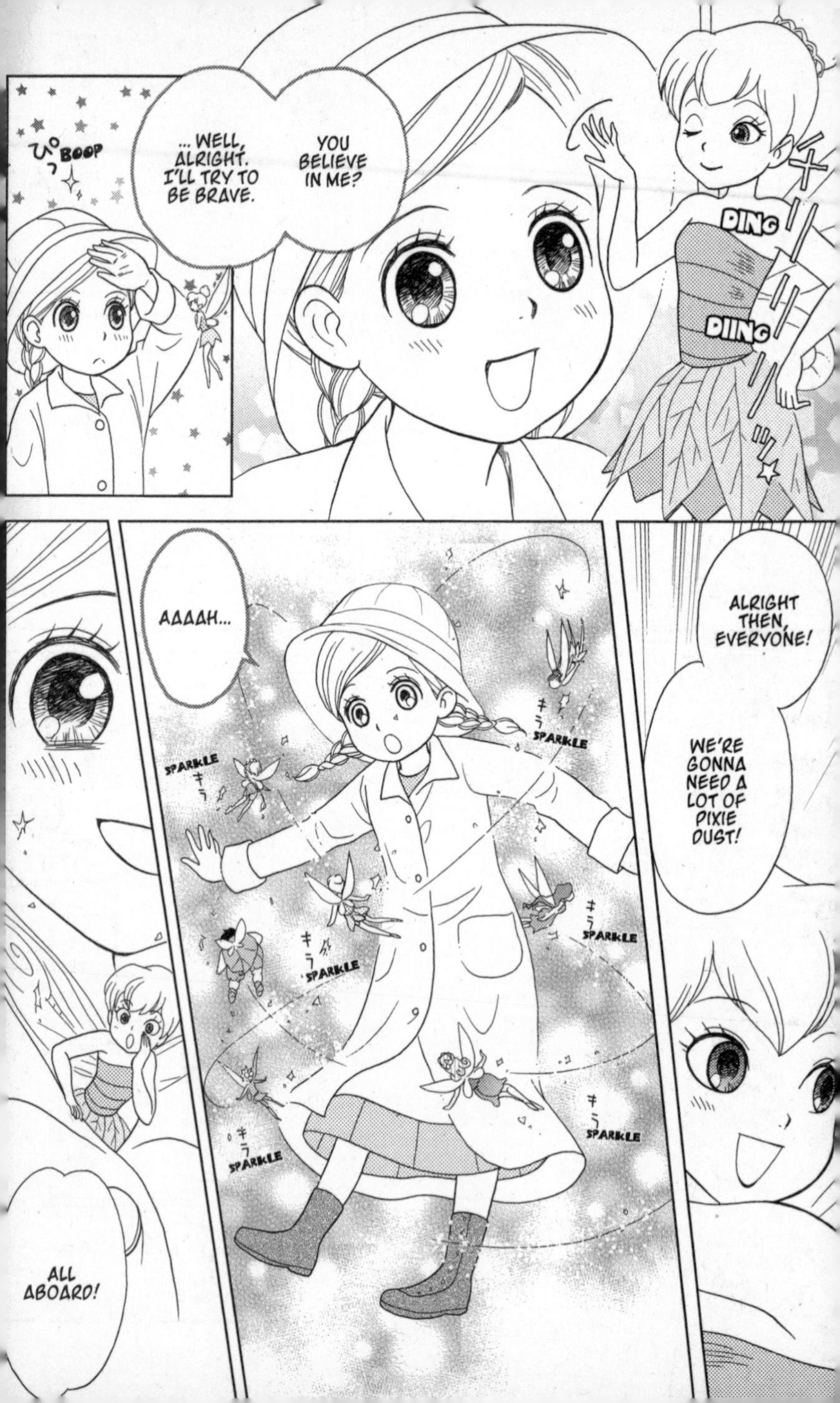
DING
DIING
YOU BELIEVE IN ME?
... WELL, ALRIGHT. I'LL TRY TO BE BRAVE.
ぴっ BOOP
ALRIGHT THEN, EVERYONE!
WE'RE GONNA NEED A LOT OF PIXIE DUST!
AAAAH...
キラ SPARKLE
キラ SPARKLE
キラ SPARKLE
キラ SPARKLE
キラ SPARKLE
キラ SPARKLE
ALL ABOARD!

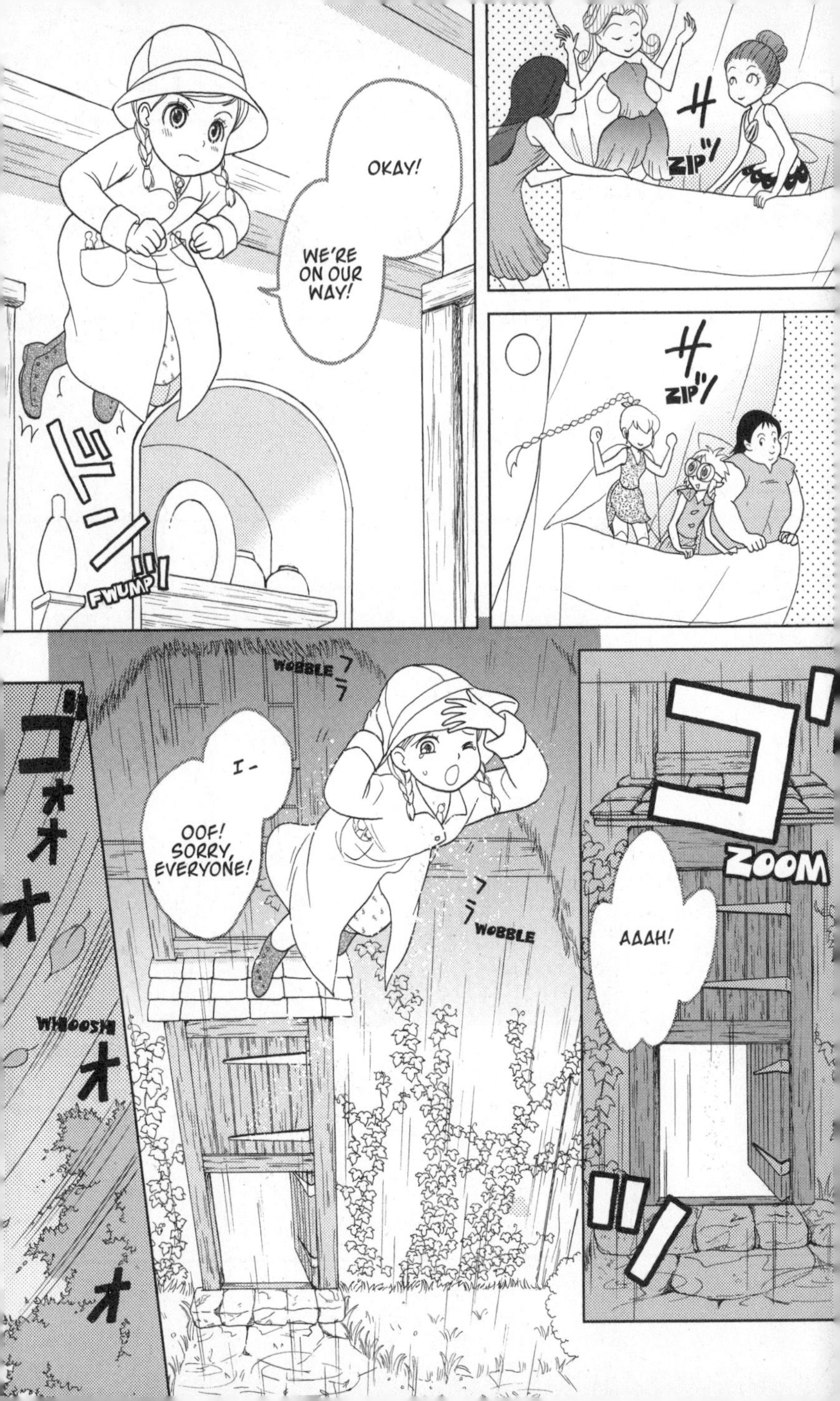
ZIP
ZIP
OKAY!
WE'RE ON OUR WAY!
FWUMP
ZOOM
AAAH!
WOBBLE
I-
OOF! SORRY, EVERYONE!
WOBBLE
WHOOSH

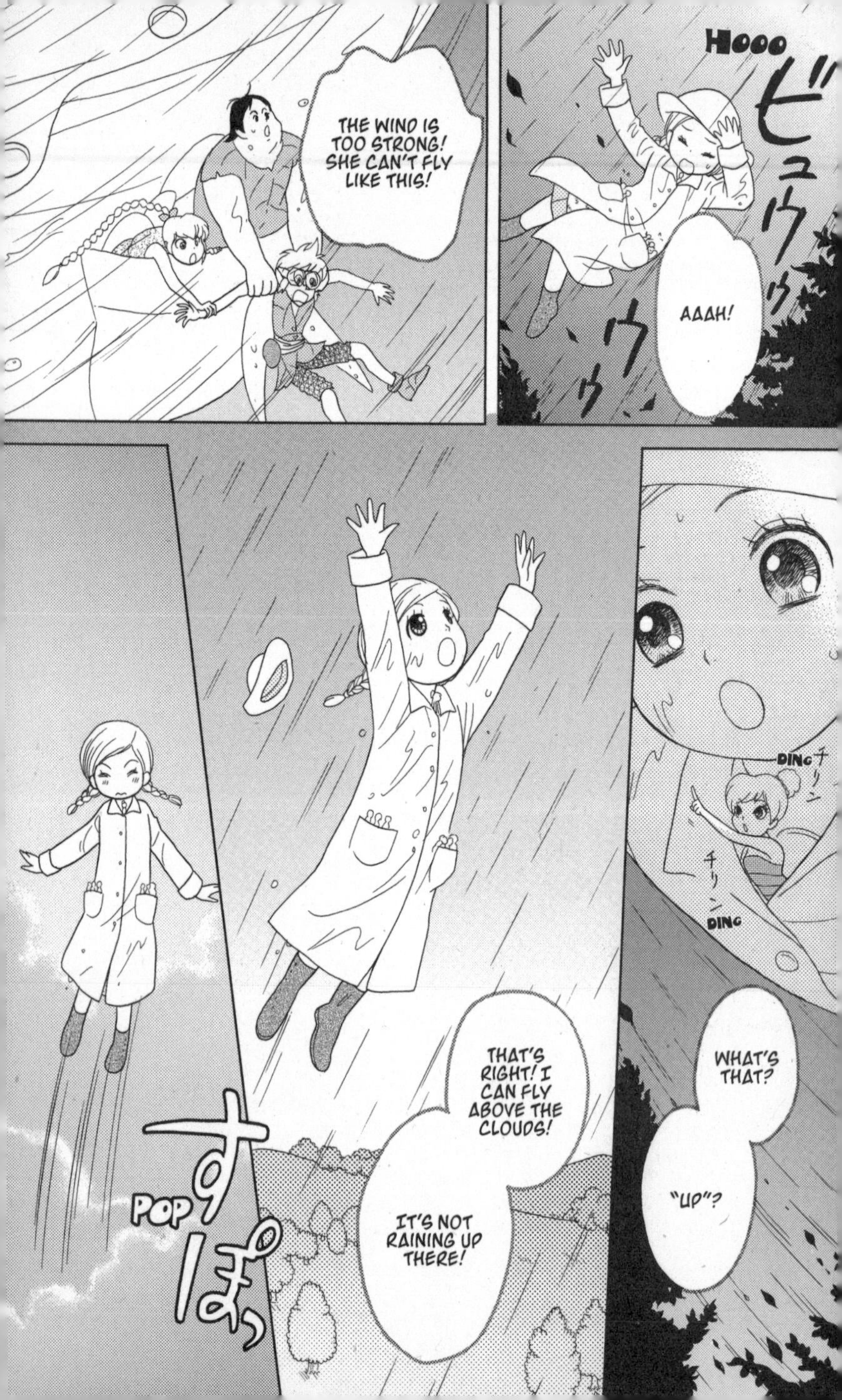
HOOO
ビュウウゥウゥ
AAAH!
THE WIND IS TOO STRONG! SHE CAN'T FLY LIKE THIS!
DING チリン
チリン DING
WHAT'S THAT?
"UP"?
THAT'S RIGHT! I CAN FLY ABOVE THE CLOUDS!
IT'S NOT RAINING UP THERE!
POP
すぽっ

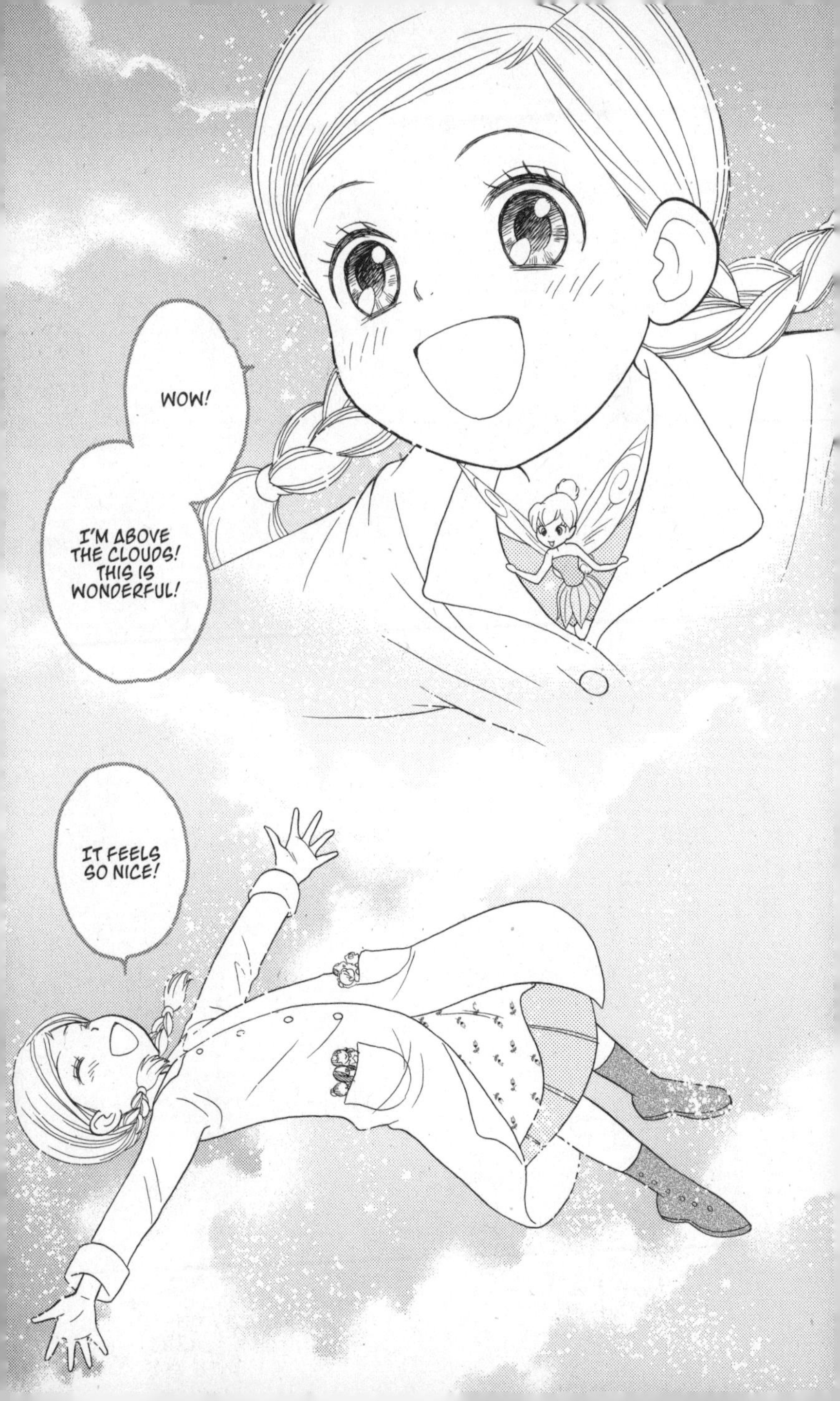

WOW!
I'M ABOVE THE CLOUDS! THIS IS WONDERFUL!
IT FEELS SO NICE!

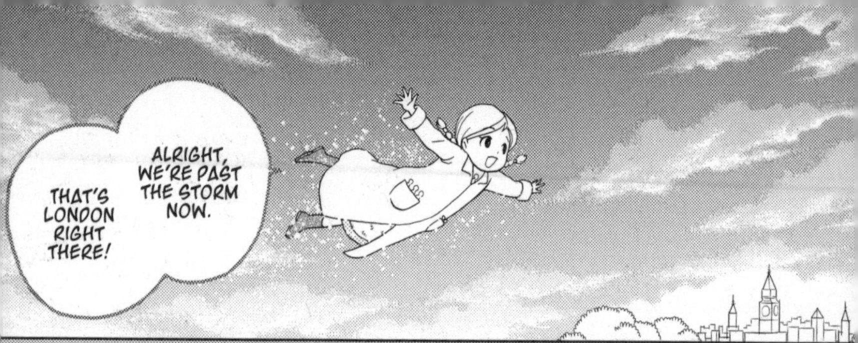
ALRIGHT, WE'RE PAST THE STORM NOW.
THAT'S LONDON RIGHT THERE!
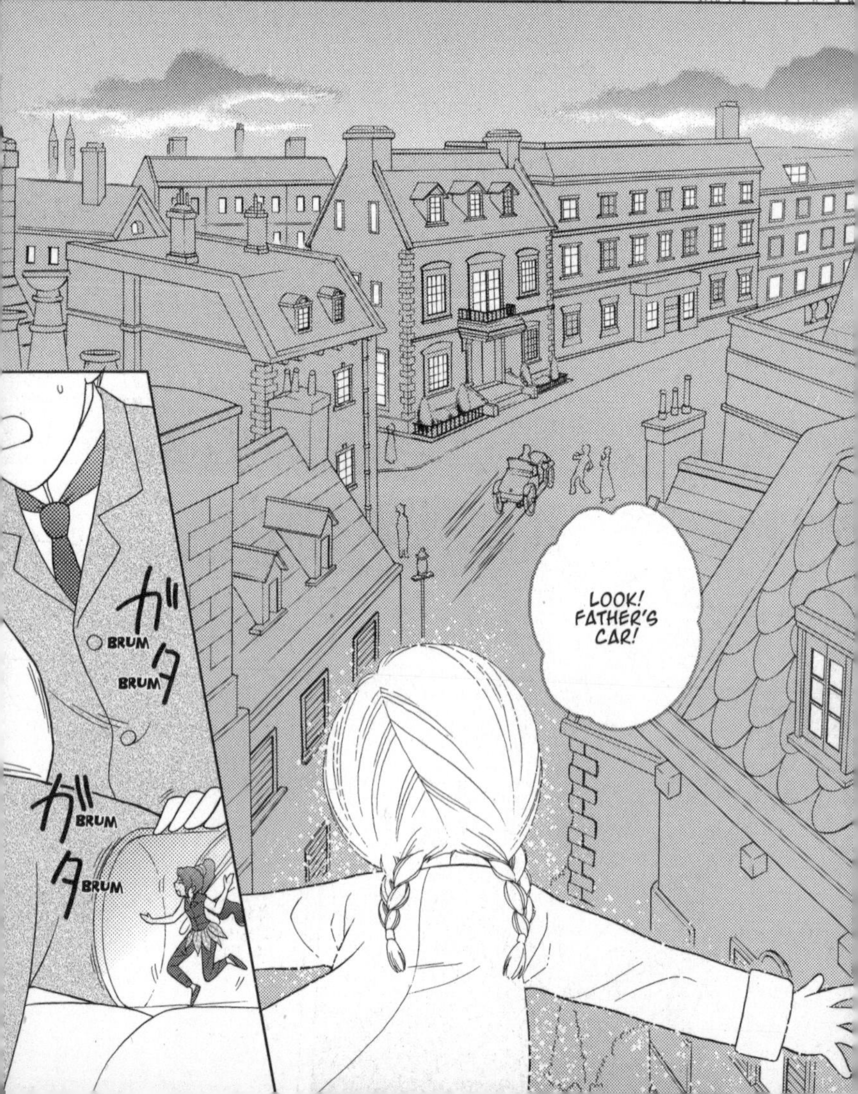
LOOK! FATHER'S CAR!
ガタ
BRUM BRUM
ガタ
BRUM BRUM

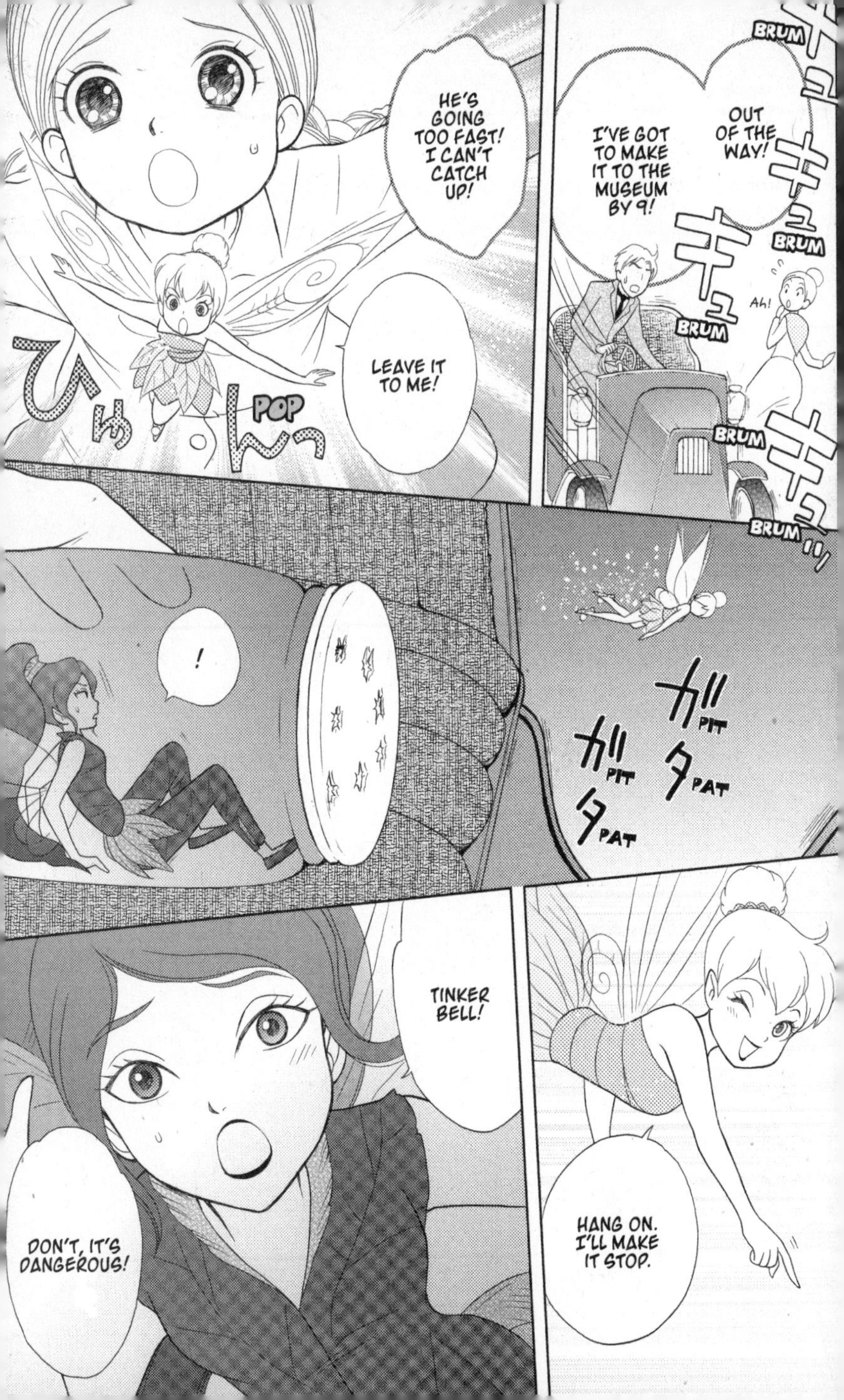

BRUM
OUT OF THE WAY!
I'VE GOT TO MAKE IT TO THE MUSEUM BY 9!
BRUM
Ah!
BRUM
BRUM
BRUM
HE'S GOING TOO FAST! I CAN'T CATCH UP!
LEAVE IT TO ME!
POP
PIT
PAT
PIT
PAT
!
HANG ON. I'LL MAKE IT STOP.
TINKER BELL!
DON'T, IT'S DANGEROUS!

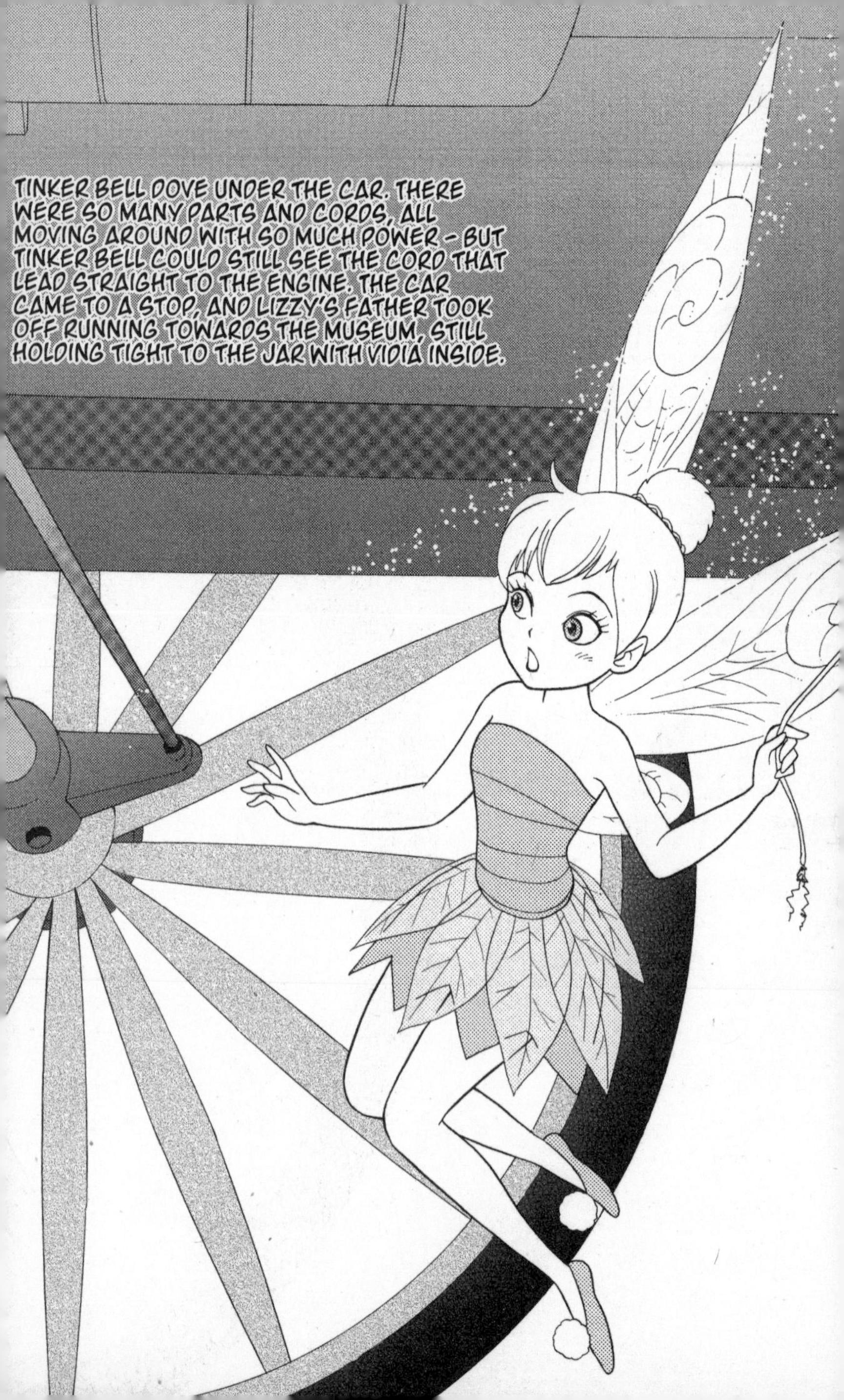
TINKER BELL DOVE UNDER THE CAR. THERE WERE SO MANY PARTS AND CORDS, ALL MOVING AROUND WITH SO MUCH POWER – BUT TINKER BELL COULD STILL SEE THE CORD THAT LEAD STRAIGHT TO THE ENGINE. THE CAR CAME TO A STOP, AND LIZZY'S FATHER TOOK OFF RUNNING TOWARDS THE MUSEUM, STILL HOLDING TIGHT TO THE JAR WITH VIDIA INSIDE.

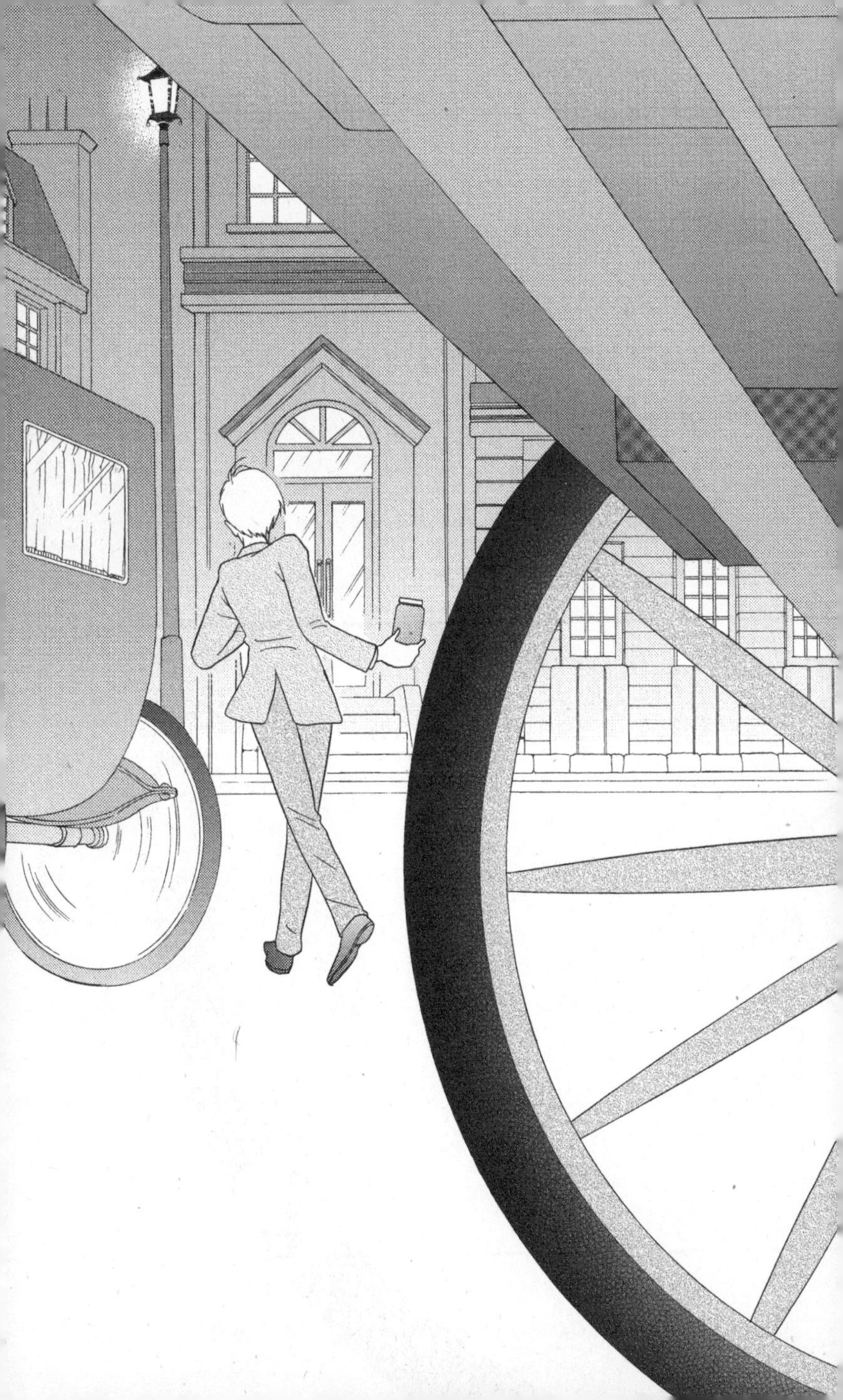

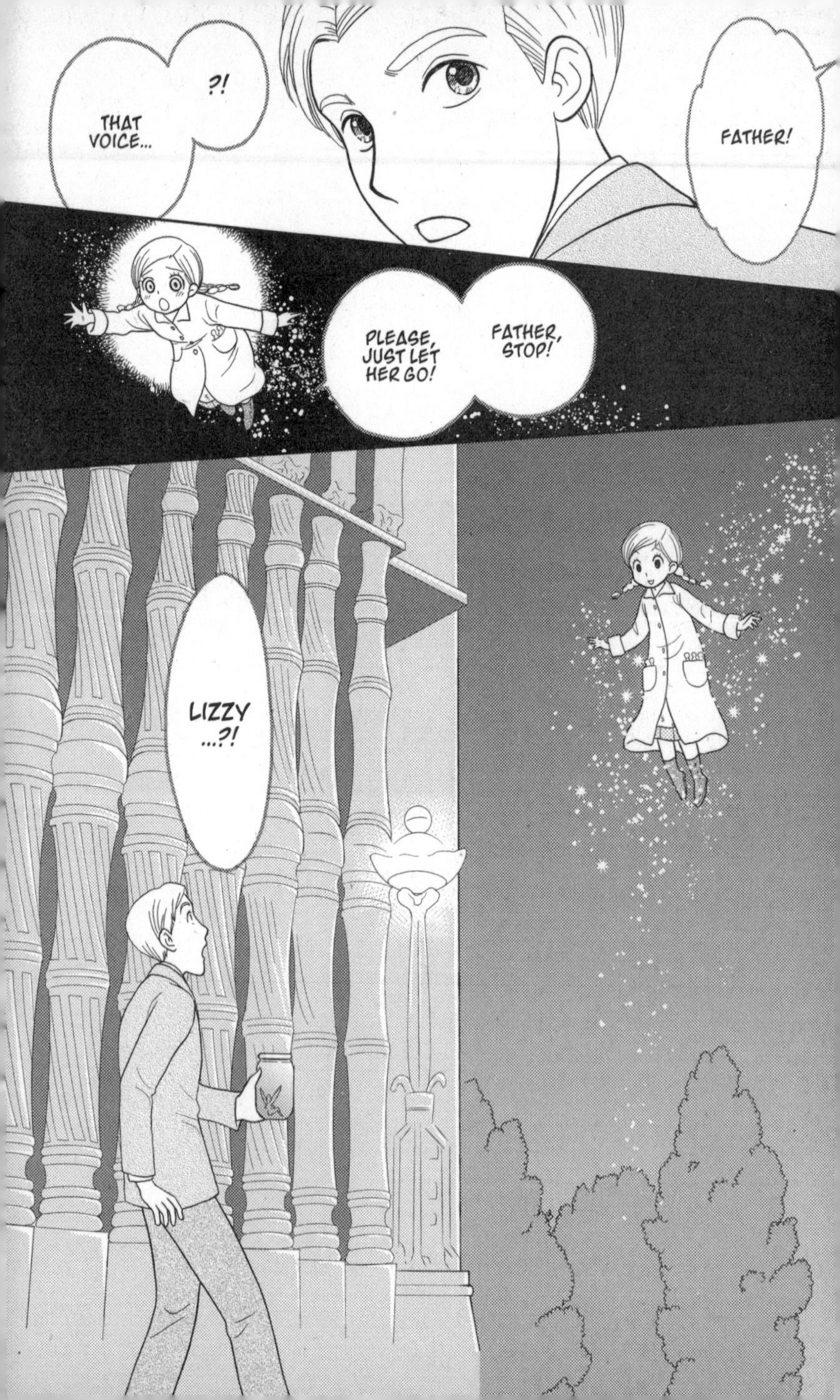
FATHER!
?!
THAT VOICE...
FATHER, STOP!
PLEASE, JUST LET HER GO!
LIZZY ...?!

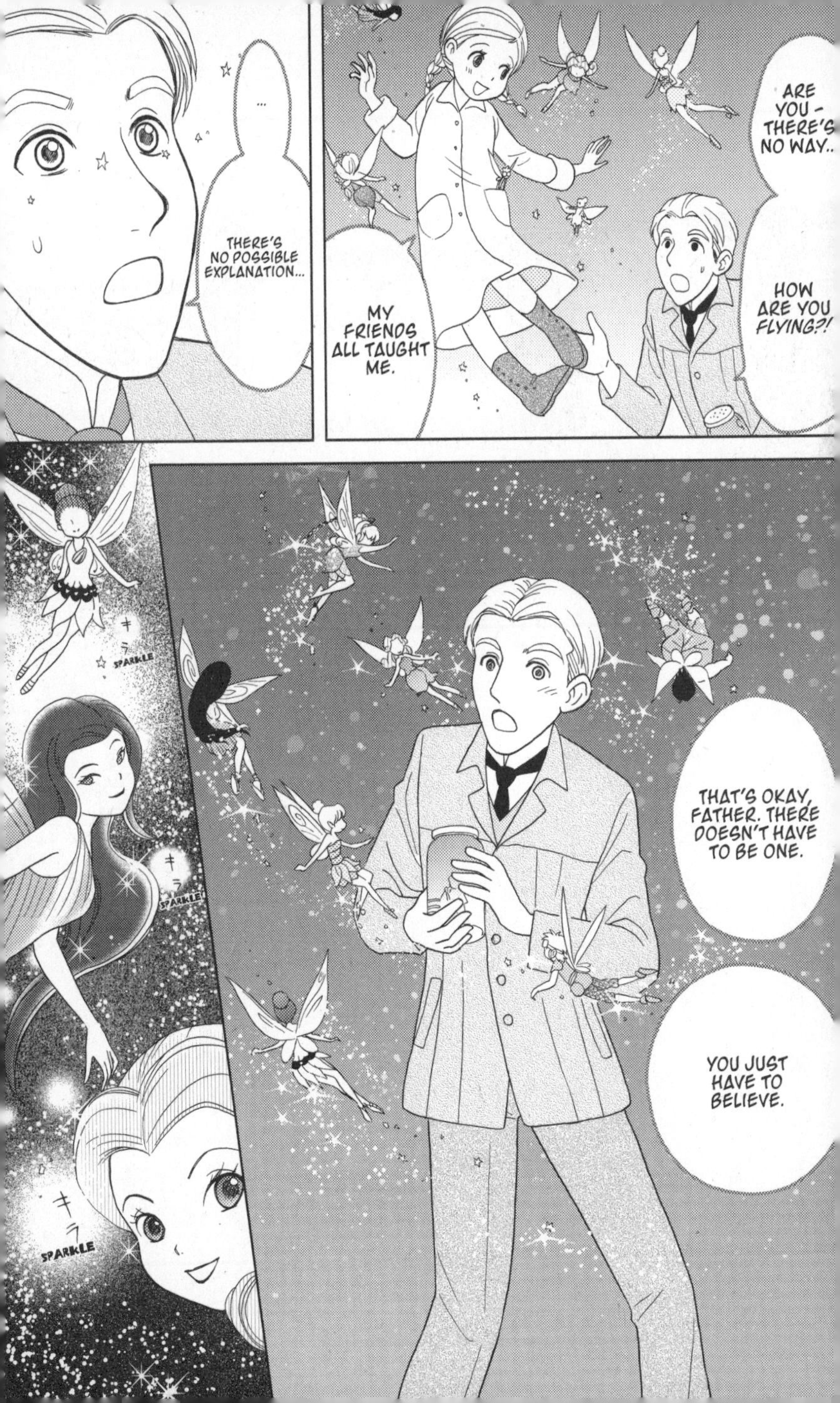
ARE YOU - THERE'S NO WAY..
HOW ARE YOU FLYING?!
MY FRIENDS ALL TAUGHT ME.
...
THERE'S NO POSSIBLE EXPLANATION...
THAT'S OKAY, FATHER. THERE DOESN'T HAVE TO BE ONE.
YOU JUST HAVE TO BELIEVE.
キラ SPARKLE
キラ SPARKLE
キラ SPARKLE

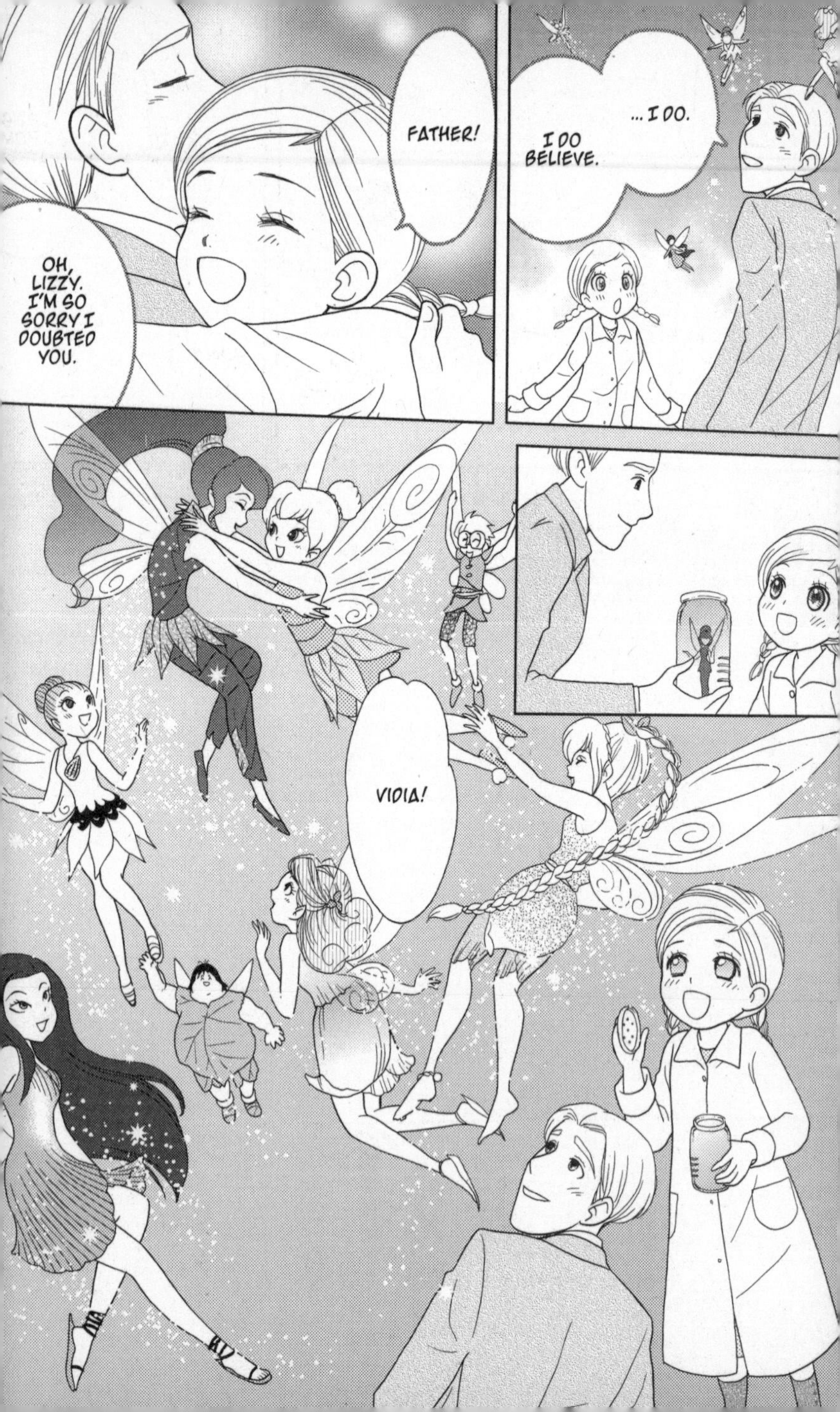
...I DO.
I DO BELIEVE.
FATHER!
OH, LIZZY. I'M SO SORRY I DOUBTED YOU.
VIDIA!

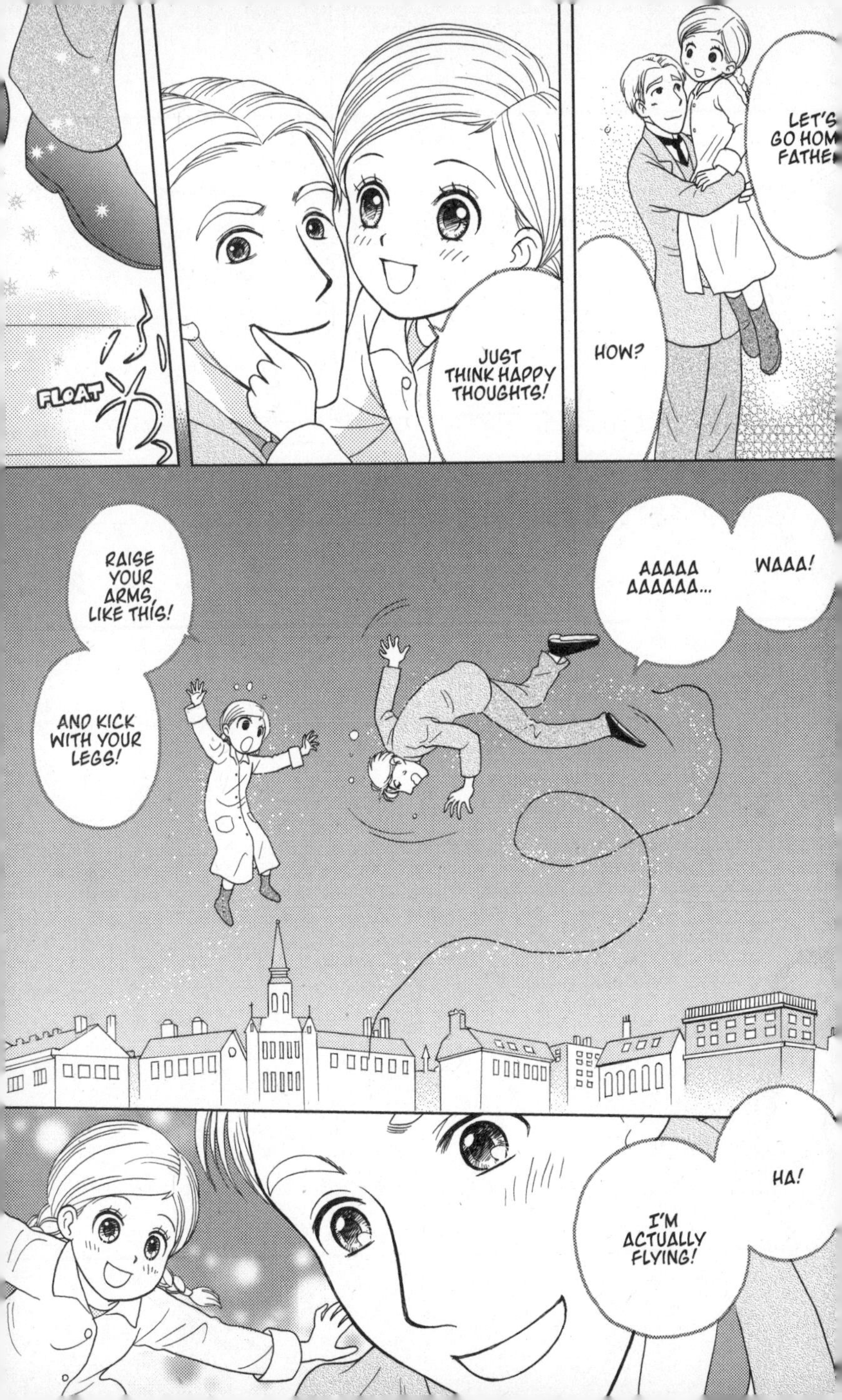
LET'S GO HOM FATHE
HOW?
JUST THINK HAPPY THOUGHTS!
FLOAT
WAAA!
AAAAA AAAAAA...
RAISE YOUR ARMS, LIKE THIS!
AND KICK WITH YOUR LEGS!
HA!
I'M ACTUALLY FLYING!

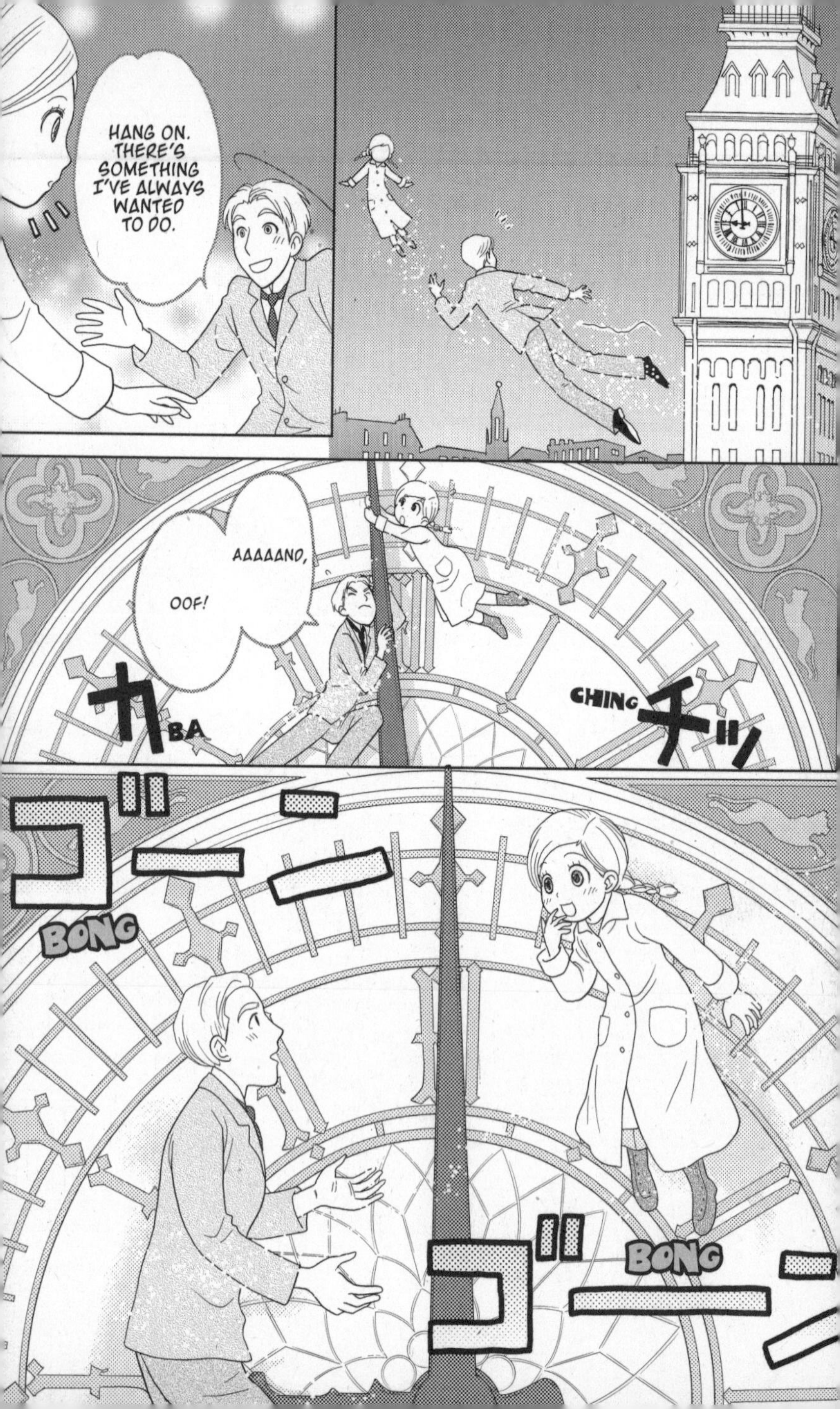

HANG ON. THERE'S SOMETHING I'VE ALWAYS WANTED TO DO.
AAAAAND,
OOF!
CHING
チッ
カ
BA
ゴーー
BONG
ゴーー
BONG

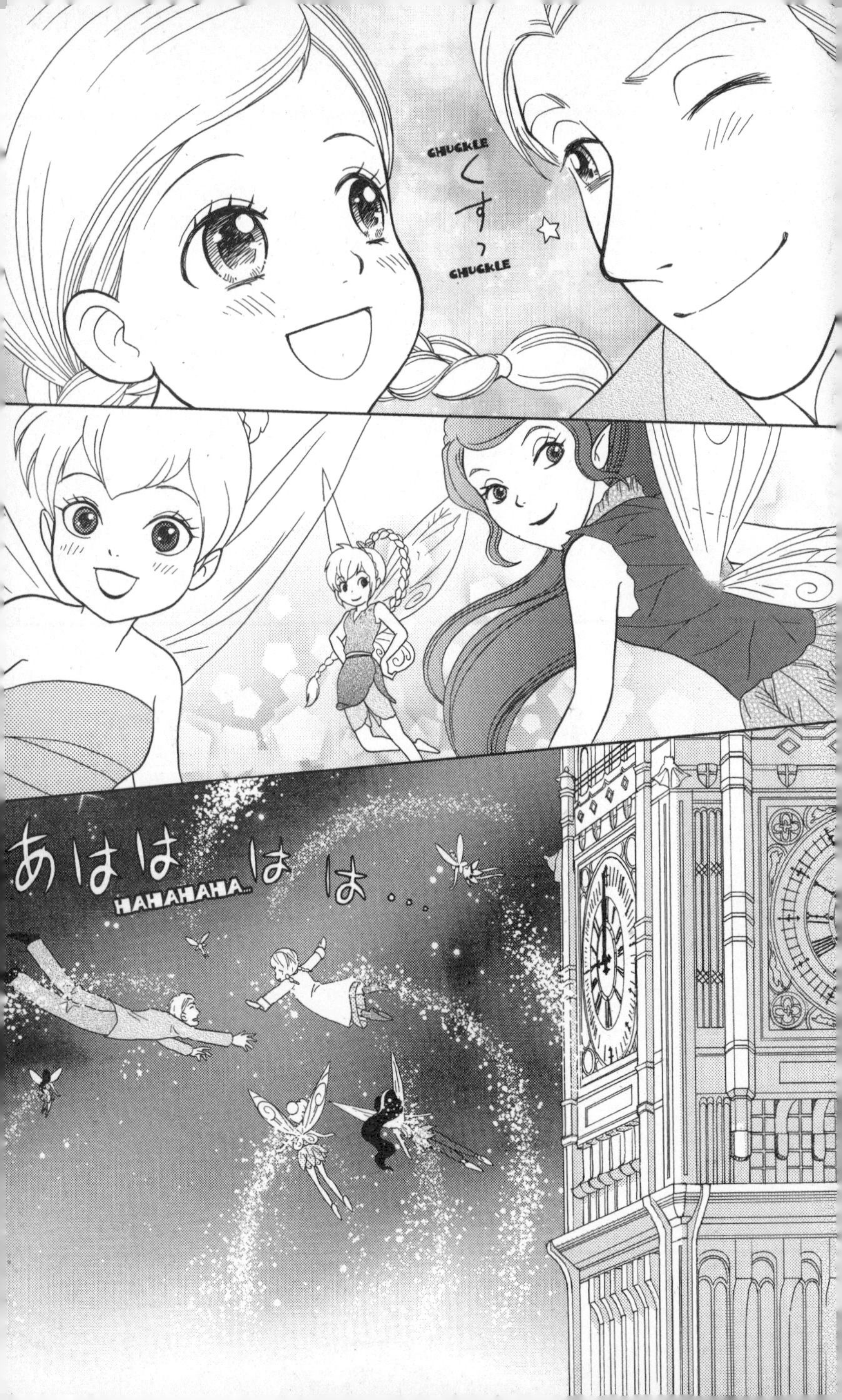
CHUCKLE
くすっ
CHUCKLE
あはははは…
HAHAHAHA...

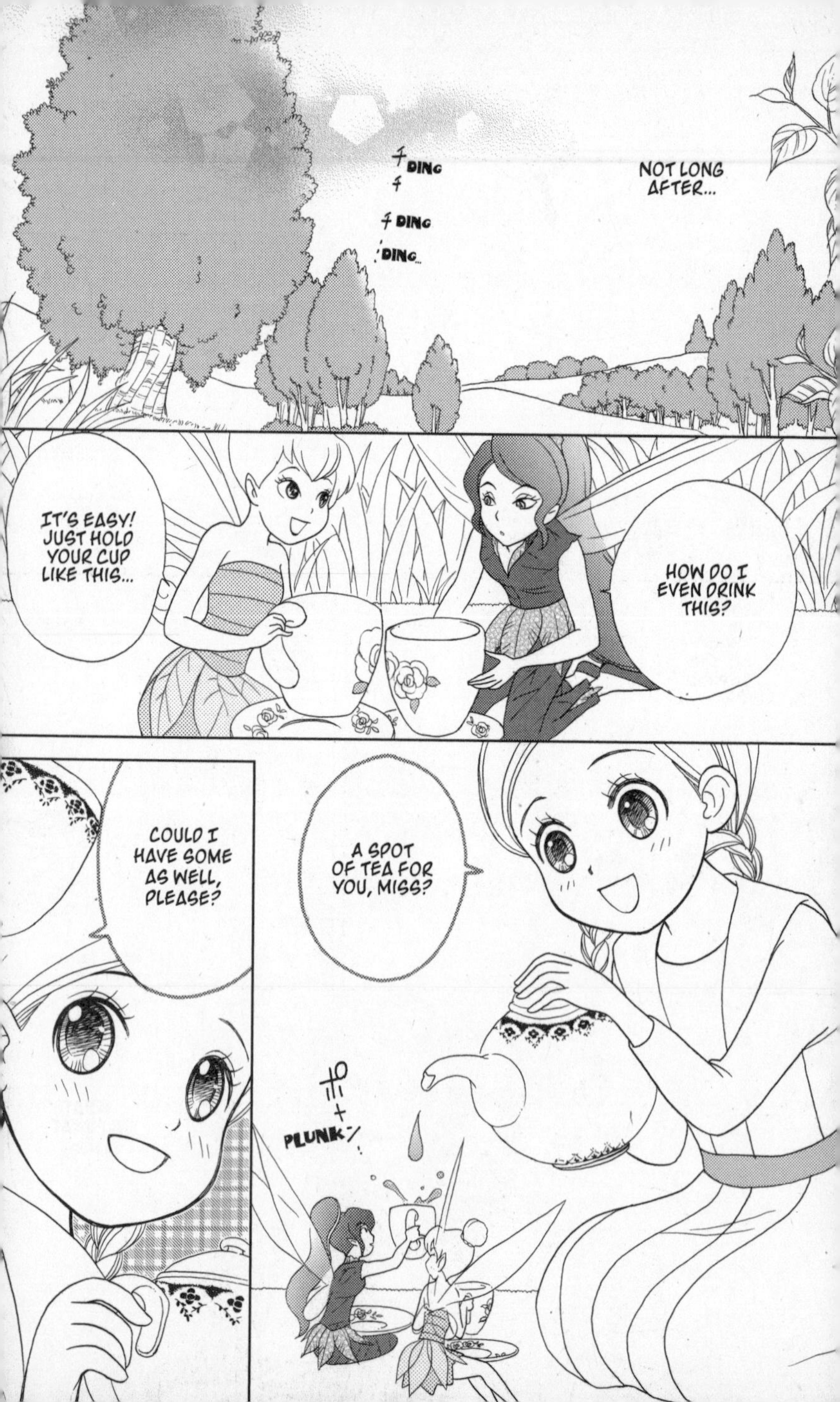
NOT LONG AFTER...
DING
DING
DING...
HOW DO I EVEN DRINK THIS?
IT'S EASY! JUST HOLD YOUR CUP LIKE THIS...
A SPOT OF TEA FOR YOU, MISS?
PLUNK
COULD I HAVE SOME AS WELL, PLEASE?

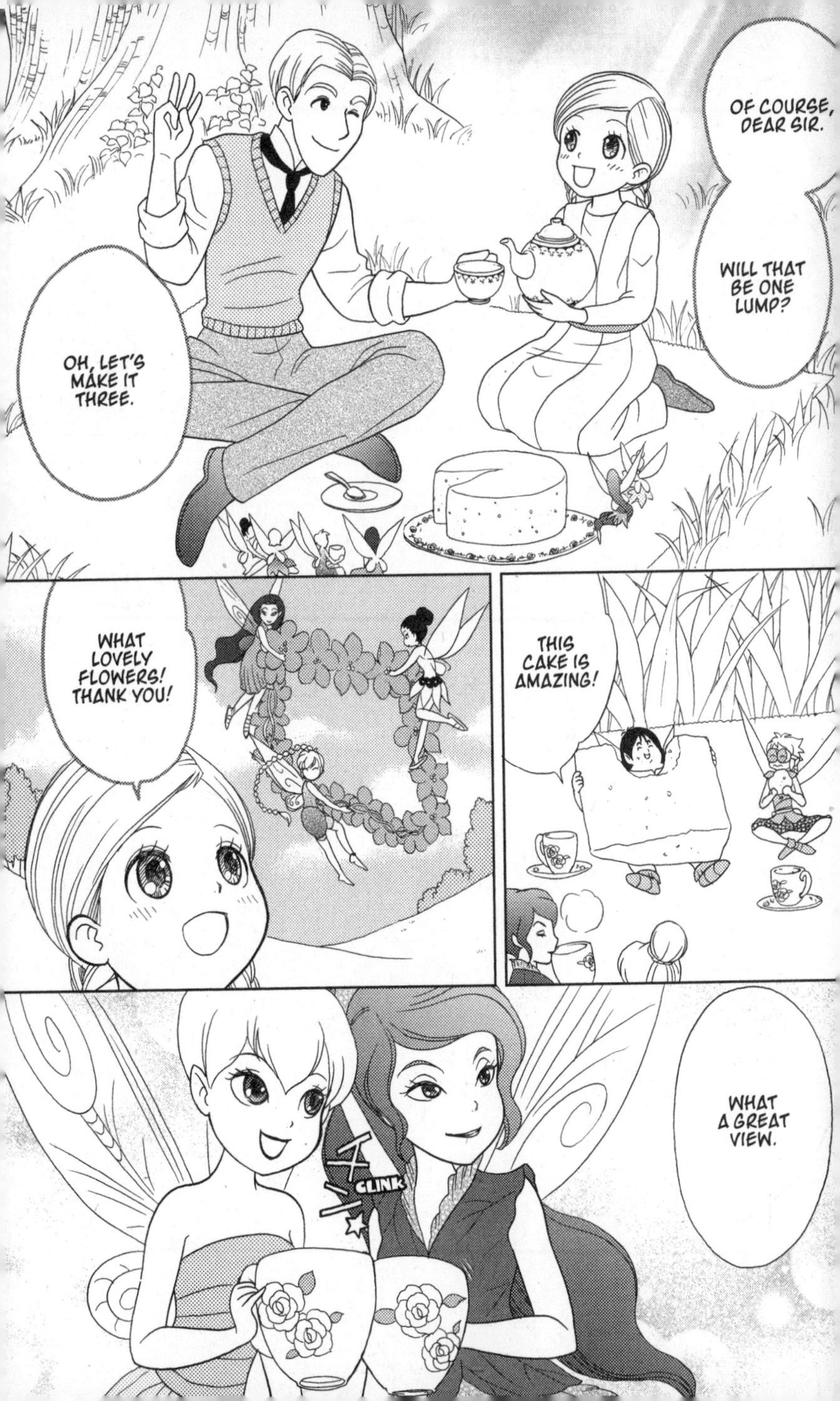
OF COURSE, DEAR SIR.
WILL THAT BE ONE LUMP?
OH, LET'S MAKE IT THREE.
THIS CAKE IS AMAZING!
WHAT LOVELY FLOWERS! THANK YOU!
WHAT A GREAT VIEW.
CLINK

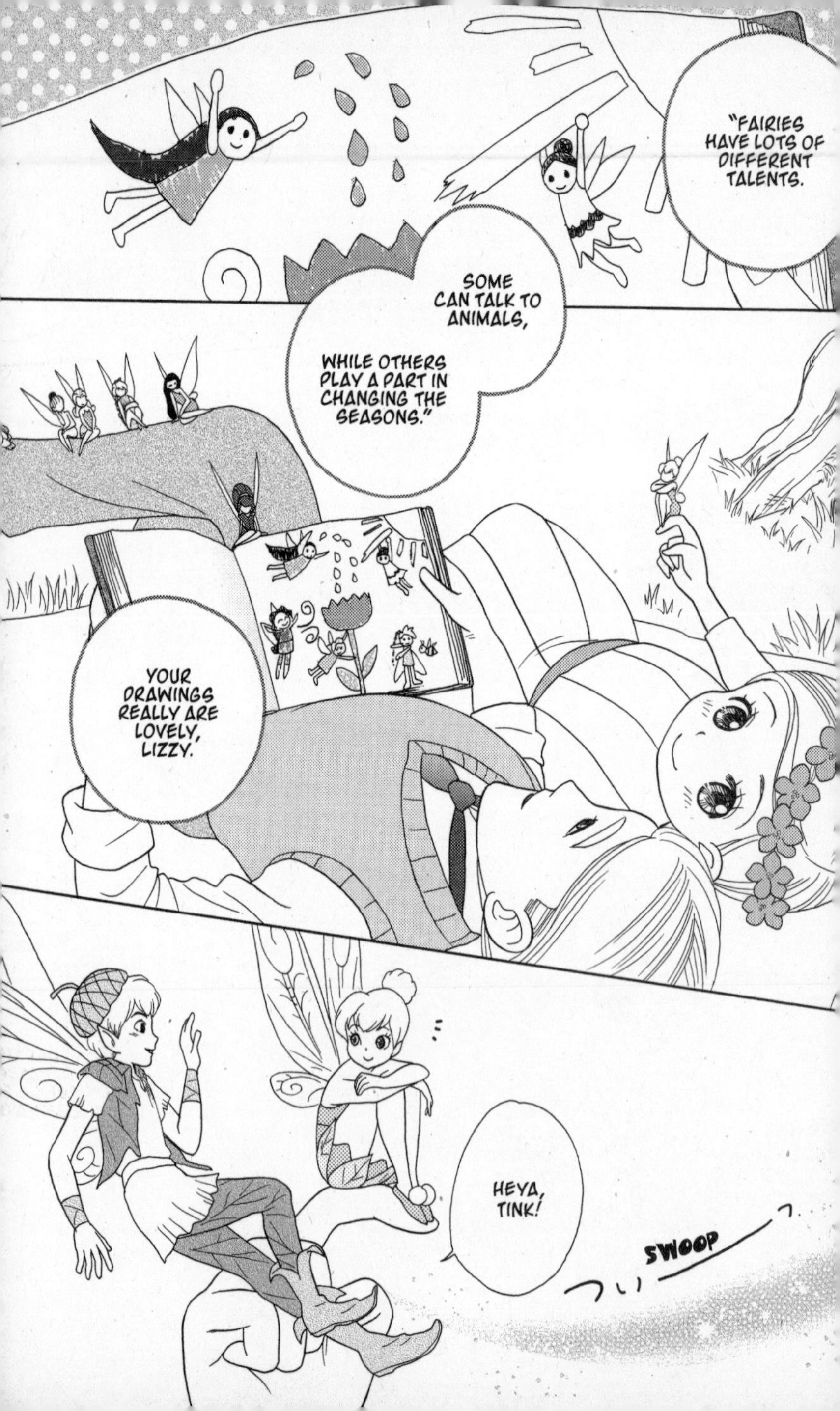
"FAIRIES HAVE LOTS OF DIFFERENT TALENTS.
SOME CAN TALK TO ANIMALS,
WHILE OTHERS PLAY A PART IN CHANGING THE SEASONS."
YOUR DRAWINGS REALLY ARE LOVELY, LIZZY.
HEYA, TINK!
SWOOP
つい

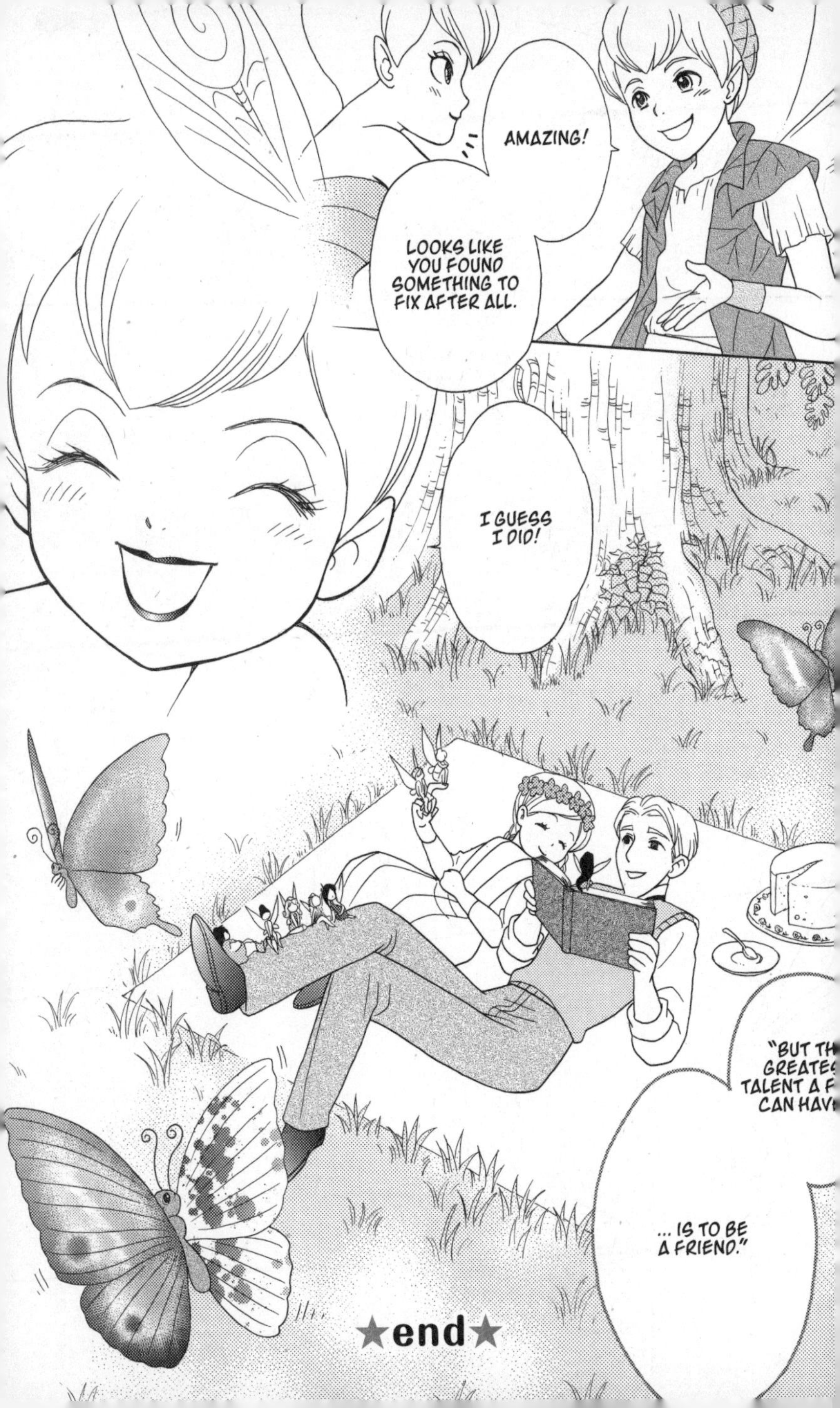
AMAZING!
LOOKS LIKE YOU FOUND SOMETHING TO FIX AFTER ALL.
I GUESS I DID!
"BUT TH GREATES TALENT A F CAN HAV
... IS TO BE A FRIEND."
★end★

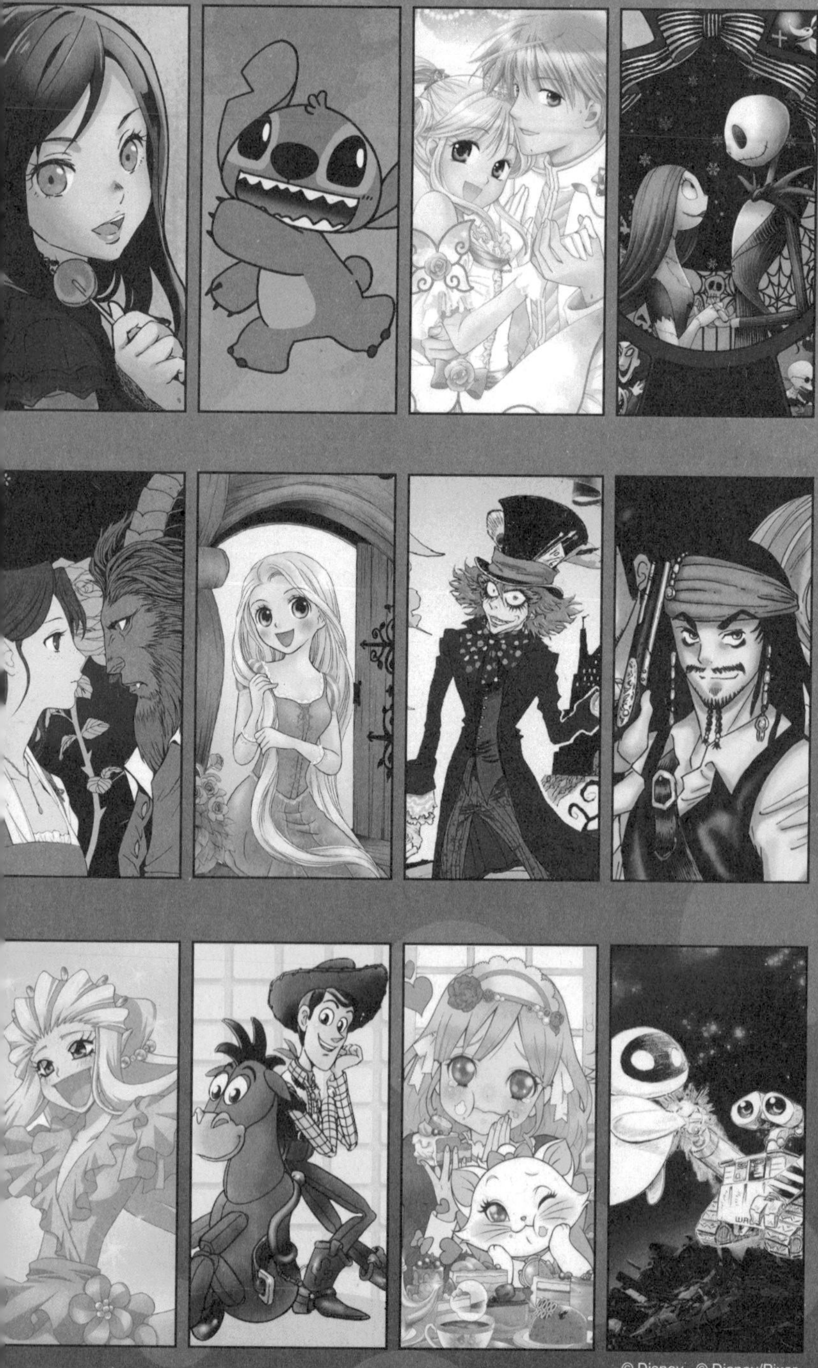

Add These Disney Manga to Your Collection Today!

SHOJO

- ☐ DISNEY BEAUTY AND THE BEAST
- ☐ DISNEY KILALA PRINCESS SERIES

FANTASY

- ☐ DISNEY DESCENDANTS SERIES
- ☐ DISNEY TANGLED
- ☐ DISNEY PRINCESS AND THE FROG
- ☐ DISNEY FAIRIES SERIES
- ☐ DISNEY MARIE: MIRIYA AND MARIE

KAWAII

- ☐ DISNEY MAGICAL DANCE
- ☐ DISNEY STITCH! SERIES

PIXAR

- ☐ DISNEY•PIXAR TOY STORY
- ☐ DISNEY•PIXAR MONSTERS, INC.
- ☐ DISNEY•PIXAR WALL-E
- ☐ DISNEY•PIXAR FINDING NEMO

ADVENTURE

- ☐ DISNEY TIM BURTON'S THE NIGHTMARE BEFORE CHRISTMAS
- ☐ DISNEY ALICE IN WONDERLAND
- ☐ DISNEY PIRATES OF THE CARIBBEAN SERIES

TOKYOPOP

Vidia and the Fairy Crown

Disney
FAIRIES
Vidia and the Fairy Crown
TOKYOPOP
Haruhi Kato

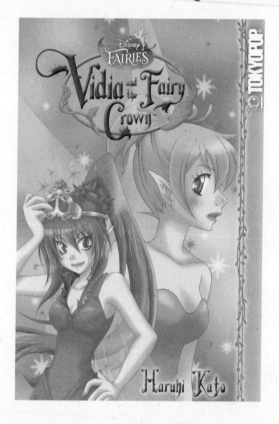

When Queen Clarion's crown goes missing on the night of Pixie Hollow's biggest bash, all fingers point to one thief - the rude and standoffish fairy Vidia! To keep from being banished from Pixie Hollow forever, Vidia goes on an outrageous hunt for the crown that takes her from one end of Never Land to the other. Can she find the crown in time to save Vidia's reputation?

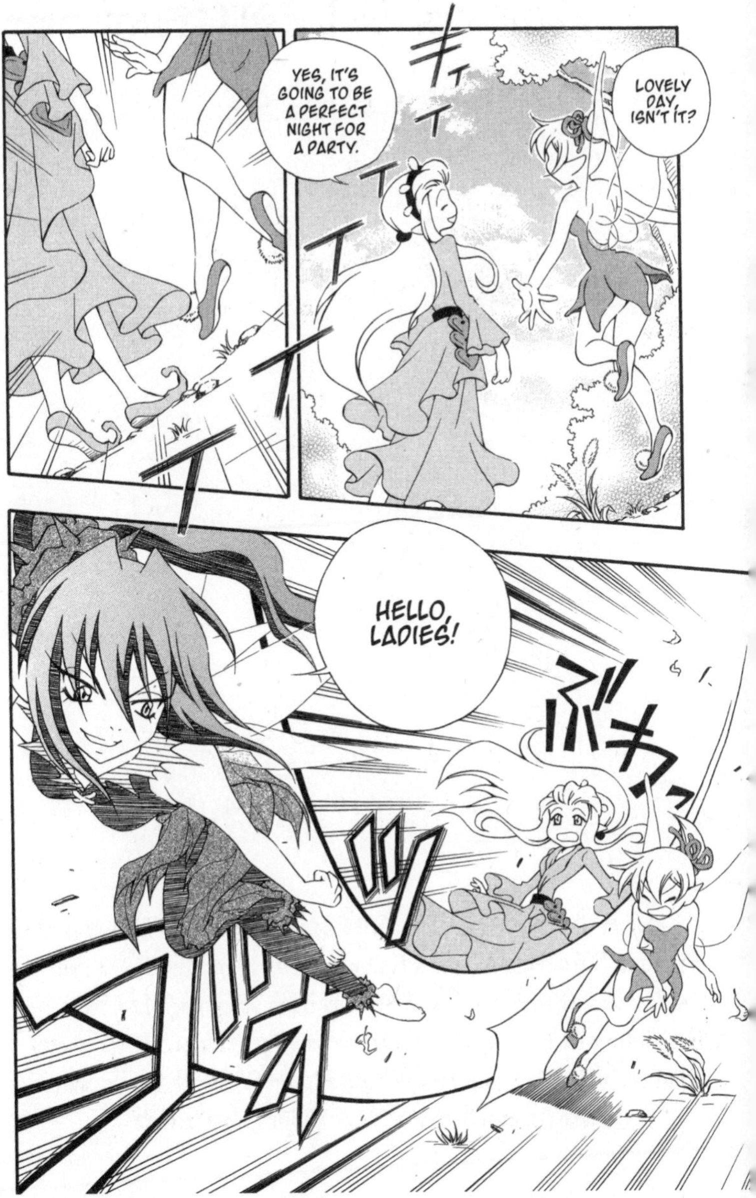
LOVELY DAY, ISN'T IT?
YES, IT'S GOING TO BE A PERFECT NIGHT FOR A PARTY.
HELLO, LADIES!

Tinker Bell's Secret

Disney
Fairies
Tinker Bell's
Secret
TOKYOPOP
Haruhi Kato

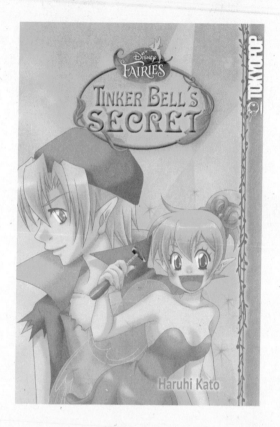

Tinker Bell is the best tinkerer in all of Pixie Hollow. She's even asked to fix Queen Lee's bath tub, the biggest honor for any tinker fairy! But when Tink loses her magical hammer in Peter Pan's secret hideout, she loses her ability to tinker! Will Tink be able to get her hammer and her talent back without being caught by Peter Pan and the Lost Boys?

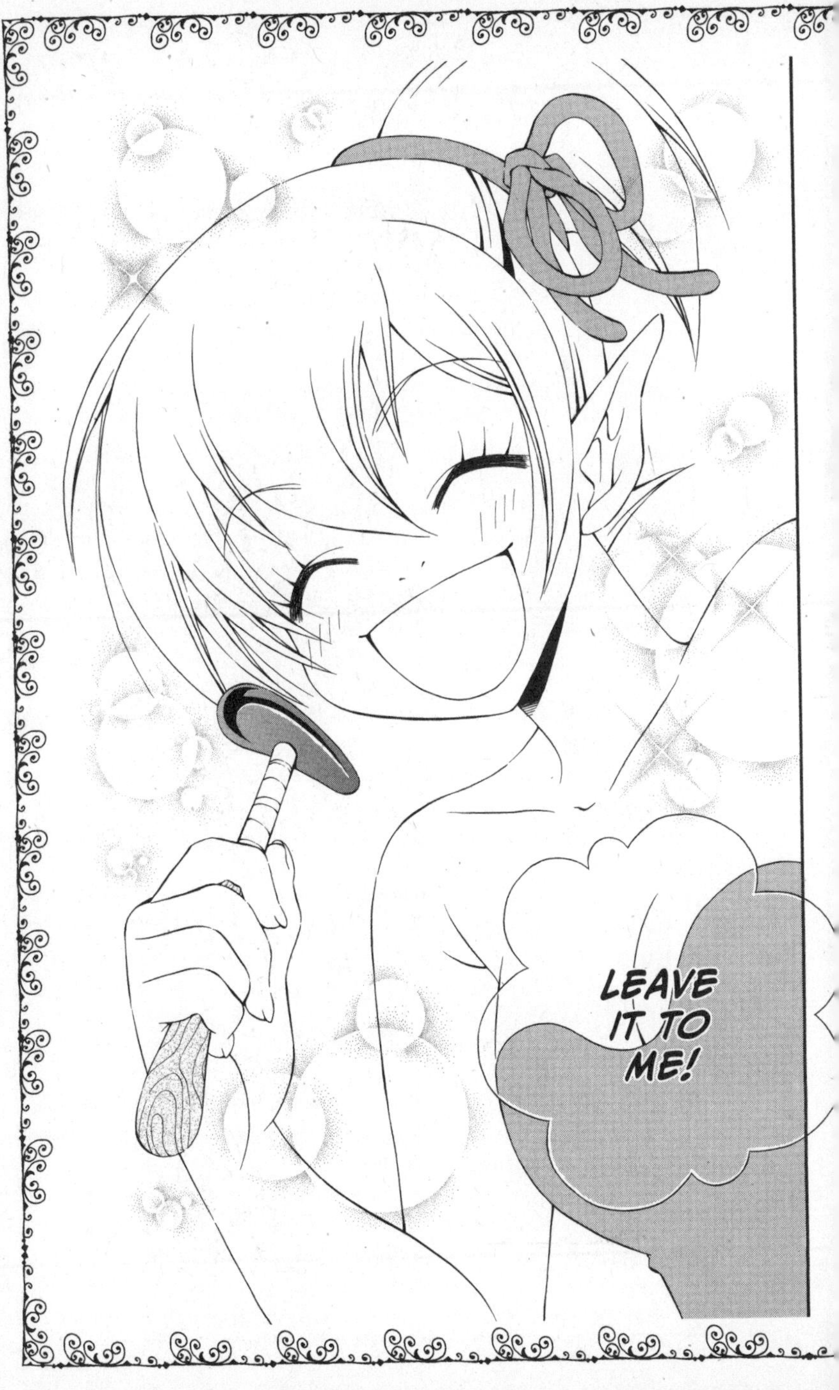
LEAVE IT TO ME!

The Petite Fairy's Diary

Disney
FAIRIES
The Petite Fairy's Diary
TOKYOPOP
Jun Asuka

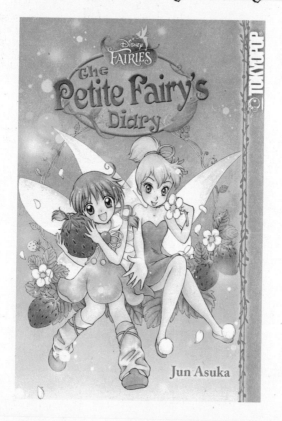

Petite is the smallest -- and clumsiest -- fairy in all of Never Land's Pixie Hollow. She's even smaller than a bug! With the Moon Ceremony coming up soon, the Fledgling Fairies are preparing to present their talents in order to graduate as Major Fairies, but Petite hasn't found hers yet! With Tinker Bell's help, can Petite discover her talent before the biggest celebration of her lifetime begins?

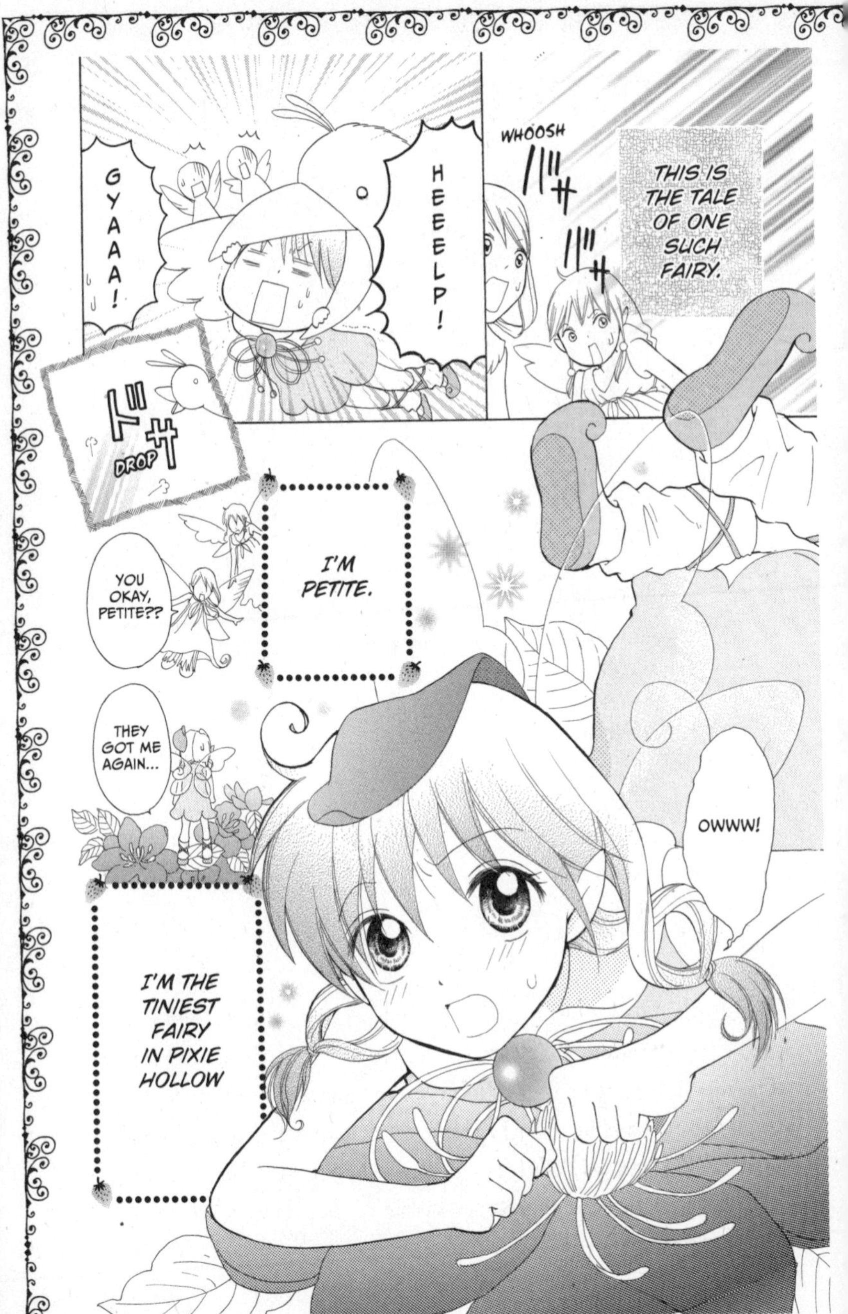
WHOOSH
THIS IS THE TALE OF ONE SUCH FAIRY.
HEEEELP!
GYAAAA!
DROP
OWWW!
I'M PETITE.
YOU OKAY, PETITE??
THEY GOT ME AGAIN...
I'M THE TINIEST FAIRY IN PIXIE HOLLOW

Rani and the Mermaid Lagoon

Rani cut off her wings to save Pixie Hollow and her
fairy friends, but a fairy who can't fly is unheard of. After a
disastrous accident at the Fairy Dance, she runs away to try and
find her own place to belong. Maybe the mermaid lagoon could be
her new home. Join Rani and the rest of the Disney fairies —
and mermaids! — on this magical adventure.

Discover what awaits Rani when she
travels beneath the mermaid lagoon!

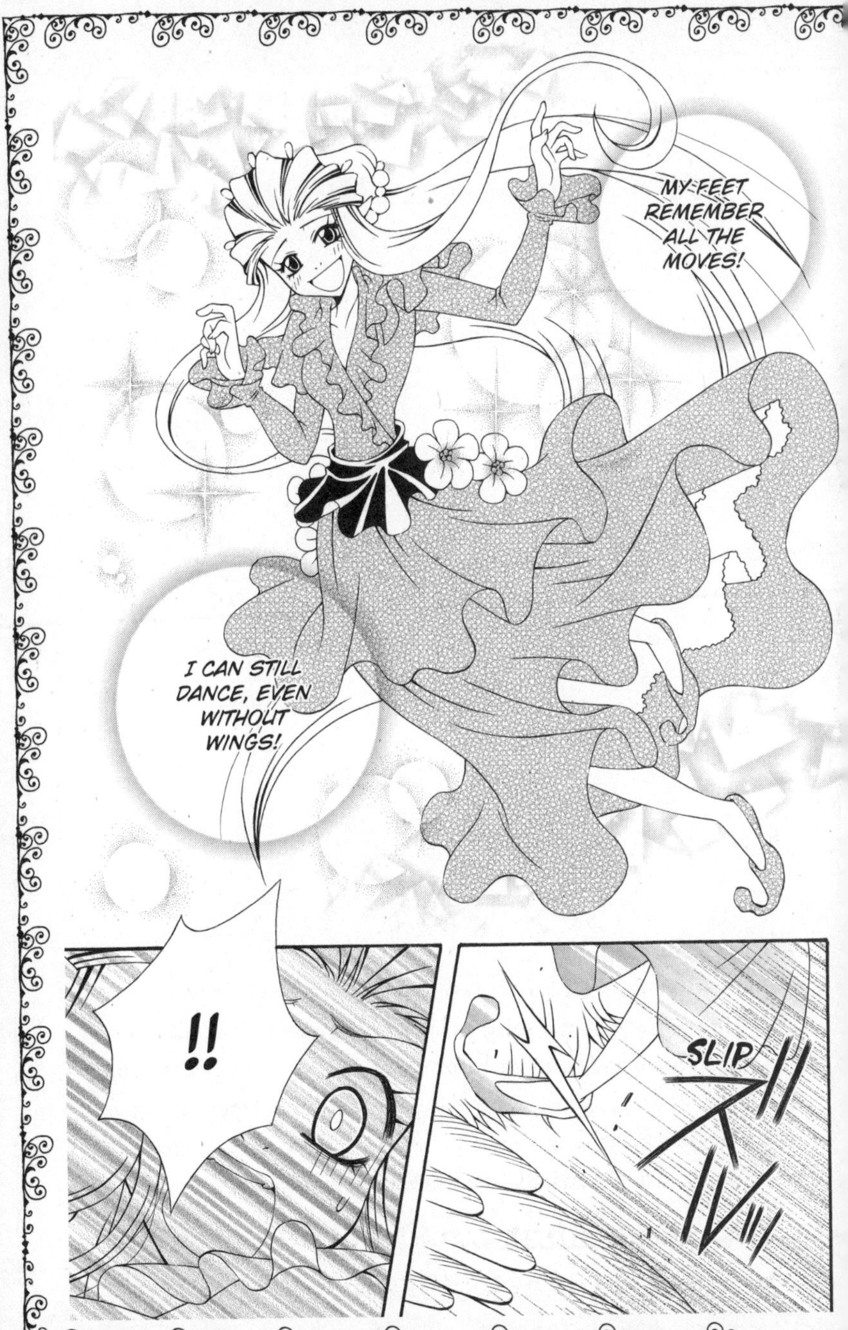
MY FEET REMEMBER ALL THE MOVES!
I CAN STILL DANCE, EVEN WITHOUT WINGS!
SLIP
!!

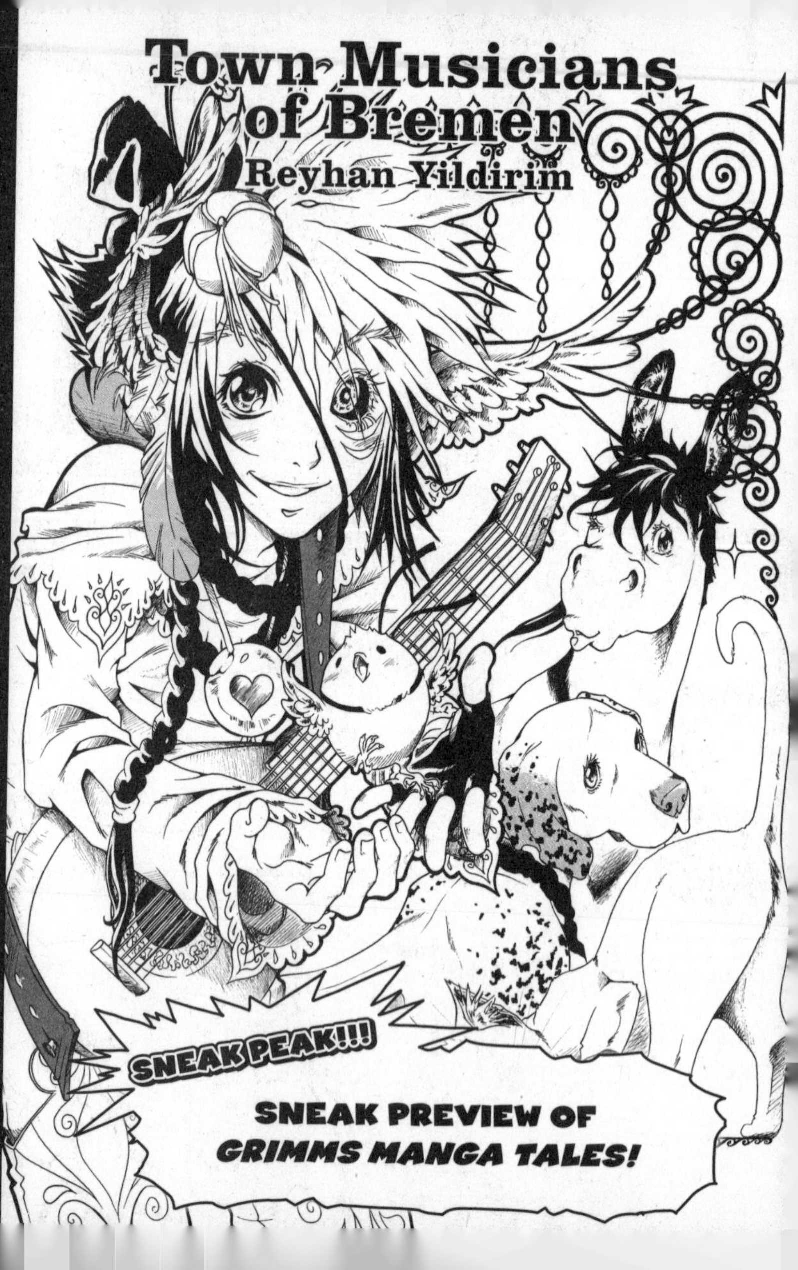
Town Musicians of Bremen
Reyhan Yildirim
SNEAK PEAK!!!
SNEAK PREVIEW OF GRIMMS MANGA TALES!

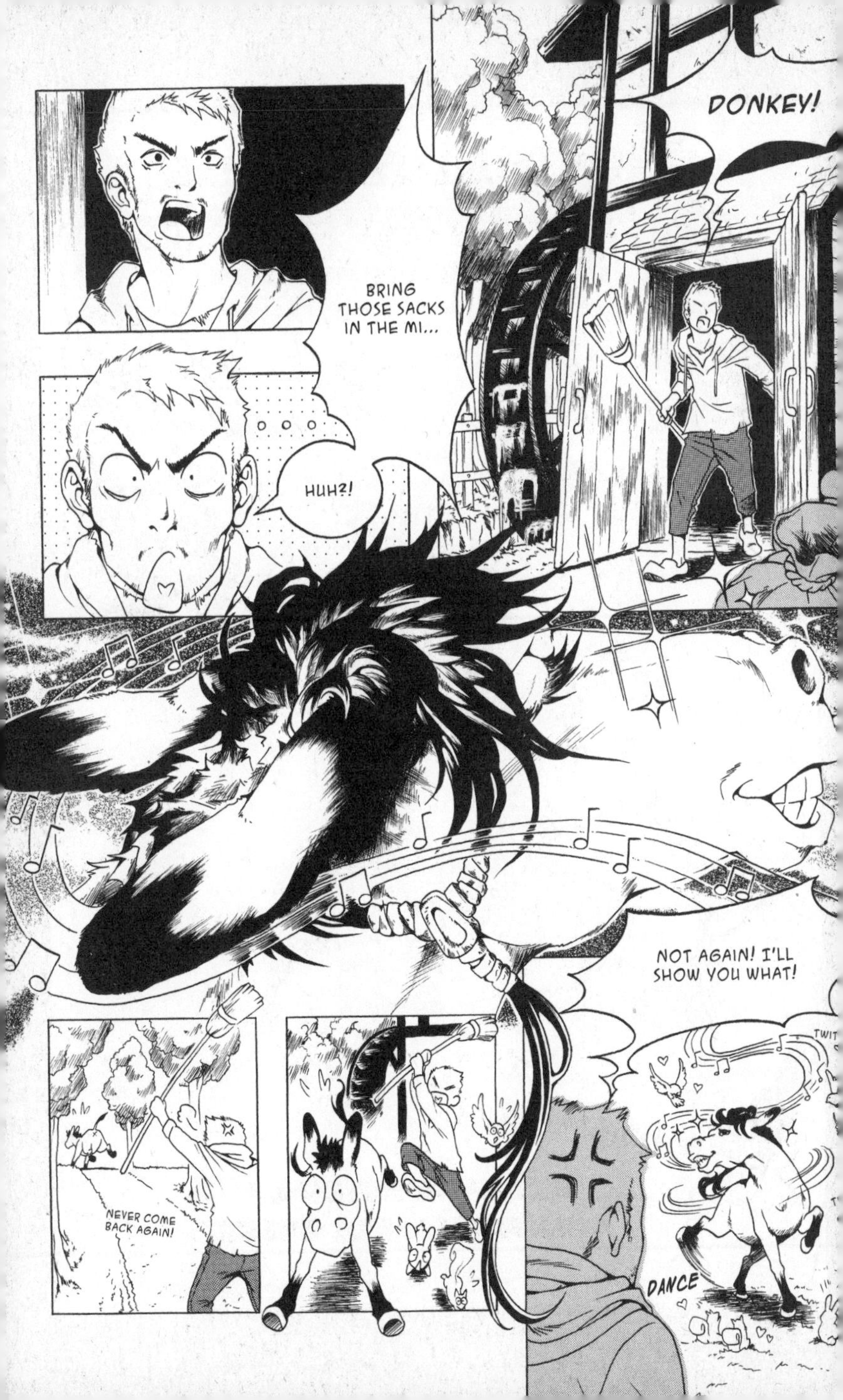
DONKEY!
BRING THOSE SACKS IN THE MI...
...
HUH?!
NOT AGAIN! I'LL SHOW YOU WHAT!
TWIT
DANCE
NEVER COME BACK AGAIN!

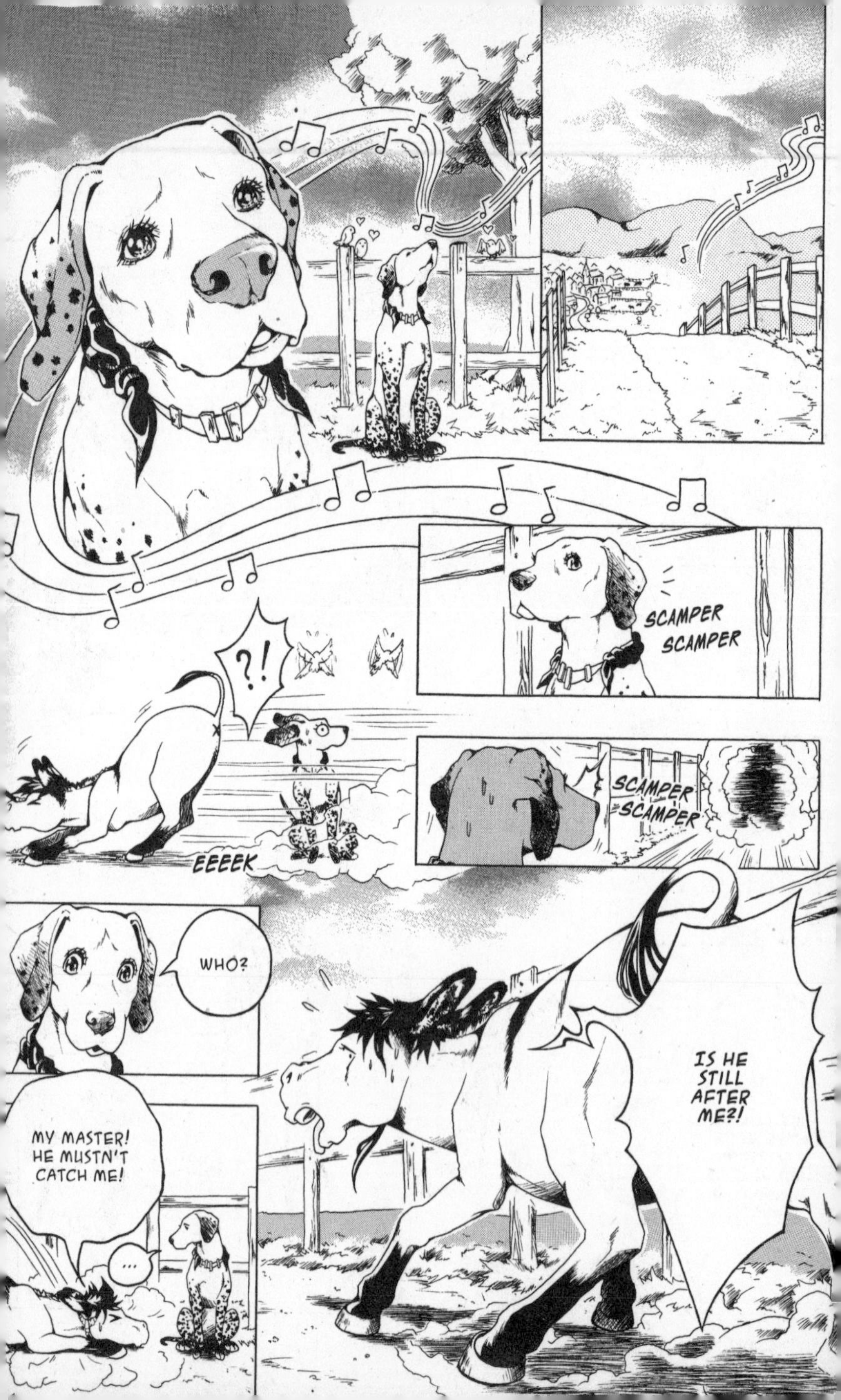
SCAMPER
SCAMPER
SCAMPER
SCAMPER
?!
EEEEK
IS HE STILL AFTER ME?!
WHO?
MY MASTER! HE MUSTN'T CATCH ME!
...

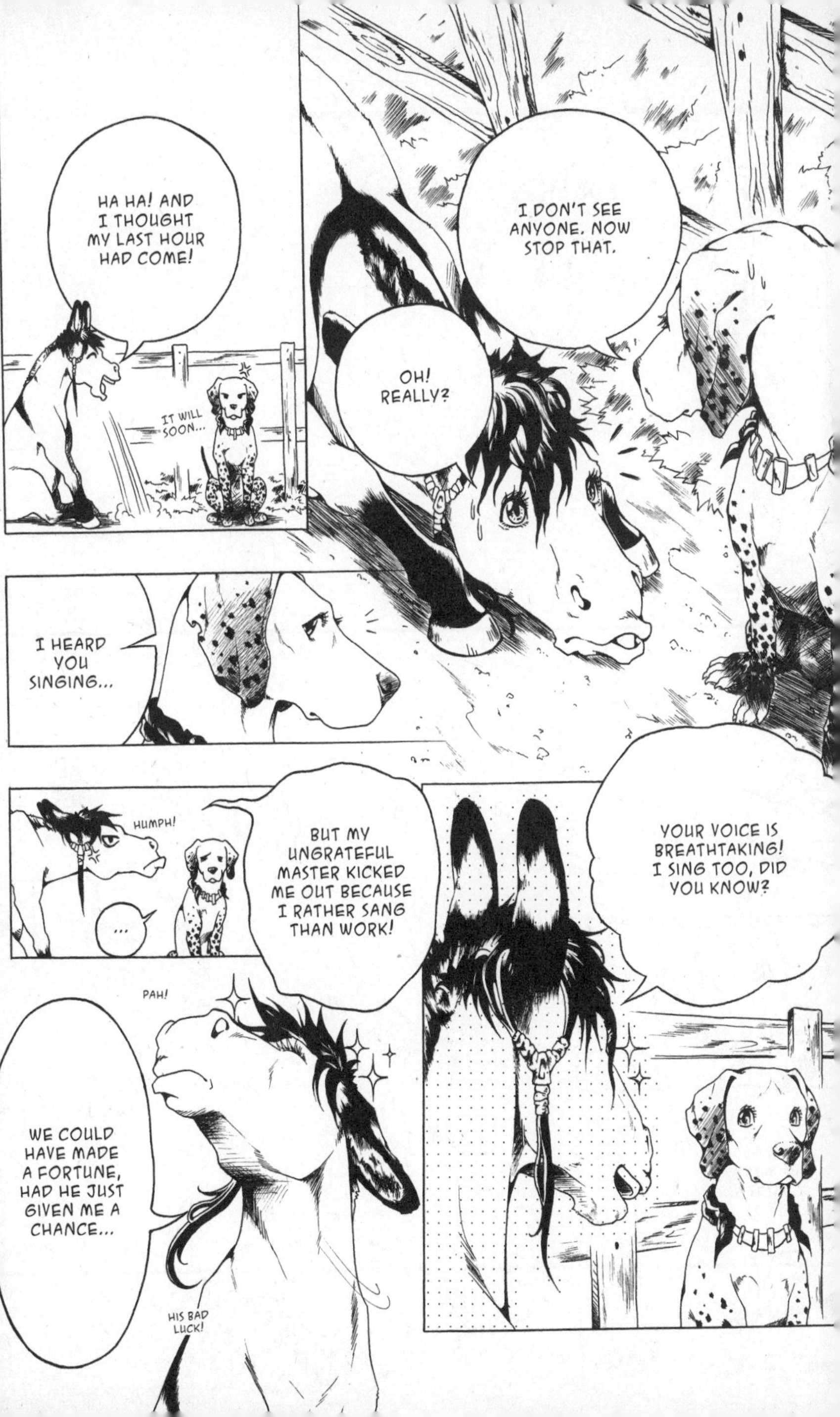
I DON'T SEE ANYONE. NOW STOP THAT.
OH! REALLY?
HA HA! AND I THOUGHT MY LAST HOUR HAD COME!
IT WILL SOON...
I HEARD YOU SINGING...
YOUR VOICE IS BREATHTAKING! I SING TOO, DID YOU KNOW?
HUMPH!
BUT MY UNGRATEFUL MASTER KICKED ME OUT BECAUSE I RATHER SANG THAN WORK!
...
PAH!
WE COULD HAVE MADE A FORTUNE, HAD HE JUST GIVEN ME A CHANCE...
HIS BAD LUCK!

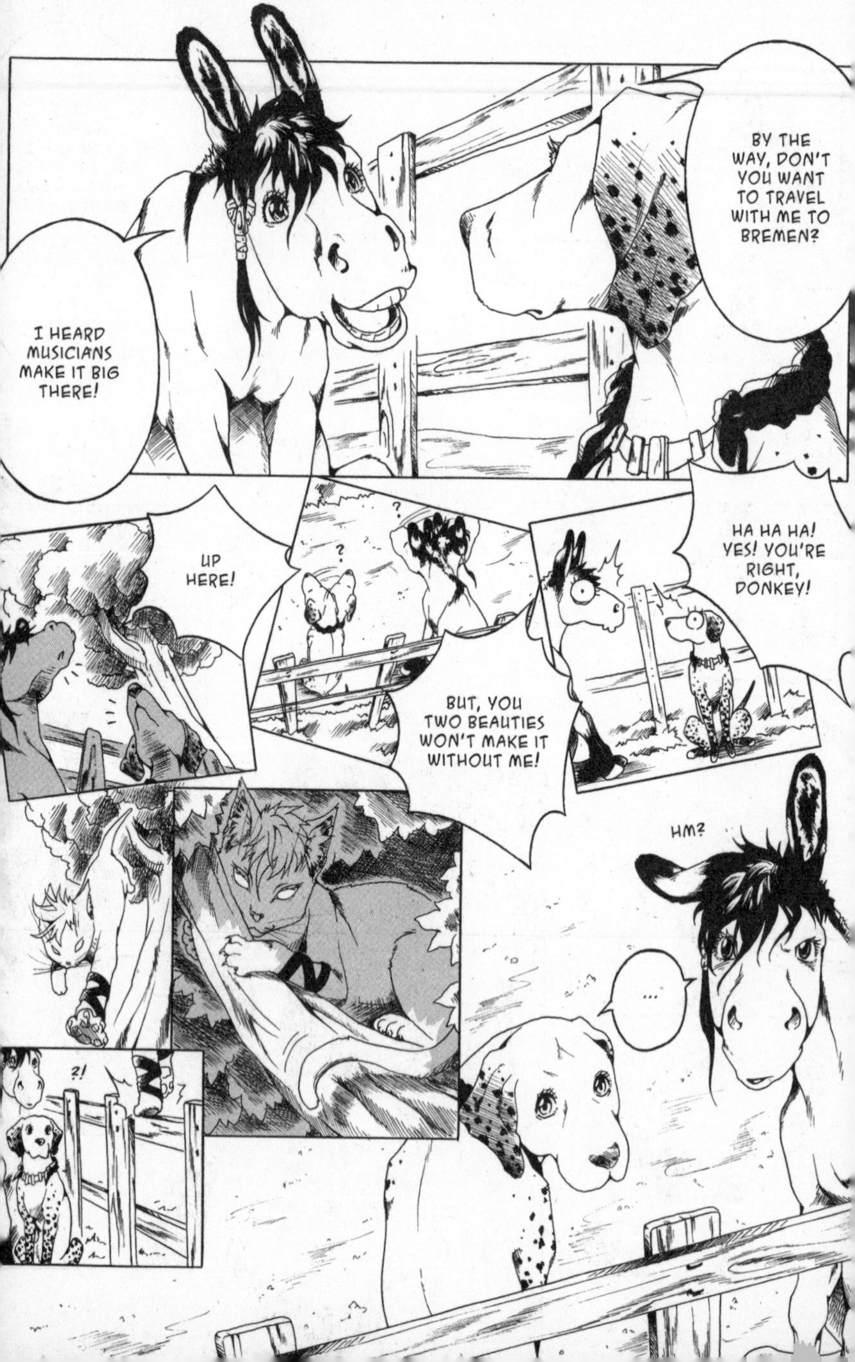
BY THE WAY, DON'T YOU WANT TO TRAVEL WITH ME TO BREMEN?
I HEARD MUSICIANS MAKE IT BIG THERE!
HA HA HA! YES! YOU'RE RIGHT, DONKEY!
BUT, YOU TWO BEAUTIES WON'T MAKE IT WITHOUT ME!
?
?
UP HERE!
HM?
...
?!

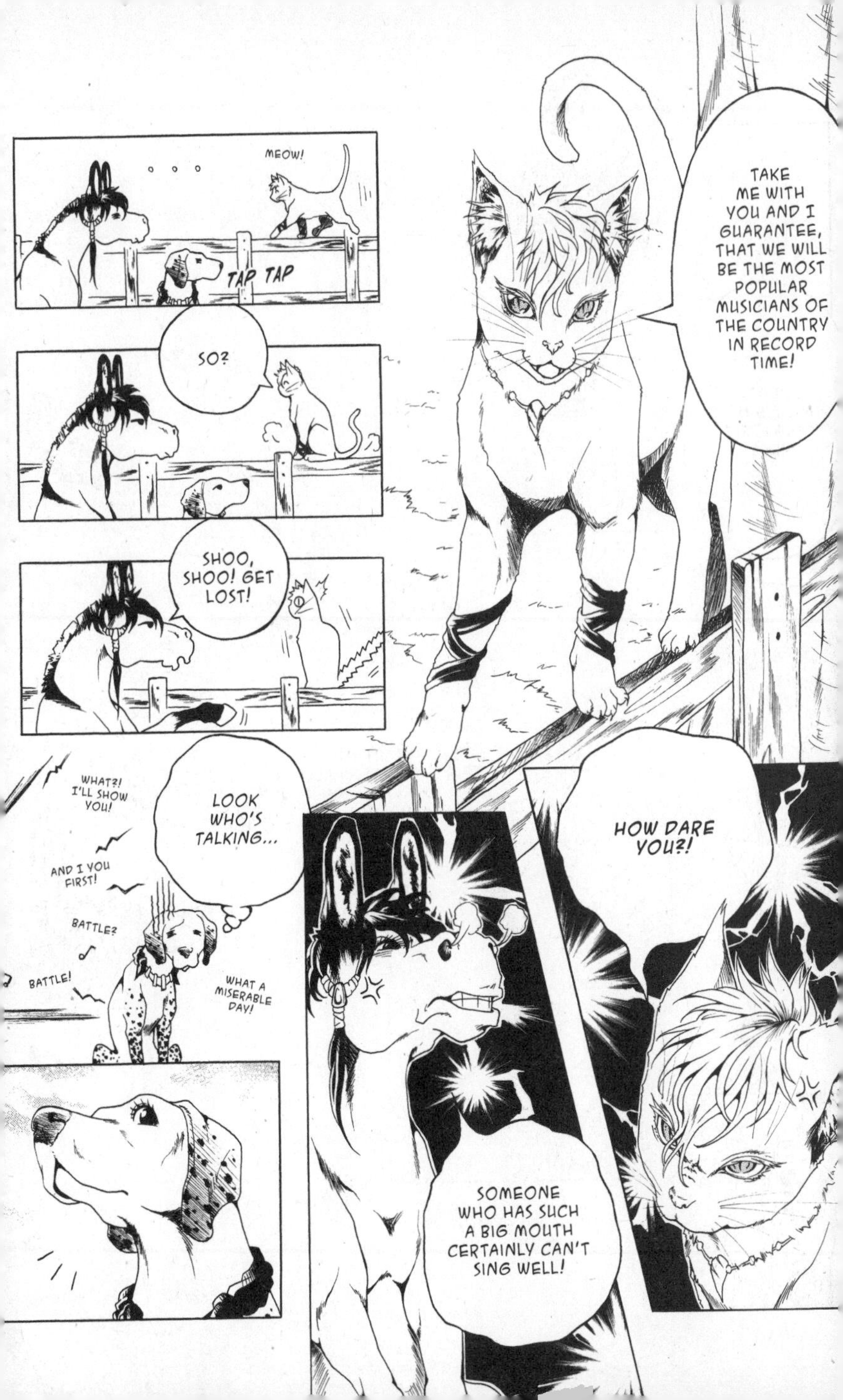
TAKE ME WITH YOU AND I GUARANTEE, THAT WE WILL BE THE MOST POPULAR MUSICIANS OF THE COUNTRY IN RECORD TIME!
MEOW!
TAP TAP
SO?
SHOO, SHOO! GET LOST!
HOW DARE YOU?!
SOMEONE WHO HAS SUCH A BIG MOUTH CERTAINLY CAN'T SING WELL!
LOOK WHO'S TALKING...
WHAT?! I'LL SHOW YOU!
AND I YOU FIRST!
BATTLE?
BATTLE!
WHAT A MISERABLE DAY!

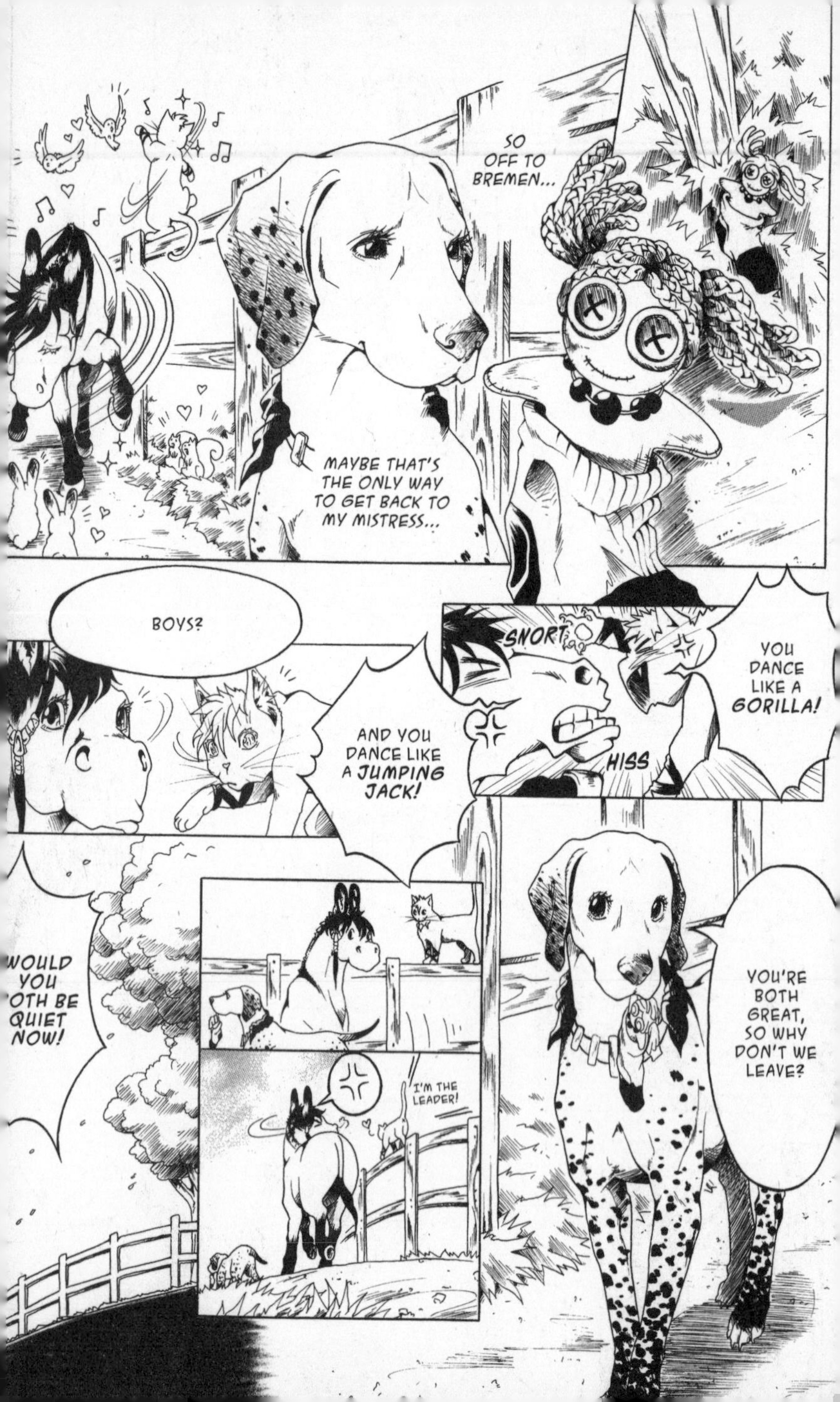
SO OFF TO BREMEN...
MAYBE THAT'S THE ONLY WAY TO GET BACK TO MY MISTRESS...
SNORT
HISS
YOU DANCE LIKE A GORILLA!
BOYS?
AND YOU DANCE LIKE A JUMPING JACK!
YOU'RE BOTH GREAT, SO WHY DON'T WE LEAVE?
I'M THE LEADER!
WOULD YOU OTH BE QUIET NOW!

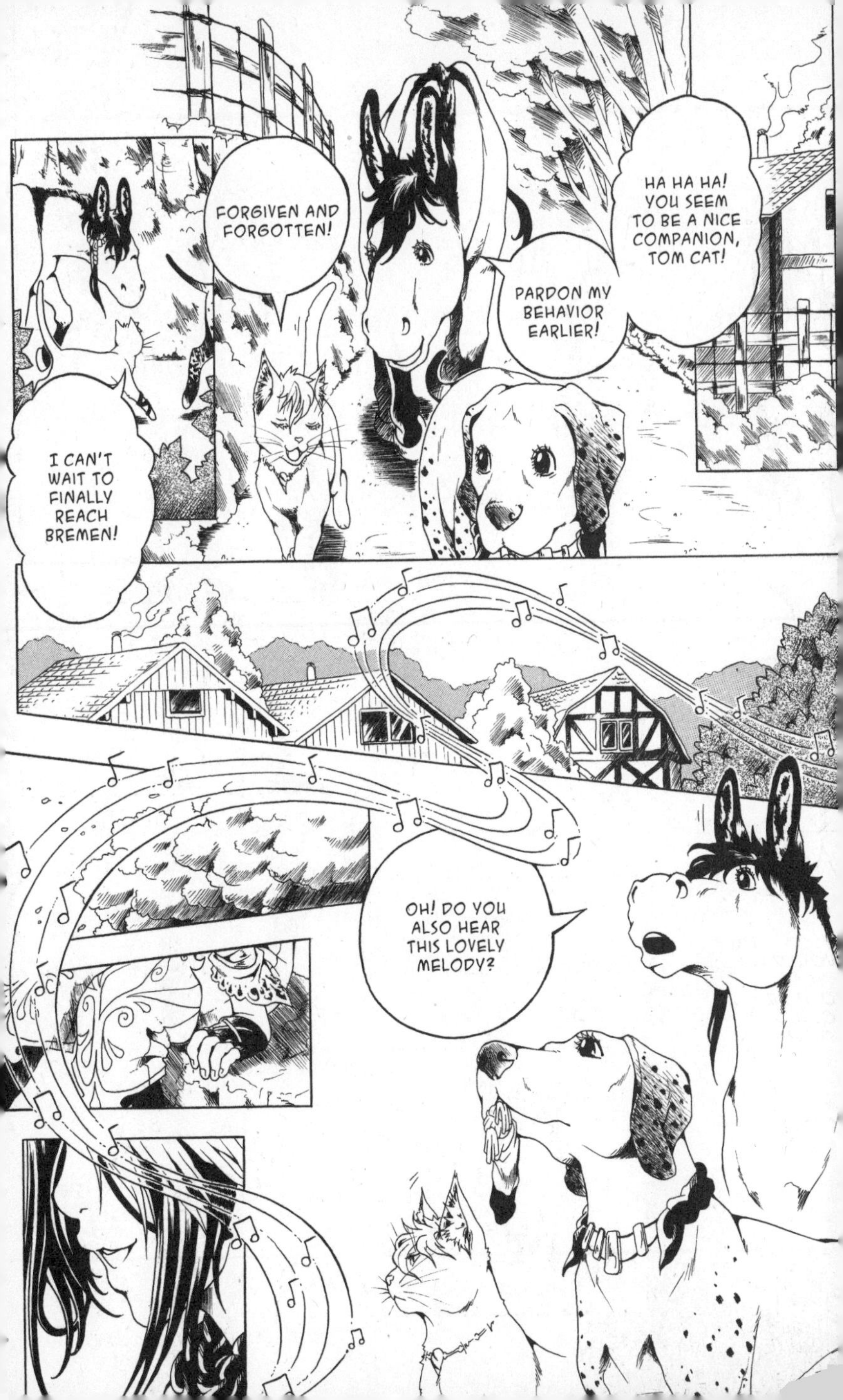
HA HA HA! YOU SEEM TO BE A NICE COMPANION, TOM CAT!
PARDON MY BEHAVIOR EARLIER!
FORGIVEN AND FORGOTTEN!
I CAN'T WAIT TO FINALLY REACH BREMEN!
OH! DO YOU ALSO HEAR THIS LOVELY MELODY?

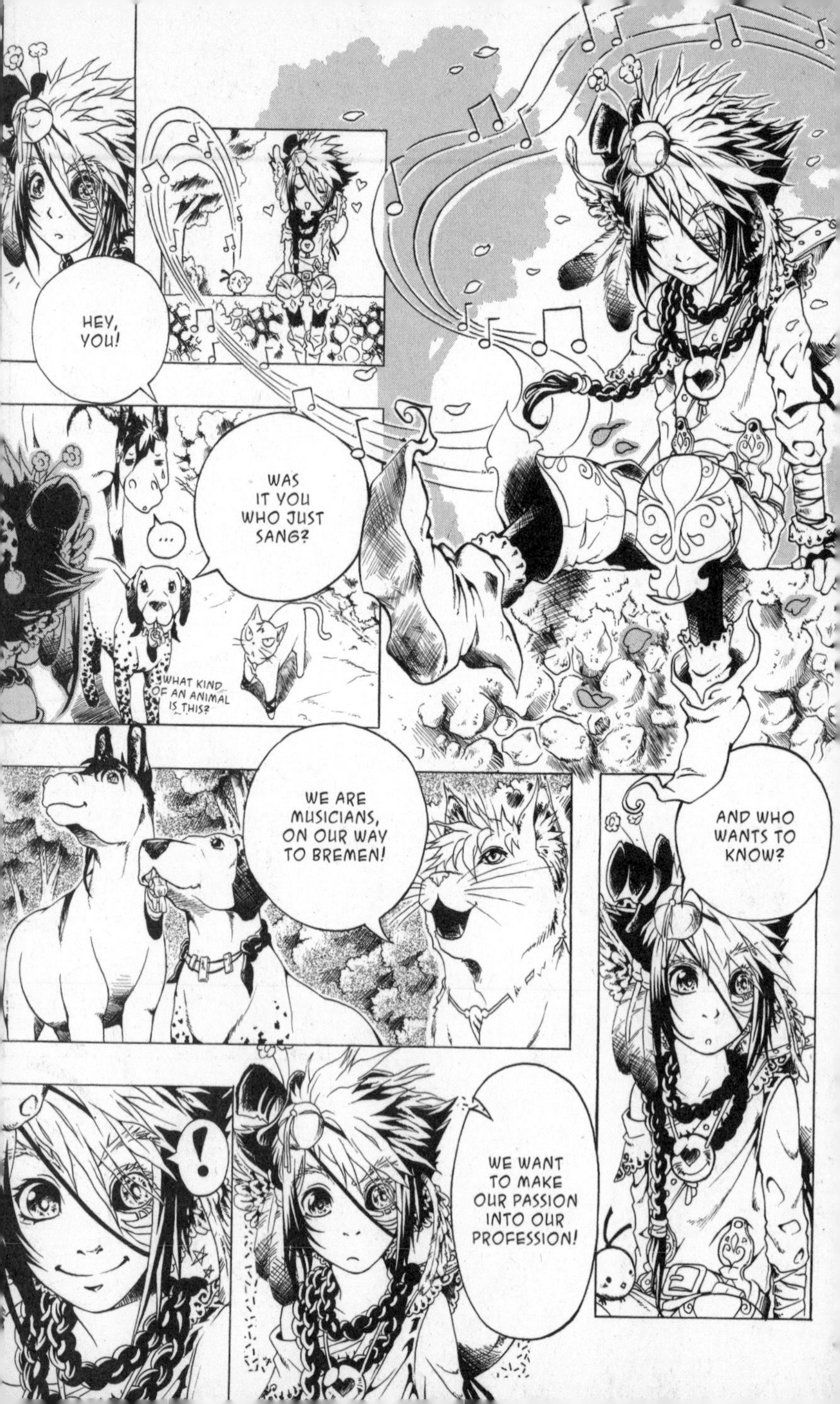
HEY, YOU!
WAS IT YOU WHO JUST SANG?
...
WHAT KIND OF AN ANIMAL IS THIS?
AND WHO WANTS TO KNOW?
WE ARE MUSICIANS, ON OUR WAY TO BREMEN!
!
WE WANT TO MAKE OUR PASSION INTO OUR PROFESSION!

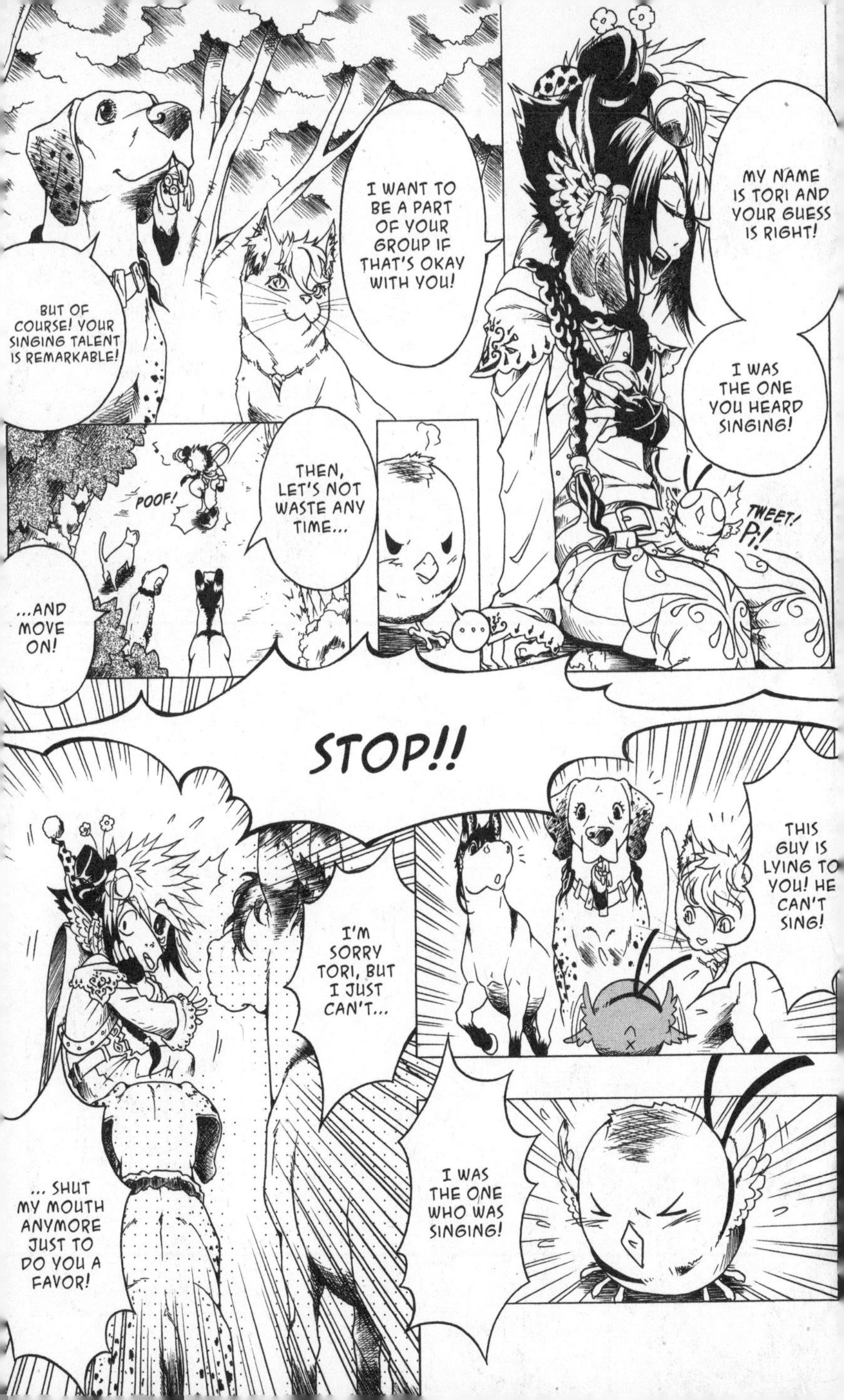
MY NAME IS TORI AND YOUR GUESS IS RIGHT!
I WAS THE ONE YOU HEARD SINGING!
TWEET! Pi!
I WANT TO BE A PART OF YOUR GROUP IF THAT'S OKAY WITH YOU!
BUT OF COURSE! YOUR SINGING TALENT IS REMARKABLE!
...
THEN, LET'S NOT WASTE ANY TIME...
POOF!
...AND MOVE ON!
STOP!!
THIS GUY IS LYING TO YOU! HE CAN'T SING!
I'M SORRY TORI, BUT I JUST CAN'T...
... SHUT MY MOUTH ANYMORE JUST TO DO YOU A FAVOR!
I WAS THE ONE WHO WAS SINGING!

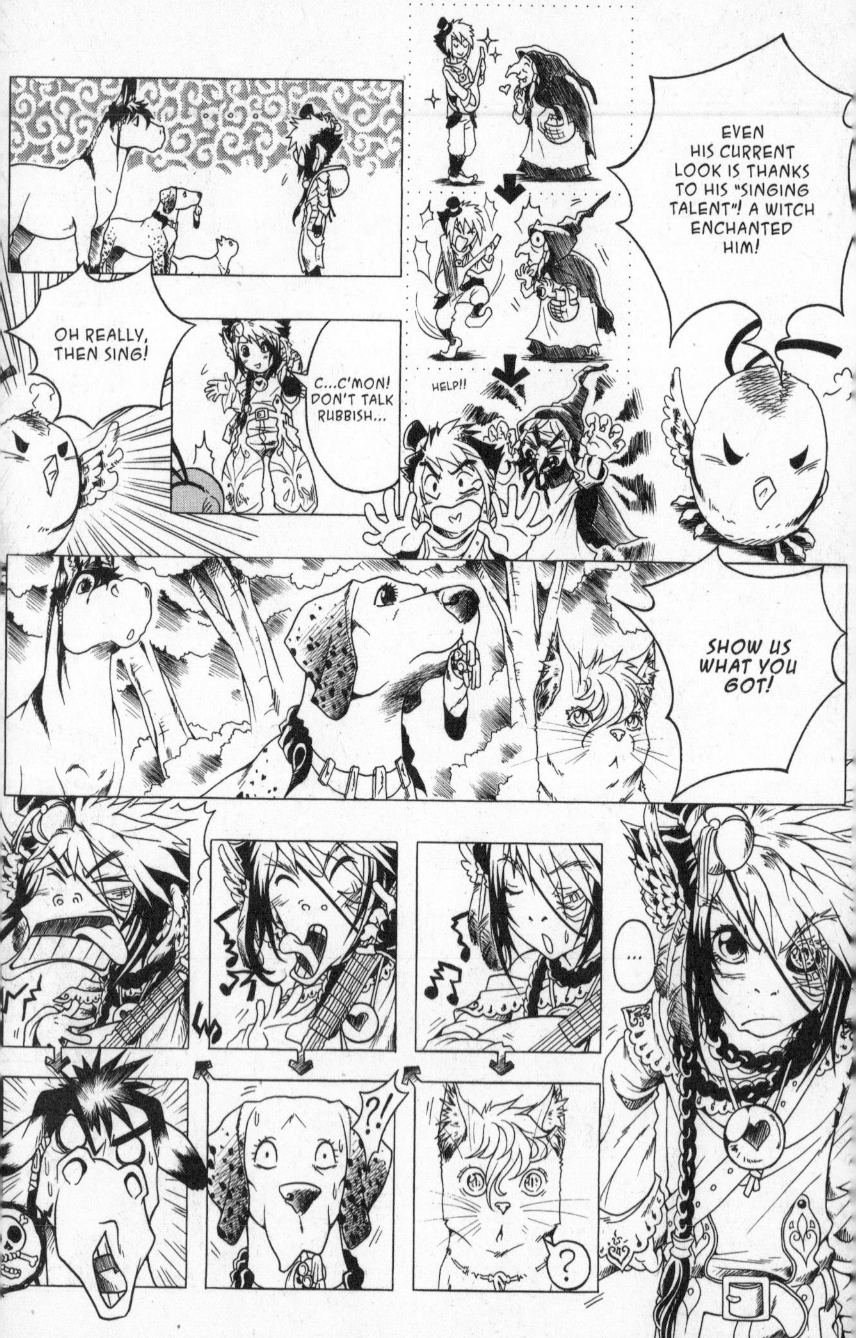
EVEN HIS CURRENT LOOK IS THANKS TO HIS "SINGING TALENT"! A WITCH ENCHANTED HIM!
HELP!!
C...C'MON! DON'T TALK RUBBISH...
OH REALLY, THEN SING!
SHOW US WHAT YOU GOT!
...
?!
?

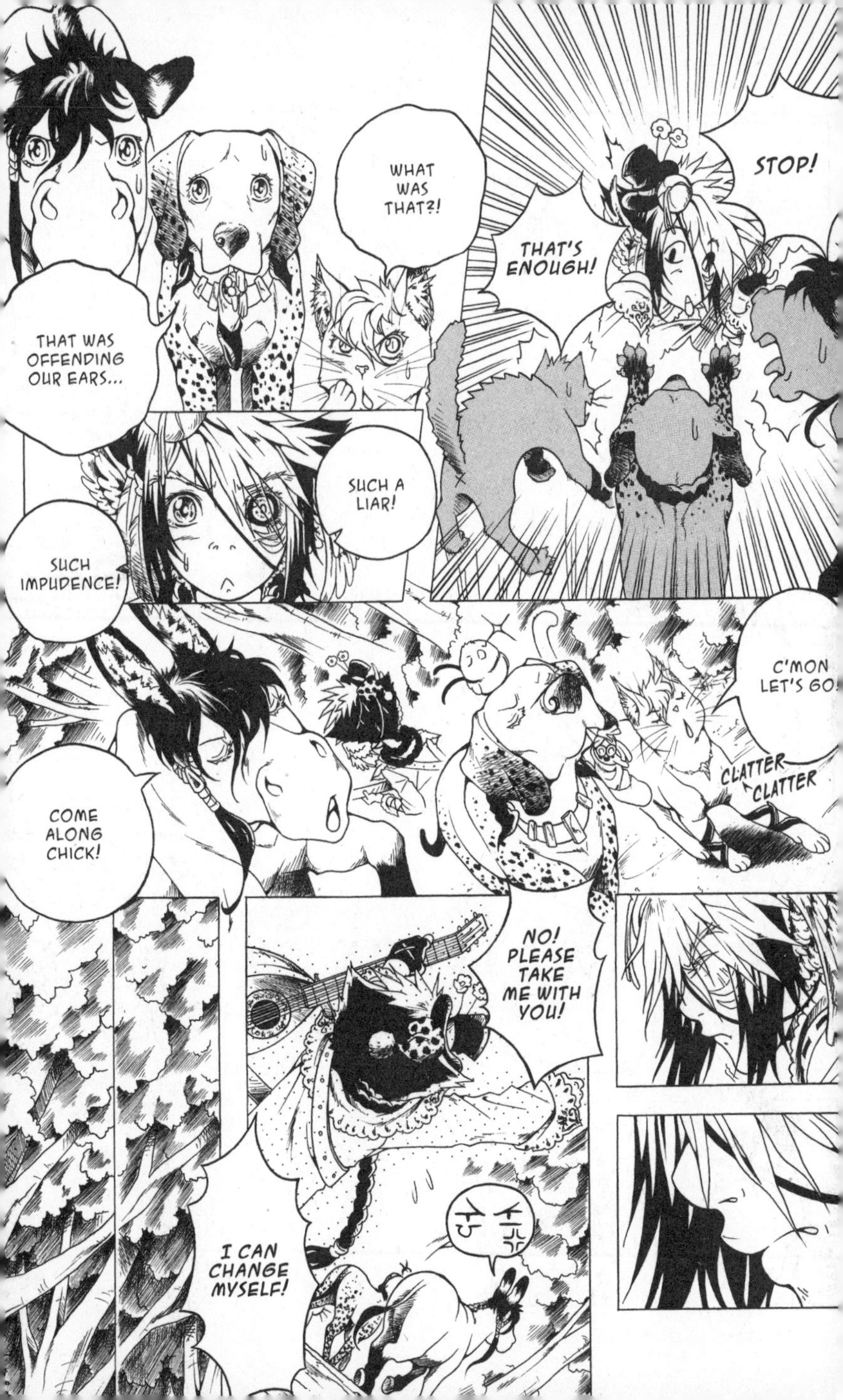
STOP!
THAT'S ENOUGH!
WHAT WAS THAT?!
THAT WAS OFFENDING OUR EARS...
SUCH A LIAR!
SUCH IMPUDENCE!
C'MON LET'S GO!
CLATTER CLATTER
COME ALONG CHICK!
NO! PLEASE TAKE ME WITH YOU!
I CAN CHANGE MYSELF!

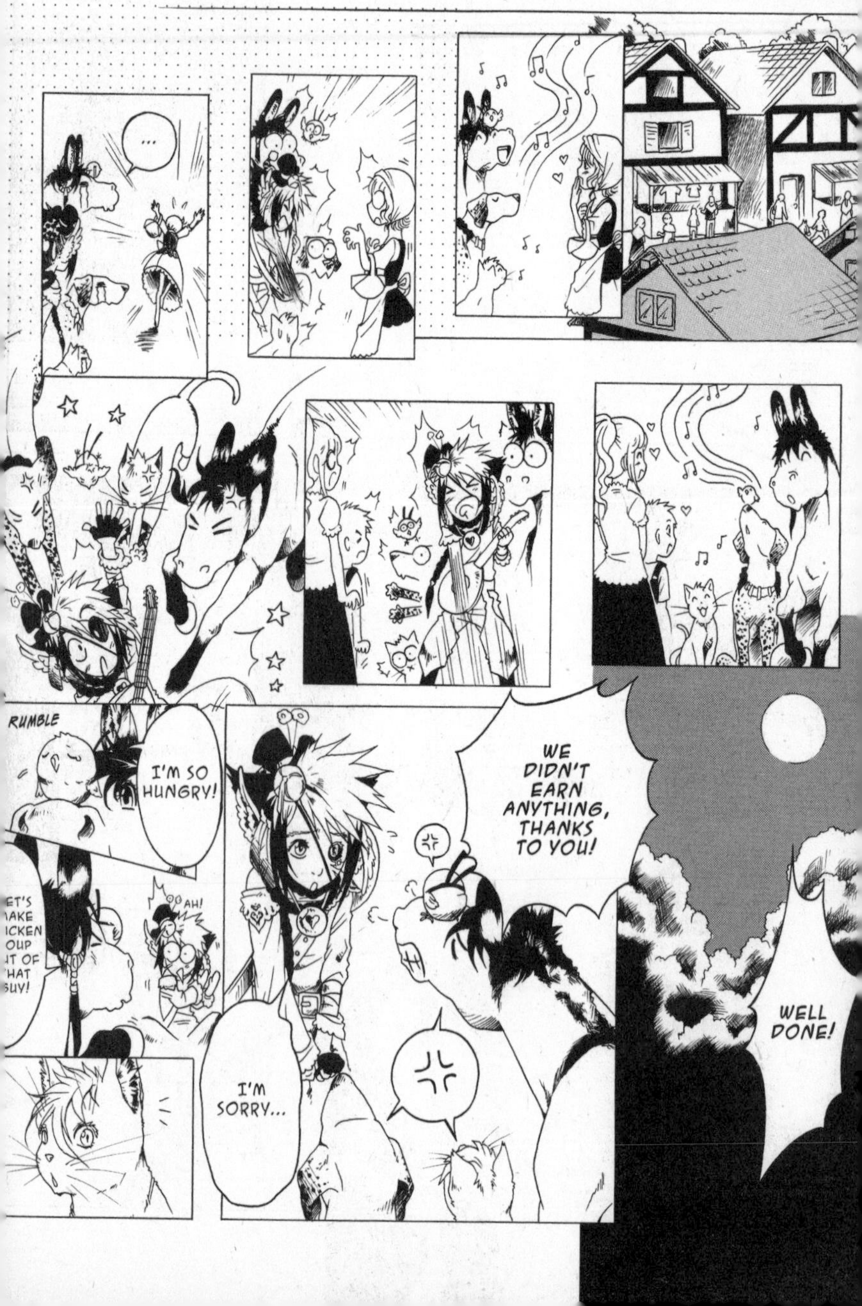
...
WE DIDN'T EARN ANYTHING, THANKS TO YOU!
WELL DONE!
I'M SORRY...
RUMBLE
I'M SO HUNGRY!
AH!
ET'S MAKE ICKEN OUP UT OF HAT UY!

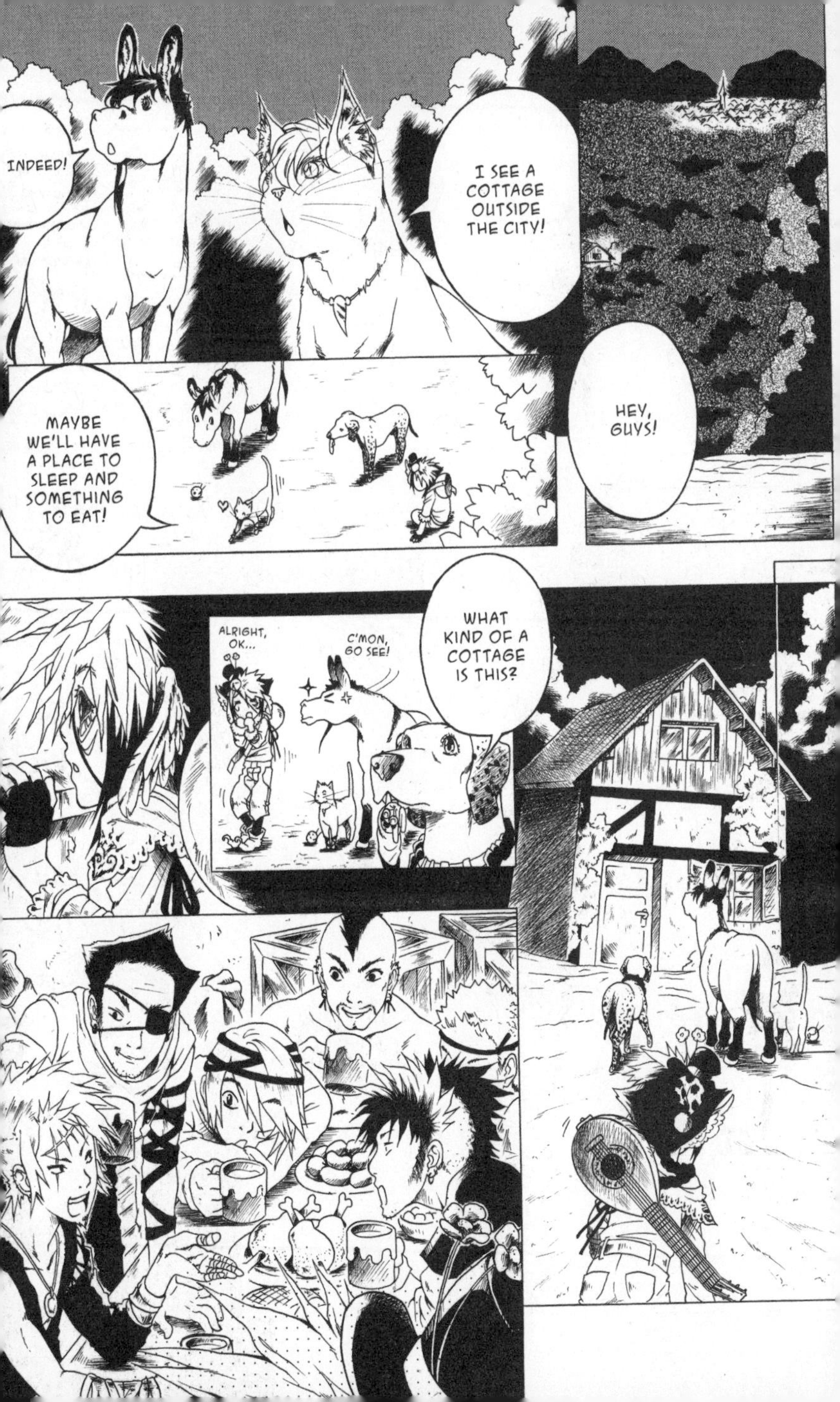
HEY, GUYS!
I SEE A COTTAGE OUTSIDE THE CITY!
INDEED!
MAYBE WE'LL HAVE A PLACE TO SLEEP AND SOMETHING TO EAT!
WHAT KIND OF A COTTAGE IS THIS?
C'MON, GO SEE!
ALRIGHT, OK...

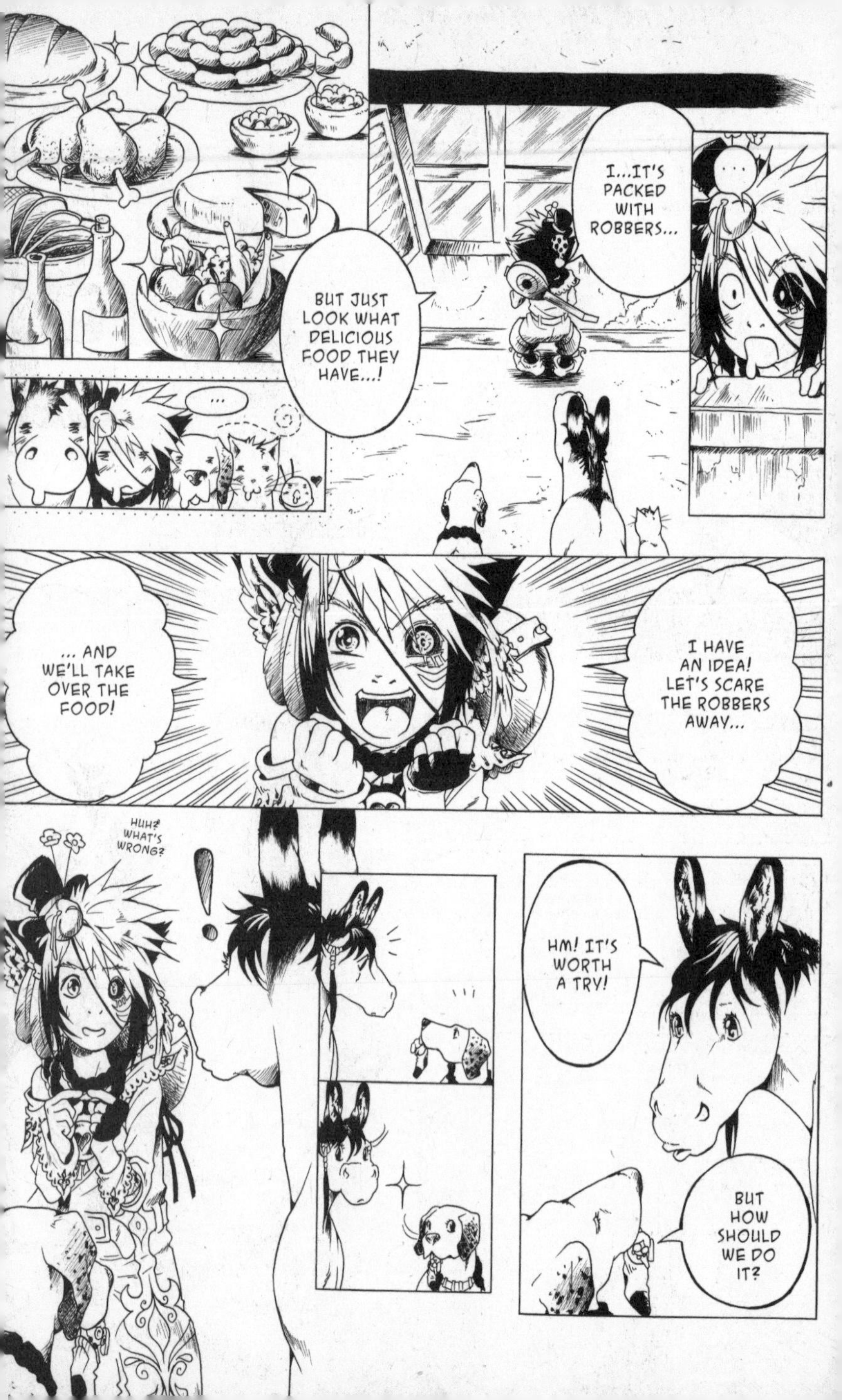
...
I...IT'S PACKED WITH ROBBERS...
BUT JUST LOOK WHAT DELICIOUS FOOD THEY HAVE...!
...
I HAVE AN IDEA! LET'S SCARE THE ROBBERS AWAY...
... AND WE'LL TAKE OVER THE FOOD!
HM! IT'S WORTH A TRY!
BUT HOW SHOULD WE DO IT?
!
HUH? WHAT'S WRONG?

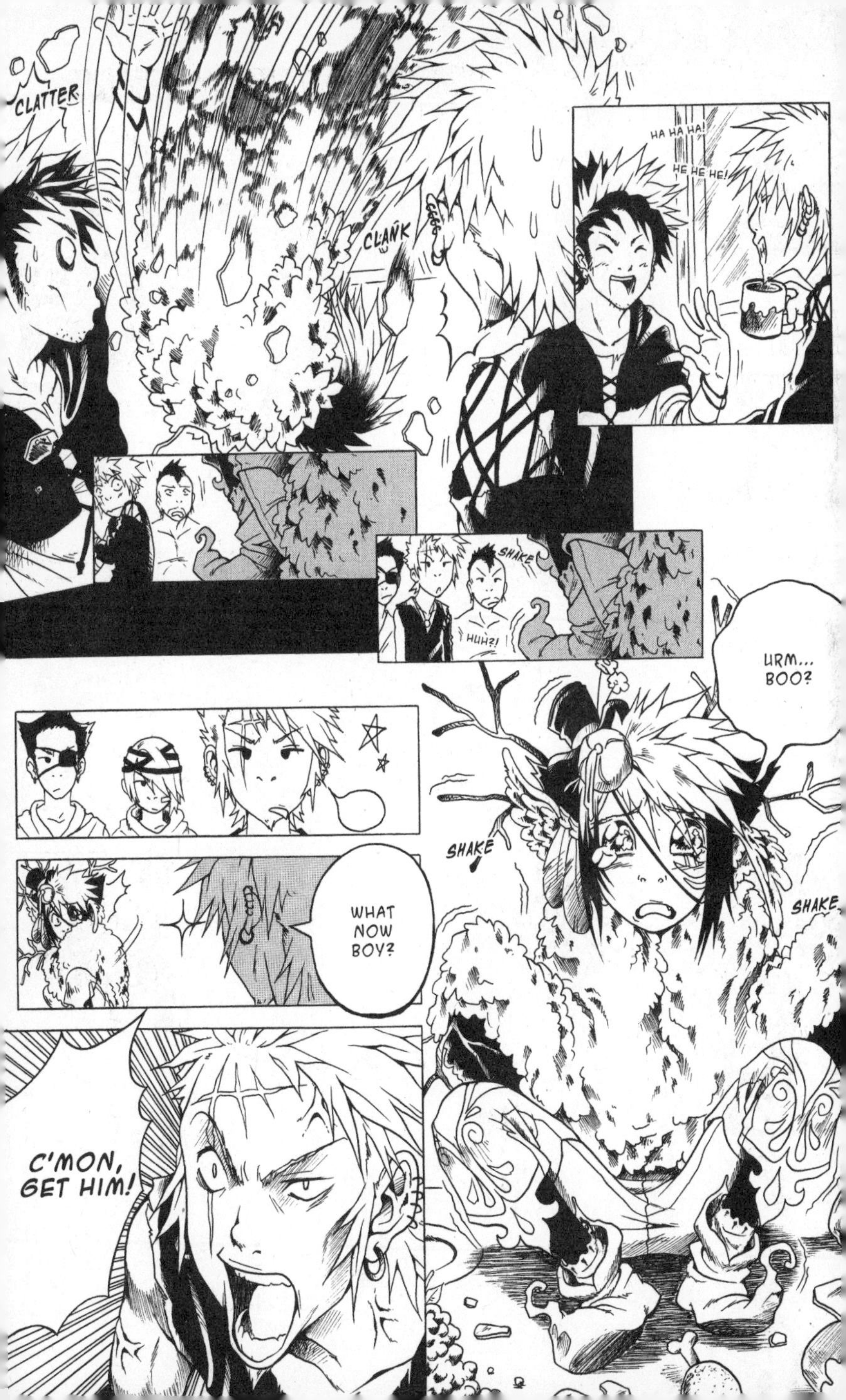
HA HA HA!
HE HE HE!
CLANK
CLATTER
SHAKE
HUH?!
URM... BOO?
SHAKE
SHAKE
WHAT NOW BOY?
C'MON, GET HIM!

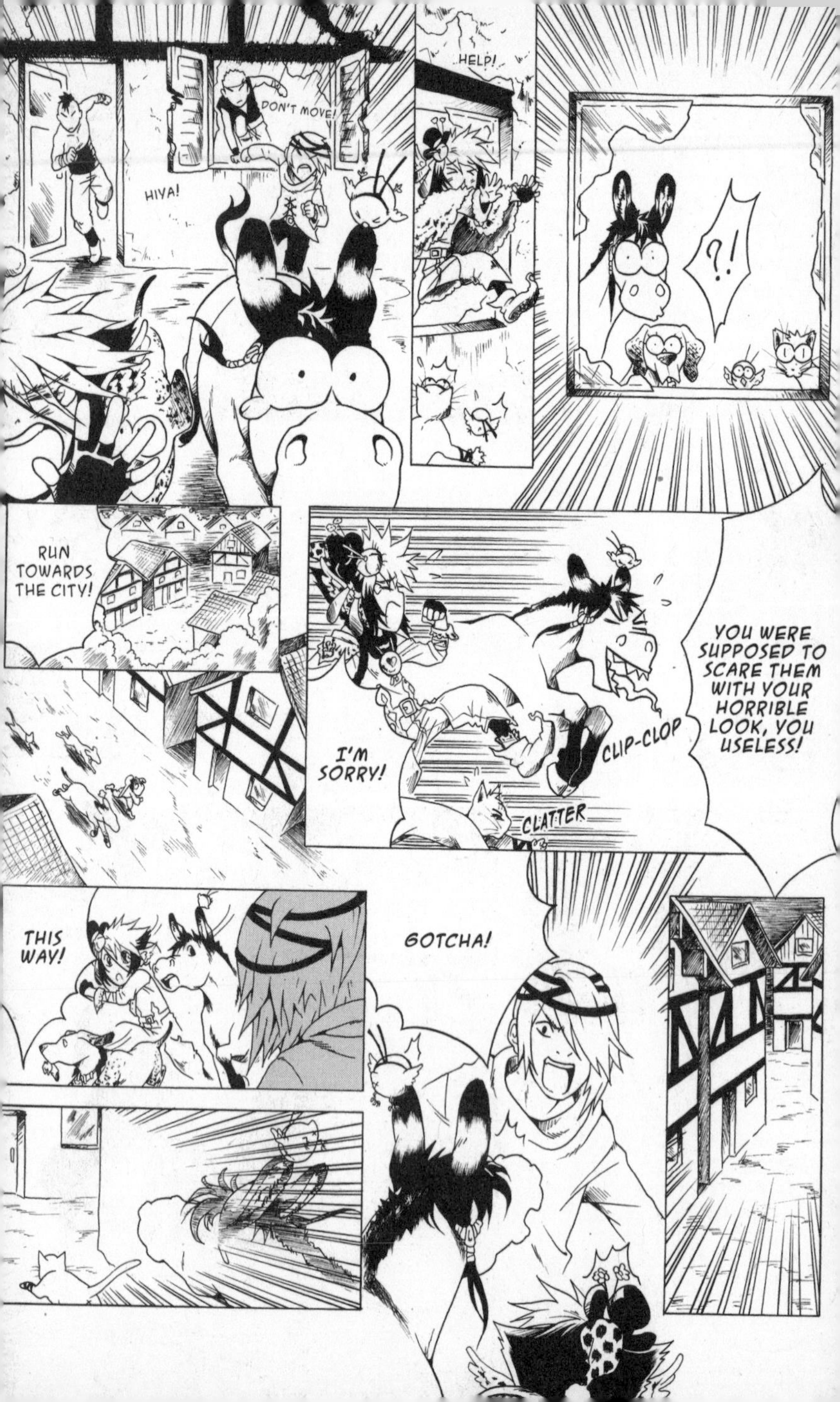
?!
...HELP!
DON'T MOVE!
HIYA!
YOU WERE SUPPOSED TO SCARE THEM WITH YOUR HORRIBLE LOOK, YOU USELESS!
CLIP-CLOP
I'M SORRY!
CLATTER
RUN TOWARDS THE CITY!
GOTCHA!
THIS WAY!

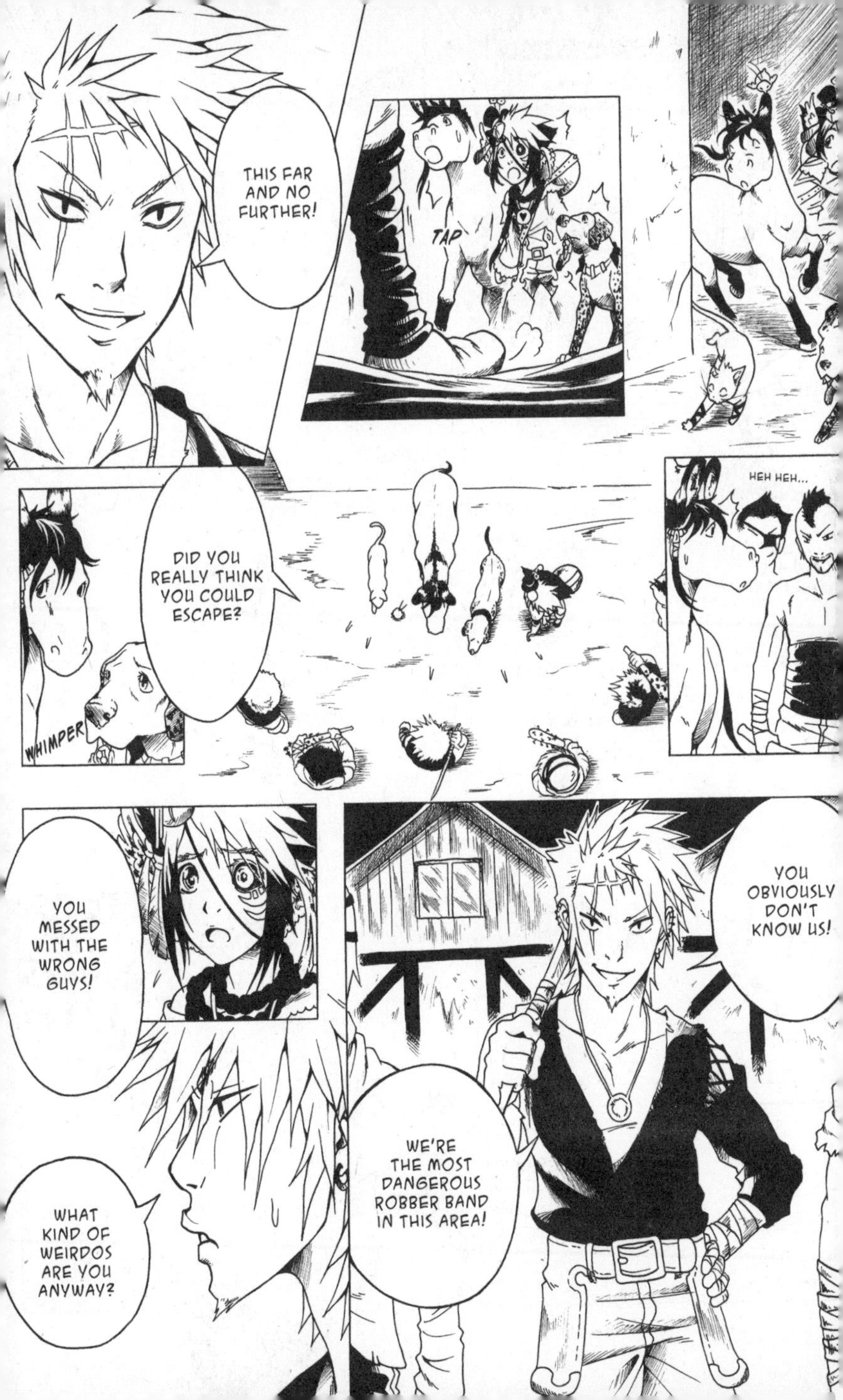
TAP
THIS FAR AND NO FURTHER!
HEH HEH...
DID YOU REALLY THINK YOU COULD ESCAPE?
WHIMPER
YOU OBVIOUSLY DON'T KNOW US!
WE'RE THE MOST DANGEROUS ROBBER BAND IN THIS AREA!
YOU MESSED WITH THE WRONG GUYS!
WHAT KIND OF WEIRDOS ARE YOU ANYWAY?

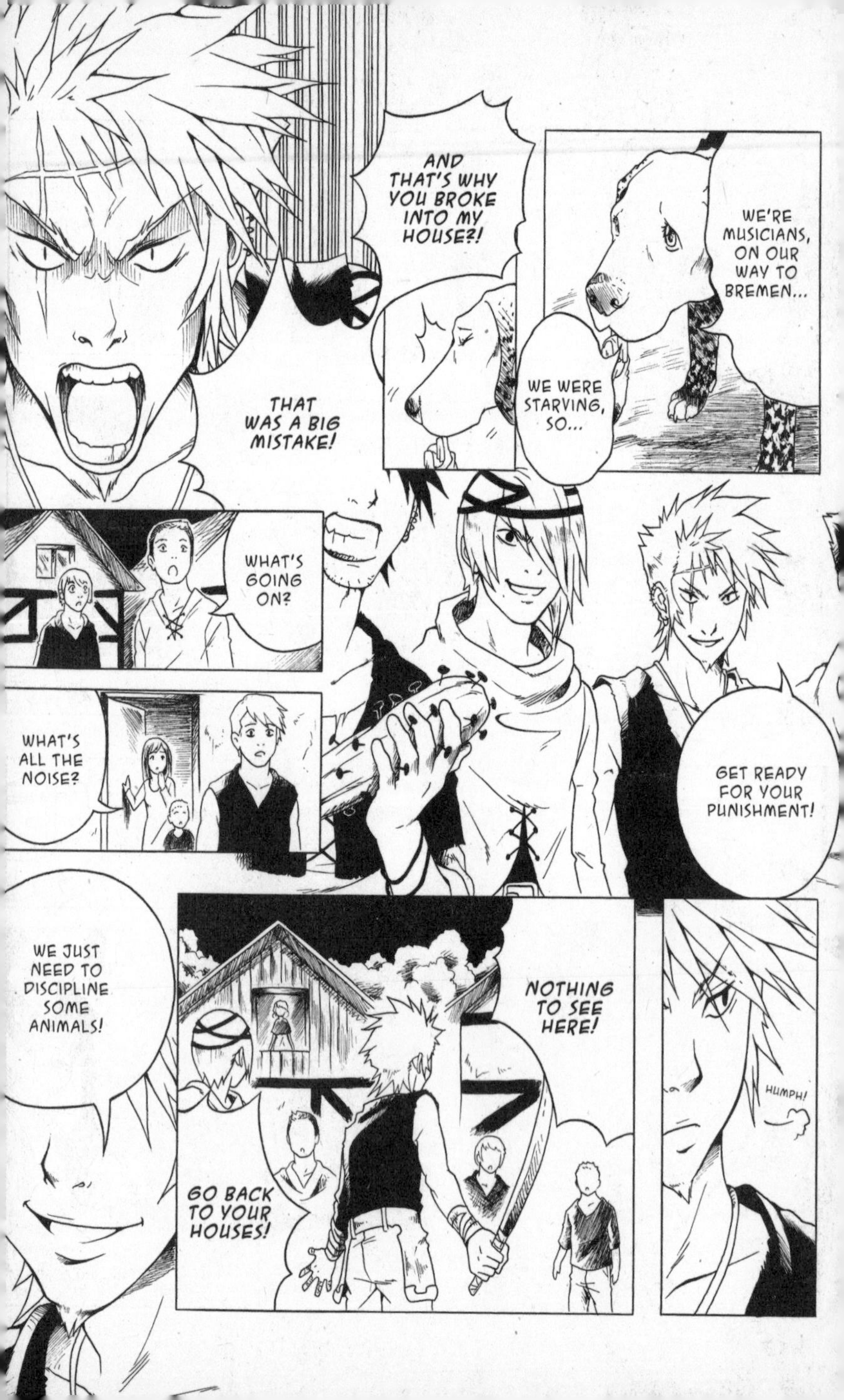
WE'RE MUSICIANS, ON OUR WAY TO BREMEN...
WE WERE STARVING, SO...
AND THAT'S WHY YOU BROKE INTO MY HOUSE?!
THAT WAS A BIG MISTAKE!
GET READY FOR YOUR PUNISHMENT!
WHAT'S GOING ON?
WHAT'S ALL THE NOISE?
HUMPH!
NOTHING TO SEE HERE!
GO BACK TO YOUR HOUSES!
WE JUST NEED TO DISCIPLINE SOME ANIMALS!

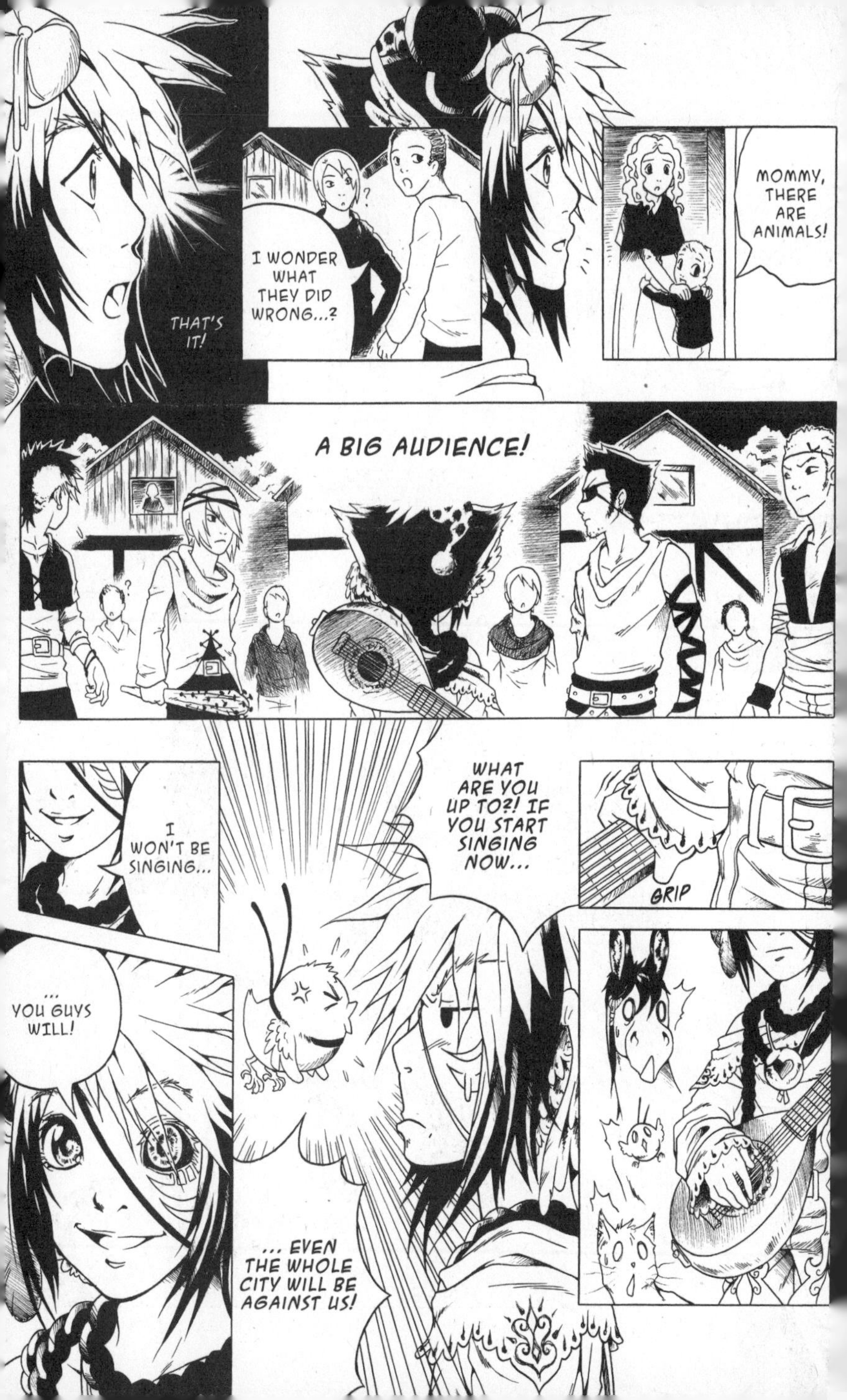
MOMMY, THERE ARE ANIMALS!
I WONDER WHAT THEY DID WRONG...?
THAT'S IT!
A BIG AUDIENCE!
GRIP
WHAT ARE YOU UP TO?! IF YOU START SINGING NOW...
... EVEN THE WHOLE CITY WILL BE AGAINST US!
I WON'T BE SINGING...
... YOU GUYS WILL!

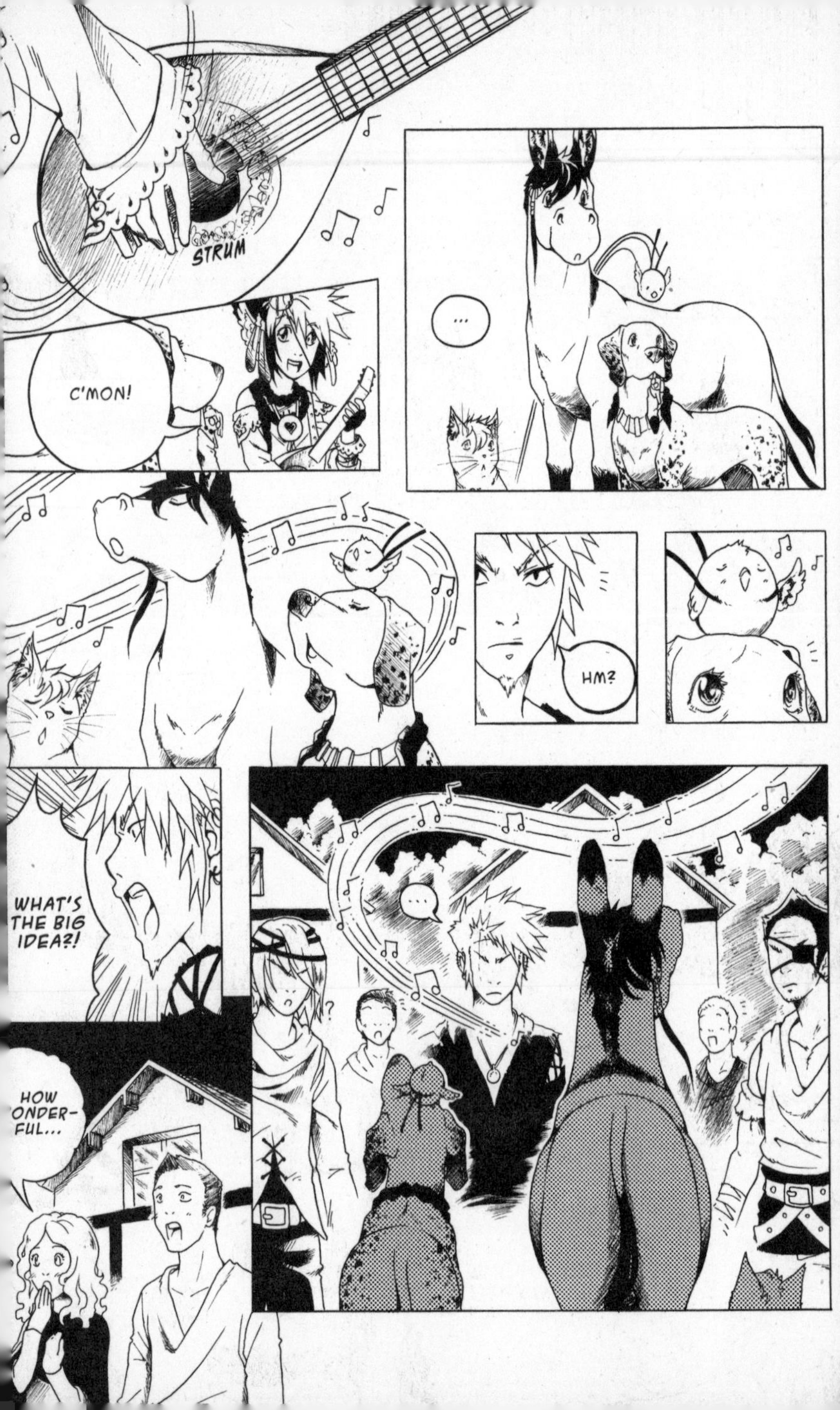
...
STRUM
C'MON!
HM?
...
WHAT'S THE BIG IDEA?!
HOW ONDER-FUL...

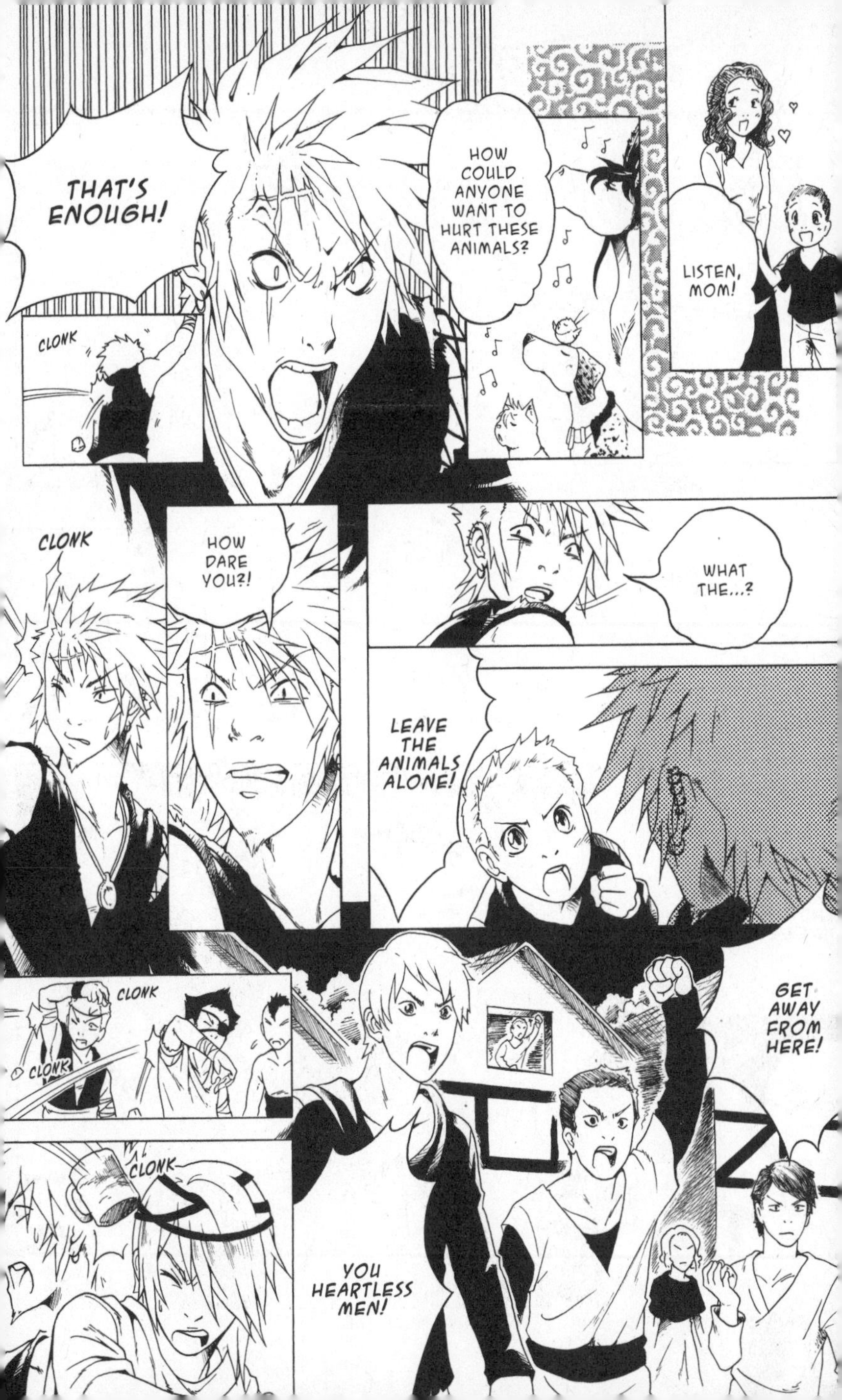
LISTEN, MOM!
HOW COULD ANYONE WANT TO HURT THESE ANIMALS?
THAT'S ENOUGH!
CLONK
WHAT THE...?
LEAVE THE ANIMALS ALONE!
HOW DARE YOU?!
CLONK
GET AWAY FROM HERE!
YOU HEARTLESS MEN!
CLONK
CLONK
CLONK

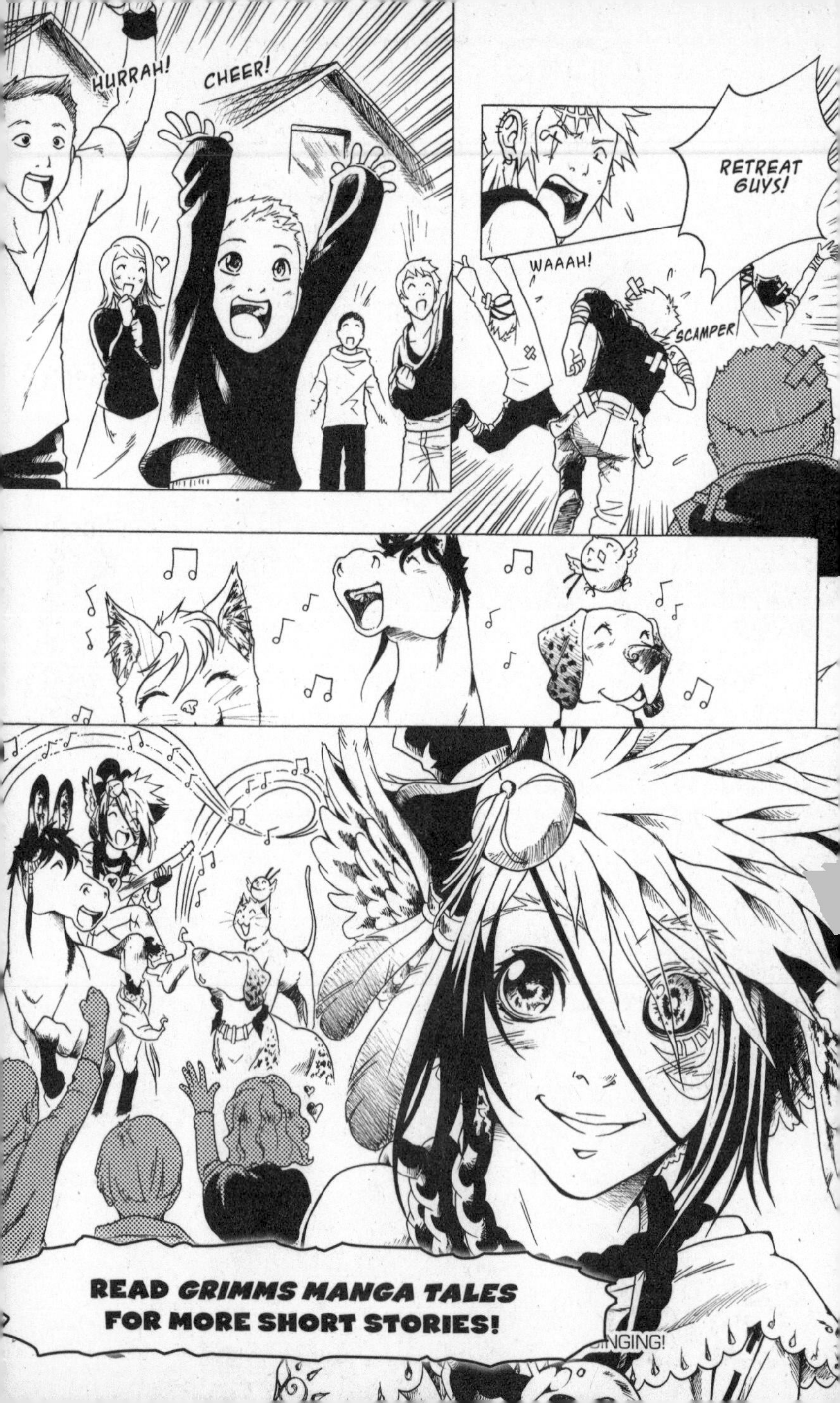
RETREAT GUYS!
WAAAH!
SCAMPER
HURRAH!
CHEER!
READ GRIMMS MANGA TALES FOR MORE SHORT STORIES!

GRIMMS manga Tales

The Grimm's Tales reimagined in manga!

Beautiful art by the talented Kei Ishiyama!

Stories from Little Red Riding Hood to Hansel and Gretel!

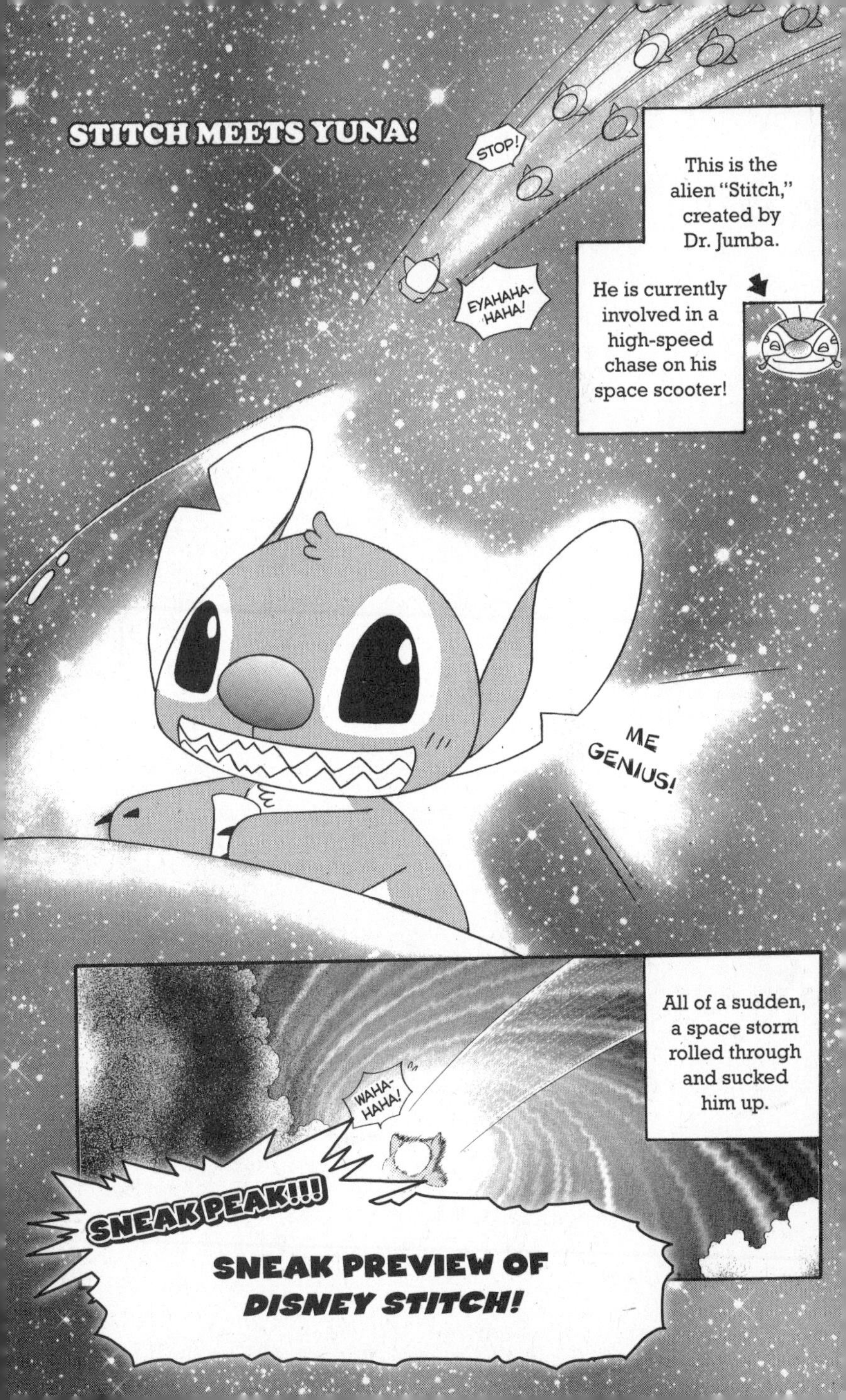
STITCH MEETS YUNA!
STOP!
This is the alien "Stitch," created by Dr. Jumba.
He is currently involved in a high-speed chase on his space scooter!
EYAHAHA-HAHA!
ME GENIUS!
All of a sudden, a space storm rolled through and sucked him up.
WAHA-HAHA!
SNEAK PEAK!!!
SNEAK PREVIEW OF DISNEY STITCH!

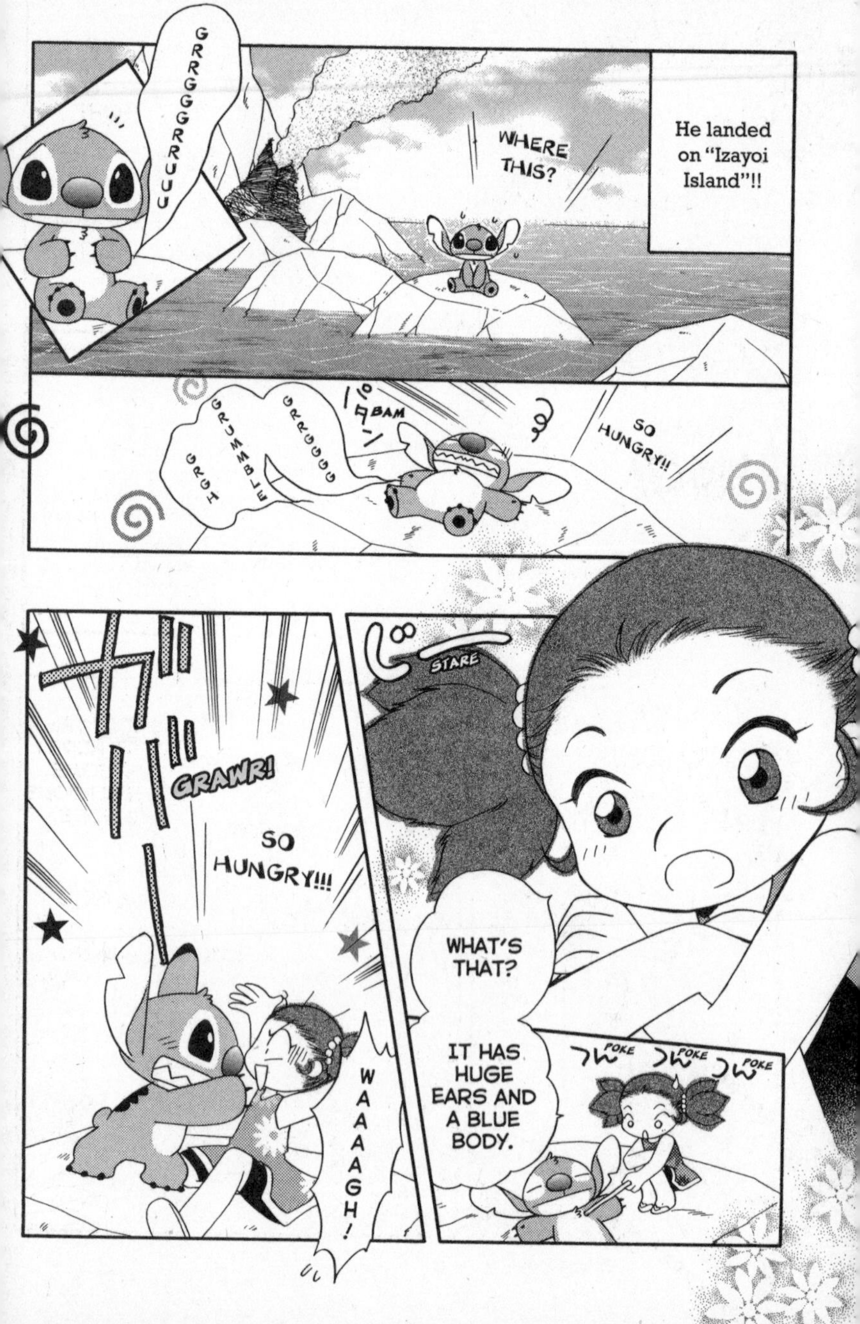
He landed on "Izayoi Island"!!
WHERE THIS?
GRRGGGRRUUU
SO HUNGRY!!
BAM
GRRGGGG
GRUMBLE
GRGH
STARE
WHAT'S THAT?
IT HAS HUGE EARS AND A BLUE BODY.
POKE POKE POKE
GRAWR!
SO HUNGRY!!!
WAAAAAGH!

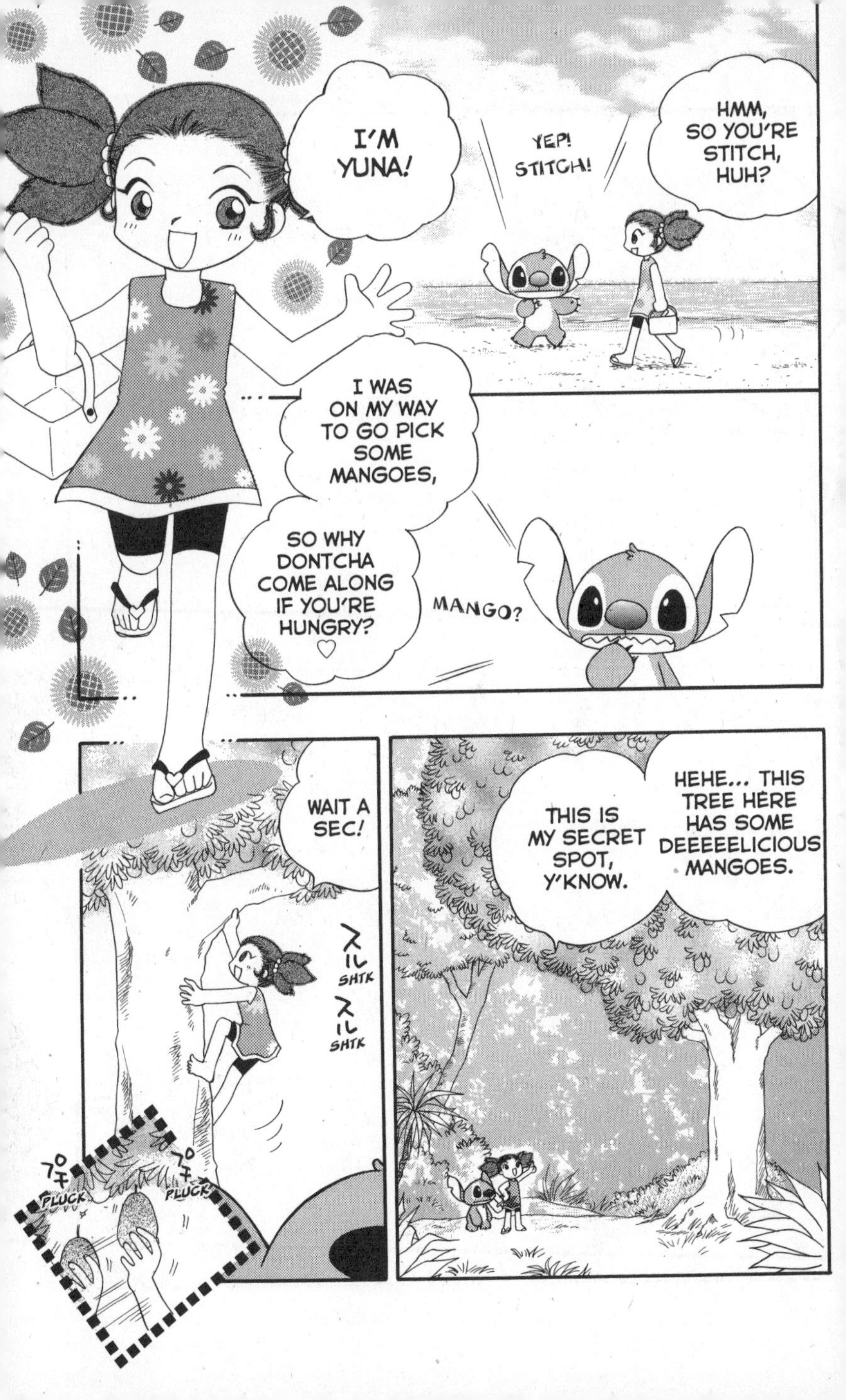
HMM, SO YOU'RE STITCH, HUH?
YEP! STITCH!
I'M YUNA!
I WAS ON MY WAY TO GO PICK SOME MANGOES,
SO WHY DONTCHA COME ALONG IF YOU'RE HUNGRY? ♡
MANGO?
HEHE... THIS TREE HERE HAS SOME DEEEEELICIOUS MANGOES.
THIS IS MY SECRET SPOT, Y'KNOW.
WAIT A SEC!
スル SHTK
スル SHTK
プチ PLUCK
プチ PLUCK

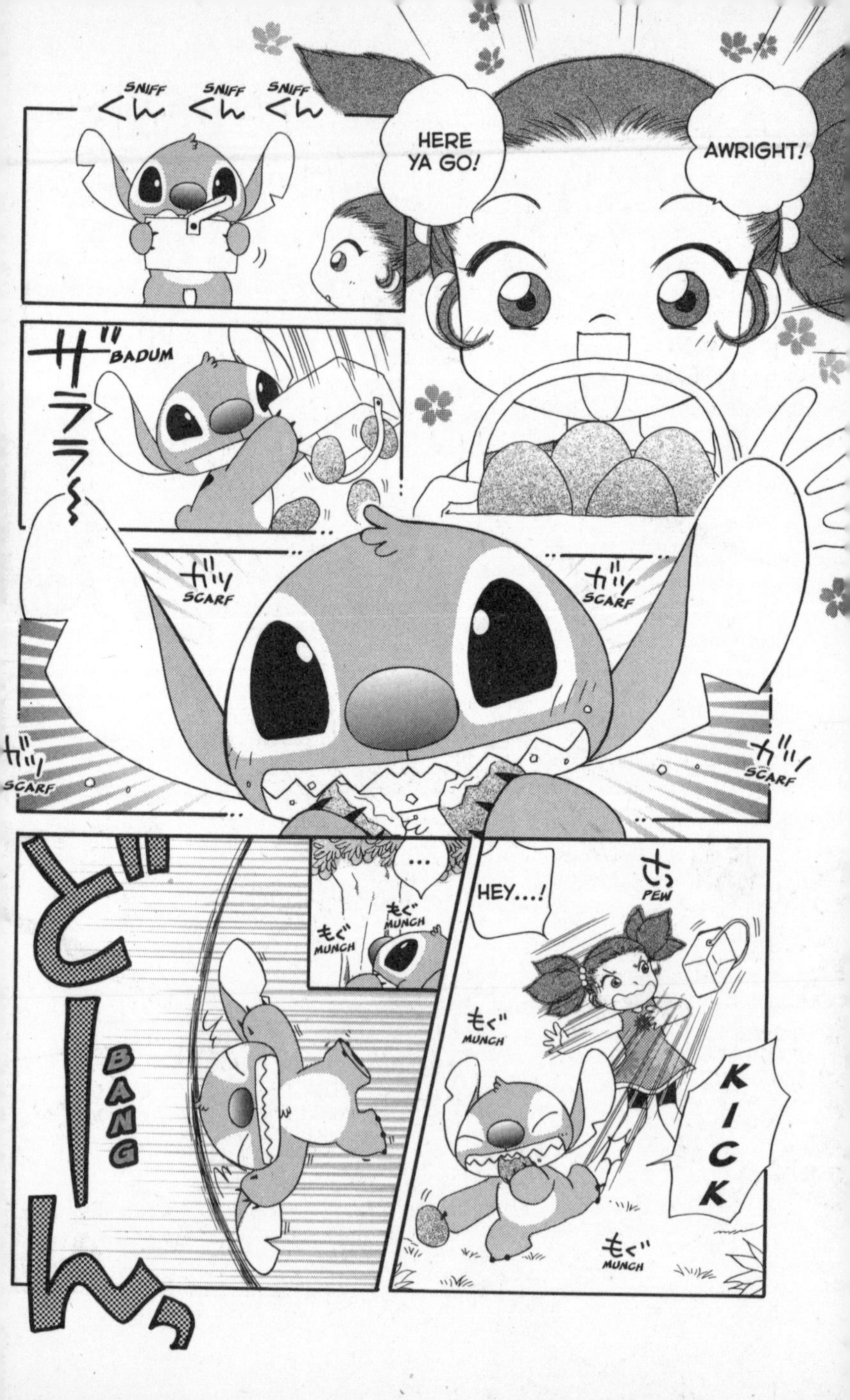
AWRIGHT!
HERE YA GO!
SNIFF SNIFF SNIFF
くん くん くん
ザ BADUM
ザラ～
ガツ SCARF
ガツ SCARF
ガツ SCARF
ガツ SCARF
さっ PEW
HEY...!
もぐ MUNCH
KICK
もぐ MUNCH
...
もぐ MUNCH
もぐ MUNCH
どーん BANG

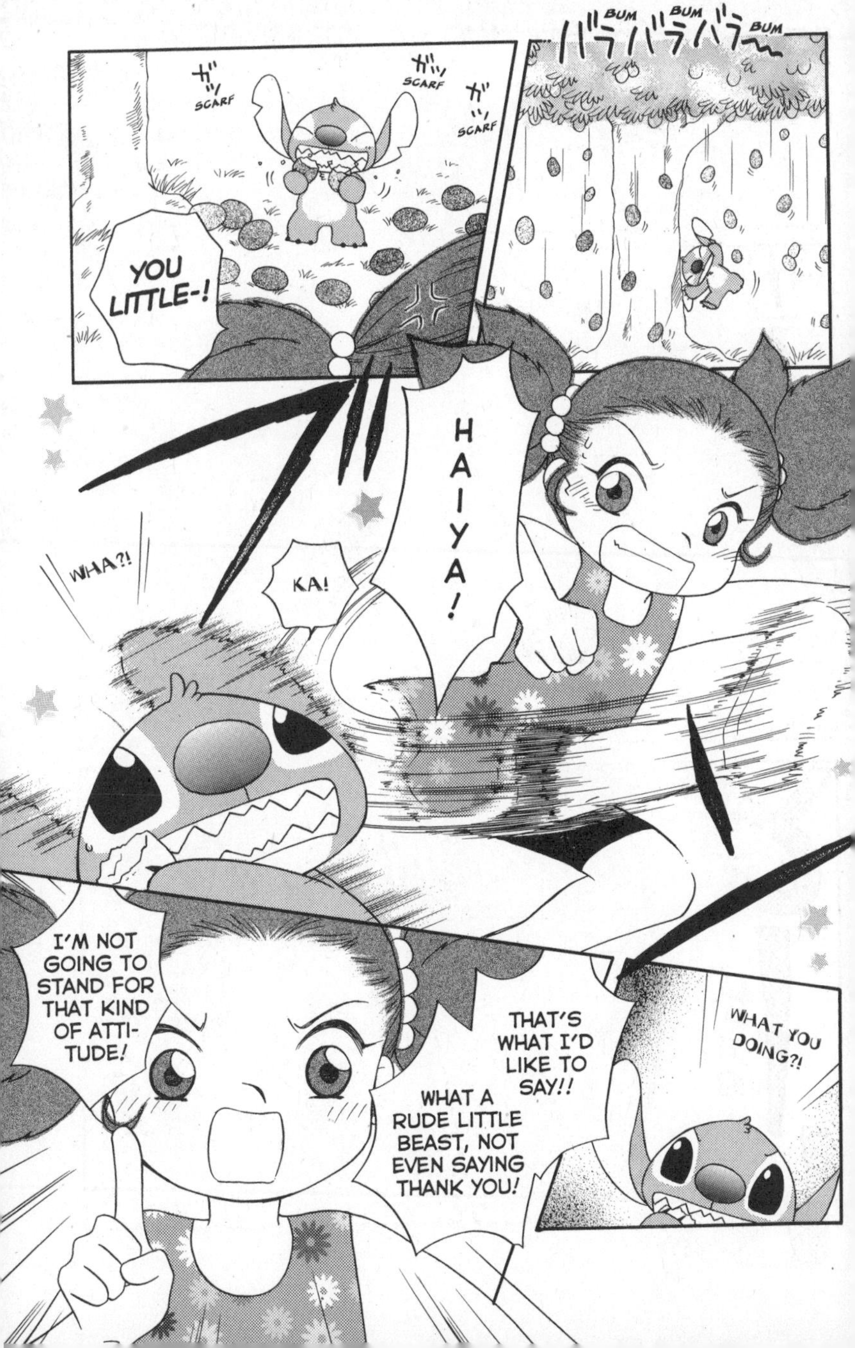

バラバラバラ〜
BUM BUM BUM
ガッ SCARF
ガッ SCARF
ガッ SCARF
YOU LITTLE-!
HAIYA!
KA!
WHA?!
WHAT YOU DOING?!
THAT'S WHAT I'D LIKE TO SAY!!
WHAT A RUDE LITTLE BEAST, NOT EVEN SAYING THANK YOU!
I'M NOT GOING TO STAND FOR THAT KIND OF ATTI-TUDE!

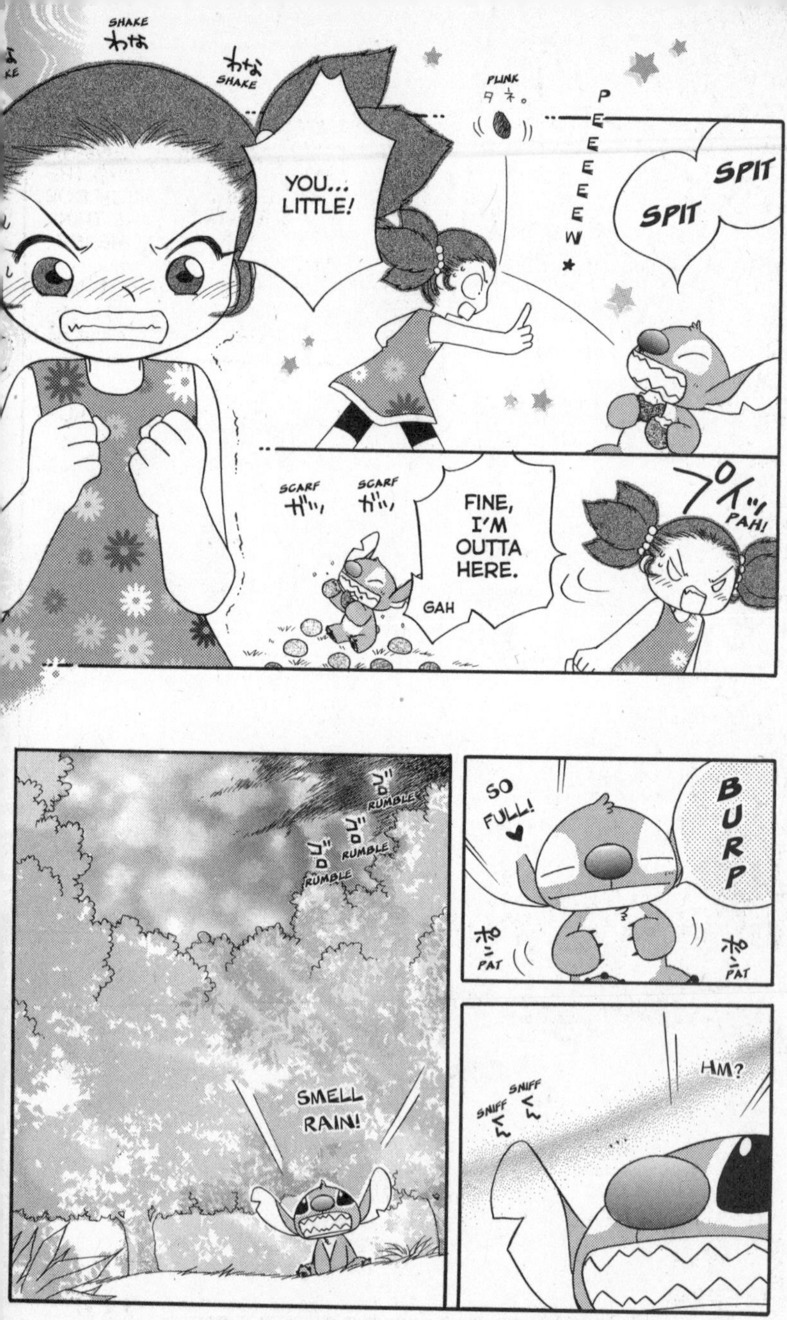
PLUNK
タネ。
PEEEEEEW★
SPIT
SPIT
プイッ
PAH!
FINE, I'M OUTTA HERE.
GAH
SCARF
ガッ
SCARF
ガッ
SHAKE
わな
SHAKE
わな
YOU... LITTLE!
BURP
SO FULL! ♥
ポン
PAT
ポン
PAT
HM?
SNIFF
くん
SNIFF
くん
ゴロ
RUMBLE
ゴロ
RUMBLE
ゴロ
RUMBLE
SMELL RAIN!

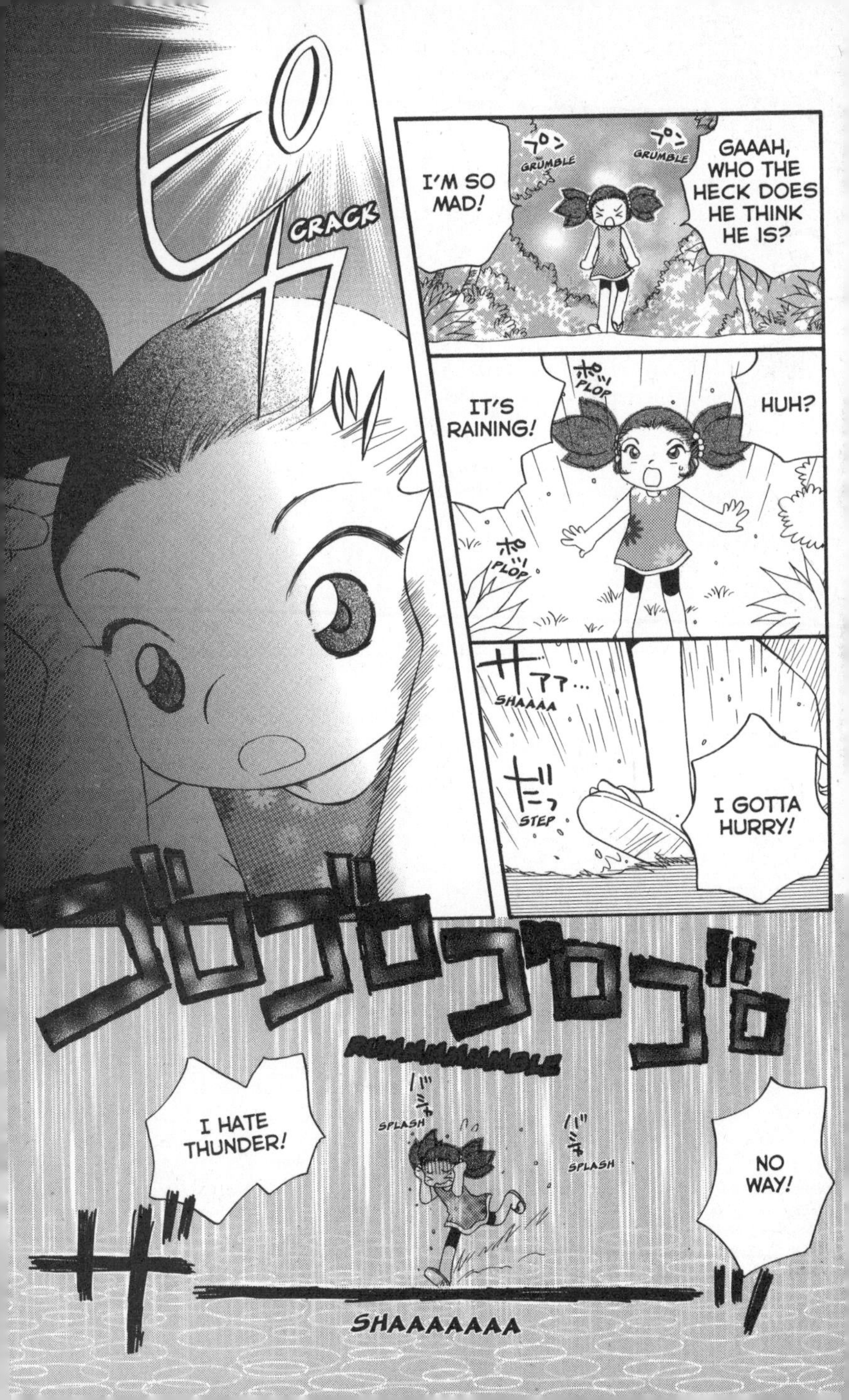
GAAAH, WHO THE HECK DOES HE THINK HE IS?
GRUMBLE
GRUMBLE
I'M SO MAD!
HUH?
PLOP
IT'S RAINING!
PLOP
I GOTTA HURRY!
SHAAAA
STEP
CRACK
NO WAY!
SPLASH
SPLASH
I HATE THUNDER!
SHAAAAAAA

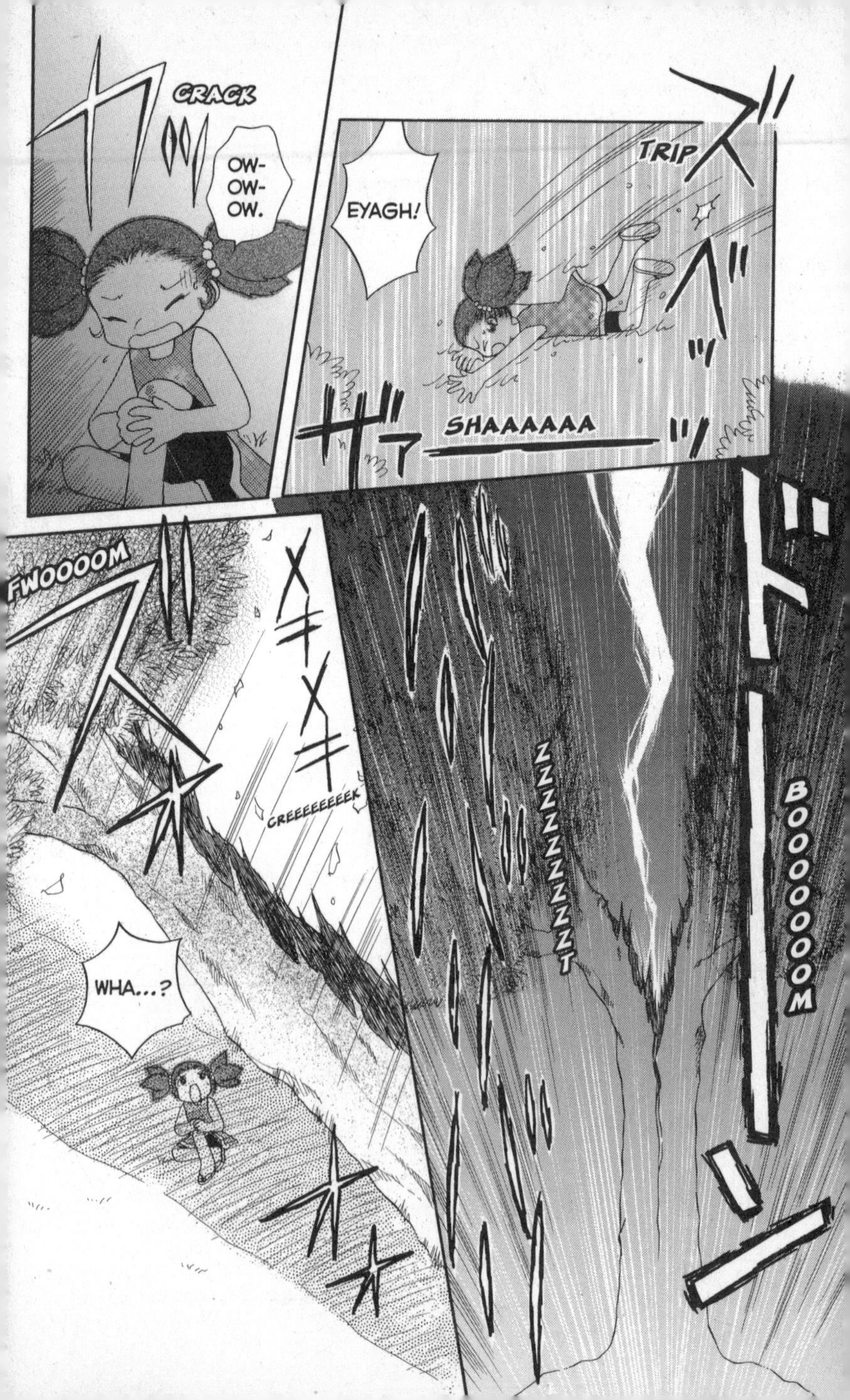
EYAGH!
TRIP
SHAAAAAA
CRACK
OW-OW-OW.
BOOOOOOOOM
ZZZZZZZZZT
FWOOOOM
CREEEEEEEEK
WHA...?

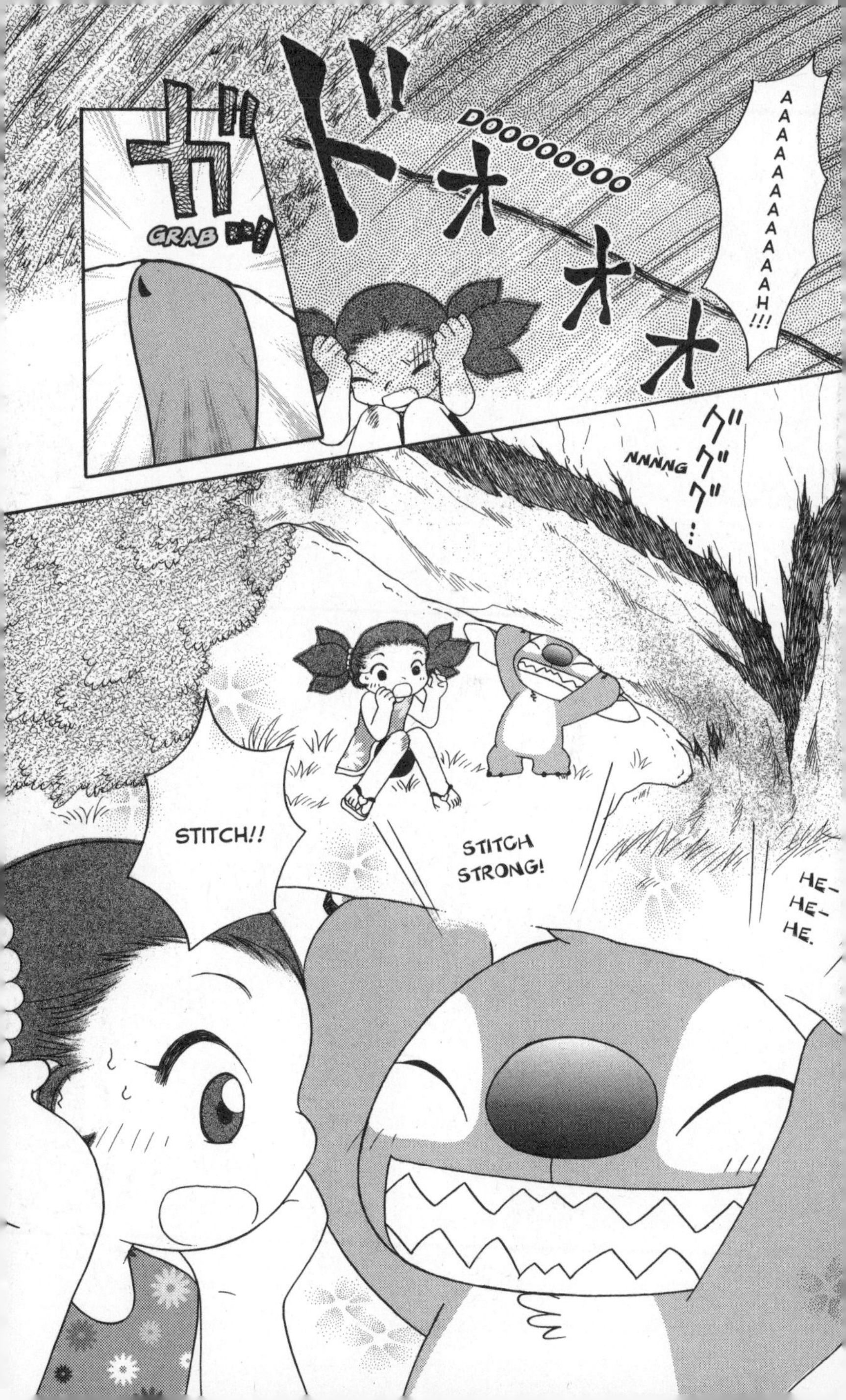
AAAAAAAAAAAAAH!!!
DOOOOOOOOO
GRAB
NNNNG
STITCH!!
STITCH STRONG!
HE-HE-HE.

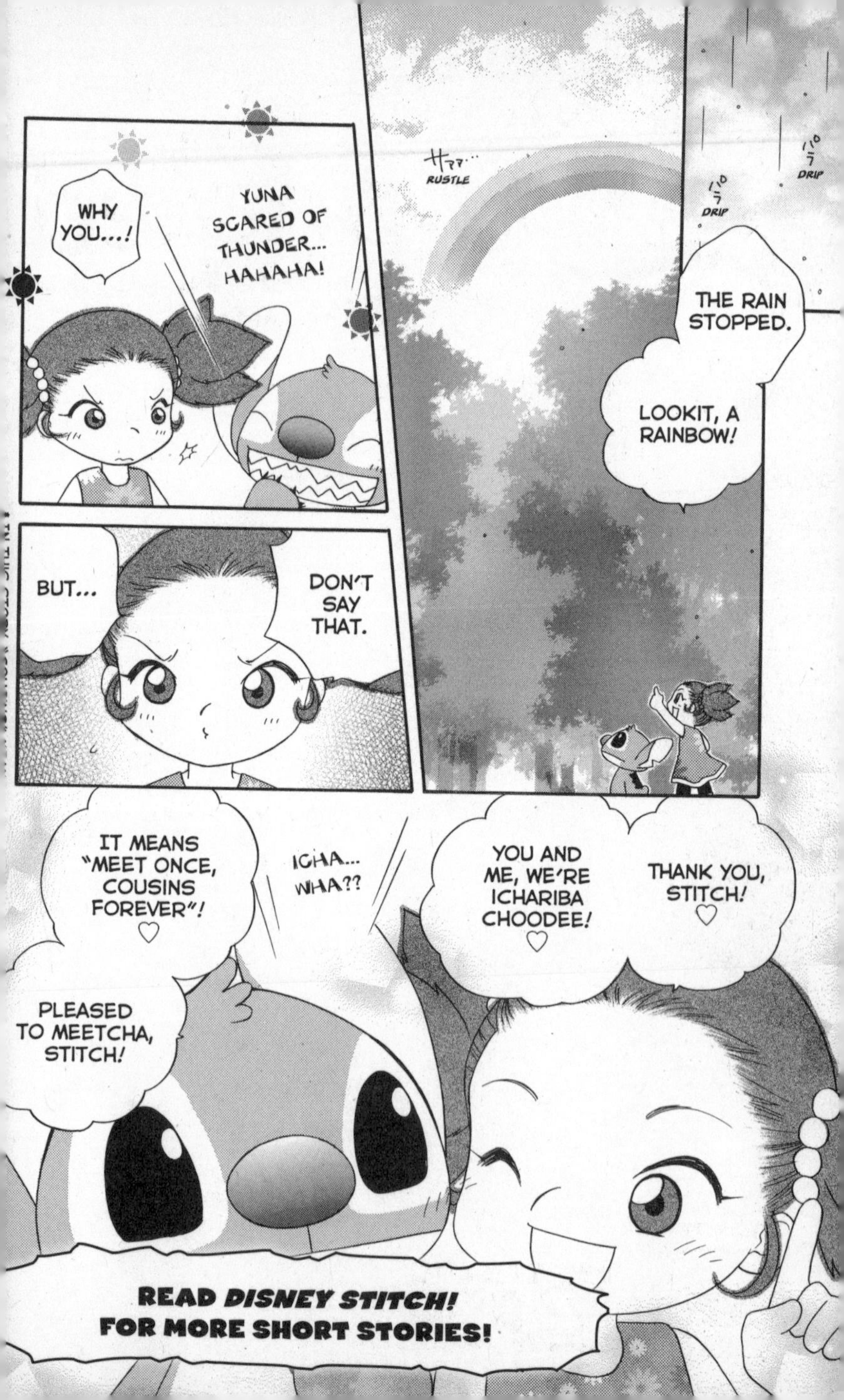

DRIP
DRIP
THE RAIN STOPPED.
RUSTLE
LOOKIT, A RAINBOW!
YUNA SCARED OF THUNDER... HAHAHA!
WHY YOU...!
DON'T SAY THAT.
BUT...
THANK YOU, STITCH! ♡
YOU AND ME, WE'RE ICHARIBA CHOODEE! ♡
ICHA... WHA??
IT MEANS "MEET ONCE, COUSINS FOREVER"! ♡
PLEASED TO MEETCHA, STITCH!
READ *DISNEY STITCH!* FOR MORE SHORT STORIES!

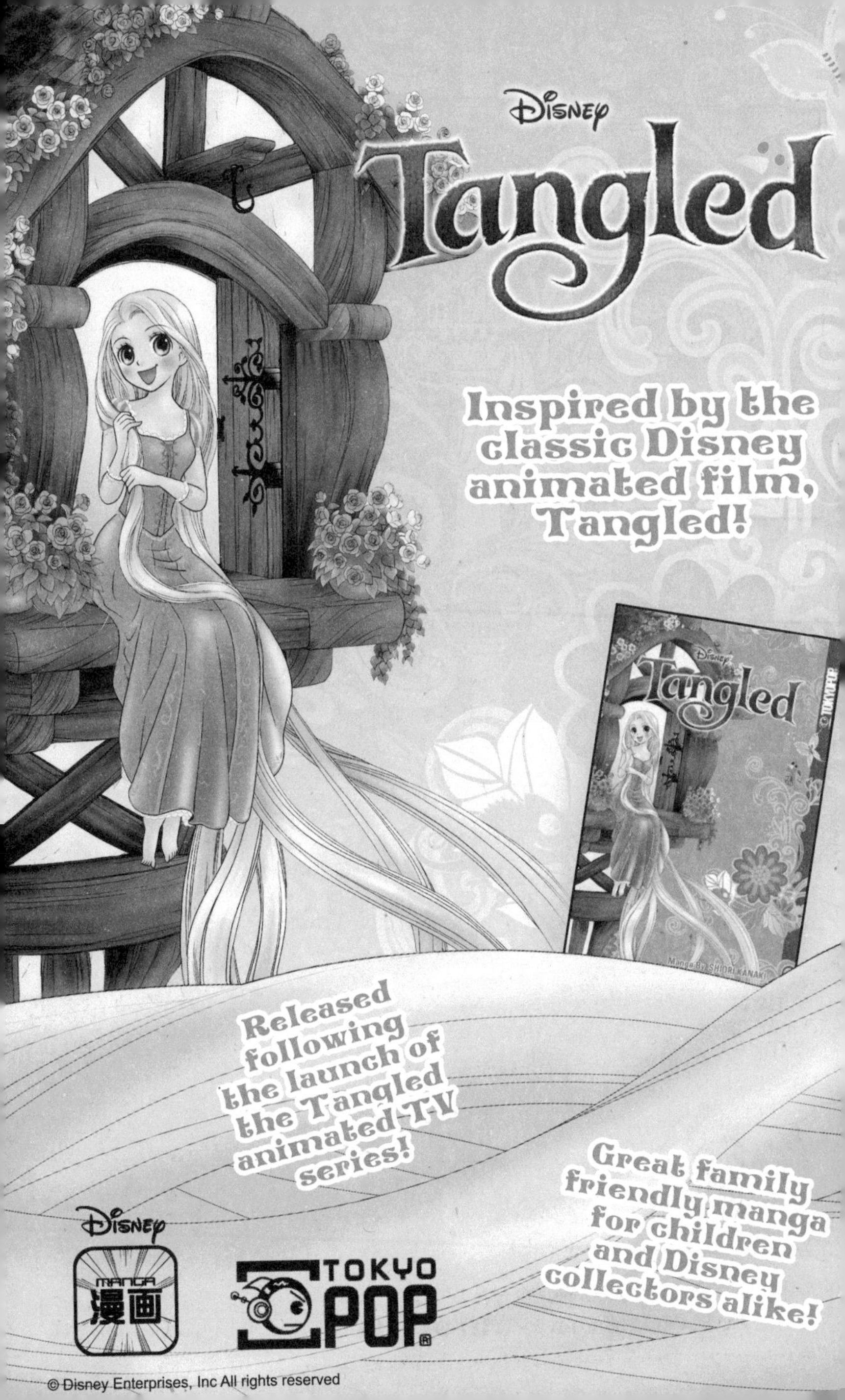
Disney
Tangled
Inspired by the classic Disney animated film, Tangled!
Disney
Tangled
TOKYOPOP
Manga By SHIORI KANAKI
Released following the launch of the Tangled animated TV series!
Great family friendly manga for children and Disney collectors alike!
Disney
MANGA 漫画
TOKYO POP
© Disney Enterprises, Inc All rights reserved

MAGICAL ★ DANCE

© TOKYOPOP

MAGICAL DANCE

COVER NOT FINAL

Rin joins a troupe with her fellow students and soon realizes that she has two left feet. She practices day and night but is discouraged by the lack of results and almost gives up on her dreams. Impressed by her passion and dedication, Tinker Bell appears to give her a little encouragement in the form of Disney magic!

FROM THE CREATOR OF DISNEY KILALA PRINCESS!

Dɪsney

漫画

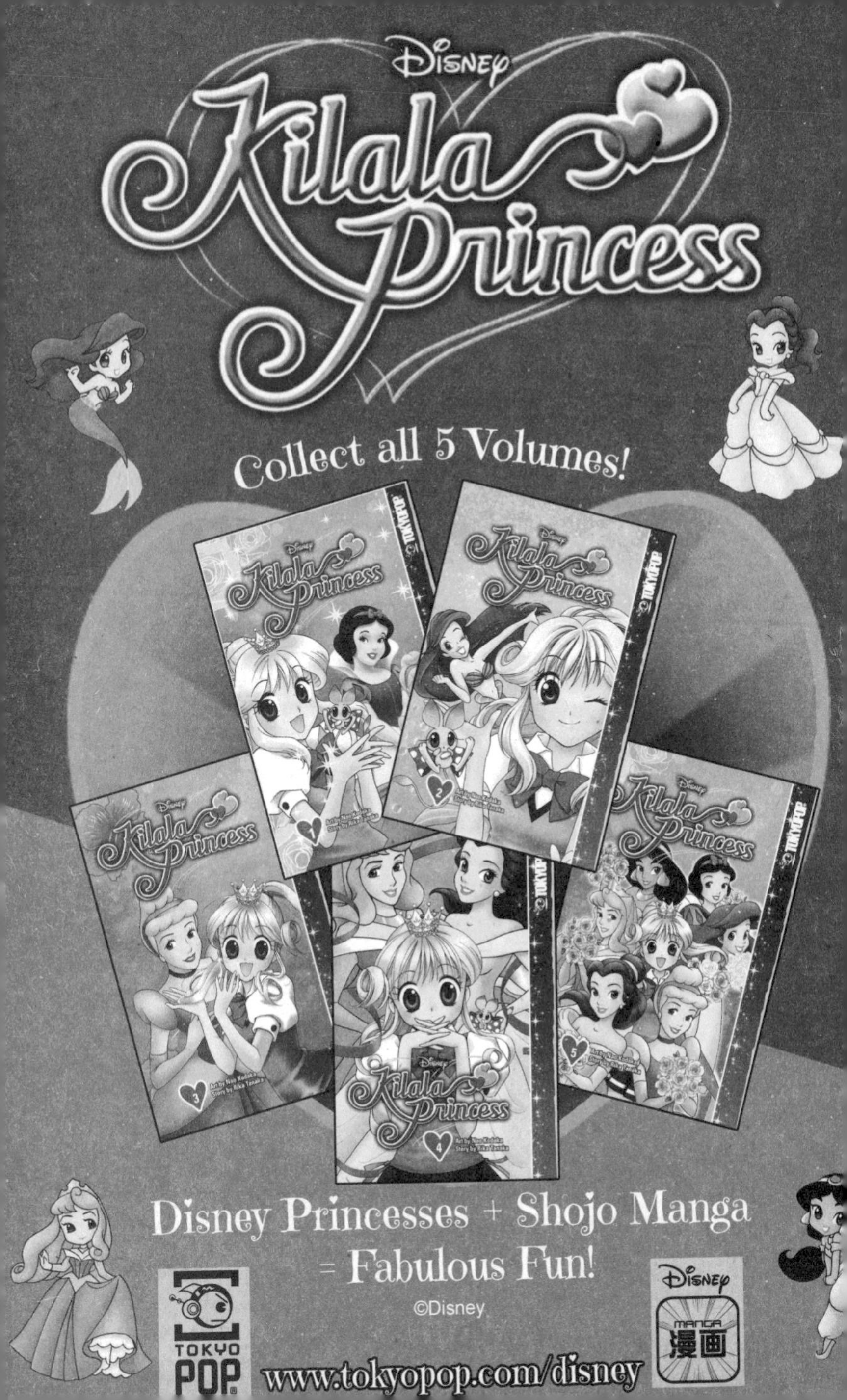
Disney
Kilala Princess
Collect all 5 Volumes!
Disney Princesses + Shojo Manga
= Fabulous Fun!
©Disney
TOKYO POP
www.tokyopop.com/disney
Disney
MANGA
漫画

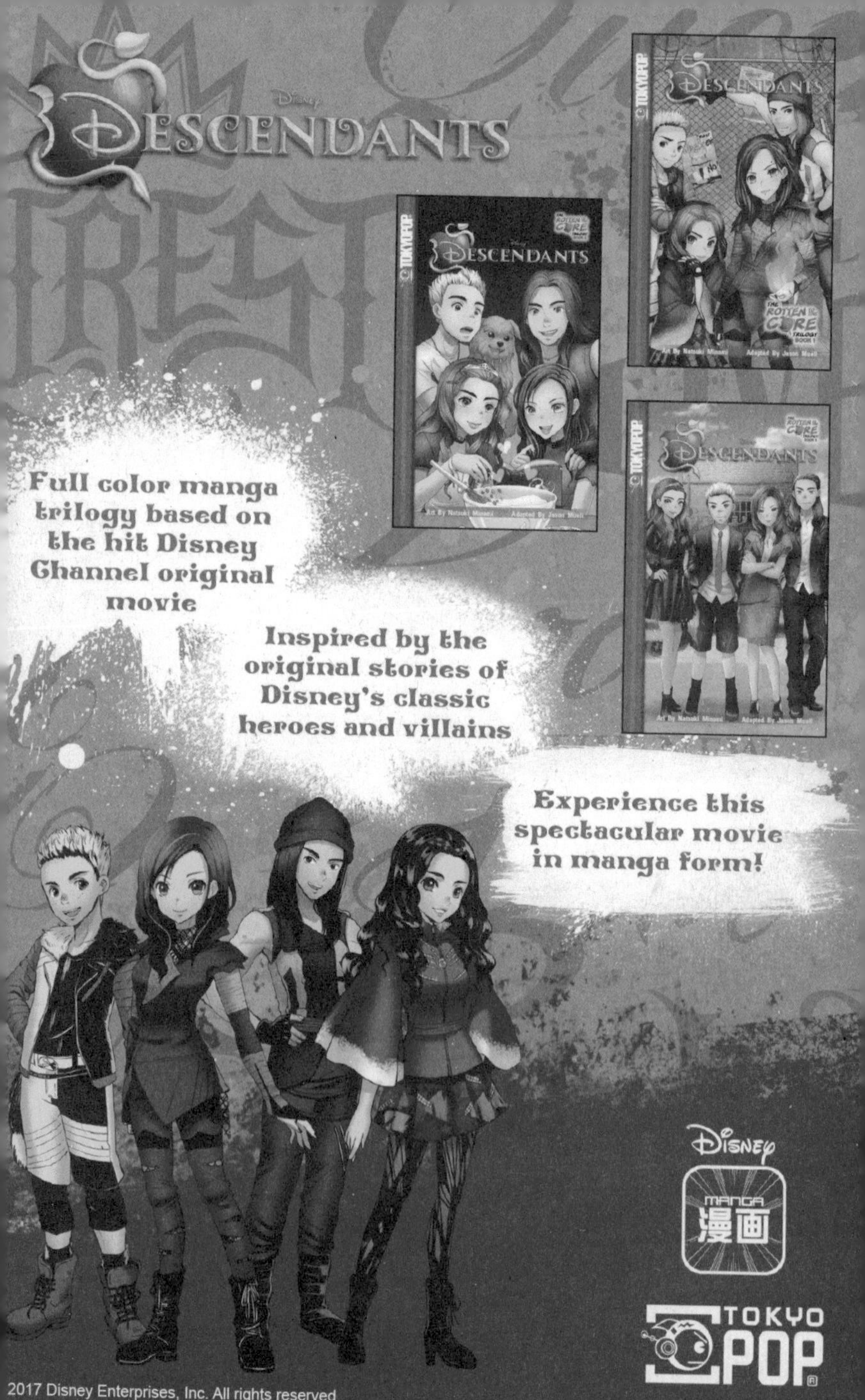
Disney
DESCENDANTS
Full color manga trilogy based on the hit Disney Channel original movie
Inspired by the original stories of Disney's classic heroes and villains
Experience this spectacular movie in manga form!
Disney
MANGA 漫画
TOKYO POP

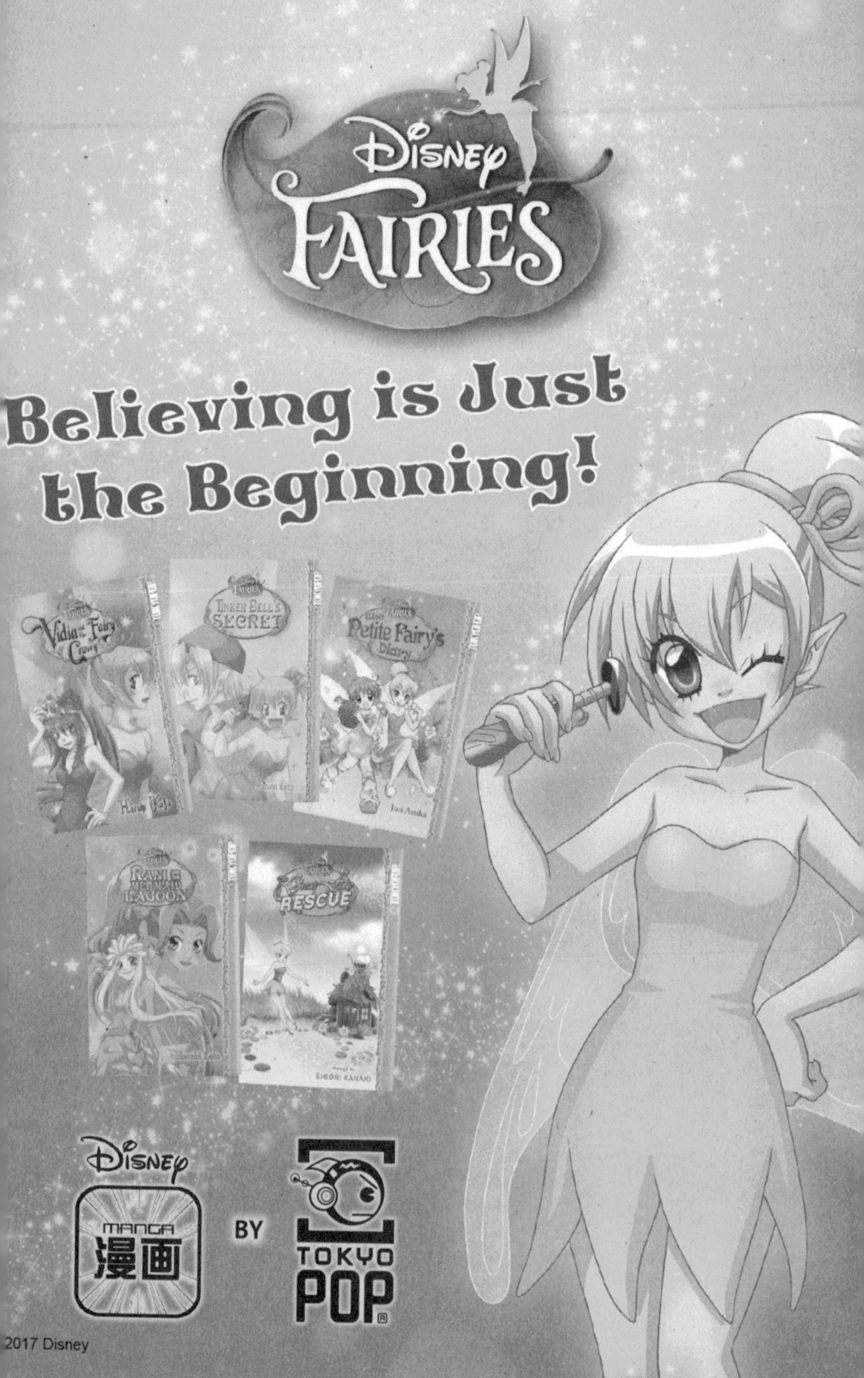

Disney Fairies
Believing is Just the Beginning!
Vidia and the Fairy Crown
Tinker Bell's Secret
Petite Fairy's Diary
Rani and the Mermaid Lagoon
Rescue
SHIORI KANAKI
Disney
MANGA 漫画
BY
TOKYOPOP

Disney Tinker Bell and the Great Fairy Rescue
Manga by: Shiori Kanaki

Editorial Associate - Janae Young
Marketing Associate - Kae Winters
Technology and Digital Media Assistant - Phillip Hong
Translator - Kelly Bergin
Copy Editor - M. Cara Carper
Graphic Designer - Phillip Hong
Retouching and Lettering - Vibrraant Publishing Studio
Editor-in-Chief & Publisher - Stu Levy
Digital Media Coordinator - Rico Brenner-Quiñonez

A  Manga

TOKYOPOP and 👁 are trademarks or registered trademarks of TOKYOPOP Inc.

TOKYOPOP inc.
5200 W Century Blvd
Suite 705
Los Angeles, CA 90045 USA

E-mail: info@TOKYOPOP.com
Come visit us online at www.TOKYOPOP.com

f www.facebook.com/TOKYOPOP
▶ www.twitter.com/TOKYOPOP
▶ www.youtube.com/TOKYOPOPTV
P www.pinterest.com/TOKYOPOP
◙ www.instagram.com/TOKYOPOP
t. TOKYOPOP.tumblr.com

ISBN: 978-1-4278-5809-2

First TOKYOPOP Printing: February 2018
10 9 8 7 6 5 4 3 2 1
Printed in CANADA

STOP

THIS IS THE BACK OF THE BOOK!

How do you read manga-style? It's simple! To learn, just start in the top right panel and follow the numbers:

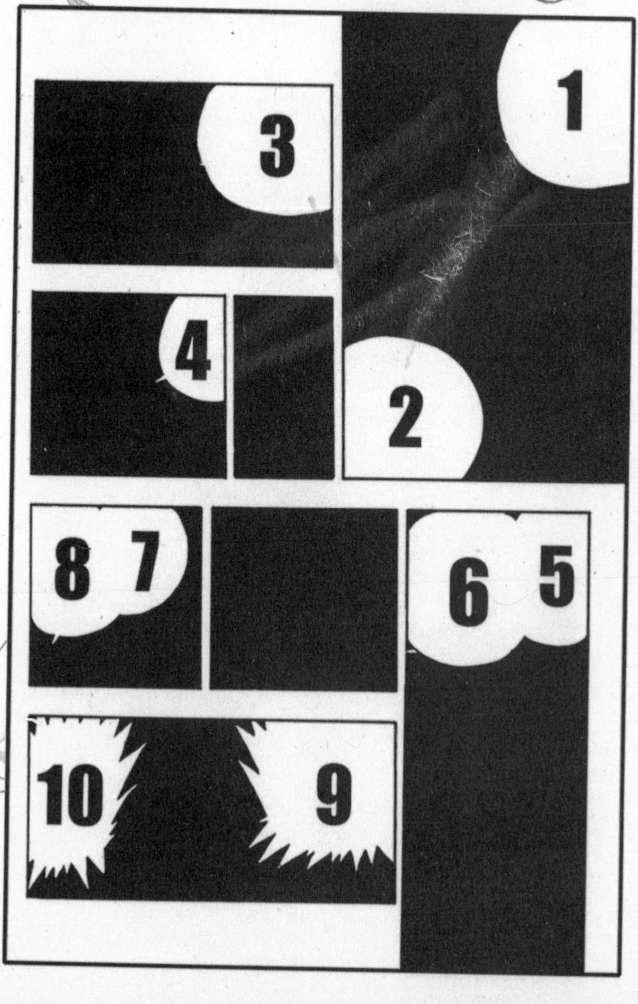
1
2
3
4
5
6
7
8
9
10